SWIM AT YOUR OWN RISK

We had come out onto the sand of the beach. Hisako daintily kicked off her shoes. "Shall we walk near the water?"

Sure, why not? The longer I stayed with Hisako, the less time I had to spend behind the desk. We strolled barefoot along the firm sand where waves lapped the shore, detouring inland when we came across one of the rock piers. Just being that close to the ocean soothed my agitation.

Until Hisako stopped dead in her tracks. She pointed to the shoreline ahead. "What is that?"

I shielded my eyes and squinted. Something large had washed up on shore. A log maybe.

No, it was a person.

Panic washed over me. I stood paralyzed for a second before my lifeguard training kicked in. I sprinted toward the body. As I drew closer, I could tell it was a woman. Her hair lay tangled about her head like seaweed, matted with sand. Her pale skin was mottled, and her lips were an odd color of blue.

My heart sank right down to my stomach. The ground seemed to tilt beneath my feet. I could hardly breathe. I dropped to my knees beside her. The ties of her halter-top bikini were tangled tight about her neck. My hands trembled as I tried to loosen them.

LINDA GERBER'S *DEATH BY* SERIES

Death by Bikini

Death by Latte

Death by Denim

OTHER SLEUTH BOOKS YOU MAY ENJOY

Double Helix	Nancy Werlin
Haunted	Judith St. George
Hunted: Fake ID	Walter Sorrells
In Darkness, Death	Dorothy and Thomas Hoobler
Lulu Dark Can See Through Walls	Bennett Madison

THE
DEATH
BY
BIKINI
mysteries

An Imprint of Penguin Group (USA) Inc.

Acknowledgments

I'm deeply indebted to all the people who have had a hand in bringing this book to life.

Heartfelt thanks to my long-suffering family and their willingness to be ignored, wear mismatched socks, and eat out. GUSH to my CPs Jen, Ginger, Nicole, Barb, Julie, Marsha, Karen, and Kate!

And, of course, there wouldn't be a book without the hard work of the entire Puffin team. I still pinch myself at my incredible good fortune to work with you all. Thanks much, Theresa and Linda, for the fabulous cover design! Gracias Grace for your editorial eyes. And Angelle, as always, I appreciate your guidance and wisdom more than I can say.

SLEUTH / SPEAK
Published by the Penguin Group
Penguin Group (USA) Inc., 345 Hudson Street, New York, New York 10014, U.S.A.
Penguin Group (Canada), 90 Eglinton Avenue East, Suite 700,
Toronto, Ontario, Canada M4P 2Y3 (a division of Pearson Penguin Canada Inc.)
Penguin Books Ltd, 80 Strand, London WC2R 0RL, England
Penguin Ireland, 25 St Stephen's Green, Dublin 2, Ireland (a division of Penguin Books Ltd)
Penguin Group (Australia), 250 Camberwell Road, Camberwell, Victoria 3124, Australia
(a division of Pearson Australia Group Pty Ltd)
Penguin Books India Pvt Ltd, 11 Community Centre, Panchsheel Park, New Delhi - 110 017, India
Penguin Group (NZ), 67 Apollo Drive, Rosedale, North Shore 0632, New Zealand
(a division of Pearson New Zealand Ltd.)
Penguin Books (South Africa) (Pty) Ltd, 24 Sturdee Avenue, Rosebank, Johannesburg 2196, South Africa

Registered Offices: Penguin Books Ltd, 80 Strand, London WC2R 0RL, England

Published by Speak, an imprint of Penguin Group (USA) Inc., 2008
This omnibus edition published by Speak, an imprint of Penguin Group (USA) Inc., 2010

1 3 5 7 9 10 8 6 4 2

LIBRARY OF CONGRESS CATALOGING-IN-PUBLICATION DATA
Gerber, Linda C.
Death by bikini / by Linda Gerber.
p. cm.
Summary: Sixteen-year-old Aphra Behn Connolly investigates why her father let an unknown family stay at their exclusive tropical island resort, who strangled a famous rock star's girlfriend with her own bikini top, and what a smoldering teenaged guest is hiding.
ISBN: 978-0-14-241117-9 (pbk.)
[1. Resorts—Fiction. 2. Murder—Fiction. 3. Fathers and daughters—Fiction.
4. Islands—Fiction. 5. Mystery and detective stories.]
I. Title. PZ7.G293567Dec 2008 [Fic]—dc22 2007046771

Speak ISBN 978-0-14-241117-9
This omnibus ISBN 978-0-14-241826-0

Printed in the United States of America

For Aaron. I love you.

DEATH BY BIKINI

PROLOGUE

He's coming.

I climb harder, but rain weighs down my clothes and stings my eyes. The downpour slicks decomposing leaves beneath my feet so that I slip and stumble up the hill. My thighs burn. My chest is hot and tight. I want to stop and catch my breath, but his footsteps crash steadily through the undergrowth below me.

Close. So close.

Inches from my head, a banana leaf jumps and rips apart. Half a breath later, a bullet splinters the palm trunk beside me. I drop to the ground, the sound of my scream caught in my throat. I swear I can feel the vibration of his footsteps coming nearer.

If only I could rewind the past three days, I'd do everything different. I would tell Seth I'm sorry. I would protect Bianca. I would do whatever it took to see my mom one last time before I die.

CHAPTER 1

Until last week, my most pressing concern had been getting ready to visit my friend Cami back home in South Carolina. On Friday, all of that changed. Not the part about going to see Cami; I still planned to do that. Let's just say I picked up a few more concerns along the way.

As days go, Friday had been normal . . . the last normal day I can remember. But with Friday evening came a string of events that, while they may have seemed unremarkable at the time, changed my quiet island life forever.

It all started when my dad had asked me to meet a new guest at the helipad. Nothing unusual about that—although we don't get many of them in the off-season. Guests, I mean. The late July heat can be brutal on the island, and those who know usually wait until the trade winds return before they flock back to the resort. Still, a new arrival here and there was to be expected.

I stood sweltering in my uniform, even as the sun hung low on the horizon, waiting for her on the hilltop as the helicopter set down.

Frank—our pilot—saluted as he brought the landing

skids down inside the painted circle. I sighed with relief at the breeze created by the wash of the rotors and waved back at him. Because of our remote location, the only way to and from the resort is by helicopter, so Frank is like our lifeline to the city. He delivers everything—mail, supplies, and guests.

I tried to smooth my hair as the rotors wound to a stop. Frank climbed from the cockpit. "Hey, darlin'! You doin' the honors tonight, eh?"

"You got it." It's not like he had to ask; the new guest was a lady from Japan, and as Frank knew, my Japanese was much better than my dad's. In fact, I served as the liaison for most of our international guests—owing to the fact that I can speak more than five languages, whereas my dad is fluent only in French. I'll admit that most of what I know is pretty basic, but it's enough to check someone in.

Frank helped the lady from his helicopter and retrieved her suitcases from the cargo hatch while she stood, predictably, admiring the view. It's the first thing any new arrival does.

The helicopter pad rests atop a hill overlooking the property, and, I have to admit, our resort makes a very good first impression. It sits on a remote stretch of shoreline sandwiched between jagged black mountains draped in rain-forest green and a cerulean ocean that stretches to an impossibly wide horizon. I remember the first time I saw it, the beauty of it made me want to cry. Or maybe that was because my mom wasn't there to share it with me.

I stiffened and raised my chin. Four years and the confusion about my mom's decision still clung to me like a sour smell. I wasn't going to let it ruin another otherwise beautiful evening.

Frank and the lady approached the cart, and I bowed in greeting. "*Konbanwa. Yokoso.*" Good evening. Welcome.

She clapped her hands. "Oh! You speak Japanese, *ne?*"

"*Sukoshi.* Very little."

She introduced herself with a bow of her own. "I am Shimizu, Hisako."

I bowed again. "*Hajimemashite.* Pleased to meet you, Shimizu-*san.*"

"Please, you must call me Hisako."

Frank loaded the bags into the back of the cart while we settled in the front. He stepped back when he was done, touching a finger to the brim of his old blue-and-gold Navy cap. "Enjoy your stay, Miz Shimizu."

Tossing a good-bye wave to Frank, I swung the cart around for the return trip. "So, what brings you to our island, Hisako-*san?*"

"I study botany. I am interested in the number of plants unique to these islands."

"Oh, yes. I just did a plant unit in my biology class, so I know more indigenous species than I care to remember."

I steered the cart around a bend in the path. "If you'd like me to take you around sometime . . ."

"Yes. I believe I would like—Oh!" She threw out a hand. "Please, stop here!"

I coasted to the side of the path, where we could see the entire resort stretched out below us, backlit by deep corals, reds, and golds. The sun hovered like a flame orange ball atop the ocean and then sank quietly behind Technicolor waves. Hisako-*san* brought one hand to her heart and murmured in Japanese, "It is perfect."

I smiled in agreement and bowed to thank her. Not that I was personally responsible for the view or anything, but I did feel a certain amount of pride, being the owner's daughter and all. Of course, the resort was his dream, not mine, but no sense in letting reality spoil the moment. I forced a smile. "Just wait until you see the stars from your veranda."

The steward delivered Hisako-*san*'s luggage to her villa while I signed her in at the Plantation House. As usual, Dad took over from there and took our new guest to her villa while I watched the desk.

He hadn't been gone two minutes before the French doors slammed open again. I jumped and reached for the two-way radio from the desk in case I needed to call security, but I relaxed as soon as I saw who it was—our resident aging rock star, trying to wrestle a suitcase away from his latest girlfriend.

This, again, was nothing out of the ordinary. The girl was just the latest of a long string of girls he'd brought to the island, but she was by far the smartest of the lot—which is probably why she was constantly threatening to leave him. We'd nicknamed the pair Mick and Bianca, since both had declined to register under their real names.

Our secluded location makes us attractive to a lot of fake-namers like them—celebrities just out of rehab, adulterous politicians, trophy wives recovering from plastic surgery, you name it. They know their secrets—and identities—are safe with us.

Mick was one of our regulars—a big spender who kept a villa at the resort and flew in every other month with a different girl on his arm. Either he didn't think we noticed or he counted on our discretion. Maybe a little of both.

Bianca tugged on her suitcase. "I'm warning you!"

Mick tugged back, whining like a little kid. "Why won't you even listen to me?"

Not for the first time, I wondered what Bianca saw in him. She was a lot younger than him, but she didn't seem as star struck as the other girls he'd been with. If she didn't like something he did, she let him know. Most of the time by packing her bags while he—a rock god who used to smash amps and breathe fire onstage for a living—ran after her like a whimpering puppy.

Bianca finally wrestled her suitcase away from him.

"You promised to stop drinking. You're such a pig when you're drunk!"

"I did stop. Alls I had was a little nip." He pinched the air, weaving like Jack Sparrow. Even from where I was standing, I could smell the sickly sweet fermented smell of alcohol on him.

"I'm outta here."

Bianca marched into the lobby, and he followed unsteadily. "But, ba-a-a-be . . ."

"Don't 'babe' me!" She plopped her vintage leather handbag on the counter. "I'd like a flight out, please."

"Ah, c'mon. No more, I promise."

He plucked at her arm, but she swatted his hand away. "You promised yesterday. And the day before. You're pathetic." She turned to me. "Am I right, or am I right?"

I gave her a neutral smile and pulled her name up on the registration screen, just in case she really did check out this time. It happened that I did think she was right, but I had a strict personal policy about getting involved with our guests' lives: Don't. Getting involved led to getting attached, and getting attached led to getting hurt. Eventually, everyone leaves. It's a lot easier not to care when they do.

It was about that time that my dad—the great mediator—arrived. I was both relieved and disappointed to see him. Despite the fact that we host more celebrities than *American Idol,* not much exciting happens at our place, and at least the fight was interesting. Dad calmed the lovebirds down, and they all went out to the lanai to talk. The show was over.

He was still out there with them when Mr. Mulo walked into the lobby. Of course, I didn't know who he was then, but I did know we weren't expecting any more incoming flights that evening. Or were we? I stood with a pasted-on smile that I hoped would mask my uncertainty. "Good evening. May I help you?"

The man hesitated for a moment, scanning the lobby before he returned my greeting. The way he did that struck me as a little odd—like he was casing the joint or something. My imposter antenna shot straight up, and I watched him closely as he approached the desk.

He was a little taller than average, with salt-and-pepper hair combed back from a wide forehead. His clothes spoke of careless elegance, and he carried himself confidently. But behind his casual air was an unmistakable watchfulness. He was definitely hiding something.

"I would like to speak to Mr. Connolly, please."

I pressed my lips together. Was I imagining it, or did his midwestern nasal tone sound forced? I thought I could detect an underlying accent, but I'd have to hear him speak a little more before I could determine what it was.

I didn't get the chance, though, because, at that moment, Dad stepped back in from the lanai. He strode toward our new arrival, hand outstretched, as if he'd been expecting the guy.

"Jack Connolly. Pleased to meet you." He gave Mr. Imposter his trademark charm-the-guest grin as he pumped the man's hand. The way he was talking, I wondered if we'd had a last-minute call-in or something, but . . . no, Dad's smiling eyes betrayed confusion. Had we somehow both missed a reservation? Since Frank was the only pilot authorized to pick up and deliver at our location, and since he would never deliver anyone who wasn't cleared through us, it seemed the only explanation. And yet none of the stewards were anywhere to be seen. Who had brought the guy down from the helipad?

I picked up the two-way radio to give Frank a squawk. With Mick on the island, it wouldn't surprise me if this guy was a paparazzo. We should probably check it out before we went handing out any rooms. A slipup like that could cost us a buttload of PR.

But then the man leaned close to my dad and said something in a low voice that I couldn't hear. The smile faded from Dad's face, and the color drained right out of it. He glanced over and gave me a small shake of his head. I set down the radio.

What just happened? Did the guy threaten him? Should I call security?

I gripped the radio again, but stopped just short of raising it to my ear. What if I was wrong? Overreacting? I inched closer so I could hear the conversation and make a better judgment.

All I caught was the last part of the man's final

sentence. ". . . just for a few days, until suitable arrangements can be made."

Dad forced a smile again. "I'll see what we have available." He brushed past me to the computer and awkwardly adjusted the flat-screen monitor.

I bit my lip, watching his obvious discomfort. Computerizing the system had been my idea. He would have been much more composed opening the huge logbook and methodically turning the pages, which was something he used to do to buy himself thinking time. It had always bugged me, but now I felt guilty for having deprived him of the ritual.

I sidled up next to him and whispered, "You want me to do it?"

He glanced back at me, but he didn't say anything. It was like he didn't even see me.

"Shall I call the concierge to arrange a pickup for his luggage?"

"No. Thank you." He blinked and seemed to come to himself again. "I'll take care of them personally."

Them? I looked up.

Mr. Imposter was not alone.

CHAPTER
2

They stood just inside the door. The woman had short dark hair and striking—almost elegant—features. But I was more interested in the guy at her side. I guessed he couldn't have been much older than me, judging from the smoothness of his face and the sharp angles in his razor-cut hair. He wore a plain black T-shirt and nondescript jeans, and, unlike the older guy, he seemed completely at ease. He watched me openly, maybe even a little curiously.

I watched him right back, probably more curious than he was. We don't get many guys my age at the resort. Okay, we don't get any. Who brings their kid on a hide-away vacation? At least that's what I assumed he was. The imposter's and the lady's kid, I mean. They did look like they belonged together—father, mother, and son. The boy had his dad's height and his mom's strong cheek-bones. He also had eyes the color of the midnight sea. Mr. Imposter's were plain dark brown. I decided I liked the blue eyes much better.

As if he could tell what I'd been thinking, the son's lips curved into a smile. I blinked and looked away, my face all hot and tight. I'm not used to people looking at me. I mean, really *looking* at me. Of course, I don't usually go around staring at them, either. At least not right out in the open. Working at the resort, I've learned the value of dealing with the guests as unobtrusively as possible—blending into the background.

Usually the blending part comes naturally for me since I happen to be what you might call unremarkable to look at—average height, average weight, average-length average brown hair. At a resort populated by beautiful people, all that averageness pretty much makes me invisible. But apparently not to this guy.

I straightened. What was I, twelve? I wasn't going to get all flustered just because some boy looked at me. I turned my attention back to Dad, who seemed to be in some sort of trance, staring at the blank registration screen.

"You want me to do that?" I offered again.

He stiffened and jerked his head in my direction, startled, like he'd forgotten I was there. "No! I'll take care of it, Aphra. You go on up to bed."

"But if you'd like me to—"

"I've got it." His voice took on a sharp edge. "Good night."

I took a step back, stung. Dad had never spoken to me in that tone before. He'd never treated me like a little kid. In fact, when we first moved to the resort, Dad brought me into his office and sat me down to talk. He knew how upset I'd been when I realized my mom wasn't coming with us, but he said we could get through it if we stuck together. He explained about his plans for the resort and his need for my cooperation, as if I were a business partner with whom he had to confer. "It's just you and me now, you understand? We've got a big job to do."

I took him at his word. I thought we were a team. So how could he send me to bed like some errant child? In front of guests!

"But I was just—"

"Aphra! Go!"

I spun and pushed through the French doors out into the sultry night air. My fists curled tight, and I had an overwhelming desire to slug something. Or someone. I paced the length of the lanai. The sweet perfume of the potted plumeria and jasmine—a scent I usually loved—suddenly smelled false and cloying.

Through the window, I could see the imposter and his family, waiting expectantly as Dad fumbled through the check-in. Again I wondered if Frank had flown them in. Had he even had time to get to the city and back after dropping off the last guest? I would like to have called him to ask, but there was no way I was going back to the office to get the two-way. Not with the mood Dad was in. His snappish tone replayed in my head, and I grew angry all over again.

I couldn't stay there. I had to move, to give the anger and frustration an outlet. I backed away from the window, bounded down the steps of the lanai, and tore across the manicured lawn to where the huge banyan tree dominates the northern seaward corner of the courtyard. Pushing my way through its hanging roots, I finally came out onto the beach. My beach. My sanctuary.

Our shoreline is broken up into little scallops of sand divided by natural lava rock piers that jut out into the water like prehistoric fingers. The finger on my beach comes all the way up to the tree line on one side, cutting it off almost completely from the other beaches. The banyan tree shields it from the courtyard. That, plus the fact that it's the farthest beach from where the villas are situated, means hardly anyone ever goes there. Except me.

I breathed deep the familiar, comforting tang of salt and seaweed. Waves curled gently inland, breaking in a steady *shush* across the beach. Moonlight shimmered across the foam. If the ocean couldn't calm me, nothing could. Kicking off my shoes, I dropped my shorts and shirt in the sand. Like a lot of our guests, I practically live in my swimsuit. Unlike them, I actually swim in mine. When I was younger, I spent so much time in the water that my mom called me her little fish. But I haven't been her little anything for a long, long time.

I jogged the last few yards to the shore, waded in, and dived under. The seawater cooled the fire in my face and raised goose bumps on my skin.

Following the current downward, I skimmed along the sandy bottom until my lungs burned, then I made myself stay underwater just a bit longer. That's my ritual—something I do when I need to clear my head.

Stay under long enough and pretty soon all you can think of is the primal need to breathe. It didn't work that night, though. All I was left with was an ache in my chest that had nothing to do with the lack of oxygen.

I shot back up to the surface and gasped in a huge gulp of salty air before diving under again. My ritual was failing me. I couldn't make my head cooperate.

I'd probably gone down half a dozen times before I noticed that the surf was starting to get rough. The wave height didn't usually bother me; we're on the windward side of the island, so I'm used to it, but the power of the surge was getting intense, which meant I should probably head for shore before it got too dangerous.

I swam toward the beach, riding the waves until I could touch the bottom and wade in. I stepped lightly, careful to avoid the sharp rocks that lurk beneath the sand. See, we're not Laguna or Mazatlán or any of those places where all the beaches have nicely padded sandy bottoms. Ours is a volcanic island where the waves can carry away the sand and leave the rock exposed, sharp as glass.

I was picking my way toward the beach when I saw him. Imposter Junior sat on the shore watching me.

Despite the coolness of the water, my face grew hot again. My calm facade rolled away with the waves. All I knew about teenage guys was what I had read in Cami's e-mails. I had no experience actually dealing with one.

What was he doing? Waiting for me? And then what? What was I supposed to say to him? What—

I heard the crash of the wave too late. It rammed into me like a bull elephant, knocking the breath out of me. The next thing I knew I was facedown in the surf, heavy water pummeling the back of my head. Stupid, stupid, stupid. I knew better.

Never turn your back to the ocean.

The wave receded and pulled me with it. I scrabbled at the sand, but the force of the water dragged me under and tumbled me like a washing machine. The rip current pulled me seaward.

I'm not one to panic, but I will admit I started to freak. It was dark. I didn't know which way was up or down. My chest felt like a crushed milk carton. Dizzy spots circled before my eyes. I was going to die.

Then pain sliced along my arm. *Yes!* The rocks. That way was down. I righted myself and swam sideways as hard as I could, out of the current's pull.

Finally, I was free. Pushing upward, I popped to the surface, coughing and gagging. It took a minute for my head to clear and another minute to figure out where I was. A deep chill settled in my gut as I realized the water had carried me nearly twenty feet out. Much farther and I would have been diced on the reef.

My muscles felt heavy and useless as I tried to swim toward the shore. It wasn't until I could touch the bottom to walk in that I realized the wave had nearly torn my bikini top off. I gasped and straightened it to cover myself, praying that the imposter kid hadn't noticed. But when I looked to the shore, he wasn't there. Not where he had been sitting, anyway. Another glance and I saw him splashing through the water about fifteen feet to my left. It took a second to register; that's where I had been when I went under. The fool was probably trying to save me. I didn't have the energy to signal him. I did try to call out to him, but a wave slapped the words from my lips and left me with a mouthful of salt water instead.

All I could do was adjust my course so that I would come in a little closer to where he was. It's a good thing, too, because he made the same mistake I had, and he went down next.

Fortunately for him, his wave wasn't quite as big as the one that had slammed into me. I lost sight of him in the churning white water, but then he popped up like a cork, just over an arm's length from me. He had time only to take a breath and give me a startled look before a larger wave rose above us. And I had time only to grab his shirt and pull him down to dive under the surge. He struggled against my grasp as we went underwater, and I lost him for a moment, but I managed to snag his ankle before he was pulled away.

We both surfaced at the same time, sputtering and gasping for breath.

"Why . . . did you . . . ," he wheezed.

"Lifeguard," I said, pointing to myself. I was too wiped out to explain the finer points of surf survival, so I just showed him the next swell as it began to rise. "We . . . ride this one . . . in. Got it?"

He nodded and followed my lead, paddling with the rush of water until it lifted us up on the crest and pushed us toward shore. I didn't have any breath left in me to tell him what to do, so I could only hope he'd bodysurfed before and could figure it out.

I concentrated on keeping my own body in a streamlined position on top of the wave. I could feel him next to me, though—and I could swear he was laughing. We rode the crest until it crashed down, tossing us and grinding us into the sand. At least there *was* sand. It would have been worse if we'd have hit rock.

Like some primordial creature, I crawled out of the water and collapsed—after checking to make sure my top was in place, of course. He dragged himself over to where I had sprawled and flopped onto his back next to me.

We lay there, not saying a word, for a long time. All I cared about in those moments was breathing in and out. My heart was still jumping around in my chest so hard it almost hurt. I stared at the stars, thinking how bright they looked. What if we had drowned? I would never have seen those stars again. Never have seen my dad. My mom . . .

He broke the silence. "Some ride, huh?"

"Huh."

We lay still a little while longer, and then he said, "I'm Adam. Adam Smith."

"Aphra Connolly."

He reached over and held his hand out to me. "Thanks for the save."

I grasped his hand—weakly, I'm afraid—and shook it. "Thanks for coming in after me."

He gave me a half nod. "So. You live here?"

"Yeah."

"You like it?"

How was I supposed to answer that? No one ever cared to ask before—not my dad and especially not a guest. I loved the island, but I missed having friends to talk to. I lived for the sun and the sea, but I would trade them both in a second if I could have my old life and my family together again. Adam was waiting for an answer, but some things are too complicated to explain. I shrugged. "S'okay."

He sat up, hooking his arms around his knees. His back and broad shoulders were plastered in sand, and his dark hair was matted with it. "What do you do for fun around here?"

I propped myself up on one elbow. "That was it."

He gave me a sideways glance and then laughed. "Oh, great. Now what am I supposed to look forward to the rest of the trip?"

"How long will that be?"

He looked away. "I don't know."

"Oh." I pushed down a little quell of uneasiness. Ours was not a drop-in, stay-till-whenever type of place. People generally knew well in advance how long they were going to visit us—they had to, in order to book a villa. I thought of Adam's imposter dad and the way he'd inspected the lobby. How my dad's face froze during their whispered conversation. Something was definitely not right, but I didn't want to look at it too closely. Not tonight. Not with the moon and the sea and someone to share it with.

I took a deep breath. "If you want, I could show you around sometime."

His smile returned. "Show me around what? I thought this was it."

Touché.

"For special patrons, we offer the near-death mountain experience as well." I pointed back toward the hills.

He caught my arm and lifted it to the moonlight. "Yow. Does that hurt?"

It wasn't until I saw the scratch that the pain began to register—faintly at first, and then stinging like the salted wound it was. A deep scratch ran the length of my forearm, oozing blood that mingled pink with the seawater. "It's not too bad," I lied, "but I should probably . . ." I glanced back toward the Plantation House.

"Right." He stood with some considerable effort. "Come on. I'll walk you." He held his hand out to me again, and this time the moonlight glinted off a ring on his finger—the ugliest, gaudiest gold and garnet thing I'd ever seen. It looked out of place.

"No, it's okay. I can—" I pulled my eyes away from the ring and started to get up, but my head tingled and my vision began to darken. I sank back down onto the sand.

He bent next to me, face all serious and concerned. "Are you all right?"

"Yeah. Fine. No worries." I sat up again—slowly this time—and he wrapped an arm around my shoulders to help me.

I stiffened. Not that I wasn't enjoying the contact or anything, but all sorts of alarm bells started going off inside my head—mainly because I *was* enjoying it. The whole thing was a little too cozy. He was a guest. Likely leaving in a few days. And even if he wasn't, nothing good could come of my letting my guard down. I thought of my mom, of the friends I'd left back home, of my dad snapping at me that night. You let people get too close, you just get hurt.

He must have sensed my hesitation because he chuckled. "Don't worry. I'm harmless."

My face started to do the burning thing again. "Oh, no. I didn't mean—"

"I know. I don't usually rescue girls on a first date, either."

He looked so ridiculous with his exaggerated contrite expression that I had to smile.

His face brightened, and he helped me to my feet. He half guided, half supported me over to where my things lay in the sand. Of course he wasn't much steadier than I was, and the two of us nearly fell over more than once. By the time we reached my clothes, we could barely stand for laughing.

I pulled on my blouse, folded my shorts, and slipped my gritty feet into my shoes.

The conversation died as we picked our way through the banyan roots and up the path toward the Plantation House. When a section of the path veered off toward the villas, I stopped. "Well, good night."

"No. I can walk you all the way up."

"But don't you go this way?" I pointed down the path.

"No, our villa is off to the left up there, by the big palm tree."

"Are you sure?" That didn't make any sense. There was only one villa to the left of the Plantation House, and it wasn't ready to be occupied.

"Yeah, I'm sure. Villa four."

"Oh, no."

"What's the matter?"

"I'm so sorry. We can move you."

"Why?"

"Are you kidding?"

"It's fine."

"It's under renovation."

"Oh. I thought the plastic sheeting was part of the decor." It took me a second to realize he was joking. That was long enough to make him laugh.

His laughter died abruptly when Adam's imposter dad, Mr. Smith, stepped out of the shadows. "Adam!" he hissed. "Where have you been?"

Adam's face darkened. He shoved his hands into his damp, sandy pockets and whispered sideways to me, "I better go. You know how it is; spies and parents never sleep."

He left with his dad, and I stood on the path, staring long after they'd gone. I felt numb. Adam's last words buzzed in my head.

My mom used to say the *exact* same thing.

CHAPTER 3

Dad was always the careful one. Mom used to make him crazy with the things she'd do, especially when she took me with her. I learned to scuba dive when I was ten. When I was eleven, she taught me to rock climb and rappel. I was supposed to go white-water rafting with her when I turned twelve, but she left before my birthday.

I used to lie on the floor in my room at night with my ear pressed to the boards and listen to my mom and dad fight. He'd say she was being reckless with me, and she'd say I was learning to be strong. He'd make her promise to be more careful, and she'd promise she would. And then we'd try something new the next day.

"Just don't tell Dad," she'd whisper.

We'd giggle like girlfriends when we talked about each new adventure, and it made me feel important that she wanted to share the things she loved with me. Mom was always the one to kiss away a tear or patch a skinned elbow. She tucked me in at night and read me bedtime stories. And when I had nightmares, Mom would always be there as soon as I woke up. She'd crawl under the covers with me, smooth back my hair, and tell stupid jokes until I laughed. Before long, I forgot to be scared.

I once asked how she knew whenever I needed her. She just smiled and said, "It comes with the territory, hon. Spies and parents never sleep."

I skipped my usual swim in the morning and went straight to the registration desk so I could look up the Smiths' information before Dad got to the office. It's possible he had forgotten villa four was under construction when he was checking them in; he did appear to be a little distracted after Adam's dad had spoken to him. If they were legitimate guests, we should move them right away.

I ran a quick computer search but couldn't find any sign-in at all listed for villa four. I checked the filing inbox next. Sometimes when Dad gets frustrated with the computer, he just does the paperwork by hand and leaves it for me or the other staff to input.

Nothing.

He walked into the lobby while I was searching the computer files again. I looked up, trying to gauge his mood. After the way he'd snapped at me the night before, I wasn't sure where I stood.

He caught my look and gave me a smile. A forced smile, perhaps, but at least it looked like things were back to normal. Maybe. "What are you working on this morning?"

I glanced almost guiltily at the computer. "I, um . . . I was updating the client list, and I can't find the Smiths' information."

He stiffened and shot me a look I couldn't decipher. Uh-oh.

"Information?"

"The check-in. There's no record of them—"

"Don't worry about it. I took care of it."

I pasted on a smile. "Oh, good. Do you want me to enter the info into the system?"

"Thank you, but that won't be necessary."

Just like that. No explanation. He stood next to me, calmly sifting through yesterday's mail as if it were perfectly normal for him to have placed guests in a villa with plastic sheeting for walls and no kitchen floor.

I reviewed the inventory sheet for Frank's next flight, matching Dad's calm with a calm of my own. Outwardly, at least. Inside I was screaming with frustration. Did he think I was stupid? I was there when the Smiths arrived. Even if he didn't know about my meeting with Adam, he had to know I'd wonder where those people went.

The worst thing was that I couldn't pursue it any further now that he had effectively closed the conversation. I knew how stubborn he could be. I'd have to fish for information elsewhere.

"Well, I'm done for a while." I signed off on the sheet and filed it away. "Do you mind if I run over to the lounge for a minute? I want to get some bandages from Darlene."

He looked up from the mail. "Hmm? What? What's wrong?"

"Nothing, really. I just scraped my arm on some rocks this morning when I went swimming." Technically, that was not a lie. It was after midnight by the time I'd gotten back to my room, so it really had been morning. I did feel bad about the half-truth, but if he knew where I'd gone the night before, I might have forfeited my trip. We had rules against swimming after dark.

He inspected the scratch, which by then had turned a nasty, puffy umber. "You'd better have her put some disinfectant on it, too."

He turned back to the mail, and I went looking for answers.

The one person on the island who keeps up with all the gossip is our lounge manager, Darlene. She's been with us at the resort since the beginning, so she's a fixture on the property and the closest thing to family that I have. Besides my dad, that is.

Darlene isn't a nurse, but she is like the resident mom, and so she's the one in charge of the first-aid kit. I headed for the lounge and found her behind the bar, stacking glasses. As I expected, the lounge was empty—with the exception of Mick, who was sleeping in the corner, his hand half wrapped around what looked like a glass of tomato juice.

Darlene's face brightened when she saw me. "Eh, Aphra! What's the haps?"

"I need a Band-Aid."

Her smile disappeared. Small bandages we had back at the Plantation House, so if I was coming to her, she had to know it was something bigger. "Oh. Lemme see."

"It's no big deal. Dad just told me to have you look at it." I slid onto a bar stool and rested my arm on the counter.

She grabbed the first-aid box from under the bar. When she saw the scratch, she grimaced. "Ai. Does it hurt?"

"Not much."

"Then I'm sorry for this." She grabbed my hand to hold it down and then spritzed my arm with antiseptic spray. "Don' want it to get infected."

I hissed in a breath. The antiseptic stung and burned, but not a whole lot worse than the salt water had.

She measured out a gauze strip. "So why you really here?"

"I'm sorry?"

"Nah. Don' be sorry. Just tell me what's up."

Darlene, it should be said, knows me a whole lot better than my dad does. I should have figured she'd see right through me. "I just wanted to ask . . . It's probably nothing."

"What's nothing?"

I hunched my shoulders. "You know villa four? Do you know if it's still torn up?"

"It just needs cabinets and flooring now. Maybe a little paint. Why ask me? You seen it."

"Yeah, but it's been a few days, so I wondered. I just thought it was weird that Dad put the Smiths there last night."

She glanced up from wrapping my arm. "The who?"

"The family that came in last night."

She taped off the end of the gauze, frowning. "What family?"

My heart dropped. That was not a good sign. As manager of the lounge, Darlene had to know the comings and goings of all the guests so she could get their meals prepared and charged to the right villa. She should have gotten the paperwork ten minutes after the Smiths checked in, if not before. Even if Dad had somehow forgotten to send it over, he always met with senior staff first thing in the morning. Why wouldn't Dad have told Darlene about them then?

I frowned. That kind of oversight was not like him at all. He's so obsessive with paperwork and procedure, he borders on anal. "Darlene, you saw my dad this morning, right? Did he seem a little off to—"

"'Scuse me." Mick called from his table, holding an empty glass. He had apparently woken up thirsty.

Darlene pressed her lips together. "Sorry, honey. Duty calls. You make sure I get that family's info, yeah?"

I walked outside, blinking in the morning sun. Something was definitely going on. Dad hadn't been himself since the moment the Smiths showed up in the lobby. I chewed on my lip, remembering how Mr. Smith's words had stolen Dad's smile. What could he have said?

I couldn't bear to go back to the office. Not with Dad being so weird. There were too many questions to be answered. What I really needed was a long swim so I could think, but I could hardly justify going to the beach when I was supposed to be working. If I went to clean the pool, however . . .

During the slow months we operate at half staff, and I make extra money by taking on more jobs. Now that I'd earned my lifeguard certification and my hourly wage had inched up, Dad had added pool upkeep to my daily list of chores. So really, going to the pool was technically justified.

There wasn't much upkeep to do since we have an automatic filtration system and everything, but there's always a bug or two to be skimmed from the surface of the water, especially when the mosquito population reaches its peak, as it does each year when the weather turns hot.

At the pool house, I hung my shorts and blouse in the employee locker and padded barefoot out to the deck. Only a sprinkling of dead insects and a handful of leaves floated in the pool, but that was enough to warrant cleaning, right?

I grabbed the skimmer and started to fish them out when I saw Bianca strolling up the walk. She looked every bit the part of a rocker chick in a retro crocheted halter-top bikini, platform sandals, and oversize white-rimmed mod sunglasses.

"Hey, girl!" She waved as she approached. "What they got you working for on a beautiful day like today?"

I gave her a resigned smile and a you-know-how-it-is shrug and continued cleaning the pool.

She skirted the edge and dropped onto a chaise near where I was working. "Hey, you wanna take a break for a bit?" She patted the chair next to her. "I won't tell if you don't."

"Oh. Thank you, but—"

"Please. Ray's off doing his thing somewhere, so I don't have anyone to talk to. You can keep me company."

Ray was Mick's island pseudonym. The one he chose for himself, that is. I have to tell you, visiting with Bianca was tempting. She was without a doubt one of the most interesting people I'd ever met on the island. But visiting with guests was just not something I did. Be helpful, yes. Be pleasant and polite, yes. But *visit*? No, thank you. It was better just to keep my distance.

"Ah, c'mon. We can talk about that new kid you were with last night."

That was all it took. I set down my pole.

She grinned triumphantly. "I saw you from our veranda last night, coming up from the beach. He's a hottie, that one. I'd hang on to him if I were you."

I could actually feel the blush creeping across my cheeks. "It's not like that."

"It's always like that."

"He's a guest."

"And?"

"It's just . . . I don't . . ."

She winked. "Of course you don't."

I fell silent, and my discomfort must have amused her because she laughed.

"I'm just giving you a hard time. Come on. Sit." She patted the seat cushion again. "I'll play nice, I promise."

I sat.

She sighed with exaggerated contentment. "See? Isn't that better?"

I nodded.

"Nice pool."

"Thank you."

"Ooh, I love it. You're so proper and polite."

"Thank you." I gave her an elaborate seated curtsy this time, which made her laugh again.

"There it is! I knew you had a personality lurking behind the mask."

I blinked. "Mask?" Me?

"Oh, yeah. I've seen you around, acting all professional and aloof. What are you, like, seventeen?"

"Sixteen."

"Even worse. You should be out partying. Or at least not being so damn careful all the time. Believe me, life's too short."

Careful? That was my dad, not me. I was . . . smart.

Smart to toe the line with school and work. Smart not to rock the boat. Smart to maintain an appropriate distance from the guests. But that remark stung. Or hit too close to home.

I fought hard for a comeback, but nothing sprang to mind except, "At least I'm not lying around a swimming pool less than two hundred yards from the beach."

"What?" She laughed, free and happy. "Well, I suppose you've got a point. However"—she crossed her long legs—"some people don't like sand."

"What's the draw of a beach resort, then? Why not vacation in Kansas or someplace with a really great pool instead of flying three thousand miles to find the ocean?"

"They have great pools in Kansas?"

I laughed. "You know what I mean."

"So this is a pet peeve of yours, is it?"

I hesitated. Maybe I should just keep my mouth shut.

"C'mon." Bianca leaned back on the chaise, grinning. "Give it to me straight."

"Okay." I took a deep breath. "Before we came here, my dad ran a resort in South Carolina that sat on the most gorgeous beach you've ever seen. White sand, crystal clear water. But that wasn't good enough for the owners. They built a huge swimming pool up on a platform so that it looked like it spilled over into the ocean. It was pretty, but it ruined the beach—and, come on. A pool just isn't the same as the ocean. It has no energy. No life."

"So true." Bianca swung her legs over the side of the

chaise. "You know what? You've inspired me. I'm tired of waiting around for Ray. I think I'll keep it real and go to the beach. And besides"—she lowered her sunglasses—"three's a crowd."

I followed her gaze to see Adam coming down the terraced steps toward the pool. He was shirtless, in a pair of royal blue board shorts that offset his tanned skin. He moved smoothly, all broad shoulders and six-pack abs. I let out an appreciative breath.

A knowing smile spread across Bianca's face. "Now that's what I'm talking about."

"No . . . I'm not—"

She laughed and stood up. "Nice hangin' with you, kid." Sliding her sunglasses into place, she strolled off toward the beach.

Adam waved when he noticed I was watching him. He took the last few steps two at a time.

"Hi!" I waved back. "What're you up to this morning?"

"Looking for you."

I swear I must have blushed all the way up from my toenails. "Really?"

"Yeah." His gaze wandered beyond me to the deserted pool. "So is this where you guard all those lives?"

I laughed. "Yes. As you can see, it's a very demanding job."

"Is it always this busy?"

"Pretty much. When the resort's full, we get a handful of sun lizards, but that's about it."

He eyed my bandage. "How's that doing?"

"This? It's fine."

"Can you get it wet?"

"I guess."

"So . . ." He gestured with his head toward the pool.

"Oh. I can't. I'm supposed to be working."

"Ah." He looked at his feet. "Got it. Do you mind if I . . . ?"

"No, not at all."

I stepped back as he kicked off his sandals and executed a perfect dive from the side of the pool. He surfaced just as gracefully, his dark hair slicked back and dripping.

"Very nice."

He didn't answer, but sank beneath the water. A second later, he came up thrashing. "Agh! Leg cramp! Help! Help!"

I laughed. "Hold on. I'll throw you a life preserver."

He stopped sloshing. "You're no fun."

"I'm working."

"And I'm drowning. As the lifeguard, isn't it your job to save me?"

I hesitated. On the one hand, I *had* been planning on going swimming. I just hadn't planned on Adam being with me. I probably shouldn't . . . but then I remembered Bianca's mocking grin. I was being careful again. What would it hurt? If she could deal with sand between her toes, I could let myself relax a little. I closed my eyes and jumped into the pool before I could change my mind.

Once I got in the water, I remembered that I hadn't finished skimming the pool. I cringed, scooping up a mosquito carcass and flinging it onto the deck.

"That's an interesting ritual."

I spotted another bloodsucker and scooped it out as well. "I should get out and get the net."

"For what? A couple of bugs? We went swimming in the lakes all the time back home. This is nothing."

I hooked my elbows over the lip of the pool and let my legs float behind me. The cement was warm under my arms. "So, where's home?"

"Uh . . . Montana."

"Where in Montana?"

He hesitated. "Butte."

"Why the pause? Can't you remember?"

"I . . . wasn't sure you'd know where it was, you know, since you live so far away."

I swatted water at him. "I've only been here four years, and I do remember my geography, thank you very much. I learned all the states and capitals before I was six."

"Me, too," he boasted. "*And* all the major freeways."

I drew back. "Seriously? I thought I was the only weird kid who did that. My mom and I used to map imaginary road trips, and I had to figure out the distance and time traveled."

He laughed. "Wow. I was just kidding, but you really know them? That *is* weird."

Well, that deserved some kind of a comeback, but I couldn't think of one, so I splashed him. He splashed me back. I splashed him again, a little harder this time. He laughed and grabbed me, trying to wrestle me under the water. I hooked my arm around his neck so he couldn't dunk me without going down himself, but it didn't faze him. We both went under. He grinned at me, cheeks all puffed up like a double-sided balloon. I grinned right back. I'd been building my endurance for years, with my swimming ritual and all. I could outlast him.

But he was still with me when my lungs started to burn. Still with me as the ache in my chest turned into desperation. Finally, I had to break free and push for the surface. He followed, but I came up first.

"Not bad for a girl."

"Yeah? Well, I was just protecting your fragile male ego."

He laughed at that, and the conversation lulled. I took the opportunity to climb from the pool so I could dry off on one of the lounge chairs. Adam followed.

We sat quietly for a moment. I turned to him. "Hey, did our dads know each other before you got here?"

He propped himself up on his elbows. "I don't think so. Why?"

"Just wondering. The way they were talking the other night..."

"Oh. I didn't hear what they were saying. Did you?"

"No. It just seemed like they might be . . . old friends."

He shrugged. "Maybe. I don't know. Dad never mentioned it."

"How did you decide to come to our resort for your vacation?"

"That's easy. I heard you had the hottest lifeguard around, and I begged until the parents gave in."

I blushed hot and looked away.

"What? No more questions? Okay. It's my turn. Is Aphra a family name? I don't think I've heard it before."

"Well, it's not really a family name, like my aunt or grandma shares it or anything, but my mom chose it, if that counts. She named me after Aphra Behn."

"Who's that?"

"Are you kidding? Only one of *the* first professional women writers. She was also a spy for King Charles II. My mom, she used to be really into spies and stuff like that."

"Used to be? So she isn't anymore?"

"I don't know. I haven't seen her for a while. She left when we moved here."

"Oh. I'm sorry."

I picked at a seam on the chaise. Well, that was one way to kill a conversation. Which was probably a good thing because it saved him the tedium of hearing how it felt to find out at twelve years old that you are going to a new place with no friends, no school, no television, no movie theaters, no malls, no fast food, and, by the way, no mom.

"Moving sucks," he said finally. "It changes everything. Each new place, you have to reinvent yourself to suit the situation. It's like you have no control over anything."

"I know! Your whole life gets rearranged, and you're just supposed to accept it."

"Well, at least you got to move here. It's a lot better than ending up in West Bloom—" He seemed to catch himself and paused for a second. "You know, a lot of people would love to live in a place like this."

"No, a lot of people would love to *visit* a place like this. There's a difference."

"So, do you miss it? Your home before here?"

I shrugged. "I was only twelve when we left South Carolina. But I miss the things I wish I was doing."

He lowered his brows. "Okay, you're going to have to explain that one."

"I have a friend back home I've kept in touch with. Every time she e-mails me about going to the latest movie or getting her driver's license or being asked to the prom, I have serious bouts of homesickness, even though I never got to do any of those things there."

He nodded. "Well, at least you *can* keep in touch."

"What about you? You've moved, too?"

"Once or twice."

"And do you still stay in contact with your old friends?"

He shrugged. "Sometimes. Through Facebook, mostly. I don't get much chance to e-mail."

"Oh! Cami has an account too. She keeps telling me I should—"

"Aphra, may I see you for a moment?"

I jumped and twisted around. Dad! I had completely forgotten I was supposed to be working. His carefully bland expression showed he wasn't happy about it, either. He wasn't the kind to yell or scold or anything like that, but when he was disappointed in me or mad at me, I knew it. He became ultra-polite and aloof. Oh, and sometimes he docked my pay—something he couldn't get away with for the other employees. To me, losing money was worse than being grounded. He may not have been aware of it, but the cash I was saving was one day going to help me find my mom. I wanted to ask her why she left.

I stood and walked over to him with as much dignity as a kid caught playing around instead of working can muster. "Yes?"

He lowered his voice. "I've been looking all over for you. Please grab your things. You're needed in the office."

I turned and gave Adam an apologetic frown.

He nodded in understanding. "I should get going anyway. I'll see you around?"

I sure hoped so.

Dad was silent most of our walk back to the Plantation House, but as we came to the courtyard, he finally spoke. His voice was tight. "What were you doing with that boy?"

"Nothing. We were just talking."

"Well, don't. I want you to keep away from those people, understand?"

Those people? What was he talking about? "You mean his family? Why? Who are they?"

He regarded me for a second and then looked away again. "They're guests who have asked for their privacy, and I would like you to respect their wishes. Now if you would hurry and get dressed, Miss Shimizu is waiting for you in the lobby."

Right. I had offered to show her around. "Oh. Yes, of course." I hurried up to my room and changed, not even bothering to rinse the chlorine out of my hair before I pulled it back into a ponytail.

Dad's warning kept turning over in my head. *I want you to keep away from those people.* Why? What was he not telling me? The frustration built again. I ground my teeth. Why couldn't he just talk to me?

When I reached the lobby, Dad was chatting with

Hisako near the lanai doors. He looked up at me. "Ah, there you are." His voice was all sunshine and roses, as if he hadn't been angry just a few short minutes before.

I forced a smile and bowed. "Hisako-*san*. So nice to see you again."

She bowed in return. "I hope this is a good time?"

"Of course." Actually, considering Dad's moodiness, the timing couldn't be better. I really wasn't sure where to take Hisako on this little nature hike of ours, but I recognized an opportunity to escape when I saw one. I figured we could start at the far side of the property and work our way back.

We took the back path, and Hisako admired the landscaping as we walked. "It is so lovely here! I suppose you meet a lot of fascinating people in such a place?"

I hated to disappoint her, but our guests really weren't as fascinating as they thought themselves to be. "I suppose . . ."

"It is such a cozy setting. Very peaceful, and so quiet."

"Well, it's actually quieter than usual now. When we're full, it can get really busy."

"Oh? So you do not have many guests at the moment? How many are here?"

"Only a handful."

Hisako nodded politely, and I snuck a glance at her. Was she bored? We hadn't come on the walk to talk about the property; we were supposed to be talking about plants, and I was failing miserably. I had to find something worth showing her, or she might decide the walk wasn't worth her trouble. Then I'd be stuck inside. With Dad.

I directed her attention to the orange-red flowers of a koki'o hibiscus. "This is one of my favorite plants. The petals remind me of flamenco dancers fanning their skirts."

"Very beautiful." She stopped to make a quick sketch in the small blue book she carried.

We continued our walk, with me pointing out some of our finer local flora and her murmuring appreciation. She was especially taken with one of the plants—a Star of Bethlehem with its cluster of small white flowers.

"Ah, *sugoi*!" She bent to examine it. "Madam Fata plant. We have these in Japan. They are very poisonous." Her voice was almost reverent. Botanists can be very weird about their plants.

"Be careful handling it," I warned. "The sap burns if it gets on your skin."

She pressed her lips together as if suppressing a smile. "Thank you, Aphra-*chan*. I will remember that."

My ears burned, and I suddenly felt like an awkward little girl. She was the botanist, and here I was lecturing her about how to handle a plant. How lame can you get? I tried to cover my humiliation by forcing more conversation. "So . . . what got you interested in botany?"

She tilted her head to one side as if this question required serious thought. "I am interested to know what plants can do. They hold much power—to soothe, to heal, even to kill."

"Oh, yeah. We did a unit on the medicinal uses of plants in my biology class. Of course, I forgot most of it as soon as I took the final."

She laughed. "What do you remember?"

I told her how the noni and kava plants can help you sleep. In turn, she shared that the nuts of the kukui could be used as a laxative—as if I really wanted to know that—and that salvia plants have psychoactive effects.

By this time, we had reached the end of the paths and had come out onto the sand of the beach. Hisako daintily kicked off her shoes. "Shall we walk near the water?"

Sure, why not? The longer I stayed with Hisako, the less time I had to spend behind the desk. We strolled barefoot along the firm sand where waves lapped the shore, detouring inland when we came across one of the rock piers. Just being that close to the ocean soothed my agitation.

Until Hisako stopped dead in her tracks. She pointed to the shoreline ahead. "What is that?"

I shielded my eyes and squinted. Something large had washed up on shore. A log maybe.

I gasped.

No, it was a person.

Panic washed over me. I stood paralyzed for a second before my lifeguard training kicked in. I sprinted toward the body. As I drew closer, I could tell who it was: Bianca.

Her hair lay tangled about her head like seaweed, matted with sand. Her pale skin was mottled, and her lips were an odd color of blue.

My heart sank right down to my stomach. The ground seemed to tilt beneath my feet. I could hardly breathe. I dropped to my knees beside her. The ties of her halter-top bikini were tangled tight about her neck. My hands trembled as I tried to loosen them.

But as soon as I touched her, I knew. She was dead.

CHAPTER 4

Over and over again, Bianca's voice echoed in my head, "You've inspired me. I think I'll go to the beach." I had challenged her. If it hadn't been for me, she would be alive and well and sunning herself at the pool.

I killed her.

I blinked hard to keep away the tears and fought the bile rising in my throat. It was my fault. My fault. My fault.

I shook my head until my whole body swayed with grief. She couldn't be dead. Not her. Not someone so . . . alive. No! It wasn't right! There had to be something I could do.

I tilted her head back and bent to blow air into her lifeless mouth. Once, twice. Her cold lips had a waxy feel to them. I shook off another rise of nausea and changed position for chest compressions.

"Aphra-*chan*. Stop. It is too late." Hisako's voice was gentle, but it cut into me like the lava rock.

I was not going to accept that. I pumped furiously on Bianca's chest, counting compressions. She did not respond.

"Aphra-*chan*." Hisako touched my shoulder. "It is over."

"No!" The word was more a plea than a denial.

The pressure of Hisako's fingers increased. Gently, but firmly, she pulled me back. Finally, my hands stilled. I realized my face was wet.

"You knew her?" Hisako asked softly.

"Yes. She is . . . *was* a guest at the resort."

"Then we must report it at once."

I straightened. "Yes. Of course." Hisako was right. I was forgetting my responsibility. There was comfort in having something practical to do. I wiped my eyes. "We should get my dad."

"I will go." Hisako bowed. "You stay with the girl."

I drew in a sharp breath. Stay with her? By myself? But of course Hisako was right. We couldn't both go; the surf was already sucking at Bianca's legs. If we left her on the beach unattended, the tide could carry her away. I couldn't let her lie there with a stranger standing beside her, either. I nodded, and Hisako jogged off across the sand.

The whole thing had a bad dream feel about it. I kept hoping I'd wake up and everything would be back the way it was.

But I couldn't pull my eyes from Bianca. She looked so peaceful, like she was just sleeping in the sand. I reached down to brush away a strand of seaweed that hung across her face, and a crab scuttled out from under her matted hair. I screamed and yanked my hand back.

After that, I kept my distance. I was afraid of what else I might find if I got too close. I hugged my knees and stared out at the sea, where a pair of terns spiraled over the whitecaps. Usually their screeches didn't bother me, but that afternoon the shrieking calls sounded eerie and ominous. I shuddered and closed my eyes, as if that could shut out their cries.

At long last I heard voices at the far end of the beach. I pushed to my feet, anxious to share my vigil with the living. That's when I saw him. Adam's dad was standing near the trees, watching me. His eyes flicked past me to the body in the sand and then toward the approaching group. With a half-perceptible nod, he turned and headed back toward villa four.

I watched him disappear into the brush, a strange, cold feeling settling in my stomach. And then my dad was beside me, hugging me, rubbing my arms, studying my face.

"Are you okay?"

I nodded, even though I still felt pretty shaken. The rest of the group ran to join us. Nothing says rush, I suppose, like one dead guest and a handful of live ones you want to keep ignorant of the fact. Dad hadn't wasted any time in gathering his containment team: Darlene, Frank, and the head of security, Junior. No, really. That's his name. Ironically, this guy is about six-four and must weigh three hundred pounds—all of it muscle.

Hisako had stopped just short of where we all stood. Dad gave her a slight bow and mouthed, "Thank you." She inclined her head, turned, and headed back down the beach.

Once she was gone, Junior crouched beside me, balancing his enormous weight on the balls of his feet. "Yup. She wen mahke a'right." "Mahke" was his way of saying dead. Yeah, nothing gets by Junior.

I glanced up. "Where's Mick?"

"Sleeping?" Darlene looked to Junior for confirmation, and then explained. "He was drinking in the lounge all morning, soused as Sinatra. Junior here had to take him back to his villa to sleep it off." I noticed that Darlene had dropped all traces of the island from her accent, something she did whenever she was truly upset. She'd been the one serving him those drinks. I wondered if she was feeling guilty.

Dad's frown deepened. "So that's why she was swimming alone."

And why she had been waiting by the pool . . . before I sent her to the beach to die. I started to cry again. The guilt was mine.

Darlene misunderstood the emotion and draped an arm around me. "We've never had a guest drown before, have we?" She turned to Junior and said in a low voice,

"How could this have happened? The water wasn't even that rough this afternoon."

Frank bent over Bianca's body. "Take a look at this." He pointed to where the ties of her halter-top bikini were wrapped around her neck. "Mebbe she got tumbled by a wave. Wouldn't have taken a big one if she wasn't a strong swimmer. Those strings could'a got caught on something and choked her."

Darlene and Junior nodded gravely.

I shook my head. Something about that scenario didn't feel right. Junior bent close to examine the bruises on Bianca's neck.

I froze, thinking back to the night before when I'd been caught by that wave. The force of the water had pretty much ripped my top off. What it didn't do was wrap the ties around my neck and choke me to death.

And the wave had dumped Adam and me on the sand. Hard sand, not the loose, drier stuff like where Bianca was lying. Her body was too far aground to have been left there by a wave. It was almost as if someone had put her there.

"I don't think she drowned," I said weakly.

Frank looked up. "Right, I think mebee she choked."

Dad cleared his throat. "We'll leave the thinking up to the coroner."

"I hear ya, brah." Junior stood and brushed the sand from his hands. "I get her into the city, fast kine, yeah?"

"Wait!" I pulled away from Darlene. I couldn't shake

the feeling that something wasn't right. They couldn't move Bianca. Not yet. "Shouldn't we leave her where she is until the police—"

Dad cut me off. "Getting the police here could take all afternoon. I am not leaving this girl to bake in the sun. She goes to the coroner."

"But . . ."

Junior looked to Frank. "How soon you can fly?"

"I was just flushing the lines when I got the squawk. Could be a couple hours."

"Where we gonna put her until then?"

Frank took off his Navy cap and ran a hand through his graying hair. "The walk-in?"

Darlene's eyes got big, and she took a step back. He was talking about her walk-in refrigerator in the lounge kitchen. "No way. If any of my staff sees her, they'll flip out. They'd never walk in there again."

Dad waved them quiet. "Lay her in my office. We'll seal it off and crank up the AC. She'll be fine until you can get off the ground." He turned to Darlene. "We'll need a diversion. Send out complimentary tapas and drinks to the villas, and let's be sure everyone is accounted for." He scrubbed his hand over his face. "I suppose I had better go get Mick and sober him up. He'll want to be with her."

It didn't seem fitting to send Bianca off to the city in just her bikini, so while Frank and Junior waited for their diversion, I ran to get a bedsheet. I wrapped her body in the linen as neatly as I could before the guys carried her off on a stretcher.

I followed them to the Plantation House and watched, numb, as they laid her next to the couch in Dad's office and sealed the place up.

Frank mumbled an apology to no one in particular and said he had to get his helicopter ready to fly. Junior plopped onto one of the couches and fanned himself, his round face red and shiny with sweat. "You know, for a little girl, she sure was heavy."

Frank lowered his thick brows and shook his head at that comment, which just made Junior's face turn even redder. He spread his hands and demanded, "What?"

Frank jerked his head in my direction.

Junior rolled his eyes and pantomimed sweeping Frank out the door. Frank left, but Junior hung around the lobby until Darlene stopped by to see how I was doing. The two of them had a low-voiced conversation in the corner of the lobby—as if I couldn't hear every word they were saying. It seems they were worried I'd be freaked out or something if I were left alone with a dead body in the next room. I admit I was a little shaky, but that's not the same thing as freaked, and not from what they thought, either.

They fussed and fretted over what to do with me until their little powwow was interrupted by a loud squawk from the two-way at Junior's waist.

It was Dad. Mick was being, shall we say, a bit hostile about the sobering-up efforts. Dad requested a little muscle as backup.

Darlene sat with me after Junior left, even though I knew she must have had a million things to do.

"I'm fine," I insisted. "I just wish I knew what happened."

She gave me a sad look. "Honey, she drowned. Her top . . ." She raised a hand to her throat.

"Yeah, I know. The strings. But . . . isn't that kind of strange?" I shuddered, thinking back on how cold Bianca's skin had felt when I had tried to loosen those strings—how they were *wrapped* around her neck, not tangled, as Frank hypothesized. She may have been caught, but not by a wave. The ties, her position on the shore . . . it didn't add up.

"What are you saying?"

"Maybe someone . "

Darlene pulled back. "Aphra, honey, I know you're upset—"

"It has nothing to do with being upset! There's something off about this whole thing. Her top—"

"Aphra. Don't."

"But it doesn't make—"

Darlene cut me off. "The dead deserve some respect, honey. Let this one go."

I chewed on my thumbnail and looked at Dad's closed

office door. Respect. I'm sure "the dead" would have preferred to be alive. I wasn't going to let it go. It was my fault Bianca was gone. If someone had killed her, I had to find out who it was.

Darlene parked herself in the lobby to work on her meal lists, but I managed to ignore her. I was busy making lists of my own.

The first thing I had to figure out was who would want to hurt Bianca? Maybe Mick; they were always fighting, and he might have believed that, the next time, she really would leave him. And Bianca did say she'd been waiting for him. He could have met her at the beach. But both Darlene and Junior had placed Mick at the lounge at the time Bianca died. In fact, I had seen him there myself when Darlene was bandaging my arm.

A chill spread through me as I remembered Adam's dad, watching from the trees. I tried to shake it off. Lots of people go to the beach. They just don't stand around looking over dead bodies and then run off without a word. Did Mr. Smith have something to do with Bianca's death? I thought of how Adam would feel if that turned out to be true, and I felt sick.

What kind of motive could Mr. Smith have? He'd just gotten to the island. What possible connection could he have with Bianca? For Adam's sake, I hoped there wasn't any. But how could I even guess? I didn't know anything about the Smiths. Not even the basic registration info, thanks to my dad. And the way he'd been acting lately, I was pretty sure he wouldn't appreciate my asking questions. I was going to have to figure it out on my own. Who were the Smiths? Where were they from?

Wait.

Didn't Adam say he was from Montana? He'd said something about West Broom. Or was that Bloom? It was West something. Was that the name of their town? Could Mr. Smith have known Bianca from before? I had no idea. But it was the only thing I had to go on. Maybe if I found out where West Bloom was, I could find more information on the mysterious Smiths.

I logged on to the computer and quickly Googled: *West Bloom Montana people search.* Point-two-three seconds later I had over a million hits. Nothing on the first page was a perfect match, but I did find a couple of hits for a Bloomfield, Montana. The rest of the page listed hits for a West Bloomfield in Michigan. I scrolled through a couple more pages. The results were similar.

I leaned back in my chair. Adam *had* said Montana, right? Not Michigan? Yes, I remembered his challenging me about knowing where Butte was. Maybe he lived in the west part of Bloomfield in Montana? Is that what he meant?

I pressed my lips together and typed: *Bloomfield Montana white pages.* Maybe I could look them up in the phone book. I opened a site and typed in Smith. All I learned was that there were eighty-eight Smiths in

Bloomfield, but that wasn't much use. And it wouldn't help me figure out what happened to Bianca.

I folded my arms and stared at the screen. I was chasing shadows. It was stupid to think I was going to find out anything sitting in the office. I should just go find Adam. And ask him what? Had his dad killed one of our guests? That would go over well.

Then I thought about something else Adam said at the pool. "Back home" he had gone swimming in lakes. There were lots of lakes in Michigan. Montana had lakes, too, of course, but they were more known for their mountains and their big sky. Michigan had thousands of lakes. And there had been all those hits for West Bloomfield in Michigan. . . .

I rubbed a hand over my face. It was worth a try. I typed in *Adam Smith West Bloomfield Michigan*. The first page was a blog for Adam Smith, a college hockey player. The second linked to an article in the *Detroit Free Press* newspaper.

"How you doing? You look a little stressed."

I about jumped out of the chair. Darlene had finished her paperwork and stood at the counter, watching me intently.

"Oh. Uh, yeah. I'm good."

"So what you working on?"

I hesitated. If she hadn't wanted to hear my theory about how Bianca didn't drown, I wasn't going to lay out my online goose chase for her to scrutinize. "Uh, just homework. Nothing exciting." I clicked on the newspaper link.

"Good for you, but how can you even think straight? My nerves are shot. It was all I could do to post the menu for tomorrow."

I think she kept blathering, but I tuned her out. My eyes were glued to an article by reporter A. Smith from Wednesday's local section of the *Detroit Free Press*. Or, more precisely, my eyes were glued to the picture accompanying the article. It showed a hulk of blackened, twisted metal that had once been a car. Inset near the lower right-hand corner was a family portrait featuring two smiling parents and a good-looking, blue-eyed son. The caption read, "Fiery crash on I-23 claims the lives of local businessman Victor Mulo, art critic Elena Mulo, and West Bloomfield High School senior Seth Mulo."

My hands suddenly felt very cold as I adjusted the resolution of the photo. My head buzzed like I had an entire hive of bees inside my skull.

I had no doubt in my mind; the dead boy and his family were at that very moment residing in villa four.

CHAPTER
5

"What's the matter, Aphra?" Darlene edged closer. "You look like you've seen a ghost."

Try three.

I stared at the screen. Adam/Seth smiled at me from the photo.

"Aphra?"

My head snapped up. "Huh?"

"What's wrong? What is that you're—"

Before she could come any closer, I switched off the monitor. "The computer . . . it's starting to give me a headache."

Darlene frowned and stepped behind the desk. She put her hand on my forehead. "Well, no wonder you don't feel good, after all you've been through. You got some aspirin in the office?"

"I dunno." We probably did, but I wasn't thinking about aspirin. I was too busy trying to rearrange what I thought I knew about Adam . . . Seth. The new name was going to take some getting used to, but even harder to wrap my head around was the fact that he and his family were supposed to be dead.

Had the . . . Mulos faked their deaths? There didn't seem to be any alternative. But why? Who were they hiding from? And what did any of that have to do with Bianca?

My stomach tightened. What did my dad know about all this? Looking back on it, he appeared to be hiding the Mulos—putting them in a villa that was not supposed to be inhabited, not keeping records . . .

"Aphra? Did you hear a word I said?"

I jumped up from my chair. "I . . . I need to get some air. Can you watch the desk for a few minutes?"

Darlene blinked. "The desk? But—"

"I'll be right back." I raced from the office before she could object.

Not that I had any idea where I was going. Or what to do with the information I'd just uncovered. But I had to do *something* or I was going to explode. This is what came of getting involved. You end up getting hurt. Seth, if that was even his real name, had lied to me from the beginning. He had said his name was Adam. He'd said he was from Montana. What else had he lied about? I could only surmise that his family had faked their deaths and were on the run from who knew what. Now it didn't seem so far-fetched to think his dad could be a murderer. Or that my dad might be hiding them. It was too much.

I had no one to turn to. Not Darlene. Certainly not my dad. What was I supposed to do now? Spill everything to the authorities? Or should I talk to Seth first and give him a chance to explain? Could I even trust a word he said?

I had to get away. To think. I took a quick glance back at the Plantation House and then slipped into the trees and took off for my beach.

I dropped my shorts, peeled off my shirt, and ran for the water. Holding my breath, I swam along the bottom. I passed through a warm current followed by a downright chilly one. Seemed apropos for the moment, like the ocean couldn't decide what it was going to do either.

When I broke the surface, I struck out swimming, my strokes awkward and jerky—which was about how my brain was working. It wasn't until I found the rhythm in my stroke that I was able to form a clear thought in my head.

What was it Mom used to say? If you can't find the answer to a problem, you need to distance yourself from the situation to see the puzzle more clearly. I couldn't help but wonder what kind of problem my dad and I represented, and why she had felt the need to distance herself from us.

I dove underwater again. I wished I could stay down forever. Then I wouldn't have to deal with moms who leave and dads who can't be trusted. People wouldn't die. Friends wouldn't lie to me.

No, the only thing I could do was to go home. Look for answers. Ask questions. What choice did I have? I swam back to shore.

I knew I was in trouble before I even made it out

of the water, and not from the waves this time. There, standing on the beach, was my dad. He marched down to the water's edge as I came in, his face tight and redder than usual.

"What do you think you're doing?"

I figured it wouldn't be a good move to state the obvious, so I didn't say anything, which turned out to be not such a great move either, judging by the way his lips pulled down at the corners.

"Do you have any idea how worried I was?"

"I told Darlene I was going out."

"To get some *air*, not, not . . ." He gestured toward the waves. "After everything that's happened today, why would you think this was a good idea?"

"Because I had to get away. *Especially* after everything that's happened today. This is where I come to unwind."

"Not anymore you don't. Not until we get this thing resolved. Now pick up your clothes, and let's go back to the house."

It was pretty clear that Dad didn't know what to do with me. Since I'd never really given him a reason to punish me before, this was new territory for him. As a dad, I mean. As a boss, it was simple for him just to dock my pay or give me the grunt work if I messed up, but in the father/daughter arena, I'd never even talked back to him. Wanted to a few times, but never did. I think I was afraid to.

I could tell he thought he should do *something* about my running off "after all that happened," but he didn't know what. He ended up putting me under house arrest. Not that he came right out and said as much, but he had me work in the office until dinner, and, even then, he asked the staff to deliver the food to the Plantation House instead of our going to the lounge. We ate in silence in the conference room.

I really wasn't hungry, anyway. I kept thinking about Bianca, who at that very moment was being flown to the city by Junior and Frank, and about the Mulos' deception. I picked at my food while fears and questions chased around in my head like a couple of drunken geckos.

I think dad may have noticed my lack of appetite because he eased up a little after dinner and didn't give me any more assignments. He did want me to stay in the lobby, though, no doubt so he could keep a warden's watch on me. I dropped onto the couch with a book, although I didn't see a word on the page.

I have no idea how long I sat there, staring out the window. The knot in my stomach grew tighter and tighter as the sky faded from purple to black and the first stars appeared.

Then I saw movement outside the window. Seth beckoned to me from the shadows. I pretended not to see him and turned back to my book. I coolly flipped the page. Inside, however, I was anything but calm. How could he show his face after the way he'd lied to me? Did he know what his dad had done? Okay, what his dad *allegedly* had done.

I snuck another glance out the window. Again Seth motioned for me to come out. His face looked pleading, anxious. I bit my lip. What if he *had* found out what his dad had . . . allegedly done, and now he needed my help? Could I ignore him?

But he had *lied* to me!

Plus, he and his family could be dangerous if they were involved in something serious enough to make them want to fake their own deaths. I'd be smart to stay clear of him like my dad wanted me to do. Like my dad—who was sneaking around, not telling me the truth, trying to hide the Mulos, treating me like a little kid instead of just telling me what it was all about—wanted me to do . . .

I set aside my book.

Leaning back in the chair, I peered into Dad's office. He was on the phone. Maybe if I just went to see what Seth had to say . . . I rushed to the door and slipped quietly outside.

Seth was waiting by the walk. "Are you okay? My dad said something happened."

I'll bet he did. "I'm good, thanks."

He shuffled his feet. "Do you want to . . . I don't know, go for a walk or something?"

"I can't."

"Oh."

"It's my dad . . ." I gestured vaguely behind me.

"Oh."

The questions inside my head screamed to be asked. Only now, facing Seth, I didn't know how to bring them up without confronting him about his fake death. I wasn't sure if I should spill that without finding out first what was going on. But I couldn't do that by keeping quiet.

"Hey, how did you guys get to the resort last night?"

His brows drew together. "The . . . um . . . helicopter dropped us on the beach."

I took a step back. The beach? Frank was the only one authorized to bring guests to the resort, and he would never land anywhere but the helipad. I thought back to the night the Mulos had arrived. I *knew* there hadn't been enough time after Hisako's arrival for Frank to have made it to the city and back before the Mulos showed up. "Who brought you?"

He shifted from one foot to the other. "I don't remember the pilot's name."

More lies. An awkward silence stretched between us. Finally, we both spoke at the same time.

"Just wanted to make sure you were all right," he said as I asked, "Are you okay?" We laughed, probably a lot more than the situation warranted.

I searched his face, looking for I don't know what. "Really. Is everything okay? With your family, I mean. Because if you need to talk . . ."

Seth never got a chance to answer. Something small and black swooped out of the darkness, aimed directly for my head. I screamed and ducked. Seth was at my side in an instant, protectively wrapping his arms around me.

"What happened?"

I trembled and pushed away, feeling foolish. "It's nothing. A bat. It startled me, is all." Just a bat. The one thing in the world I was most afraid of. Until now.

Seth started to laugh, but then he nudged me and jerked his head toward the office. Through the window, I could see Dad heading toward the door.

"Oh, crap. Go. Go!"

Seth slipped back into the shadows. The sound of his footsteps faded into the shrubbery as the door opened behind me.

"Aphra?"

I turned around, pasting what I hoped was an innocent look on my face. "Yes?"

"Are you all right? What was that noise?"

"There was a bat. . . ."

"What are you doing out here in the first place?"

"I . . . needed some fresh air."

He folded his arms. "I see. And who was that with you?"

"What?"

"I told you, Aphra. I want you to stay away from that boy."

I pressed my lips together. I wanted things, too. I wanted Bianca to be alive. I wanted to see my mom again. I wanted my dad to be straight with me. I opened my mouth to tell him that, but I couldn't make the words come.

I followed him inside, but I wasn't in the mood to pretend-read anymore. "Dad, I'm really tired. I think I'm going to go up to bed now."

He narrowed his eyes. "Bed? Now?"

What was he thinking? That I was going to sneak outside again? I said good night and trudged up to my room. I didn't even turn on the light, but went straight to my window seat and sat staring out over the trees. I hated that my dad and I couldn't trust each other anymore. We may not have had the closest of relationships, but it had worked on some levels. We'd always had a mutual respect. I just wasn't sure it was there anymore.

I must have fallen asleep at the window because when I awoke, I was curled up on the seat, cold and stiff from lying in a weird position all night.

A soft wind blew in a salt water tang from the ocean. It smelled fresh and clean. If only the new day could erase all that had happened the day before.

I showered and dressed and headed down to the lobby, braced for more terse words from my dad. But Dad wasn't there, which was strange; he always began each day promptly at seven o'clock. It was well past eight.

I didn't have time to think too much about it, because just then, Darlene trudged into the lobby, propping up a man in a rumpled navy suit. The collar of his crisp white shirt lay open, and his silk tie hung at a crazy angle. Frank followed close behind with the man's suitcase—a big, blocky thing that appeared to be heavy, the way he was straining with it.

I stared at the procession as they made their way across the room. Another check-in I knew nothing about.

"Aphra, honey, do you know where your dad is?" Darlene sounded irritated. "Frank had to call me to help with Mr. Watson here."

"Watts," the man said.

Darlene gave him a reassuring smile and patted him on the arm like a little child. "No worry, beef curry. We get you settled fast kine, yeah? Guaranz." She lowered her voice and told me, "He got sick on the flight."

Maybe. But even pale and sweating, the man had a threatening air about him that made me want to hide. It was the way he looked at me, with black, veiled eyes . . . like a shark's. Sharp eyes that felt like they were trying to probe my thoughts. Heavy brows hung over those eyes, already disapproving of whatever he might find.

I shuddered and pasted on a courteous smile. "I'm sorry to hear that, Mr. Watson. Let's get you to your room so you can rest."

"Watts." He scowled. "Damian Watts."

I typed in the name and a registration screen came up immediately. It looked like Dad had taken the reservation just a couple of hours before. "Oh. Yes. Here you are. You'll be in villa ten."

"Wait." Mr. Watts pulled away from Darlene and leaned heavily on the desk. He fixed me with those dark eyes. "Mr. Connolly . . . is expecting . . . me. I need to . . . speak to him."

"I'm sorry, Mr. Connolly is assisting another guest at the moment, sir, but I can let him know you're here." I gave him a shaky smile. "Until then, we should get you to your villa so you can lie down."

His thin lips tightened and curved into a frown. "Mr. Connolly—" He swayed, and I thought he was going to pass out right there in the office.

Darlene hurried to prop him up again. "Frank, help me get Mr. Watts out to the cart. You can take him to his room, yeah?"

Mr. Watts shook his head emphatically. "No. I . . . need . . . to—"

"You need to rest," Darlene said with finality.

I promised to pass along his message to Dad, and Darlene and Frank helped Mr. Watts outside. Once they were gone, I closed out the registration screen as fast as I could. Even having the man's name staring at me gave me the creeps. I didn't know what he wanted with my dad, but whatever it was, I had a sick feeling it wouldn't be good.

Dad showed up around nine that morning with a file folder tucked under his arm. When I asked him where he'd been, he didn't directly answer, but he did ask if Mr. Watts had made it in.

"He's all taken care of. When did we get the reservation? It wasn't on the calendar."

"Late call-in." Dad thumbed the edge of the folder and looked beyond me to the conference room. "Please hold my calls until we're done."

I frowned. "Until who's done?"

"Mr. Watts and I." He paused. "You did show him into the conference room, didn't you?"

"No, he's in his villa. He got sick on the flight. Who is he, anyway? What's this meeting about?"

"Insurance," Dad said too quickly. "It's time to update our policy."

Insurance? Did he think I was a complete idiot? I knew full well our policy was current. Besides, there was no way Watts was an insurance salesman.

"Well, he was looking pretty rough, but I'm sure he'll call when he's conscious."

Dad nodded without saying a word and stepped into his office, taking the file folder with him. I stared after him. Who was Watts, really? And what kind of business could my dad have with a person like that? I watched as he slid the file folder into his desk drawer. One thing was certain: I was going to find out.

Lunchtime came and went. My stomach growled, but I wasn't going to leave the office until I had a look at that file.

Darlene called around one and asked to speak to my

dad. I'm not sure what she had to say, but whatever it was, he hung up frowning. "Aphra, I need you to keep an eye on the office for a moment. If Mr. Watts comes in, tell him I will be right back."

I nodded nonchalantly, watching, hoping, praying that he wouldn't take the file folder with him. He didn't. I waited, blood drumming in my ears, until he cleared the lobby, and then I rushed into his office.

Slowly, quietly, I inched open his desk drawer. The file lay on top of a pile of papers. The label on the tab said simply, SMITH. My breath caught. I *knew* he had to have recorded the information somewhere. But why would he be sharing private guest information with Mr. Watts?

An uneasy feeling coiled in my stomach. Seth's family had gone through a lot of trouble to disappear. Was Watts there to help them or to hunt them down?

I opened the file. Paper-clipped to the inside of the folder were a couple of Polaroid snapshots of the Mulos that had obviously been taken around our resort. Several lined sheets of paper, all filled with my dad's neat handwriting, made up the rest of the file. On the top right-hand corner of the first page was written a notation in red ink: *Watts.*

I wanted to read what the handwritten notes said, but suddenly I heard voices outside the office—my dad and someone else. They seemed to be getting closer. I slapped the file closed and slipped it back where it was.

I probably should have tried to hide or something,

but I couldn't move. The walls seemed to be closing in. Outside the confines of the office, we had a murderer on the loose, an imposter family, and now perhaps a... what? What would Watts be? I had to find out, before my dad said the wrong thing and something happened to Seth.

Dad looked puzzled when he returned to his office to find me standing there. I managed to give him a bland hello and reminded him that Darlene had sent over some invoices for his signature. I fished them out of his in-box and handed them to him.

He looked them over. "Any word from Mr. Watts?"

"The insurance guy? No."

He pulled open his drawer to grab a pen and began signing on the dotted lines.

I watched Dad bend over his paperwork, frustration building until I wanted to scream. How could he act like everything was normal? Why couldn't he just talk to me? He could tell me what he knew, and I would tell him what I knew, and maybe we'd be able to make sense of it all. But I didn't have to ask what he thought of the Mulos. That much he had made clear. If I wanted answers, I had to go out and find them myself.

I cleared my throat. "Excuse me, Dad? I'm not feeling very well. Do you need me any more this morning? I think I'd like to lie down."

"No, no. That's fine." He didn't even look up from his papers. "Go rest."

I murmured my thanks and trudged up the stairs, sighing and moaning all the way. In my room, I flopped onto my bed and waited.

Sure enough, Dad showed up at the door within just a few minutes. "Are you sick? Should I get Darlene?" His face was pinched with concern. Made me feel the slightest bit guilty for what I was about to do. But what's fair is fair. If he was lying to me, why should I be honest with him?

"No. It's just . . . you know . . . that time of the month. I get really bad cramps."

His ears turned brick red, and he looked down the hall. I could tell he wanted to escape.

"I think I just need to rest. Is it okay if I skip the office today?"

"Yes. Sure. Fine. I'll, uh . . ." He'd grasped the knob and was already pulling the door shut. "I'll check in on you later."

"Thanks," I called weakly.

I waited until I could hear his footsteps fade away down the stairs and then crossed stealthily to the door. "I'm sorry," I whispered, and depressed the lock.

CHAPTER 6

The trellis looked sturdy enough. A tangle of Kuhio vine clung to the little slats of wood, hot pink flowers long gone in the summer heat. I had no idea if it would hold my weight—I'd never done this sort of thing before.

I threw my uniform clothes on the bed and pulled a pair of worn jeans shorts and a faded OP T-shirt over my swimsuit. Into the pocket of my shorts I tucked the vial of pepper spray my dad kept around for emergencies—just in case I needed protection. Fingers shaking, I tied the laces of my beat-up Pumas and tiptoed back to the window.

My room overlooks the courtyard. It's a great location—it gives me a front-row seat for watching people come and go—but it does make sneaking out a dicey proposition. I watched and waited until I was certain the courtyard was deserted before swinging my leg over the windowsill.

I found a foothold in the latticework and tested my weight against the thin wood. It held. I stepped down with my other foot. So far, so good. I let go of the casement. Not a bright idea. The wood splintered beneath my feet with a sharp crack. In a panic, I grasped at the vines to break my fall, but they pulled away in my hands. I landed smack on my butt, vines snaking down around me.

Actually, it wasn't as bad as I thought it would be. Couldn't breathe for a moment there, but I'd suffered no broken bones. No serious injuries—except to the trellis. I untangled myself from the pile of vines, hoping the rest of the plant was full enough to cover the damage I'd done. Shoving the fallen tendrils behind the trellis, I tried to fluff up the foliage I had crushed at the base. It looked pretty sad but would have to do.

As I turned around, brushing the dirt off my shorts, I noticed Hisako standing near the edge of the courtyard, black eyes alight with amusement. She smiled and bowed to me. My face went hot, and I bowed in return, trying to come up with the Japanese words to explain what the heck I was doing. She placed one finger to her lips and continued on the path as if she had seen nothing out of the ordinary. See, I knew there was a reason I liked her.

I slipped off in the other direction. I had to find out who Watts was and what he was up to before he had that meeting with Dad.

I skirted the main courtyard and headed straight for the maintenance shed. Our grounds crew was working on the other side of the resort that day, but Watts wouldn't know that. I found a uniform shirt hanging on a peg in the shed and slipped it on. It smelled vaguely of old sweat and stale cigarettes, but a dirty shirt was a small price to pay for the truth.

To be clear, I had no idea who the Mulos were running from—or even whether they were running. I didn't know if they were the good guys or if I should be taking Watts straight to them. I didn't know if Seth's dad had anything to do with Bianca's death. All I knew was that I had to get to the bottom of whatever was going on before someone else got hurt.

I grabbed a rake and a pair of canvas gloves and headed to villa ten.

I started raking just up the path from the villa, working my way closer with each stroke. You wouldn't even know anyone had checked into the place, it was that still. No movement in the windows, no lights, nothing. I got bold and worked my way close to the front-room window. I couldn't see a thing for the glare on the glass, though.

Then I heard a voice—no, more like a groan—coming from the veranda. I clutched the rake and snuck around the side of the building.

Watts sat hunched over in a chair, holding a cloth to his forehead. On the table next to him sat a glass of water and a bottle of aspirin. He had removed his tie and undone the top buttons of his shirt, which hung open so that the white scoop of his undershirt showed. When he moved, I caught a glimpse of a brown leather strap cutting into the flesh near his shoulder. My stomach curdled. He was no insurance salesman. The man was wearing a holster.

I retreated backward until I reached the corner of the villa, then spun around and ran all the way back to the maintenance shed.

My hands shook as I undid the buttons of the borrowed shirt. He had a gun. A gun! How had he gotten that past airport security? How had he gotten it past Frank?

I tossed the shirt at the hook and missed. I had just bent to retrieve it when I heard footsteps outside. I froze, my pulse beating in my throat. Had Watts seen me? Followed me here? My eyes darted about the shed. There was no place to hide.

"What are you doing out here?" The voice did not belong to Watts. I'd recognize that fake midwestern accent anywhere. It was Mr. Mulo.

I was about to turn and explain myself when Seth's voice replied, "Nothing. Just walking."

"You can't keep doing this! You know we need to be careful."

"Careful? Dad, there's hardly anyone here! Who's going to see me? I thought we came here so we didn't have to hide."

"No," Victor Mulo said. "We came here *to* hide. You can't be gallivanting around out in the open. We can't risk standing out."

"Then this was a stupid place to come. At least in a big city we could blend in."

"It's only temporary."

"And then what?"

"And then we—" He stopped. "Wait. Did you hear something?"

The voices fell silent.

I held my breath.

"Come. We should get back to the house."

I waited until their footsteps faded away before I dared peek outside the shed. By then Mr. Mulo was at the far end of the path, just starting to turn toward their villa. Seth lagged behind, shoulders hunched, hands dug deep into his pockets. Suddenly he stopped. He turned and looked directly at me. He did not look happy.

My breath caught, and my face flamed hot. I'd been caught spying. Not knowing what else to do, I ducked behind the shed and slipped into the hillside jungle. It's actually a rain forest, if you want to get technical; but with bamboo, banyan, mango, and palms shooting up from the mossy ground, it feels like a jungle. Whatever you call it, it provided a chance to escape while I tried to come up with an explanation to give Seth about why I'd been watching him and his dad.

One of the distinct disadvantages of hanging around in there, though, is that it harbors island mosquitoes. They're about the size of small birds, have tiny needles for noses, and they attack in swarms. Usually I'm careful about dousing myself with repellant before hiking, but in this particular instance I hadn't had the opportunity.

By the time I reached the first ridge, I was covered with itchy, red welts.

Mosquitoes aside, I felt some peace among the ferns and palms. I'd been exploring the hills since the day I arrived on the island, and they had become a refuge to me, just like my beach. Better yet, a few years before I had found a cove tucked back in a little crack of a valley about a mile or so from the property. I liked to think of it as my own private hideaway, which was exactly what I needed at the moment. I didn't know what I would do up there, but at least I had a destination.

In all the time we'd been on the island, I had never seen anyone else at the cove, which isn't much of a surprise because it's easy to miss through the trees, even from the air. I know, because I looked for it last time we flew into the city. I probably wouldn't have seen it at all if I hadn't known it was there. Besides, I doubted any of our guests would expend the effort to climb up that far. You have to hike up to the third ridge, cross a fallen log over a twenty-foot ravine, and slog through an abandoned taro patch. But, oh! Is it ever worth it! A little sliver of paradise, all my own.

On either side of the cove, rocky walls covered in velvet green stretch up to the sky. In the center of the valley, a long, narrow waterfall hangs like a bride's veil and empties into a sapphire pool. The coolest thing of all, though, is the secret cave hidden behind the falls. And no one knew about it but me.

My mom would have appreciated it. We used to go hiking together before Dad and I left for the island, and she was always on the lookout for "little pockets of tranquillity," as she called them.

"Gather peace whenever you find it," she told me once. "Bask in it. Store it up. You never know when you might need it."

Peace was exactly what I needed. Peace and answers. I hoped if I could find the first, I'd be able to figure out the second.

When I reached the pond, I peeled away my shorts and T-shirt and climbed down to the ledge, where I kicked off my Pumas. The rock was warm beneath my feet as I padded to the edge and dived into the chilly water.

Swimming downward, I counted slowly. One-one-thousand, two-one-thousand . . . I could hold my breath for about 239 seconds—pretty good, I think. I once read that pearl divers can stay underwater for three and a half minutes, and I've got them beat. It took just over two minutes to wriggle through the little underwater crevice into the hidden cave, so I had plenty of time to spare.

I popped up to the surface on the other side, gasping for breath. On the rocky bank, I rolled onto my back, staring at the shadowed front wall of the cavern. A long fissure high above me allowed a small amount of light to penetrate the blackness. Crashing down on the other side of the fissure was the waterfall, through which the filtered sunlight cast a jumping, greenish glow across the low ceiling. When I closed my eyes, the light still danced in negative patterns behind my eyelids.

From the upper chamber of the cave came a rustling sound. I went stiff. Bats. I'd always known they lived somewhere deep in the caves, but I had fortunately never run into them. Hearing them from time to time was enough to keep me from exploring beyond the front cavern. I inhaled slow, deep breaths and tried to close my mind to their presence. I couldn't find a tranquil place, though; the events of the past couple of days crowded tranquillity right out of the picture. Bianca was dead, my dad was acting weird, Seth was lying to me, and now we'd added a man with a gun to the mix.

I swatted the water, the splash echoing in a hollow *ploink* throughout the cave. I felt out of control and helpless. More than ever, I needed my mom. She'd always been able to help me talk through my problems until I saw a solution. Who could I talk to now? Darlene? She'd freak out and probably cause more trouble than we were in already. My dad? Not likely. Seth? I didn't know if I could trust him.

My dad sure didn't. Trust him, that is. I thought back on the night the Mulos had arrived—Dad all grins and handshakes until Mr. Mulo's whisper put an end to the party. I wished I knew what he'd said.

Guilt panged at the thought of Dad, despite the fact that I wasn't happy with him. How long before he discovered I was gone? He'd be worried if he saw I wasn't in my room. I should get back. With Watts on the island, time was crucial. If he wanted to talk to Dad about the Mulos, I would just have to beat him to it.

I slid back into the water, took a deep breath, and dived under again. Before going to my dad, I should probably talk to Seth. If I could get him to tell me what was going on, I could go to my dad with crucial information. Maybe then I could convince him to stay clear of Watts.

Wriggling through the tunnel, I mapped out a plan: How I would sneak over to Seth's villa. How I would get his attention. How I would get answers no matter what it took.

Back on the pool side, I glided up to the surface, so fixated on the next piece of the puzzle that I didn't see it standing right in front of me.

"Where did you come from?" Seth stood on the rocks, mouth hanging open, holding my T-shirt in one hand and my shorts in the other. How did he find me? I treaded water, gawking at him.

He returned the gawk. "How did you do that?"

I just shook my head. "Hold on. I'm coming up." I swam to the shore and pulled myself out of the water, all the while trying to come up with a way to ask Seth about the newspaper article. It was a whole lot easier in the cave deciding what had to be done than it was standing in front of Seth and trying to do it. I forced my wet feet into my shoes and climbed the rocks slowly to where he stood.

"No, really," he said. "Where were you? I've been

searching around here for probably ten minutes. I thought maybe you'd drowned or something."

I forced a laugh. "Hey, you should know better than that, after our ocean adventure the other night. I'm indestructible."

"I'll try to remember that."

"How did you get up here anyway? What'd you do, follow me?"

"Well, yeah. I wanted to talk to you. Why did you run away?"

I hesitated. "I was . . . afraid."

He laughed. "Afraid? Of what? I thought you were indestructible."

"I'm not joking."

"Neither am I. See?" He handed me my clothes and spread his hands. "I'm totally harmless."

I looked him square in the eye. "Then tell me your name."

He frowned, hesitating just a fraction too long. "You know my name. It's Adam Smith."

Wrong answer. I turned and started to walk away.

"Aphra, wait."

I waved good-bye with my shirt and kept walking. He ran ahead of me and blocked my path.

"I don't get it. What did I *do?*"

"I know who you are, *Seth.*" I drew out his name and watched the shock register on his face. "I know about you and your dead family, so you can stop pretending."

His jaw dropped. "How . . . how could you know?"

"It doesn't matter. I—"

He grabbed my shoulders and shook me. Hard. "It does matter," he said. "How did you find out?"

I tried to break away, but his fingers dug into my shoulders. Now I really was scared. I fumbled with my shorts, trying to get to the vial of pepper spray in the pocket. It wasn't there. It must have fallen out. I searched the ground. It had to be there somewhere.

Seth lowered his voice, though there was no one around to hear. "Did she tell you?"

"What? Who?"

"Natalie. Did she tell you our names? She promised not to tell anyone our names."

I felt like he'd just slammed me in the stomach. My world spun sideways. I couldn't breathe.

"How," I whispered, "do you know my mom?"

CHAPTER 7

Seth made his face go blank, but not before I saw the "oh, crap" panic pass through his eyes.

"Tell me how you know my mom!"

He shook his head. "I can't."

"Then I can't tell you how I found out your names, either." I twisted out of his grasp and took off down the hill.

"Aphra, wait!"

I could hear him crashing through the brush behind me, and I pushed myself harder. Tears blurred my vision and spilled onto my cheeks. This was a piece of the puzzle I couldn't have seen coming.

Seth caught up with me just past the taro bog. He grabbed my hand and pulled me to a stop. "Aphra, please. I need to know. It's important."

"Yeah? Well, my mom is important to me."

"Please. You don't understand."

"And neither do you."

All of a sudden Seth froze, his eyes darting about the bamboo and ferns.

"What is it?"

He yanked my hand and signaled to me to be quiet.

Then I heard it. From just below the first ridge came a rustling noise. I didn't know of any animals in the area big enough to make that kind of sound, which could mean only one thing. Someone else was in the forest. And obviously Seth didn't want to be seen.

The rustling grew louder, sending a flock of ʻiʻiwi finches into the air in a burst of scarlet and black. Seth flinched, and his grasp on my hand slackened. That was all I needed. I tore away from him and ran down the hill. Seth didn't follow.

I burst through the trees and stumbled to a stop. As if I hadn't had enough surprises for the day, there in the clearing stood my dad and Hisako.

They stared at me like I was some kind of apparition. I stared right back. Out of all of us, Dad recovered first. "Aphra! What's going on?"

I could ask them the same thing.

Hisako bowed. "Jack-*sama,* thank you for showing me the plants of your rain forest. It is a great help for my thesis." She tactfully took her leave.

Without a word, Dad took my arm and steered me down the hill toward home. We'd made it about halfway there before he finally spoke.

"You must be feeling better now." It sounded like an accusation.

Oh, yeah. I was supposed to be sick in my room. "Uh, right. I am. Much better. Thanks."

"You've been swimming?"

I wished I could have come up with something better than, "Um . . . no?"

In the long run it would have been easier just to admit I had been swimming, but I didn't think Dad knew about my cove in the hills, and I wanted to keep it that way.

"I see." Dad folded his arms and walked away. I followed silently. Neither one of us spoke until we had nearly reached the Plantation House.

"I don't know what I'm going to do with you." Dad's voice sounded tired.

"*Do* with me?" What was that supposed to mean?

"Sneaking around. Lying. It's not like you, Aphra."

"I'm not—"

"I told you to stay away from them."

"What are you talking about?"

"Don't play games with me, young lady. You were with that Smith boy, weren't you?"

"No!" Hey, I was telling the truth. His name was not Smith.

"Ever since they came to this island you haven't been yourself. You don't know the first thing about those people, Aphra. I want you to stay away."

I didn't know about them? *He* didn't even know their real names!

"You've left me no choice. You are to stay in your room the rest of the afternoon."

"But—"

"That's final."

"Fine." I turned and stomped up the stairs, making as much noise as I could to let him know I was just as mad as he was. It wasn't until I reached the upstairs landing that I remembered one little hitch. My bedroom door was locked. From the inside.

Now, I don't do this sort of thing all the time, so don't get the wrong idea. I've had to pick a few locks here and there, but nothing illegal, I swear. It's just that in a business like ours, occasions do arise when locks have to be opened, and a key is not always readily available. I learned how to pick locks from our super the first year we were here. We still have the old pin-tumbler types on all the doors, so it really isn't that hard. It just takes time, and I wasn't sure how much I had.

As long as I could hear my dad slamming around downstairs, I knew I was safe, but he could come up to check on me at any moment. I rushed into the bathroom to find something to work the lock. Nothing. Listening for more movement from below, I tiptoed to Dad's bedroom.

His door squeaked as I opened it, and I froze, cursing under my breath. I was supposed to have asked maintenance to oil the hinges weeks ago. The banging downstairs continued, so I slipped inside his room, stealthily crossing to his desk. *Come on, come on.* I rifled through the top drawer until I found two large paper clips. Good enough.

Back out in the hallway, I straightened the paper clips. All I could hear from below was silence. Where was Dad? No time to find out. I tiptoed to my door and dropped to my knees. With a feather touch, I manipulated the paper clips, feeling for the pin stack inside the lock, gently lining them up. I could feel the plug turning. Almost there.

"What are you doing?"

I shot to my feet, palming my improvised tools as I spun around. Dad glowered at me.

"Nothing." I jiggled the handle of my door. *Yes!* I'd done it. I stepped inside and closed the door behind me.

Trembling, I stumbled over to my bed. That was too close. Before the sweat on my palms even dried, Dad cracked open my door.

"You are not to step one foot outside this room for the remainder of the day. Is that clear?"

"Fine."

Beads of sweat stood out on his pale forehead, and he wiped them away with the back of his hand before closing the door. Okay, I knew he was mad, but come on. That was a little much.

Besides, shouldn't I be the one who was angry? I paced back and forth across the room. More pieces of the puzzle were falling into place, and I didn't like what I saw. Thanks to Seth's slipup, I now knew that the Mulos had some connection with my mom. What that connection was, I didn't know, but I could bet my dad did. That night when they came—Papa Mulo probably told Dad about the connection then. That was probably what he had whispered—how he got Dad to let them stay. And it was safe to guess that Dad learned the Mulos were on the run. That would be why he hid them in villa four, and why he thought they were dangerous.

It all began to make sense, except . . . why didn't my dad think he could tell me about it? The Mulos were the first connection we'd had with my mom in four years. Didn't I deserve to know? And what about Bianca? What did any of this have to do with her?

I sank down on the window seat. My chest felt heavy, as if I were buried under a ton of rocks. I stared out at the ocean, realizing, with the kind of clarity that comes with self-pity, that I was utterly and completely alone.

When we first got here, I used to stand at the shore and imagine my mom standing on the other side of the water. I thought it connected us somehow. I was sure one day she would follow the water to where I was. But then the weeks and months and years passed, and I realized that Mom was never coming back to us. I'd never felt so lonely and isolated in my life.

Until now.

Outside, both sea and sky had gone gray. Storm clouds roiled and white caps frothed on the water—a fitting backdrop for my mood.

Just then, I caught sight of my dad as he cut across the lawn and disappeared down one of the many paths into the trees. It was like a sign from God: I wasn't supposed to just sit there and go all emo. For the next few minutes, my dad's office would be empty. At least I could solve one piece of the puzzle. If the Mulos knew my mom, then they likely knew where my mom *was*. That meant that Dad probably knew where she was, too. And I was going to find out.

Forgetting my promise—which, by the way, dealt with stepping one foot outside the room, but said nothing about two—I rushed downstairs, carrying my paperclip tools just in case.

As I figured it would be, Dad's office door was locked. Crouching in front of the knob, I jiggled the paper clips into the key opening.

"Excuse me, miss?"

I whirled around so fast I nearly fell over. It was Mr. Watts. He looked at me with those cold, appraising eyes, and I nearly swallowed my tongue. Somehow I managed to make myself speak.

"Good afternoon, Mr. Watts. I hope you're feeling better."

"Much, thank you. Is your father in?"

"No, I'm afraid he isn't at the moment."

He frowned. "I need to speak with him. It's a matter of some urgency. Do you know when he'll be back?"

I shook my head. Unfortunately, since I had no idea where Dad had gone off to, I also didn't know when he might return. I glanced nervously at the door. Chances were, it would be any minute.

Watts folded his arms. "I'll wait."

No. That was the one thing he couldn't do. I didn't want him and his gun in the lobby, and I definitely didn't want him talking to my dad. Not yet. I needed more time to sort things out. Besides, if he was there, how was I going to break into the office? "It may be a while."

"Oh? Where is he?"

More important, where was he *not*? Because that's the only place I could send Watts. "He had an emergency to attend to."

"Where?"

"I could have him drop by your villa when he gets back."

He leaned an arm on the counter and glared at me with those cold shark eyes. "I'd like you to tell me where he is."

Suppressing a chill, I put on my most honest expression and gave Mr. Watts directions to the old lava tubes a few miles down the shoreline . . . only you can't walk straight because there's no road, so he had a little workout ahead of him. I hoped it would keep him occupied for a couple of hours and buy me some time to figure out what was going on.

I was afraid those sharp eyes would see right through my deception, but, fortunately, he believed me. "Thank you, miss." He dipped his head. "You've been a great help."

As soon as he was gone, I returned to Dad's office door. It wasn't a difficult lock to pick; I made it through in less than a minute and flipped on the light.

My dad borders on neurotic about his record keeping. He can't not file things away. If he found out where my mom was, I knew beyond the smallest doubt that he would keep a record of some sort. Probably a paper file.

Since I was all too familiar with the filing system, I knew where the information wasn't—in any of the cabinets that lined the far wall of the office. So either the file was in his desk or in the fireproof metal box he kept in the floor under the desk to hold all the important documents like birth certificates, life insurance papers, and stuff. I'd always known the thing was there, but it's not like I've ever had the opportunity to use my passport or anything. I'd never once gotten into the box.

If he felt he needed to keep something hidden from me, it made sense that he'd put it in the firebox, since his desk didn't lock. Just to be sure, I checked the desk anyway, and noticed with disappointment that the file on the Mulos was no longer in the top drawer. As I had suspected, there was also no information on my mom.

Kneeling down behind the desk, I pushed back the rug to uncover the small two-foot-by-two-foot inset in the floor, which housed the firebox. I suppose it was meant to be really secret, but the square lid didn't quite match up with the rest of the floor, so it was completely obvious if anyone cared to look under the rug. I used a letter opener to pry up the lid. It was too easy. Worse, the lock on the metal box inside was a wafer type that was even easier to pick than the door. When we were speaking again, I'd have to have a serious talk with my dad about security.

I rifled through his files until I found a thick manila file folder with the heading NATALIE.

My mom.

My breath caught. I swear I could feel my heart pounding all the way down to my fingertips as I opened the file.

There was no information on her whereabouts. Not that I could see through my tears, anyway. Just dozens of colorful envelopes, all addressed to me. I sorted through them. Each one was postmarked from a different place. The earliest was dated just weeks after Dad and I came to the island, when I was twelve years old. The latest was postmarked a couple of months ago. I tore open one envelope. It was a birthday card. I tore open another envelope and another and another. I could barely breathe. Birthday cards, Christmas cards, "just because" cards covering the past four years. They were all there.

"What do you think you're doing?"

My dad stood at the open door, his hand grasping the doorknob so tightly that his knuckles were white. His ashen face contorted into a mask of anger, the veins standing out like pale crawling worms.

I suddenly found my breath. As if *he* had the right to be angry at *me* after lying to me for all these years! I waved a handful of cards at him. "What is this?"

When he saw what I was holding, his skin took on an even pastier shade than that of his knuckles. "Aphra—"

I slapped the cards on the desk and sprang to my feet, chair banging against the wall behind me. "You told me she was off 'finding' herself! You said you didn't know where she was! You *lied* to me!"

"You don't understand."

"No, I don't. I will *never* understand how you could do this!"

"Now, Aphra, calm down."

"I will *not* calm down!" I snatched up the folder and threw it at him. It didn't quite have the effect I'd hoped for but sort of just wavered in the air before flopping at his feet. He stepped over it and came toward me. I backed away. "She didn't leave us, did she? What did you do, send her away?"

"It was for the best."

"Best for who? All these years I thought she left because she didn't want me! How could you do that to me?"

"I was protecting you."

"From what? What's going on, Dad? Where is she?"

"I don't know."

"I don't believe you!"

"It's true. She moves around."

"Why? What are you not telling me? How does she know the Mulos?"

"The who?"

"The Smiths. Their real name is Mulo. How does she know them? Is that what Mr. Mulo whispered to you the night they came? Is that why you let them stay?"

He mopped his face again.

"Come on, Dad. Out with it."

"You watch your tone with me, young lady." His voice had an edge to it I had never heard before. It only served to make me angrier.

"Or what? You'll restrict me? Take away my privileges? No watching TV or going to the movies? No allowance? Or, wait—why don't you ground me from hanging out with my friends? News flash, Dad: I don't *have* any here. Do you know how it feels to read Cami's e-mails and see what I've been missing, being stuck on the island with you? I haven't seen a movie in four years! We've never once been on a family vacation. And while Cami's off going to the prom, I've never even been on a date. You can't *possibly* make my life any more miserable than you have already."

With that, I stormed out of the office and left him, white-faced and trembling, a defeated droop to his shoulders. He didn't try to stop me, though he may have if he'd known where I was headed. If he wasn't going to tell me what I wanted to know, I'd have to ask someone who would. I didn't stop until I reached villa four.

CHAPTER 8

If Mrs. Mulo was surprised to see me, she didn't show it. She stood at the door like the lady of the manor and invited me inside. I peered into the front room, which was still stripped down to the bare walls.

"I need you to tell me about my mother," I blurted. So much for social graces.

She stepped cordially aside to allow me to enter and then closed the door behind me, shutting out the light. Her face held no expression as she looked me over, sizing me up—as if I'd been the one running around, hiding things. "Why don't we step into the kitchen?"

I followed her down a short, bare hallway. The kitchen was not quite as desolate as the front room, but it wasn't exactly luxurious, either. A table and four chairs sat next to the shuttered window and a stainless steel refrigerator stood in the corner, but the makeshift counter consisted of a length of two-by-four stretched across a couple of sawhorses, and underfoot, the flooring had been pulled up to expose the plywood subfloor. No cabinets hung on the spackled walls.

"Please have a seat," Mrs. Mulo said. "May I offer you something to drink? To eat?"

"No, thank you." I perched uneasily on the edge of

one of the wicker chairs, and she took the seat opposite. I remembered the first night I had seen her in the lobby. I hadn't noticed then that her inquisitive eyes were the same deep blue as Seth's. I tried to ignore the little tug in my chest when I thought of him.

Mrs. Mulo leaned back in her chair. "I'm pleased to see you again, Aphra. Seth has enjoyed visiting with you. He's told us so much about you."

I'll bet, I thought darkly. Still, hearing his name gave me an unexpected thrill. I wanted to blurt, "Oh, really? What did he say?" but I asked instead, "Do you know my mother well?"

She pressed her lips together and folded delicate hands in her lap. At length she answered. "As well as can be expected, I suppose."

"Where is she?"

Her eyes widened for an instant, brows arching, but she hid any further reaction. "I'm sorry. I can't—"

"Does she live in West Bloomfield?"

"I'm afraid I can't tell you that."

"How does she know about your secret? Is she involved?"

Mrs. Mulo reached across the table and took my hand. "Aphra, I can't answer your questions. I'm sorry. Your mother has worked very hard to keep our . . . secret safe. I realize that is not what you came to hear, but please know that digging further could place us all in very real danger—yourself included."

Before I could process what she was saying, she glanced up. "Ah. There you are."

Victor Mulo—the possible murderer—walked into the room. My hands went cold.

"What is this Mata Hari doing in my house?"

I blinked. Was he talking about me?

Mrs. Mulo shot him a look. "Victor, please."

"Please, nothing!" He pointed a finger at me. "You! Knowing the danger our son faces, you lure him up into the hillside—"

"Lure?" I pushed back in my chair. "Is that what he said? Excuse me, but I didn't lure Seth anywhere. He *followed* me. Uninvited, I might add."

"Please. You think I don't know your kind?"

"My *kind?*"

"Victor, please. This is Natalie's daughter!"

He snorted. "Is that supposed to mean something to me? Natalie betrayed us. Her daughter—"

"We don't know that she betrayed anything. We—"

"How else could this girl have known?"

"Stop!" I scraped my chair back and stood. "My mom didn't tell me anything. How could she? She hasn't spoken to me in four years."

Mr. Mulo's brows lowered, and he frowned like he didn't understand what I had just said. I should have stopped then, but I couldn't keep my mouth shut. "Besides, you betrayed *yourself*. You know, yesterday? On the beach?"

He flinched and exchanged a look with Mrs. Mulo. It was all the reaction I needed. In that moment, I had no doubt. He was the one who had killed Bianca. All at once, my bravado crumbled. I couldn't believe this was happening. I'd gotten too close. Would Mr. Mulo feel the need to silence me the way he had Bianca? I backed to the door.

"Look, I won't tell anyone who you are or what you did, but you . . . you can't stay here anymore. Just . . . go!"

With that, I spun to run out the way I had come in. That's when I saw Seth in the hallway, watching me with a sad frown on his face. He looked achingly wonderful in his jeans and T-shirt. Made me want to forget everything that had just happened and stay right there forever. But of course I couldn't do that. I pushed past him and out the front door.

He could have tried to stop me, but he didn't.

Wind whipped my hair into my eyes as I ran aimlessly down the path. Angry tears slid down my cheeks. I swiped them away with the back of my hand. What was I supposed to do now? Everything I had known as truth had crumbled like a house of sand. I had no one to trust, nowhere to go.

"Ho, Aphra, I been looking for you!" Darlene caught my arm. I hadn't even seen her. "Where you been?"

I pushed away. "Not right now. I need to be alone."

She looked me over, no doubt taking in my tears, and shook her head. "No, honey. That is exactly what you don't need." She wrapped an arm firmly around my shoulders and drew me close. I struggled to get away, but she only tightened her grip. "Hey, now. You're gonna hurt my feelings. I'm not such a bad listener, you know." She glanced up at the darkening sky. "Tropical storm moving in. Come on. We can go to my place. I got Häagen-Dazs in my freezer. Chocolate. What d'ya say?"

Well, it wasn't like I had a whole lot of other options. I allowed Darlene to lead me to her place. Like the rest of the staff, she lived in an apartment on the property—except, as a manager, she didn't have to share with anyone. She had a bungalow near the lounge. She'd done it up in an island motif that was about as genuine as her accent, from the tropical leaf–print wallpaper to the fake bird-of-paradise on the bamboo coffee table. True Darlene.

Once she had me settled on the wicker couch with a bowl of mocha almond fudge in my hands, she sat back. "Now tell me," she said. "What's going on?"

I stared out the window to where the wind clinked and moaned through the bamboo chimes hanging from the ceiling of her lanai. "Nothing," I said finally. Nothing I could tell her about, anyway.

"Aphra . . ."

I shoveled a scoop of ice cream into my mouth so I wouldn't have to talk.

Darlene waited. I swallowed my ice cream. She waited some more. I licked my spoon. She cleared her throat. "Aphra. Talk to me. Your father said you were—"

"You've been talking to my dad?"

"He's very concerned about you."

I smacked the bowl down on the table so hard the spoon clattered against the ceramic. "Concerned about me? He ruined my life!"

"He did what he thought was best."

I drew back against the couch cushions. "Wait. You *knew* about it? You knew he was keeping me from my mom?"

"I don't know all the details, but listen—"

"No! Not if you're just going to take his side."

"Come on now. There are no sides. You need to trust your dad."

I snorted. "Trust? Trust is for people who earn it. Four years of lying to your daughter does not cut it."

"He was trying to protect you."

"By letting me believe my mom abandoned me?" My voice grew shrill. "Do you have any idea what it's like to grow up thinking your mother never loved you?"

"Actually, I do. But I didn't have a father who cared enough to try to pick up the pieces. You don't know how lucky you are."

"Oh, yeah. Lucky me. With an absent mom and a dad who can't even be straight with me about why she went away."

Darlene reached for my hand, but I pulled back.

"You've got it all wrong," she said.

"Oh, like you know! You're only taking his side because he's your boss."

"Honey—"

"He made her go away, did you know that? And he never gave me any of the cards she sent. What kind of a father does that? What kind of a sadistic, twisted, rotten, underhanded—"

"Your mother was involved with some dangerous people, Aphra." Darlene's voice rose to match my own. "Your dad hoped that by coming here, she could leave them behind. Start over. But either she couldn't or she wouldn't come. *She* made the choice to stay behind."

"No! I don't believe it."

"His main concern was you, baby girl; you've got to believe that. Your mama loved you, but she could have hurt you. You can see that, can't you?"

"No, I can't."

"I'm so sorry, honey." Her voice was all soft and gushy now. It made me want to hit her.

I just shrugged and looked away.

"And I apologize for this, but there is one more thing I need to speak to you about."

I snorted. "Sure. Why not?"

She cleared her throat. "Your father is a little concerned about your relationship with that Smith boy. You can't be sneaking out with—"

"You don't know anything about Se—Adam! And I

have not been sneaking out!" Well, okay, I actually had, but I hadn't snuck out to meet Seth. It just kind of happened that way.

"Honey, listen to me. Your father says these Smiths are shady characters. Very evasive. I need you to promise you will—"

"Give me a break. If he thinks they're so dangerous, why would he let them stay here in the first place?"

She chewed on her lip. For the first time, she looked doubtful. "I'm sure he—"

Darlene's two-way squawked, and she jumped at the sound. She shot me a "hold on" look, pressed the receiver to her ear. "Speak." Her face fell as she listened. "Yeah? Yeah? No!" She turned from me slightly, cupping a hand over the receiver. "No," she said in a low voice. "Do not move him. I'll be right there."

Darlene signed off, pursing her lips. "Well . . ." She smiled shakily and stood. "There's . . . ah . . . a little problem I need to take care of. You wait for me here, okay?"

I shrugged.

"You get hungry, help yourself to anything in the fridge." She hurried to the door, but paused with her hand on the knob and looked me in the eye. "Promise me you will stay right here."

"Fine."

But promises easily made are easily broken.

•••

As soon as she disappeared down the path, I began to have second thoughts. It's not that I don't respect Darlene. Generally I do. But it was clear she was going to take my dad's side on everything, so we really didn't have anything else to talk about. I eased out her door and shut it firmly behind me.

The wind had picked up. Dark clouds boiled overhead. Darlene may have been right about the storm, but she was dead wrong about everything else, and I wasn't going to hang around to be lectured.

Up ahead I saw Hisako, long black hair dancing tangos with the wind. Her face was set in a serious frown, and she looked about as lonely as I felt.

She glanced up and saw me watching her. Crap. I cussed under my breath and gave her a polite bow. I would have turned away then, but she gestured to me to wait. I sighed. The last thing I wanted was another forced conversation, but four years of conditioning dies hard. She was a guest. I waited.

"Looks like rain," I said as she neared.

She studied the sky for a moment, then shook her head. "Soon. Not yet." She held out her hand. "Come. Walk with me."

I hesitated. "But the storm . . ."

"I don't mind the little wind." She slipped her hand into the crook of my arm. "Come."

We walked silently, though my mind was anything

but quiet. It was on overload after everything that had happened that day. So much so that I didn't even hear Hisako when she finally spoke to me.

"Aphra-*chan*. Are you here?"

"I'm sorry."

"Do you want to talk?"

I shook my head. I wouldn't know where to start.

Hisako stopped walking and looked me in the eye. "In Japan we have a saying, '*Iwanu ga hana*.' It means to not speak is a flower. But there are times, Aphra-*chan*, when it is not a flower. There are times you must speak the things in your head."

"I'm fine, really."

She regarded me for a moment. "Yes, you are strong. But know this, silence is not always bravery."

"I'll remember that."

She smiled. "I am sure you will." Hisako deftly changed the subject. "All your guests are prepared for the storm, *ne*?"

"Yeah. Everyone should be snug in their villas."

As if on cue, thunder growled overhead. Hisako peered up at the darkened sky. "It will start soon."

"Yeah. I should probably go help bring in the awnings and stack the deck chairs."

"Perhaps the work is already done."

"Probably." I felt a little guilty for not helping prepare for the storm, though I don't know why I should have, after what my dad had done.

She bowed when we reached her villa. "Thank you for the walk, Aphra-*chan*. We will talk again later."

I bowed in return and high-tailed it back toward the Plantation House just as the first fat raindrops fell.

I had nearly made it to the courtyard when Seth stepped out from behind the trees. He took an aggressive stance, chest all puffed out in anger. I drew up short.

"Came to thank you for your compassion and understanding." His lip curled up on one side in what could best be described as a snarl. Water ran in rivulets down his face. He didn't seem to notice. I did. It slicked back his hair and clung to his eyelashes. I wanted to brush the raindrops from his cheeks, his chin, his lips.

"I thought I told your family to go away," I muttered.

"Yeah, well, we'll be on the next charter out, thanks to you."

My heart plummeted. That was what I wanted, right? But if the Mulos went, the answers about my mom went with them. "You can't leave yet. The storm—"

He laughed without humor. "Make up your mind."

I stared up at him, blinking away rain. "Where's my mom, Seth?"

He looked away. "I don't know."

"Don't lie to me! How did you know her? Tell me!"

"I can't."

I stepped back. "Then go ahead and leave. Just go."

"Whatever." He threw a wad of soggy blue fabric at me. "I brought you your shirt."

My face flushed hot. I must have dropped it when we were up at the cove. I threw it back at him. "Drop dead."

He didn't attempt to catch it, but let my shirt fall into the mud.

"Forget it." I tried to push past him, but he grabbed my wrist.

"Aphra, wait."

"Let go of me."

He didn't let go. Instead, he pulled me to him so that we were standing face-to-face—or, in this instance, face-to-chin. I pushed against him, but he held fast. "Listen!"

I glared up at him and he glowered down at me, and when our eyes met . . . well, I can't say exactly what it was. Some sort of chemistry or electricity or something completely unrelated to science zinged between us. A look of surprise crossed Seth's face. His expression softened, and I could have melted right there.

"Aphra, my dad didn't do it."

"What?"

"The girl on the beach. That's what you think, isn't it? That he killed her?"

I swallowed.

"He didn't do it, and he would have tried to save her if he could, Aphra, but it was too late."

"Then . . . why did he just leave?"

Seth shook his head. "We can't be seen. You know that."

Yes, I did know that. What I didn't know was why. "Seth—"

"Aphra!" Darlene's voice cut through the air, driving an immediate wedge between Seth and me. Literally. We must have jumped about three feet apart. She stood at the head of the path, with hands on her hips and murder in her eyes. I watched as those eyes went from me to Seth to my shirt on the ground and back up to me. Her nostrils flared with indignation.

"I've been looking all over for you!"

"I'm sorry, I . . ." My face burned as I bent to retrieve my sodden shirt. "What is it?"

"Something's wrong with your dad," she said. "You had better come with me."

CHAPTER
9

Darlene stalked back to the Plantation House without another word. I mumbled good-bye to Seth and ran after her.

"Wait!" I grabbed her hand. "What is it?"

"You promised, Aphra," she said. "I asked you to stay put."

"But the storm. I . . . thought I should go stack the deck chairs and—"

"That's not what it looked like to me." She pulled away and stomped up the stairs onto the lanai.

"Darlene! What's up with my dad?"

The anger cracked as she turned to look at me, and I caught a glimpse of the worry behind it. That scared me even more. She ran a hand through her wet hair. "I don't know what it is for sure. He's having trouble breathing. I think he might be having some kind of an allergic reaction. We've got to get him to the hospital."

"How? The closest one is—"

"I know. That's what I need you for. After Mr. Watts came in, Frank went back to the city to grab Junior. They should be coming in any minute. You need to get up there and tell Frank to wait. I'll get Jack ready. Send

Junior down to help me get your dad to the landing pad. We've got to put him on the return flight to the city."

She didn't have to tell me twice. I threw down my shirt and raced around to the side of the lanai, where the guest cart sat in the middle of a huge puddle of water. I sloshed to the cart, slid onto the seat, and reached down to turn the switch. Nothing. I tried again. Not even a whimper. Battery must've been dead. Probably shorted out from the rain. I took off on foot.

Rain lashed against my face and ran in rivers down the hill toward me. The steps were slick with mud. I stumbled and fell twice, the second time scraping my shin on the sharp corner of one of the stone steps. By the time I limped to the top of the hill, the helicopter was sitting in the middle of the giant painted circle, rotors turning slowly in the wind.

Frank was already unloading boxes from the cargo hold.

"Hey, Frank! Where's Junior?"

He waved to me and shouted over the wind, "Hey, darlin'! Had to leave him back in the city." He looked over my shoulder. "Where's your daddy?"

"That's why I'm here. He's sick! Darlene says he needs to go to the hospital, and she wants you to wait so you can take him back with you."

"No can do." He closed the door and fastened the latches. "This bird's not leavin' the ground till the storm passes. Squall just about took us down comin' 'round the Point. Too dangerous."

"But he needs a doctor!"

"He'll need a mortician if I try to take off in this wind." He opened a small compartment and pulled out a length of rope.

I stepped over the landing skid and ducked to peer under the belly of the chopper, where Frank bent over the securing line, threading it through a mooring anchor. "Listen! Those ropes won't hold if the wind gets as strong as you say. She'll tip right over. You should get back to the city, where you can dock in a nice, safe hangar. And take my dad with you."

He sat back on his heels and frowned at me, shaking his head. "Wish I could, darlin', but I can't. Wouldn't be safe."

"But he needs help!"

"Give me a minute. I finish tyin' her down, and I'm all yours. We'll think of somethin'."

Instinctively I knew I didn't have a minute. "Meet me down there," I shouted, and took off back down the hill.

I'm not ashamed to admit I was scared. As angry as I'd been with Dad, the thought of losing him was too much to bear. I didn't even know what was wrong with him, but judging from the worry I had seen on Darlene's face, whatever it was, it was serious.

I had just made it to the bottom of the hill when I stopped dead in my tracks, my stomach turning to ice.

Mr. Watts stomped up the path toward me, water streaming down his face. He was clearly not happy. "Miss! A word with you!"

"I'm sorry! Emergency!"

I tried to run by him, but he caught up with me and grabbed my arm. Tight. He narrowed his black eyes at me. "No more games. I need to speak to your father."

It took every ounce of control I had to keep from shrieking and running back to Frank. "I'm sorry, Mr. Watts, but my father is very ill. So if you will excuse me—"

"Perhaps I could be of some assistance," he said. His fingers tightened, digging into my skin.

I shivered. No way was that man getting anywhere near my dad. "Mr. Watts, please. Go back inside."

"I haven't *been* inside. I've been hiking all over the property looking for your father, thanks to you. And now you say he's sick—"

"He *is* sick. And I'm busy. Excuse me."

But Watts wouldn't take no for an answer. He followed me to the Plantation House. I planned to run inside and lock the door on him, but Darlene was in the way.

"Hello again, Mr. . . ."

"Watts. I was just telling the girl here that I have some field training, if you'd like me to take a look at Mr. Connolly."

I desperately shook my head no, but Darlene didn't see me. She went limp with relief.

"Oh, thank you." She pumped his hand, pulling him inside. "Jack's not doing too good. Maybe you could help us get him back up to the chopper, yeah?"

"Frank says no," I said. "He says the winds are too strong."

"But—"

"I know. I told him what you said, but he still says he can't fly until the storm passes." I looked beyond her. "Where is he?"

"In his office. Come on."

We tracked mud across the lobby.

My dad lay on the couch shivering, his face even paler than I remembered and shiny with sweat. His lips had a bluish tint to them. I dropped to my knees and grabbed his hand, the clammy skin like death under my fingertips . . . not unlike Bianca's had been. I trembled. "Dad? It's Aphra. Can you hear me?"

His lids fluttered open, and red-rimmed eyes stared at me. A spark of recognition burned behind the dull torpor but quickly faded. His eyes drifted shut once more.

"Dad?" I shook him. "Dad!"

He wheezed in a breath.

Mr. Watts cleared his throat. "Sounds bad. He asthmatic?"

"No," Darlene said. "I thought he was having an allergic reaction or something, but I gave him an epi shot and he's not responding to it."

"How's his pressure?"

"Dropping steadily for the past half hour."

"Shock?"

"Not yet, but I'm worried."

"Can he talk?"

"What do you think?"

I watched them go back and forth like a tennis match. The end conclusion was that Mr. Watts really didn't have any more medical expertise than Darlene. The conversation died down, and he just hovered. Like a vulture. The intense way in which he stared down at my dad looked very predatory. I jumped to my feet.

"Thank you for your help, Mr. Watts."

"Not at all. If you'd like me to stay—"

"That won't be necessary." I steered him from the office.

"If he wakes up . . ."

"Yes, we'll let you know."

Frank appeared in the doorway at that moment, shaking water from his gray hair like a sheepdog. "Where is he?"

I rushed to talk to him. "Dad's resting in his office. Darlene's with him." Lowering my voice, I said, "What happened in the city? Why didn't Junior come back with you?"

Frank leaned close. "Mick took off the minute we landed. Junior went after him. Seems Mr. Rock Star had some possession issues he didn't want to discuss with the authorities. Paperwork got complicated. Thought

Junior woulda been done by the time I went back to get him, but he wasn't, quite. He sent me on ahead and he said he'd follow, but with the storm—"

"Follow? How?"

"The city police want to come have a look-see at the resort."

"Oh, Dad's just going to love that."

Dad. I glanced at his office, and my chest tightened.

"Want me to take a look?" Frank asked.

"Actually, could you make sure this guy gets back to his villa first? He's making me nervous. Just . . . be careful."

"You got it, darlin'."

Frank strode across the lobby and laid a heavy hand on Watts's shoulder. "If you'll come with me . . ."

I ran back into the office where Darlene knelt by the side of the couch. Worry pinched her features as she mopped Dad's face with a cool washcloth. His breathing sounded raspy, and his chest rose and fell in rapid jerky movements.

"Is . . . is he going to be all right?"

"I don't know," she murmured. "I don't know how to help him."

"There has to be something we can do. Call the hospital! Talk to a doctor."

"I called earlier. They said to bring him in."

"We need to call them again. If we can't get him there, they should at least tell us what to do!"

Darlene looked up and nodded at me. I didn't like the

expression on her face. Like she was already mourning his death.

I crossed to the phone and picked up the receiver.

Silence.

The line was dead.

Chapter 10

I allowed myself about ten seconds to panic, but that's all. With the phones down, the Internet would be out, too. Our only lines to outside help were gone. But I wasn't about to sit around and act powerless. Not when my dad's life depended on it.

"Think, Darlene!" I insisted. "You are the island guru. What would the locals do in this situation? Isn't there some folk remedy or some kind of herb or . . ." My voice trailed off. Of course. Why hadn't I thought of it before?

"What is it?"

"Hisako! She knows all about plants and herbs and all that. Maybe she could find something to help until we can get Dad to a doctor."

Darlene pursed her lips together and gave a little shrug. I supposed that was her way of saying it couldn't hurt, but anyway, I wasn't waiting for permission. I ran all the way to Hisako's villa, rain plastering my hair to my head and squelching in my shoes. The light in her window shone like a beacon in the proverbial storm. I could see her inside, seated on the floor in a lotus position, facing the wall. Her black hair hung in a single braid down the center of her back. She wore exercise clothes—stretch pants and a tank top. As I got closer, I could see a tattoo decorating one muscular shoulder. I wouldn't have expected that from her—she seemed so demure. I stared at the ornate dragon tattoo and tapped timidly on the glass.

As if she were expecting my company, she rose gracefully to her feet and pulled on a *yukata* robe, tying the sash at her waist as she turned unhurriedly to open the door. When she saw me standing on the stoop, the calm on her face dissolved as she must have read the concern on mine. "Aphra-*chan!* Come in, come in." She stepped aside and motioned for me to enter, but I didn't have time for that.

"I need your help," I shouted, my voice carried away by the wind.

She gripped my hand and leaned closer, worry creasing her delicate brow. "What is it?"

"My dad."

Her grip tightened. "Jack-*sama?*"

"Something's wrong. He can't breathe and he... he..." The weight of the past couple of days became too much, and I burst into tears.

She grabbed my shoulders and shook me. "Aphra! Tell me what is happening!"

I hesitated. This was all wrong. Hisako was a guest. I shouldn't say too much. I shouldn't—

"Aphra!"

I couldn't help it. One look in her troubled, black eyes, and it all tumbled out. "He... looks bad, but we can't get him to a hospital because of the storm, and I . . . I should have noticed something was wrong this afternoon; he was getting all pale and sweaty and everything, but I was too obsessed with the Mulos, and now there's this man looking for them, and I probably should have told him where they were, but I really like Seth and I think that guy might hurt him, and I don't know that I can trust him and—"

"Aphra-*chan!*" She shook me again. "You are making no sense. Please talk slowly. I cannot help if I do not understand."

I told her as much as I could in those urgent minutes, and she listened intently. "I do not believe I have met this Seth. Is he a guest?"

I bobbed my head. "Yes. No. His family is hiding out here. Probably from Mr. Watts, I don't know. That doesn't matter. We need to help my dad!"

Hisako took my hand. "We will, Aphra-*chan*, but we must also stop this man," she said. "Do you think he is dangerous?"

I nodded.

Her mouth set in a straight line. "Then you must see to this Mr. Watts," she said. "I will gather medicines and go to Jack."

"Thank you. Thank you!" I bowed deeply.

"I will meet you there." She gave me a quick bow and then stepped inside to change her clothes.

I left her villa, mind churning. She said I should deal

with Mr. Watts, but couldn't that wait? First I wanted to make sure my dad was okay. I started up the path toward the Plantation House, but I couldn't shake the image of Mr. Watts's cold smile from my head. My gut told me he was dangerous. I could feel it.

But were the Mulos dangerous, too? Seth's face swam before my eyes, and for one delicious moment, I could feel his arms around me. Danger did not fit my image of him at all, but was I thinking clearly?

At the head of the path, I hesitated. I didn't have time to sort out who was good and who was bad. And if I chose wrong, how could I undo it?

The branch of a coral tree blew into my path, and I kicked it out of the way.

Then I had an idea.

When Mr. Watts answered the door, he blinked at me, surprised. "What is it? Your dad doing better?"

"Uh, soon I hope. Thanks. I, um . . ." I raised the domed silver tray I held in my hands. "The kitchen will be closed until further notice because of the storm, so the chef sent me down with a complimentary supper."

"In this weather?"

"Yeah. You're my last delivery, and then I can go home. May I come in and set this down?"

He stood back, holding the door open with one arm. I stepped into his lair. My hands were shaking so bad that the silverware on the tray rattled. I slipped off my muddy shoes and padded barefoot into the entry, trailing water in my wake. "Where would you like it?"

"There is fine." He pointed to a small table near the front window.

I set the tray down gently and raised the lid with a flourish. I have to say that the salad was artfully arranged: cucumber, tomato, and carrot curls atop butterhead and romaine, set off with a sprinkling of bright red coral seeds. Not a bad job, given my haste.

Next to the salad plate sat a basket of rolls with butter, and a small cruet of dressing, specially doctored by yours truly. Even if he ate it all it wouldn't do permanent damage, but the amount of salvia leaves I used in conjunction with the coral should knock him out for a good couple of hours. And just in case he wasn't a salad fan, I had brewed a small pot of jasmine tea, careful to include kava root in the blend.

He stood uncertainly and then bent to sniff the aroma of the fresh-baked rolls. Well, not exactly fresh baked since the kitchen truly was closed, but I had zapped them in the microwave before tucking them into the basket. As he reached forward to grab a roll, I noticed a bulge under his shirt, just below his left arm. The gun. I swallowed hard and backed to the door. "*Bon appétit.*" With a hasty bow, I ducked out the door and closed it behind me.

I couldn't get out of there fast enough. Still, as I reached the top of the path, I ducked behind a tree and looked back toward the villa. Through the bucking branches, I could see Mr. Watts pull a chair up to the table and unfold the napkin onto his lap. He ate like a starved man, barely pausing between bites to take a sip of tea. Rain pelted me with increasing fury, but I hugged my arms and waited. I wanted to get back to the Plantation House, but not before I made sure the job was done.

It didn't take long. Before he even completed his meal, Watts yawned and stretched like a satiated cat. Standing unsteadily, he staggered to the couch, where he flopped down for what I hoped would be a very long nap.

Hisako hadn't gotten there before I returned to the Plantation House. Darlene stood at the door to the office, wringing her hands. "Well?"

"She's coming. She had to gather some things together."

"Does she know what to do, then?"

"I hope so. How's Dad doing?"

She didn't answer with words, but the look on her face spoke volumes. My heart fell. I stood in the doorway with her, dripping water on the floor and feeling very small. On the office couch, Dad lay on his back, one arm thrown over his eyes. His face was gray as a corpse. Small gasps escaped his lips as he struggled for each shallow breath.

"Daddy," I whispered, "please don't leave me."

With uncanny timing, the front door blew open with a loud crash. I jumped and whirled around to see Mr. Mulo framed by the doorway, backlit by the raging storm, his raincoat whipping in the wind. He strode into the lobby carrying a black bag. Mrs. Mulo and Seth followed close behind.

"Where is he?" Seth asked.

Mrs. Mulo rushed to the office and peered inside. "Victor! Come quick!"

He pushed past me and bent over my dad.

Elena Mulo touched her husband's arm. "You must help him. He looks very bad."

He threw an anxious glance at Darlene and me.

"Victor." Mrs. Mulo's voice grew sharp. "Aphra knows already, and Miss . . ." She looked to Darlene with raised eyebrows.

"Darlene," I supplied.

"Miss Darlene will not utter a word of what she sees here, will you?"

Darlene shook her head dumbly, obviously confused. As was I. What was she talking about?

Mr. Mulo dropped to one knee beside the couch and placed a knowing hand on my father's forehead. He opened his black bag and pulled out a wooden tongue depressor and a silver flashlight with a narrow black tip—the kind they use for physical exams in the doctor's office.

He glanced up impatiently. "How long has he been like this?"

I shook my head, still bewildered. "I . . . I'm not sure."

"He passed out about two hours ago," Darlene offered. "I gave him an epi shot."

Mr. Mulo shook his head. "This does not appear to be an allergic reaction."

"I don't understand," Darlene said.

"Victor was a doctor . . . before," Mrs. Mulo whispered, as if that explained everything. She peeled off her raincoat and dumped it on the counter and then hurried to assist her husband.

"I don't have the right equipment, Elena," Dr. Mulo said. That title would take some getting used to. What else didn't I know about Seth's family? Whatever it might be, I did feel better watching Dr. Mulo poke and prod my dad. The man obviously knew what he was doing.

"I know you wanted us to leave the island, but they can help. I had to tell them." Seth's voice rolled over me like a summer zephyr, warming me despite my sodden clothes.

"Thanks," I murmured.

Darlene planted her hands on her hips. "Anyone mind telling me what is going on?"

I waited for Seth to explain, but he said nothing. "Their name is not really Smith," I said simply, and left it at that.

Dr. Mulo gestured to Darlene to come closer. I followed.

"His airway is compromised. If this continues, we may need to intervene."

"Intervene?"

"Tracheotomy." He scribbled notes on a small piece of

paper and handed it to her. "Here is a list of things I will need in order to be prepared. We shall hope it doesn't come to that."

"Hisako will bring us something," I said hopefully. "She said she would come."

"Who is this Hisako?" Dr. Mulo looked alarmed. "We cannot be exposed to anyone else."

I didn't have the heart to tell him that Hisako already knew all about them. "She'll be discreet."

"What is it she is bringing?"

"I'm not sure. Some kind of herbs or something. She's a botanist. She's looking for something to help."

He grunted. "She can give you these herbs without coming in here, can she not?"

"I . . . I guess so."

"Go see what she has and bring it back directly." Then, turning to Darlene, "You gather these items, just in case."

I ran to the door, and Seth followed. "I'm coming with you!"

I wasn't about to argue.

The storm nearly whipped the door from its hinges when I opened it. It probably would have knocked me right over if I hadn't been holding on to the door frame. Seth took my hand, and we struggled together against the wind, heads ducked to keep the rain from stinging our eyes. I led him to Hisako's villa. Her windows were dark, but I pounded on her door anyway and called her name.

"She must still be out gathering the plants," I yelled. "We should look for her."

"Where?"

"I'm not sure. She'd probably be able to find more variety up there." I pointed to the jungle behind the property.

"What are we going to do? Comb the entire hillside? We'd never find her."

"We've got to try!"

He shook his head. "Aphra, it's getting dangerous out here. We can hardly see as it is."

"Seth, I need her. For my dad."

He nodded without a word and took my hand again. We followed the trail that led to the far south corner of the property. Bits of sand and twigs flew through the air, stinging my skin like needles. A branch of a tree shot out of the darkness like a javelin. It missed Seth's head by inches. It was stupid being out in that weather, but I didn't know what else to do.

As we rounded the corner of the shuttered lounge building I saw a figure sprawled on the ground. Even in the darkness, I could tell it was too big to be Hisako. Stumbling toward the body, I swiped water from my eyes. "Frank!" I dropped into the mud beside him and shook his shoulder. "Are you all right? Frank, talk to me!" I slipped my hand under his head to lift it from the water, and my fingers touched a huge knot at the back of his skull.

"He's been hit on the head!"

"Something in the wind, maybe?"

"Probably." Or . . . maybe some*one*. But who? Watts was dead asleep in his villa. My stomach seemed to fold in on itself. What if Watts wasn't working alone? If the Mulos had managed to get on the island without Frank, what would've stopped someone else from dropping in? That person could be prowling about the resort right now! He could have been the one to kill Bianca. The Mulos could be in more danger than I had thought.

"Seth! I need you to get Frank back to the office. Have your dad check him for a possible concussion. I've got to go see something."

"I'm not leaving you out here alone!"

"I'll be right behind you. I just need to do this." I took off before he had a chance to protest and ran as fast as the wind and the mud would allow, all the way to villa ten.

Just like Hisako's had been, Watts's windows were completely dark. A tickle of fear caught in my throat. If Mr. Watts was still sleeping as I'd left him, who had turned off the lights? I crept to the front window and pressed my face against the glass to peer inside. A flash of lightning lit the front room where I had seen Mr. Watts drop onto the couch.

As I had feared, the couch, the room, and all that I could see was empty.

CHAPTER 11

Panic lashed at me like the wind and the rain. How could he have eaten everything I gave him and not have it affect him at all? Maybe he had help. Maybe they knew I had been trying to drug him, which meant that I could have placed us all in more danger. Someone had already attacked Frank. My stomach dropped. Hisako was out there looking for plants. What if they went after her, too? I had to get help.

I wheeled around and tore back to the Plantation House. Slamming through the doors, I ran smack into Seth. He grabbed me to keep me from falling.

"What is it? What's wrong?"

Everything. I clung to his arms and wished I could die right there so that I wouldn't have to face him and tell him how I had betrayed his family. I should have told the Mulos the moment I realized Watts had come looking for them. Should have warned them that someone else might be on the island. Now they were trapped. At that point, I didn't even care who the Mulos really were or what they may have done. All I could go on was the feeling of dread gnawing at my chest.

"Seth, you and your family are in danger."

He tensed and held me from him. "What are you talking about?"

I looked away, unable to let him see the guilt written on my face. "There's a man. Here on the island. Looking for you—for your family."

Seth's eyes slid to the office, where his parents were busy attending to the needs of my father. I felt like such slime. "I didn't tell him anything." My voice sounded whiny. Pleading. Like I was trying to convince myself as well as him that I had done all I could to protect them. It just wasn't true. "Seth, he may not be alone. Whoever hurt Frank could be coming after you next."

Seth's grip tightened, pinching the skin on my arms. "Mom! Dad!"

Elena Mulo was the first to respond. She appeared at the office door, clearly shaken by the urgency in Seth's voice. "What is it?" Dr. Mulo joined her, his face showing the strain of the past hour.

"They found us."

Dr. Mulo looked stricken. "How can it be possible?"

Mrs. Mulo didn't say a word, but shook her head, the color draining from her face.

"A man came today," I said. "Asking about you."

Darlene came down the stairs at that moment. "Frank is resting comfortably. I gave him the icepack. . . ." Her voice trailed off. "What is it?"

The lights flickered, and then everything went dark.

Mrs. Mulo gasped. Darlene tried to reassure her. "The storm."

I knew better. The resort's emergency generator would have kicked in the instant power was interrupted. This was no accident. First the phones and now the power.

"Lock the doors." I pulled away from Seth. "Hurry!"

I have to give Darlene credit. She didn't even ask why, but rushed to the front doors and drew the bolt. I ran to the back entry and did the same. I even checked the French doors that led out to the lanai, although I knew that, with its flimsy lock, if someone wanted in, all it would take was one well-placed kick and we were done for.

"Victor . . ." Elena Mulo's voice cut through the shadows, tight as an overwound piano wire.

Darlene looked from one to the other. "Someone tell me this instant what is going on!"

"Everyone just calm down," ordered Dr. Mulo. "Hysteria will do us no good. Aphra, you will tell us what happened. In the back room. I need to monitor your father."

Silently, we filed into the office. The only light came from a battery-operated clock on the wall. It washed the room with an eerie yellow glow.

Dr. Mulo squatted near the couch next to my dad, and Mrs. Mulo sank onto the rolling chair behind the desk. Dad's breathing still sounded labored, but not as raspy as earlier. Seth edged into the crowded office beside me. I wanted to draw comfort from his closeness, but my guilt wouldn't let me.

"Tell me." Darlene folded her arms in the tough-girl stance that was supposed to show she wasn't scared. She didn't fool me for a minute.

I repeated what I had told Seth. "Frank's the one who took Watts to his villa," I said. "Maybe he was asking too many questions, I don't know, but I think someone hit Frank over the head and left him out in the storm."

"Why would anyone do that?"

"They're looking for us." Mrs. Mulo's voice was so soft that I could hardly hear her for the wind outside. She held up her hand as Dr. Mulo began to protest. "We may as well tell them the entire truth, Victor. They could be in danger because of us."

His shoulders drooped. "We never thought it would come to this. We were certain no one would find us here."

"Even the agency does not know where we are," Mrs. Mulo added.

"Agency?"

"The bureaucrats nearly got us killed—although we may not have done much better ourselves."

"Why would anyone want to kill you?" From what I could see of Darlene's face in the dark, she was at once captivated and horrified.

"It was my fault," Elena Mulo said. "I crossed the wrong man, and now he's after us. Our only option, if we wanted to live, was to not exist anymore. Victor arranged the accident to make it appear as if we were dead. We thought we had forgotten nothing—"

"But it did not take long for Aphra to see through our guise," said Dr. Mulo. "We apparently did not cover our tracks as well as we thought."

Darlene frowned at me, no doubt peeved that I had kept this secret from her. I frowned back, just as confused as she was.

"Seth was our conscientious objector," Dr. Mulo continued. "He warned us that this would not work. He said that we would only endanger those who tried to help us. I am sorry to say we did not listen. He was right. We should not have come."

I stared at Seth's parents, trying to process what they were saying. If Mrs. Mulo had witnessed a crime or something like that, they had probably been in the Witness Protection Program.

Dr. Mulo looked at me with sad eyes. "I'm afraid your friend on the beach may have died because of our folly. I had feared as much when I saw her—that her death may be some kind of warning—and if what you say is true . . ." His voice cracked. "I am so very sorry."

Seth shifted beside me, and his arm brushed mine. I flinched. There was plenty of blame to go around. I may not have been able to stop Bianca's killer, but I could have warned Seth's family—if I hadn't suspected his dad to be a cold-blooded killer.

A change in Dad's breathing brought an end to the self-recrimination. He gasped and gurgled as if he were being strangled.

Dr. Mulo checked my dad's throat. "The swelling has gotten worse." He looked to Darlene. "You have the items I asked for?"

She nodded, looking unsure. "Do you have to cut him? Isn't there anything else? The herbs?"

My stomach sank. In my panic, I had forgotten about Hisako. She was out there alone. "I . . . I didn't find—"

"There is no time to wait." Dr. Mulo rolled up his sleeves. "I will need light."

"I'll get the flashlights!"

Seth followed me to the registration desk, where I grabbed a halogen flashlight. "Give this to him." I handed it off. "There's another big one in the utility closet."

The lobby was darker than the caves at midnight, except for the occasional strobe of lightning. I felt my way to the utility closet and fumbled in the blackness for the lantern flashlight. I grasped the handle and turned around just as a tremendous flash bathed the lobby and the surrounding lanai in brilliant white light. In that instant, I thought I saw a figure duck behind one of the pillars. I swallowed a scream, nearly dropping the lantern. Fingers trembling, I switched it on, shining the powerful light along the length of the lanai. Nothing. Still, my heart was doing ninety. There had been someone out there, I was sure of it.

"Aphra! The light!"

I ran back to the office. Darlene directed the beam of the smaller flashlight to where Seth was pouring the alcohol over his father's hands. The excess dribbled into a small metal bowl on the desk. Dad sounded even worse by now. His whole body arched with the strain of drawing each new breath. He was suffocating to death while someone lurked outside to kill the only person on the island who could give my dad a chance at life.

I handed the flashlight to Darlene. "Here, hold this. I . . . I think there's another one upstairs." I rushed out of the office, snagging Mrs. Mulo's raincoat on my way past the front desk.

No matter what the Mulos' story was, one thing I knew for sure: I should have given them a fighting chance. I had placed them in danger with my silence. The only way I could think of to set things right was to protect Seth's family and ensure that Dr. Mulo had time to perform the procedure on my dad. It was up to me to get that assassin away from the Plantation House.

In the darkness of my room, I yanked out dresser drawers, dumping them on my bed and pawing through my clothes until I found what I needed—long black pants and a white T-shirt. I wiggled into them and fumbled in my desk drawer for the flashlight and a pair of scissors.

In the bathroom, I locked the door and set the flashlight on the counter. The yellow beam of light cast weird shadows on the walls and made my face look alien in the mirror. I closed my eyes, lifted a handful of hair, and cut it off. It didn't matter if it was perfect, just so long as no one saw me up close. If I was lucky, that wouldn't happen. Before long, dark hair carpeted the sink, the counter, and the bathroom floor. I slipped on Mrs. Mulo's raincoat and stared at my altered reflection in the mirror.

It would have to do.

Lightning strobed through the windows as I tiptoed down the back stairs. A clap of thunder shook the house. I took that opportunity to slip out into the storm.

I am Elena Mulo. Come and get me.

The wind whipped her coat around my legs. Rain pelted me like liquid marbles. I ducked my head and ran toward the front of the house, where I had seen the man hiding. My idea was to get his attention and draw him into the jungle, where I had the advantage. I knew every inch of the hillside, and he did not. If I managed to lose him up there, he could wander for hours before finding his way back down—just enough time for Dr. Mulo to perform his magic.

Only the killer didn't follow the script.

Before I had even rounded the corner, a bullet zipped past my ear. I wasn't sure what it was until it slammed into the pillar next to me, sending splinters of wood flying. I screamed and dropped to the ground. Sodden blades of grass poked my cheek, and water soaked through my clothes.

This wasn't exactly what I had planned. I hugged

the ground, frozen with fear. A spray of grass and mud jumped up not six inches from my face. I choked back a scream. It wasn't going to do me any good to lie there like a fish on a platter. He could finish me off, and then what? My dad would die. I had to give Dr. Mulo more time.

I pushed myself up from the ground and ran in a zigzag to the tree line, hoping he would follow—only not too close.

Sure enough, his footsteps crashed through the undergrowth behind me. He was coming.

I climbed harder, but the heavy rain weighted my clothes and stung my eyes. I slipped and stumbled up the hill, decomposing leaves slick and wet beneath my feet. My thighs burned. My chest grew hot and tight. I wanted to stop and catch my breath, but I could hear him behind me.

Close. So close.

Inches from my head, a banana leaf jumped and ripped apart. Half a breath later, a bullet splintered the palm trunk beside me. I dropped to the ground once more, the sound of my scream caught in my throat. I swore I could feel the vibration of his footsteps coming nearer.

I held my breath, wishing and praying. . . . I wished I could tell Seth how sorry I was. I wished I could have protected Bianca. I prayed for the chance to see my mom one more time before I died.

The footsteps hesitated and then stilled. I squeezed my eyes shut. *Please, oh please, oh please.*

He headed off in the other direction.

I could have cried with relief . . . until I realized that he was heading back down the hill. No! I jumped up. He couldn't go back to the Plantation House.

The sound must have drawn his attention, because the course of the footsteps changed once again. I spun and scrambled through the tangle of trees and vines, the crack of branches sharp and clear behind me. Mud sucked at my feet as I struggled up the hill. Mrs. Mulo's coat kept getting caught on branches, slowing me down. I should just dump it right here, I thought. I should—

The sleeve of the coat jerked as if someone had tugged on it. Something hot zipped over my skin. I clamped my hand over the burn, and ducked behind a jambu tree. I couldn't breathe. The earth tilted and my head buzzed as I looked down at the small hole in the fabric of Mrs. Mulo's coat. The bullet had just barely missed my flesh.

Adrenaline fueled by cold, raw fear spurred me on. I broke from the tree and raced through the shadows to a stand of bamboo. Wind snaked through the narrow trunks with a haunted, moaning sound that chilled me even more than the rain. I didn't have to look back to know he was close behind me. My back tingled with the kind of dread you feel when you know someone could jump out and grab you at any second.

With the weight of the coat and the way it kept snagging on branches, I tired much quicker than I would have otherwise. Still, as much as I wanted to, I didn't dare take it off. Not yet. I had to preserve the illusion a little longer. My thigh muscles burned as I climbed up the hill. My breath came in tearing rasps, and my side ached as if someone had stabbed me with a hot poker. Finally the ground leveled off and I could breathe a little easier, though I didn't dare slow my steps. I wasn't going to give the assassin another chance to take aim. Ducking in and out of the trees, I led him farther up the mountain.

He was gaining on me. I would never lose him. Unless . . . I changed direction and scrambled under low-hanging branches toward my hidden cove.

The rain began to taper off by the time I reached the ravine. I thanked the gods; the old log was dangerous enough to cross on the best of days. Water in my eyes wouldn't do much to improve the situation.

I hesitated at the tree line. Crossing the log, I would be completely exposed with nowhere to go but down. Still, it was my only chance. I took a deep breath and went for it.

The log shifted after I had taken several steps—the ground beneath it no doubt eroding in the rivulets of water that continued to flow down the hill. I froze. My chest felt like it was clamped in a vise. If the log fell . . . I glanced down and was instantly seized by a grip of vertigo. Only the knowledge that a killer was close on my trail kept me going. I took another tentative step. The log held.

A shot exploded behind me. I screamed and lost my footing. My arms windmilled in the air before I fell. I reached out for the log and slammed against it with a thud.

I hugged the log, fingers gripping the rough bark, feet treading empty air. I could hear the killer and twisted around to see a black figure moving among the shadows. Out there on the log I was as good as dead, which wouldn't do my dad or the Mulos any good. And I'd never get the chance to find my mom. That thought gave me the surge of strength I needed to swing one leg high enough to hook it over the log. Grunting from the effort, I pulled myself up. I shimmied the rest of the way along the log until I reached the muddy ledge on the far side of the ravine. Solid ground! I rolled onto my back. I never wanted to move again.

Of course, I didn't have much choice. He was coming, and I couldn't leave the log in place for him to cross. I pushed myself into a sitting position, braced my back against some rocks, and pushed my feet against the end of the log until it gave way and tumbled down into the ravine. The rotted wood smashed into pieces at the bottom. I let out a breath. At least he wouldn't be able to reach me.

My relief didn't last long; a bullet ricocheted off the rock next to my head. I screamed and rolled to the side, scrabbling in the mud to reach the safety of the trees. In the shadows, I stood shakily and turned back just in time to see my pursuer running at full speed toward the ravine.

Time slowed, and I watched frame by frame as he flew through the air, arms and legs working for more distance. His feet hit the edge but slid backward in the mud. I was sure he was a goner, but at the last moment, he pitched forward onto his stomach and grabbed handfuls of weeds before the momentum could drag him down.

I didn't wait to see more, but spun around and ran, the focus of my world narrowing to one objective: staying alive.

CHAPTER 12

The weird thing about being terrified is that it heightens your senses. I would have thought that your mind would shut down and you'd obsess about what was making you scared, but that's not how it happened. Everything around me came into sharp focus, from the spongy texture of the jungle floor to the clean rain scent mixed with the earthy smell of humus. The hum of insects and tree frogs finding their voices after the storm seemed to be calling out to me. Run. Hide. Run. Hide.

I became acutely aware of the noise I made smashing through the undergrowth and winced at every footfall, knowing that he must be hearing it, too. I could hear him. Not clearly, but enough to know he was back there. Coming. My aim was to put enough distance between us that I could slip into the cove without leaving a trace.

Thing was, between my sanctuary and me lay the marshy old taro patch. On the best of days it's a challenge to slog through. After the rains, it was even worse. Wild and overgrown and about the width of a football field, I knew it was going to slow me down, but there was nothing I could do about it. I slipped into the bog, hip-deep in water and sludge that sucked and pulled at my legs as if it wanted to root me to the hill forever.

I hadn't made it far before I heard a crack in the jungle behind me. I dropped to my knees so that the muck closed around my chest and the huge, arrow-shaped leaves formed a canopy over my head. At least that was something to be grateful for; I'd be well hidden while I made my escape. I slid through the putrid water like a snake, navigating between the rows of taro plants.

Another rustling came from the undergrowth, much closer than before. I froze. Sheltered under the shadow of the clouded sky and the protective leaves of the taro, I considered the merits of staying right where I was. Except for one thing. The stagnant waters of the taro patch were the perfect breeding ground for mosquitoes. The rain had stopped now, and the mosquitoes had resumed their hunt for blood. There I sat—a living, breathing smorgasbord. They were all over me. I tried my best to wave them away, but there were too many of them. One landed on my face and sunk its proboscis into my skin. I flinched and reflexively swatted my cheek. Not a smart move. The noise apparently caught the killer's attention because the rustling behind me became louder, more distinct. Even though I couldn't see him, I knew he would be looking over the taro field now. It would be only a matter of time before he found me.

I eased toward the bank, gauging the distance between the end of the bog and the line of trees beyond. I had enough of a head start that I could probably lose him in the jungle. The questions were, how well he could aim in the dark, and was I willing to take the chance?

A splash at the opposite end of the field made the decision for me. He wasn't going to wait until I showed myself; he was coming to find me. I couldn't let him do that.

I slogged to the edge of the bog and tried to climb out, but the banks had turned to mud and kept coming away in handfuls. Behind me, I could hear him sloshing through the muck, tearing the plants out of his way.

In desperation, I dived at the bank, throwing myself as high aground as I could. When I was able to pull myself up, I crouched and ran for the trees.

I didn't stop until I reached the clearing that surrounded my hidden pool. In the darkness it looked like a different place. Instead of the serene, magical escape I found during the day, the shadows were menacing, the lulling sound of the waterfall now like the roar of a feral beast.

The plan was simple enough: to swim to my cave and hide there for as long as it took for the assassin to go away. Of course, life seldom works out the way you plan.

I ran toward the ledge, but my foot hit something and I stumbled. Whatever it was went skittering across the rocks. I squinted through the dark. My vial! I reached for it, but it tumbled over the ledge and clattered to the rocks below.

Those extra moments cost me a clean escape. The unmistakable sound of movement among the trees sent new tremors of fear through my body. I spun around, looking for someplace to hide. I couldn't jump into the pool now. The splash would alert him that I was here. I rushed into the shadows of the huge stones near the cliff wall just as he emerged from the jungle. Holding my breath, I watched as he scanned the clearing. In the darkness, I could make out only his shape as he crept like an animal on the prowl, light-footed and feline. He paused at the ledge and surveyed the empty water below before climbing down the rocks to patrol the banks of the pool. With any luck, he would move on when he found the place deserted.

Moonlight broke through the clouds, and I pressed my back against the stones, sending frantic telepathic messages. *Don't turn around. Keep walking.* But he stopped. He bent to pick something up from the water's edge and turned it over in his hands. My vial. Great. That's just what I needed—a signal that someone's been here.

The assassin turned around. He lifted his head. I drew in a breath.

He was not a *he* at all.

I almost called out to her. After worrying about her being lost alone in the storm with a killer on the loose, the only thing my brain could accept was that she was here, safe. And then I focused on the gun in her hand.

In the ghostly light of the moon, Hisako's mouth curved into a wicked smile as she held up my pepper spray. "I know you are here, Elena," she called. "It is no use to hide."

I sank back against the stones, my mind reeling. Wait. Was Hisako working with Watts? Or was she the real hit man? Hit woman? Hit person? Had she killed Bianca? Was she trying to kill my dad? I couldn't believe it was true. All those questions she asked earlier . . . she'd been using me to get at the Mulos! I shook my head. It couldn't be real. And yet, there she was, and she wasn't going to go away.

Disbelief quickly turned to anger. I narrowed my eyes at her dark shape. No way was I going to let her get away with this.

Watching her from the shadows, I considered my limited options. If Hisako got close enough to realize it was me she'd been chasing, she might just head back down to the Plantation House and waste the real Elena Mulo. Then she'd kill Dr. Mulo, who wouldn't be able to save my dad. And what about Darlene? And Seth. No, I couldn't let that happen. I didn't have much time to think it through, but an idea formed in my head. It could work. . . .

Eventually, Hisako climbed back up the rocks and tossed the vial aside. She scanned the area again before heading back toward the trees. Just a little bit farther and I could make my move. I edged away from the stones, praying that my luck would hold. I tiptoed to the ledge. When I was in good diving position, I kicked at a loose stone.

It worked. The noise caught Hisako's attention, and she spun to face me. She raised her gun.

Then, out of nowhere, came a dark shape, flying straight at me. I screamed. A shot echoed through the cove as the shape slammed into me, hurtling us both over the edge.

Seth.

The force of the impact knocked the breath from me, and I didn't have time to take another before we plunged into the water. I sank downward in the blackness, pulled by the weight of Mrs. Mulo's coat. My lungs were already burning as I wriggled out of it and let it drift away. Even without the extra burden, I knew I was in trouble. If I popped back up to the surface to take a breath, I was dead. If I didn't get air, I was dead. My only chance was to get to the cave. Seth brushed by me, and I tugged on his arm, signaling for him to follow.

The waterfall churned above my head as I groped along the rocks, desperately feeling for the opening. I forced the small amount of air in my lungs into my mouth and then swallowed it again to give myself more time. It prolonged the inevitable a few more seconds, but that was not nearly enough. A small stream of bubbles escaped my lips as my chest constricted. Sparks of light danced in my vision. My ears began to ring. With a strange sense of calm, I realized that I wasn't going to make it.

It was then that Seth's hand closed around mine and he pulled me close. I tried to push away, but my strength, like the oxygen, was gone. Weakly, I tried to signal that we needed to find the entrance to the cave. He didn't seem to be getting the message. Instead, his free hand snaked around the back of my head. He drew me to him.

I've never felt such an electric shock pass through my body as when his lips touched mine. Every muscle, every nerve came alive, even as my life was slipping away.

I returned his kiss, parting my lips and letting my tongue slide tentatively along his. And then . . .

He pinched my nose and blew a breath into my mouth.

Too shocked at first to take it in, I pulled back, eyes opened wide. He grabbed me again and gave me another breath. I could feel my head clearing, which wasn't such a great thing, because now that I could think straight, I felt like a total idiot.

Seth was buddy-breathing, not kissing me. What a fool. What a . . .

I didn't have time to worry about it. Above our heads came a watery *plink!* followed by a zinging noise. Hisako was shooting into the water. I didn't know if she could see us in the darkness or if she was just shooting randomly into the pool, but either way, we were like the proverbial fish in a barrel.

I grabbed Seth's hand again and pulled him to where I hoped the opening was. Nothing. Solid rock. Another shot zinged by very close. I started to panic. Disoriented from the fall from the ledge and from the lack of oxygen, I had completely lost my bearings. It was too dark to see clearly among the shadows. Either we were going to drown, or Hisako was going to shoot us. Neither option sounded particularly appealing.

Seth pulled me close again. I shook my head. He couldn't keep breathing for me, giving up his own air. With an exasperated grunt, he grabbed my hand and slapped it against the rocks, then moved it downward so that I could feel the emptiness below. The tunnel! Without hesitation, I dove for it and wriggled my way through.

It wasn't until I had surfaced in the cave and sucked in a lungful of sweet, cool air that I began to worry about Seth. If it was tricky for 110-pound me to get through the opening, how was he, with his broad shoulders and football physique, ever going to make it?

I took a deep breath and dived back under, feeling along the rocks until I found Seth. He was straining to push himself through the opening, his muscles rigid and his chest all puffed up with the breath he was holding.

I pounded on his torso and blew out a mouthful of air. The bubbles burbled to the surface. Seth continued to struggle. He wasn't getting my message. I knocked on his chest again. *Exhale, stupid!*

As if he could hear my thoughts, he released his breath so that he had just enough give to push the rest of the way through. We came out of the water at the same time, our dual gasps for air echoing through the blackness of the cave.

I dragged myself out of the water, coughing and sputtering as I rolled onto my back on the cold, hard rocks. Seth flopped down beside me. I couldn't see him in the dark, nor was I touching him, but I could feel he was there. The energy radiated from him like an electromagnet, surrounding me, vibrating through me. Just like our underwater kiss. Or *un*kiss.

My face burned as I thought of what I had done. What was I thinking? *Sure, Seth. You're trying to save me? Here. Let me stick my tongue in your mouth.* Stupid, stupid, stupid! I could just imagine what must be going through his head. He would probably rag me about what I'd done. That thought made me want to hit him. Especially when it occurred to me that the whole thing was his fault anyway, so I shouldn't be the one feeling dumb.

I sat up and glared through the darkness to where I knew he was lying. "Well, I hope you're happy."

He grunted.

"I had everything under control. All I had to do was

let Hisako take a shot at me so I could fall into the water. I would have disappeared into the cave, and she'd have thought I was dead. But then you had to come along and try to be the big hero. You just about got us both killed!"

Again he grunted, which made me even angrier.

"One disappearing body she might have bought," I raged, "but two? She's going to figure out where we are. Caves behind waterfalls are not that uncommon. What happens when she comes after us? Did you think about that? Did you think at all?"

This time he didn't make a sound.

"See? You have no answer to that, do you?"

Silence.

"Seth?"

I reached for him in the dark. His arm lay right next to me. Limp. I followed it up to his shoulder. His neck. My fingers moved up over his face, reading his features like Braille. He was out cold.

And he was deathly still.

My heart dropped as I realized he wasn't breathing. Leaning close, I felt along his neck for a pulse and panicked when I couldn't find one. "No! Oh, no. Seth!"

I shook him hard. "Come on, come on." Kneeling beside him, I put my ear to his chest to listen for his heartbeat. What I felt about stopped my own heart cold.

Hot. Wet. Blood.

I bolted upright and fumbled with his shirt, ripping it away and feeling for where the blood was coming from.

The coppery smell of it filled the air. My fingers found an oozing hole on his left arm, just below his shoulder.

The shot. Right before we fell. Ice gripped my chest when I realized that Seth must have taken the bullet. He had saved my life. Again. No way was I going to sit there and let him die.

I grabbed his face. "Seth!"

Hands trembling, I tilted his head back, lowering his chin to make sure his airway was clear. With a strange sense of déjà vu, I pinched his nose and sealed my lips over his to give him a breath. It was a lot harder on a real person than on the dummies they use for lifeguard certification. I had to try several times before I could feel his chest rise. I gave him another quick breath and switched positions to start chest compressions.

I'm not ashamed to admit that I was all kinds of scared, not the least of which was the knowledge that there was an assassin lurking nearby ready to kill us. My immediate fear, though, was not knowing what to do with Seth. What if the CPR got his heart pumping stronger just so he could bleed to death from the gunshot wound? The rational part of me knew that wasn't likely, but I was way beyond rational by then.

I wished my dad were with me. I wished Seth's dad was with him. I wished I could talk to my mom. I wished for a whole lot of things as I counted compressions. The Red Cross says thirty, hard and fast, between rescue breaths.

That's hard work. I pumped rhythmically. Overwhelmed. Exhausted. Terrified.

"Please," I whispered into the darkness, "please don't let him die."

CHAPTER 13

Emotions that had been trapped inside for too long came tumbling out as I struggled to keep Seth alive. I vaguely remember tears, but I don't know exactly who they were for. Perhaps for Seth. More likely for myself.

Something about being responsible for another person's life thrusts your own under the microscope. You feel small, inadequate. At least I did. Every fault, every shortcoming magnified until I knew I wasn't worthy. I would screw up yet again, and Seth would die.

"Come on, Seth." Pump, pump, pump, pump. "Keep fighting." Strong breath. Listen. Strong breath. Pump, pump, pump, pump.

I kept giving him chest compressions and rescue breaths for I don't know how long. My head grew light, my muscles tight and weak, but I continued. I never realized it would be such exhausting work. And still no response from Seth.

"Seth! Please! Don't give up!"

I kept up an endless monologue. Mostly it was for my own benefit, but I hoped somewhere in his subconscious Seth could hear me. Maybe if he knew how I really felt about him, he might fight harder. I just hoped it wasn't too late to admit it.

Pump, pump, pump, pump. Twenty-seven, twenty-eight, twenty-nine, thirty. Big breath. Listen. Big breath.

"Too late" was the story of my life. I thought of my dad lying on the couch in his office, and new tears rolled down my cheeks. All these years I had been so fixated on the mom who had gone that I'd never let myself get close to the dad who had stayed. So, all right, maybe my dad did have a hand in her leaving, but we could work that out. At least I knew now that she hadn't gone because she didn't want me. That meant more to me than anything. If we ever got out of this mess, things were going to be different. All I needed was another chance.

Pump, pump, pump. Big breath. Big breath.

Seth had reached a part of me I'd kept hidden for years. He saw right through the walls I'd built to keep people out. I thought of his easy smile and gentle humor. Of how he'd made me feel, standing there in the storm. Letting my guard down hadn't been scary. It felt . . . good. Right.

I bent to give him another breath, and for the first time, I was sure I felt a response, a movement of his lips. He had my full attention now. "Seth?" I listened for a heartbeat. Nothing. I breathed for him again, feeling his chest rise and fall. Laid my head on his chest to listen for the heartbeat once more. Thunk, thunk. Thunk, thunk.

It was faint, maybe a little erratic, but it was definitely there.

"Yes! That's it! Come on!"

I still couldn't tell if he was breathing on his own. I covered his mouth with mine and forced air into his lungs. Thunk, thunk. Thunk, thunk.

Again, I breathed for him.

And his lips did move. Unmistakably. Everything in the world narrowed to that point of contact between his lips and mine. Awakening. Life. Now I knew I was crying.

I sat up, wiping my eyes with the back of my hand, and tried to laugh. "I hope you don't think that qualified as our first kiss."

He coughed. I took that as a good sign.

"I'll need one when you're well. A kiss, I mean. To make up for all the trouble you've caused."

His hand closed over mine. "I'll . . . think . . . about it."

I wanted to dance, to sing, to swim, to laugh. But we weren't out of the woods yet. There was still the matter of Seth's gunshot wound. Not to mention Hisako, who was waiting outside to kill us both. Seth needed medical attention, and we were trapped. Somehow we had to get out of this cave.

"Seth, I'm going to go for help."

His hand tightened, squeezing on my fingers. "Don't . . . go."

"But you're hurt. If we don't—"

"I'll be . . . okay. Just . . . need rest."

I hesitated. Everything I knew about first aid told me I should seek immediate attention for Seth. But the first-aid rules don't generally take into consideration an assassin trying to hunt you down and kill you. If I left Seth, and something happened to me, who would know where to look for him? He could lay up there all alone and die. That didn't seem like the best scenario for either of us. I was going to have to take him with me, but until he was stronger, that wasn't going to happen either.

I propped my back against the cave wall and let Seth's head rest on my lap. And no, it wasn't quite as romantic as it sounds. I was keeping steady pressure on his wound, which, to be honest, was pretty gross. Plus, we were both cold and wet, and scared. Or at least I was. I can't tell you what Seth was thinking, because, as you may imagine, he was rather quiet.

I didn't feel like talking, anyway. I was too busy beating myself up. For someone who prides herself on reading people, I had missed Hisako by a long shot.

"Aphra?" Seth felt for my hand again.

"Yeah?"

"I'm sorry."

"What? No. Listen, I didn't mean what—"

"I mean . . . for coming here. We . . . should never have come . . . to your island."

"But I'm glad you did," I said softly.

His grip on my hand relaxed. "So what . . . do we do . . . now?"

"I don't know. Hisako could still be out there."

"What? Your friend?"

"Not anymore."

Seth tried to sit up. "I don't understand."

I pushed him back down. "Save your strength."

"I'm fine." He struggled upright again, but the way he groaned told me he was far from fine.

"You just about drowned! And in case you haven't noticed, you've been shot!"

"It's just . . . a flesh wound."

"What is this, Monty Python? Lie still."

"I thought you said . . . she was still out there. That she would . . . figure out where we were."

He was right. "Well, we'll just have to find another way out." I hoped there *was* another way. I'd only come in through the pool before. But then, I had never attempted to climb to the upper chamber because there were hordes of bats up there. Those bats had to get in and out somehow, though, right? That meant there had to be another opening. Problem was, I'd have to join the bats to find it. "You wait here. I'll climb up there and find a way out, then I'll come back to get you."

"I'm coming . . . with you."

"No. Are you crazy? You'll start bleeding again."

"I won't let you . . . go alone. It could be . . . dangerous."

"You're very gallant. But listen to yourself. You don't even have the energy to complete an entire sentence without pausing. You really think you're going to be able to protect me? Let's get real. I'm going to tie your shirt around your arm . . . there. It feels like it stopped bleeding, but you don't want to take any chances, so keep it elevated and—"

"I'm coming with you."

"What is it about this concept that you're not getting? You stay here, and I'll go look for—"

"I. Am. Coming. With. You."

"Seth, don't be an idiot. There's no way—"

From outside came a crash, followed by another.

"She knows we're in here," Seth said in a low voice.

"Don't worry," I whispered. "She can't get in."

"What's to stop her from going through the pool?"

"If she does that, we'll pounce her when she comes up on this side."

"It's pitch black in here. We'd never see her."

"Then she couldn't see us, either."

"Unless she has a flashli—"

Another crash. What was she doing? Trying to claw her way in? I didn't want to wait to find out.

"Okay, you win. Let's go."

CHAPTER 14

My plan was simple: to get Seth far enough away from the front of the cavern that Hisako couldn't see him if she somehow got inside. Then I'd figure out what to do next.

We felt our way up the clammy, sloping rock to the back of the cavern. Seth's breathing came in raspy fits, and he had to sit down every few feet. I was beginning to wonder if what we were doing was such a good idea. The back of the cave was blacker than a bat's behind. I had no idea where we were going or what lay ahead. Of course, the alternative was to do nothing, and that didn't seem like such a good idea, either.

As we climbed farther, the ceiling of the front chamber dropped so that I could feel the cold, damp rock just above my head. Before long, we had to crouch, and then crawl as the passage became shorter and shorter. Then the texture of stone beneath us abruptly changed. Coarse fragments in the rock bit into my hands and knees.

"Great." I muttered.

"What is it?"

"I'm not sure, but this feels like *pahoehoe*. It's a kind of lava rock. This is not going to be fun to cross."

"Wait." I heard tearing sounds and then Seth touched

my leg. "Give me your hands." I reached back, and he handed me some strips of his shirt. "Wrap this around them."

I quickly did as he suggested, and then I made him sit still so I could wrap his shoulder back up with the remains. The fabric helped some, but my hands still hurt. Of course, I wasn't about to complain. Seth was keeping pace with me over the same rough rock even though he had to gimp along like a three-legged dog.

The ceiling continued to drop. Before long we'd have to make like soldiers and crawl on our elbows. It would not be easy for him. He was already breathing heavily, so it was probably a good time for him to rest.

"Wait here," I said. "I'm going to go scout ahead and see where this leads."

This time he didn't argue, and that scared me. Either he was giving up, or he was too far gone to care. Fueled by the fear, I crawled forward again. I had to find a way out. For Seth.

The walls seemed to be closing in on me. Literally. Not because I was freaking out or anything. I really could feel the passage getting narrower and narrower until I realized that I must be in a sort of lava tube. How many tubes might run throughout the cave, I had no idea. I tried not to panic. I couldn't see a thing in there. What if I made a wrong turn going back to get Seth and got stuck in a maze of tubes forever?

I called out to him. "Seth?"

"Here! Did you . . . find anything?"

"Not yet. I'm still looking."

I breathed a little easier. At least if I could hear him, I could find my way back to that spot.

I pressed on. The rocks continued to narrow until I had just enough room to lay flat, cheek pressed against the rough, cold stone. And then my hand hit solid rock ahead. Dead end.

My eyes stung with tears of frustration. All that work for nothing. I was going to have to try another route, and we didn't have much time. But then I discovered an even bigger problem. As I tried to push myself back, I found that the space was too tight, and I couldn't move enough to turn around. Cold fear caught in my throat.

"Seth?" I called. "I need help."

Silence.

"Seth? Are you okay?"

More silence.

The fear intensified. My heart began to race uncomfortably. I was alone and blind and stuck under several tons of rock. Despite the chill, I began to sweat. My chest tightened up. I couldn't breathe. I could feel the beginnings of a full-on panic attack. But that wouldn't do Seth or me any good. I closed my eyes—not that it made a difference in the blackness of the cave—and made myself breathe deeply.

Think.

I had been crawling straight forward, no twists or

turns. It stood to reason that if I just backed up, I would find Seth. And once I did, I would have to get smarter about finding the nearest exit. If there were indeed several lava tubes in the cave, I'd better figure out a strategy for choosing the right one.

Again, I thought of the bats.

I have to tell you that just thinking about those things makes my skin crawl. I'm not talking about a surface fear. I am *terrified* of them. It's not rational. And it didn't make my realization any easier.

Bats are nocturnal hunters, which meant that, at that very moment, they would be winging their way in and out of the cave through some opening somewhere. To get out of the cave, I would have to follow the bats. But since I couldn't see where that opening might be, I would have to adapt their sonar sense to find the way out. I had to become one with them. I might have laughed at the irony if I hadn't been so disgusted.

If I could just get back to Seth, we could listen for the bats together. Problem was, I was stuck, and I had no idea where Seth was. Or where I was, for that matter. But now I had hope, and that gave me enough courage to try again. By lifting up on my toes, I was able to gain enough leverage to inch backward. My shirt got shredded, and the rock raked my stomach, but at least I was moving. Finally, the ceiling raised enough that I could sit. I turned around and crab-walked to where I thought Seth would be.

He wasn't there.

"Seth? Where are you?"

Nothing. And I couldn't see him. I couldn't even see my own hands if I held them right in front of my face. The panic started to set in again.

I reached out. "Seth?" I moved a little to my left. Nothing. A little more. Nothing. I struck out blindly. "Come on. This isn't funny."

Finally I felt my foot touch something soft. I nudged it. "Seth?"

"Unh . . ."

It's hard to describe the relief I felt at that moment. I almost started to cry again.

"Did you . . . ," he said groggily. "The opening . . ."

"Not yet," I said. "But I think I know how to find it now."

We sat very still and listened. Behind us, the falls rushed over the cliff and into the pool. Nearer, water dripped steadily on stone. And ahead to the left came the agitated rustling of tiny bodies. My insides curdled while, at the same time, I felt giddy with relief.

"Come on. This way."

Seth and I slowly, carefully, crawled toward the sound. The way was narrow, but the sounds grew louder as we pressed forward. Finally, the darkness faded into lesser shades of black. Somewhere ahead, light was getting into the cave. There must be an opening!

Unfortunately, the bats began to sense our presence, and they weren't happy. They started making anxious squeaking noises and shifting around. I gritted my teeth and tried to shut out the sound. Something brushed against my hair. Instinctively, I raised my hand to swat it away. Big mistake. I aroused protective bat mamas who swooped at me, leathery wings beating the air, furry little bodies bumping against me, tiny feet catching my hair.

I threw my arms over my head. This only caused the bats to become even more agitated.

"Be still!" Seth's voice hissed from the darkness.

"I am!"

He grabbed my hand and pulled me to him. I tried to focus only on my contact with Seth and to ignore the creatures flying around my head. For the first time, I was glad for the darkness so that he couldn't see that I was crying again.

It seemed to take forever, but eventually the bats settled down. Now all I had to do was crawl through their domain. No problem. Tentatively, I placed a hand down on the rock in front of me . . . right onto something squishy and cold. Bat poop. I recoiled, wiping my hand on my pants. "Ugh! That's nasty!"

"Don't be a wimp."

Wimp? I don't think so. I crawled right through the middle of the bat colony. Over the gushy, guano-covered rocks. The smell was overwhelming. More than once I thought I was going to lose it, but I wasn't about to give Seth the satisfaction.

Finally—and just in time—I caught a whiff of fresh air. Outside air. It was enough to keep me going. The blackness turned to gray. I could see dark shapes darting through the air ahead. Through the ceiling.

I don't believe I have ever been as happy to see the night sky as I was when I reached that opening. Eagerly, I stood and wriggled through. Ghosts of clouds were all that remained of the storm. Stars sparkled as if the gods had tossed a handful of glitter into the air. Moonlight frosted the rocks around me in a silvery wash. It was the most beautiful thing I had ever seen.

From my narrow ledge of rock, I could look out over the tops of the jungle trees and down toward the valley. Toward home. I closed my eyes and thanked the bats.

The next problem would be figuring out where we were going to go from there. On one side of the cliff, I could hear the steady rush of the waterfall. On the other side, the rocks looked loose and unstable. Above me, slabs of stone jutted outward in a way that would make climbing up impossible.

It would have to be down, then.

Down to where Hisako was waiting with her gun.

CHAPTER
15

Seth was in no condition to go rock climbing. His arm was weak from the gunshot, and he was still a little woozy from the drowning thing. But there was no alternative.

With the trees below and the way the rock face was situated, we couldn't see all the way down to the clearing. I hoped that meant Hisako could not see us. With luck, the sound of the waterfall would also drown out any noise that we made.

"You keep a lookout while I climb," I told Seth, "and I'll watch while you climb."

He just nodded and peered over the ledge. A little cautiously, I thought.

"Don't tell me you're afraid of heights."

"Hah!" He gave me an arrogant tough-guy look, but I noticed that he didn't deny the acrophobia.

"Don't worry." I felt among the vines that clung to the cliff face to find some sturdy enough to support our weight. "I climb up here all the time." Of course, when I go rock climbing, I use the proper gear, but I wasn't going to tell him that. "Besides, we're just climbing from one ledge to another. It's not really that far if you look at it that way."

He gave me a dark look.

"I'm just saying."

The drop to the next ledge was probably only about eight feet, but I worried that, with Seth's shoulder, he wouldn't be able to climb even that far. I climbed down first. Not that I'd be able to catch him if he fell or anything like that, but at least I could try to guide him to the next foothold.

As it was, I shouldn't have worried. Seth had the natural grace of an athlete, and even though his left arm dangled uselessly at his side, he made it to the next level without a problem—except for the amount of strength it took from him. He looked like he was going to pass out. I pulled him away from the ledge. "How 'bout we sit for a minute."

He shook his head. "I'm fine."

"Stop already. What is it that you're trying to prove? That you can be tough? Okay, I believe you. Now sit."

He sat, but only because he was getting too weak to stand. I knelt beside him and checked his shoulder. Now that I could see it in the moonlight, I was even more amazed that he'd made it this far. The bullet had passed straight through his arm. The skin around the puckered wounds was puffy and swollen, like a rising omelet. I was careful not to let the shock show on my face as I tied the torn shirt around it neatly.

"You're going to want to have your dad look at that."

He nodded.

I sat next to him and looked out over the moonlit trees. "I've never been up here at night. It's kinda peaceful."

He wasn't as impressed. "We need to get down."

I figured he was just nervous on account of the height thing, and I tried to reassure him.

He scowled. "I was thinking of my parents. They're still not safe."

"Oh." I looked down at my hands. The silence stretched between us. Finally I got up the nerve to ask. "Who are you running from, Seth?"

"A crazy woman with a gun."

"Funny. Who sent her? Why is she after you?"

"Huh. And here I thought you knew it all."

"My guess is you're hiding from the Mob."

He bunched up his shoulders and looked away.

"Tell me. Who's your family hiding from? Does it have something to do with organized crime?"

His voice took on a tone I hadn't heard before. "It's bigger than that."

"Bigger than a crime cartel? Because that's pretty big."

"As big as an entire government?"

"What?"

He snorted. "You had no clue, did you? 'Oh, I know all about you and your family, Seth,'" he mimicked.

"Hey. I said I knew you weren't who you were claiming to be. I never said I knew why."

He shot me a sharp look. "Because we don't know who to trust anymore."

I touched his arm. "You can trust me."

"That's what they said."

"Look around, Seth. Who am I going to tell your secrets to?"

He regarded me for a moment, and then dropped his gaze. When he looked up again, I could tell he had made up his mind to confide in me, but I wasn't sure if the decision was born of assurance or defeat. "I don't know all the details." He drew in a deep breath, like this story was going to take some effort to tell. "I didn't know anything, as a matter of fact, until I was thirteen. My name was Dylan then."

He didn't look like a Dylan to me, but I didn't want to say anything to stop the flow. I just nodded.

"They pulled me out of school one afternoon. Said we were going on an early vacation and headed straight for the airport. We ended up in Michigan. That's where I found out my whole life was a lie." He ran a hand through his hair, looking at once bewildered and lost. It was all I could do to keep from reaching up and smoothing the hair back down again.

"My real name wasn't Dylan," he said softly. "That was the name they gave me when they moved us the first time. I don't remember that. They said I used to be Mikhael."

"That's a nice name." Stupid, but I didn't know what else to say.

His face clouded. "They recruited my parents, you know. And now it's like they want to get them killed."

"Who?"

"The government."

I realized my mouth was hanging wide open and closed it. "Wait. Our government? Why?"

He shook his head and looked away. He didn't say anything for a long time. I laid a tentative hand on his arm. He looked into my eyes then, as if trying to see if I was really worthy of his trust.

Finally, he spoke. "You know what sleeper cells are, right?"

"Of course."

"My mom and dad used to be part of one."

My mouth dropped open again. "No way."

"Yeah. They don't talk much about it, but from what I understand, when they first came over, they weren't even married. It was just a cover. To be together, you know? And then . . ."

"They fell in love," I breathed. You have to admit that was romantic.

"And then I came along." He picked up a rock and ran his thumb along the rough edges. "They knew they had to do something." He glanced up at me. "Having a kid changed everything for them. They wanted out, but they knew they would never be allowed to just walk away from the program. And then they found out they wouldn't be able to keep me, either. That's when they defected."

I sucked in a breath. "And they went to the government."

He nodded. "They agreed to give the U.S. government information in exchange for protection. That's when they entered the Witness Protection Program the first time . . . but not before my mom fingered one of the cell leaders. He was a big catch for the government because his minions had infiltrated about every level of intelligence there was. They called him 'The Mole.'

"It wasn't long before the CIA came knocking. Mom and Dad knew a lot of people and a lot of secrets, and the government wanted in. The whole time we were living in California, I thought my dad was in exotic-car sales. He was really working for the CIA."

"Then what happened?"

"The Mole escaped."

"Oh."

"Yeah. That's when my mom and dad knew the CIA could no longer protect them. So they left. We moved to Michigan, and I became Seth."

"And now?"

He gave me a look like I was as dumb as the rock he held in his hand. "The Mole found us."

I had to take a minute to let it all sink in. "But what does that have to do with Hisako?"

Seth shrugged. "I'm sure this guy doesn't do his own dirty work."

"So she's his hit man."

"That would be my guess."

"Can't you go back to the CIA and ask for protection again?"

"My dad thinks it was someone in the agency who gave us up."

I could only shake my head. "But . . . why?"

Seth shrugged. "All I know is what my dad said. That if they didn't think we were already dead, they'd kill us themselves."

I sat still for a moment, digesting what he had told me and wondering how my mom figured into the equation. "Is my mom with the CIA?"

He didn't answer me.

"Is that how you came to us? Did she send you?"

His hand closed over mine. "You can never say I told you. Promise?"

I didn't dare breathe. "I promise."

"She was our contact in the CIA. I never knew that until I was older; I just thought she was a family friend. And she *was* a friend. She kept in touch even after she had been reassigned, which I guess is strictly forbidden. She was the one who came and got us when The Mole escaped." He looked into my eyes. "Four years ago."

I swear, my heart stopped beating. Four years. That was when we came to the island.

"That's all I know."

I murmured my thanks. There were still a lot of questions, but his story explained a lot. My mom hadn't left to find herself; she had gone to save a family. I only hoped it wasn't too late to save ours.

I stared down at his large hand folded over my smaller one and blinked away the tears. "One last question. With all those identities . . . which name do you prefer?"

He thought for a moment. "Seth, I guess. It's been too long since I've answered to anything else."

"Okay . . . Seth."

He squeezed my fingers, and the edge of his garnet ring bit into my skin. "You know, I have to tell you"—I tried to make my voice bright to lighten the mood—"this ring of yours has got to be the ugliest thing I have ever seen."

"I'm insulted." He held his hand up to the moonlight and straightened the monstrosity on his finger. "My dad gave this to me when we moved to Michigan. 'To remember the old life,' he said. I've never taken it off. I look at it and see California."

"Remind me never to visit California."

He slugged me. Softly, though. "We should go."

Seth still had to take a break between every ledge, but bit by bit we worked our way down the rocks. It was never easy, and once we got below the tree line it got even scarier. We could see the clearing then, well lit in the moonlight. I only hoped that if Hisako was down there she wouldn't look up, because if she did, she'd be sure to see us.

Every time I went over the side, I felt like I had a huge bull's-eye painted on my back. I was an open target for Hisako, wherever she was.

Finally, we made it to the ground. It wasn't pretty, but we did it.

After we rested again, Seth took my hand once more, and we crept through the shadows. I tried not to read too much into the hand-holding, but it made me happy just the same. Moonlight shone in patches through the trees, shifting as the branches moved with the lingering wind. Dodging those patches, we wove our way through the soggy undergrowth toward the clearing.

Something dull and white lay on the ground ahead. I squinted through the shadows. My vial of pepper spray! It seemed like a lifetime ago I had lost it. Could it have only been earlier that afternoon? The vial rested on its side. When we got closer, I could see that the top had broken off and most of the contents had spilled out. It lay nestled among the leaves of a Star of Bethlehem plant. Hisako's favorite, I thought grimly. Then I stopped.

"Wait a minute." I stooped down and grabbed the vial.

"What are you doing?" Seth asked.

"Hold on."

I crawled down to the water's edge and filled the broken vial with water, careful not to lose the small remains of the pepper spray. When I returned to the plant, I broke off a stem and stuck the torn end into the vial. I made sure not to get any of the milky sap on my skin.

"I don't get it," Seth whispered.

"You will. I'm trying to—"

"Do not move." Hisako's voice sent creepie-crawlies down my spine.

Chapter
16

Seth moved protectively in front of me. It made me feel warm inside—or it would have, if I hadn't been staring down the barrel of a particularly nasty-looking pistol.

I tucked the vial behind the plant and raised my hands in surrender. "*Konbanwa,* Hisako."

Confusion passed over her face for a moment. She squinted through the shadows. "Aphra-*chan?*"

I nodded.

"So. It appears you have tricked me." She shifted the gun in her hand. "You were never the target, Aphra-*chan.*" She had the grace to look sorry as she added, "You have now made yourself such."

Seth tensed, his muscles taut like a coil ready to spring. I touched his arm, hoping he would get my message. *Not yet.* If I was going to catch her off guard, I had to stall, to wait for the moment. I only hoped she'd keep talking.

"What about my dad? What did he ever do to you?"

"That could not be helped." She turned to Seth. "If your father had tried to help the girl, Jack-*sama*'s demise would not have been necessary."

"What are you talking about?"

Hisako shook her head, as if she were surprised by our stupidity. "I was quite certain I could draw your father out of hiding if he could see that his doctoring skills were needed. But I underestimated him. He allowed the girl to die."

Seth tensed. "No. You're wrong."

Hisako shot him a contemptuous look and continued. "Surely if his host became ill, I thought, he would risk exposure to help him . . ."

"But how?" Understanding dawned before I finished the question. "The plants. You drugged him."

The triumphant look on her face told me I was right.

"You're sick!"

She blinked. "Did you not employ the same methods to dispose of Watts-*sama?*"

Now Seth shot me a look, and he shifted slightly. Away from me.

"No! The plants I used were to put him to sleep. Not permanently. Just . . . until . . ."

"Aphra-*chan.* Didn't you wonder at his illness when he arrived? I had already arranged for him to receive a small . . . token of my esteem, shall we say, before he boarded the helicopter to come to the island. Combined with your creation . . ."

I felt the blood drain from my face. She'd used me. Again. But I wasn't going to sit there and take it like the meek little eager-to-please Aphra I had once been. Not after the weekend I'd had.

I felt behind me with one hand until my fingers wrapped around the vial. "Hisako?" She turned her attention to me. I sprang to my feet and threw the plant-sap-firewater in her face.

She screeched and clawed at her eyes, inadvertantly dropping the gun.

"Grab it! Grab it!" I ran at Hisako, knocking her to the ground. Straddling her chest, I smacked her hard on one side of the face and then the other, all my anger welling up inside and coming out through my fists.

Seth pulled me off her. "What are you doing? Come on! Let's go!"

I glanced back over my shoulder as he dragged me into the woods. Hisako howled like a she-wolf and groped about, unable to open her eyes. There was still fight left in her. Plenty of fight. Maybe we should have finished her off. The thought made me sick to my stomach.

We hadn't gone far before Seth had to slow to a walk to catch his breath.

"You . . . have security . . . at the resort?"

"Just a night watchman. Our head of security got stuck in the city last night."

"Is the watchman armed?"

I looked at the gun in Seth's hand. "He is now."

"She might have more weapons." His voice was grim.

I hoped he was wrong.

•••

It didn't take long to reach the edge of the taro patch. Seth jumped down into the muck first and reached back to help me down. This time, I accepted his chivalry.

"Wow, such a gentleman."

He raised a brow. "You say that as if you're surprised."

"Only a little."

I couldn't help but notice that he hadn't let go of my hand. I smiled up at him. He smiled back.

The sound of a gunshot tore through our peaceful cocoon. Hisako stood on the bank, a miniature revolver leveled at me. So Seth was right about the other weapon.

He raised his gun, but she fired at him, knocking it from his hand. It hit the water with a splash. She turned her glare on me, eyes swollen, tears flowing freely down her cheeks. My heart dropped. The plant juice had not blinded her after all.

Seth and I exchanged a quick look. Hisako would not waste her breath monologuing this time; we were in trouble. I glanced pointedly at the water, and he inclined his head. Hisako directed her aim at me. I took a deep breath and dropped beneath the surface before she had time to fire. The bullet *ploinked* into the sludge above me. One one-thousand, two-one-thousand . . . I slid under the muck toward her, praying that she would play her part. I could feel Seth somewhere nearby. The knowledge soothed my nerves and gave me the strength for what I had to do next.

The human brain is a funny thing. It's conditioned to base expectancy on experience. Above me on the shore, I imagined that Hisako would be scanning the taro field, waiting for us to surface. Reason would tell her we couldn't stay under much longer. Of course, up at the cove she had seen us disappear into the pool, but she probably figured we had found someplace to hide. This time there were no hiding places except the leaves of the taro plants. The direction we would reasonably go would be far away from her. With luck, when she didn't see us come up for air, she would take the bait and hunt us down.

As I had hoped, I felt the water slosh as she jumped into the bog. She would be ahead of me now. I zeroed in on her location, then sprang up from the water to tackle her from behind.

She must have sensed me coming. At the last moment, she spun, foot sloshing through the rancid water as she kicked up and hit me square in the chest. I stumbled backward and landed on the row of taro plants, gripping the stems to keep from falling under. I wheezed for breath and tried to stand. She steadied her stance to take aim at me once more. At that moment, Seth jumped at her from the other side. He wrestled away the pistol, but not without a fight. She slugged him on the chin and followed through with an elbow. Seth fell into the water. She lunged at him.

I reacted by instinct. Yanking on the stem in my

hands, I pulled out a taro root and swung the football-size corm at Hisako's head. It knocked her sideways long enough for Seth to regain his balance. He used the momentum to push her off her feet. She landed facedown in the water. He grabbed the back of her head in his one good hand, holding it under.

Heart jumping crazily, I sloshed to where he was and helped to keep her down. She thrashed and bucked, much stronger than I had expected. A sick feeling curled around me. Could we really do this?

Eventually her struggles weakened. She went limp. I backed away, but Seth continued to hold her under.

"That's enough, Seth."

He didn't move.

"Seth!"

He blinked and let go. Hisako floated facedown in the water.

We dragged her body through the taro patch. My insides knotted tighter with every step. I'd never hurt anyone before.

"Hurry," I urged. "Help me get her on land."

We rolled Hisako's body out of the taro bog and climbed out after it. Seth bent over her.

"Is she breathing?" I asked.

He ran a worried hand over his face. "I don't think so."

"Help me lift her up." Trembling, I knelt behind her and grasped her around the ribs, driving my hand and fist upward into her abdomen in a Heimlich maneuver to make sure she didn't have any water or gunk in her lungs before I began CPR.

After about four good tries, Hisako coughed and sputtered. We laid her back down, listening to make sure she was breathing on her own. I lifted one eyelid. Her eyes were rolled back so that only the whites were showing.

"One of us should stand guard while the other goes for help," I said. "I'm the certified lifeguard, so I can stay with her."

"If you think I'm leaving you alone with a killer, you're crazy."

"She can't do anything while she's unconscious. Go. Hurry back before she wakes up."

He shook his head. "No way."

"Well, then, just what do you propose we do?"

Without a word, Seth grabbed her by the arms and pulled her into a sitting position. Bending down, he hoisted her onto his one good shoulder. Of course, then he didn't have enough strength to stand.

"What are you doing?" I pulled her limp body away from him. "You're *not* thinking of taking her with us."

"Why not?"

"This entire night was about keeping her away from the Plantation House. Why would we want to take her there now?"

"Well, we can't leave her here. And like you said, she can't do anything while she's unconscious. We'll just have to make sure she stays that way."

He was right, but I still didn't like it. I grumbled as much under my breath as we lashed together a kind of stretcher out of palm fronds and sticks and Madeira vines. We rolled Hisako onto the stretcher, and I wrapped a few extra vines around her hands and feet, just to be safe. Seth raised a brow at that and looked as if he were holding back a smile.

I huffed. "She wakes up, I'm letting her get you first."

Hisako may have been small, but she felt heavier with every step. The sticks we had used for the frame of her stretcher bit into my hands, and my fingers grew numb from gripping them. The muscles in my arms and across my shoulders strained and ached. Not that I was going to complain—Seth was carrying the same load with an injured shoulder. And I'm sure he longed for the same thing I did—for us to get down the hill and then to get as far away from Hisako as the island would allow.

Unfortunately, I had forgotten about the ravine.

Seth had been leading the way, and so I hadn't even been thinking about the route; I just followed behind. When his step slowed, I peered around him and immediately recognized the void ahead.

My stomach sank. "Great," I mumbled.

Seth glanced back over his shoulder. "What?"

"The ravine. I pushed the log off the ledge."

"No problem. We'll just—"

"It wouldn't have been easy hauling her across anyway, but without the log—"

"We don't need the log."

"What are we supposed to do? Swing across on vines? We're going to have to find another way. We—"

"Aphra," Seth cut in, "shut up, would you? Just follow me."

Like I had a choice. He led the way uphill along the lip of the ravine. The space between the two sides seemed to be getting narrower. Not seemed to, was. Huh. For all my exploring, I had never come up this far.

"How did you know?" I asked.

"How did you think I crossed it the first time?"

The gap narrowed until the two sides were two or three feet apart—close enough to jump, but far enough apart that you could still fall down into the crevice if you weren't careful. I swallowed dryly, remembering how the log had smashed when it hit the bottom.

"How are we going to do this?" I asked. "With Hisako, I mean."

"Very carefully," he said.

He set Hisako's stretcher down and I did the same. I flexed my fingers, trying to work some feeling back into them.

"Here's what we're going to do . . ." Seth sounded like he was making it up as he went along, but seeing as how I didn't have any better ideas, I was more than happy to give him the responsibility.

He cleared the gap in one easy jump, and then knelt

on the edge, facing me. He reached out a hand. "Okay. Slowly, now."

I pushed Hisako, feet first, toward him. Inch by inch, her stretcher extended over the void. The further out she got, the more the balance shifted until I had to practically sit on the handles to keep her from upending and toppling downward.

Finally, Seth was able to grab hold of her from the other side and pulled her toward him—quickly, not slow and careful like I had been doing. My breath caught as the end of the stretcher slipped out of my hands and off my side of the ravine, but just as quick, Seth had yanked her over to his side and sat panting as she lay, oblivious, beside him.

I took a couple of running steps and jumped over the gap to join them. In the fading moonlight, Seth's face looked especially pale. The fabric I had wrapped around his shoulder glistened darkly. He was bleeding again.

"Do you want to rest for a minute?" I asked.

His lips set into a grim line. "No. Let's just go." He pushed to his feet and picked up his end of the stretcher. I scrambled to do the same on my end, my hands past feeling by that point. Once again, I followed Seth through the jungle.

By the time we made it down the hill, the gray light of predawn lined the horizon. Soon a new day would be here, and this nightmare would be over.

Or so I thought.

Dr. Mulo was the first to see us coming. He had been standing near the lanai doors and nearly tore them off their hinges to get to us.

He helped Seth carry Hisako inside, checking her vitals along the way.

"This is your friend?" he asked me. "Your Hisako? What has happened to her?" They laid her on the wicker couch in the reception area. "Elena! The lamp!"

Mrs. Mulo quickly appeared at our sides, holding the lantern high. That's when she saw her son's arm. "Seth! What have you done?"

"It's nothing," he said. "I'm fine."

"That doesn't look like nothing to me."

"Really, I'm okay."

"Victor . . ."

"Elena, leave the boy alone." Dr. Mulo completed his examination of Hisako before turning to Seth himself. "Now," he said, "suppose you tell us what happened."

Seth gave him the SparkNotes version of the night's events, leaving out the part about his nearly dying, I noticed. When Seth told him who Hisako really was, his dad uttered what I am reasonably sure was a very bad swear word in his native tongue.

"My dad," I said. "Is he—?"

Mrs. Mulo laid a hand on my arm. "He'll be fine. He's resting."

I nodded, numb with relief. "I . . . I'm sorry I lost your coat."

"Coat? Aphra, I don't care about the coat. You could have been killed!" She shook her head. "Why? After all the worry we've caused, why would you do that for us?"

I straightened. My mom had shown me by example what it was to be strong. All those things we did together . . . she was teaching me, guiding me to be like her. Though I hadn't known it until a few hours ago, she had sacrificed everything to save the lives of the people she was sworn to protect. I realized that I had just done the same. Why would I do that? I raised my chin proudly.

Because I'm my mother's daughter.

CHAPTER 17

Once Hisako was taken care of, Dr. Mulo began to examine Seth's wound, and soon Mrs. Mulo's attention was drawn to what they were saying. I took the opportunity to slip away from them and go looking for my dad.

He wasn't in the office, though I found Darlene in there, slumped over the desk, snoring softly with her head on her arms. I tiptoed over and touched her shoulder.

Darlene startled and jumped up from the chair as soon as she saw it was me. "Oh, Aphra! Honey!" She nearly tackled me as she gathered me in her arms. Her shoulders shook as she hiccupped and sobbed. "I thought you were gone to us." She pulled back, cupping her hands around my cheeks. "Don't you ever sneak off like that again! I couldn't bear it if we lost you."

I wiggled free, assuring her I was fine. "Where's my dad? I need to talk to him."

She dabbed a tissue at her eyes. "Not until we get you cleaned up. He's had a rough night of it. Your Dr. Mulo says we shouldn't upset him. He'll have a heart attack as it is when he sees what you've done with your hair." She gingerly lifted an uneven lank and eyed it with disapproval.

Darlene said Dad was asleep in his bed. I did as she

said and took a quick shower. I toweled off, staring at my reflection in the mirror. It wasn't pretty. My face was covered with scratches and mosquito welts, and the dark shadows under my eyes made me look like some kind of ghoul. At least, if I slicked my hair back, he might not be able to tell how badly it had been hacked.

The first weak rays of morning sun lit my room as I dressed in clean clothes. Finally, as presentable as I was going to get, I tiptoed to my dad's door and cracked it open.

He lay on his bed, propped up with pillows. White gauze encircled his neck like a priest's collar. A plastic tube ran from the front of the bandages to some kind of contraption on his nightstand made out of mason jars and yet more tubing.

I stepped inside the room. The hinges squeaked, and I made a mental note that I really would have to get them fixed.

Slowly, Dad opened his eyes.

"Daddy!"

I couldn't help it. I ran to his bedside and laid my head on his chest, blubbering incoherently as he stroked my short, wet hair.

Only when Dad made a weird noise in his throat did I raise my head. "Are you all ri—" I followed his gaze to see Dr. Mulo and Seth standing at the door. Gripped with a sudden shyness, I lost my tongue. Dad motioned for them to come in.

Seth had cleaned up and changed into faded blue jeans and a soft white T-shirt. I would like to have gone to him to find out just how soft, but Darlene and Mrs. Mulo followed close behind.

"I told your father the truth about why we came here," Dr. Mulo said to me. "I think all the misunderstandings between us have been cleared up."

Dad nodded, though he grimaced in pain as he did so.

"Please, tell us once again what happened last night—for your father's benefit."

One more time, Seth and I recited the events as they had transpired, from the moment the lights went out at the Plantation House until we returned with Hisako, each filling in gaps that the other left out. I learned that Seth had seen me slip out into the storm and had followed me right from the start.

My dad listened silently—not that he could have talked if he'd wanted to—gesturing when he needed us to back up or explain something more clearly.

When we concluded, Dr. Mulo shook his head. "One thing I do not understand," he said. "Aphra, last night you warned us that we were in danger because a man had come to the island and was asking questions about us, and yet the alleged assassin lying on the couch downstairs is most assuredly a woman."

"Oh, no! I forgot all about Mr. Watts!"

At the mention of his name, Dad became very

agitated. He tried to speak more than once, but only managed choking noises. I rummaged through his desk drawer and grabbed him a note pad and a pencil.

Watts agency, he wrote.

"Oh. Oh, my." Darlene pressed her hands to her face. "Jack, is this the man you told me about?"

Dad nodded as best he could.

Looking from one to the other, Dr. Mulo asked, "What?"

Darlene cleared her throat. "Jack, uh . . . Wow, how do I say this? He called the CIA when you arrived."

Dr. and Mrs. Mulo exchanged grave looks.

"He was worried." Darlene rushed to explain. "You have to understand. Knowing the . . . *element* Natalie works with, he had to be sure you weren't dangerous. He called the agency to verify that Natalie had sent you."

Dr. Mulo shook his head. "She no longer works with the CIA."

Darlene worried the hem of her uniform blouse. "But . . . Watts was her partner."

Mrs. Mulo grasped her husband's arm. "Oh, Victor. If the agency found us, then—"

Mr. Mulo nodded. "The Mole won't be far behind." He turned to me. "Where is this man now?"

I shook my head. "I don't know. He wasn't where I left him. He couldn't have gone far, though. I . . . I kind of drugged him."

"You what?"

"Well . . ." I twisted my hands. "I thought he was after you. I just gave him something to help him sleep until you had a chance to get away." An awful feeling gnawed at my gut. "There's something else. I told Hisako about him, and she said she had already drugged him. What if what I gave him accidentally . . . um . . . finished him off?"

Dr. Mulo pressed his lips together. He turned to Mrs. Mulo with a grim look on his face. "Elena, come with me. Seth, you keep watch over Miss Shimizu."

"I'll have to show you where his villa is." I rose to my feet. Dad squeezed my hand, and I looked down at him, a lump rising in my throat. "I'll be right back."

We hurried down the path, the silence weighing on me every step of the way. I was afraid we'd walk into the villa and find Watts dead.

Dr. Mulo finally spoke as we turned off the main path. "What exactly did you use to drug this man?"

I told him as much as I could remember, and he nodded but said nothing.

We knocked on the door when we reached the villa, but, as expected, there was no answer. My hands trembled as I slid the master key into the lock. I opened the door but couldn't bring myself to go inside. Mrs. Mulo stood with me on the lanai as Dr. Mulo searched the premises.

He returned rather quickly, one hand to his face. Took me a moment to realize he was chuckling.

Seems I'd chosen a bad combination of herbs. Agent Watts had spent a very long night—not asleep, as I had intended, but in the loo with an awfully bad case of Kapua's revenge.

It must have chapped Watts to have his quarry right there in front of him and not be able to do anything about it. If he'd had the energy, I'm sure he would have attempted to drag the Mulos in right then like a good little agent.

As it was, his temporary weakness bought us some time. Not much, though. Frank had said Junior would be coming back from the city with the police. Now that the storm had passed, they could arrive at any moment. We hurried back to the Plantation House.

Mrs. Mulo leaned close to her husband. "We are no longer safe here."

I didn't like the sound of that. It felt like a nail being driven into a coffin. "You could hide. We can tell Agent Watts that you've already gone, and then once he leaves—"

She shook her head. "Both Hisako and Watts found us. Others could, too. It is time for us to move on."

As much as I didn't want to hear that, I knew she was right.

Dr. Mulo agreed. "We don't have much time. As soon as Agent Watts regains his strength, we are lost. We need to leave immediately, but how?"

"Frank can take you," I offered.

"No good. He has suffered a concussion. He's not fit to fly."

"Better not let him hear you say that. Frank's a combat veteran. I'm sure he's flown with worse than a bump on the head."

"Excellent." Dr. Mulo brightened. "Then I should check in on him now."

My shoulders drooped. I was going to have to stop volunteering information that would help send Seth away.

Back in the lobby, he stood guard over Hisako's prone body. I trudged over to join him. She was still sleeping, her eyes bandaged and the vines around her hands and feet replaced with nylon cording.

"My dad gave her a sedative," Seth said. "She should be out until the CIA comes to get her."

"If he's not openly practicing, where does your dad get this medication?"

Seth grimaced. "Don't ask."

I watched Hisako's sleeping face. She looked so innocent and peaceful when she was unconscious. "Do you think we did the right thing? What if she has some kind of permanent damage from oxygen deprivation or something?"

"I don't know what else we could have done. She was trying to kill us, Aphra. At least we didn't sink to her level. The authorities will take care of her."

"But how will they know to be prepared? To take her into custody, I mean. We've no phones, no power—"

"Hell, I already roused the cavalry." Frank stood on the stairs with Darlene close behind, fussing over him and holding an ice pack to his head.

"Hey, Frank. You feeling okay?"

"This thing? It's just a bump." He pushed aside the ice pack as if to illustrate his burliness. "I radioed Junior this morning. He's on his way with a whole passel of law folk."

Radio. I'd forgotten Frank had a short wave in his helicopter.

He looked to Seth. "Get your gear together. We'd better get moving."

"You're going to fly them to the city?" I asked.

"I'm goin' to fly 'em somewhere."

"So soon?"

"Way I hear it, there's no time to lose."

I felt hollow. It was all happening too fast. "I'll come help."

"Shouldn't you watch the lady?"

My heart sank. I wasn't ready to say good-bye to Seth just yet.

Darlene cleared her throat. "I'll watch. Go."

As it turned out, Frank didn't get much help from either Seth or me. We tried, but kept tripping over lines, fumbling with latches, and generally messing things up until he told us to get out of his way. We stood together on the landing pad, silent. There were just too many things to say and not enough time to say them.

Seth's parents arrived within just a few minutes, carrying their luggage. Mrs. Mulo wore a light blue floral-print dress and had brushed her hair into short, soft waves. Dr. Mulo had also gone casual, in jeans and a golf shirt. I liked them much better this way. They looked . . . regular.

Mrs. Mulo gave me a quick hug. "I want to tell you something," she whispered close to my ear. "I knew your mother well enough to know that she loves you very much. She'd be proud of what you've done." She tucked a piece of paper into my pocket. "I think you've earned this. I don't have to tell you how important it is that you keep it secret." She gave me another little squeeze, and with that she pulled away and climbed on board the helicopter, where Dr. Mulo already sat, motioning for Seth to join them.

The whine of the engines raised in pitch as the rotors began to move faster.

"All right," Frank yelled. "Let's go!"

My throat closed up. I could hardly breathe, let alone say good-bye. Biting my lip, I looked into Seth's eyes one last time.

"I have to go," he said.

I nodded, still unable to speak.

"Seth!" Dr. Mulo called.

"I guess this is good-bye," I managed to whisper.

"For now, anyway. Remember, I know where you live."

I laughed. "I'll never forget you, Adam Smith."

He took my hand and pressed something hard into it. "Aphra, I—"

"Seth!"

He pulled me close and brushed his lips against mine. "Remember," he whispered, and ran for the helicopter.

I opened my hand, and a lump rose in my throat. Seth's ring. Gold and garnet never looked so beautiful. I hugged the ring to my chest and waited for the pain I knew was about to come.

Seth climbed inside and closed the door behind him. The tug in my chest grew stronger as the helicopter lifted into the air, as if a part of me was attached to the runners and was slowly unraveling as they pulled away. But I didn't crumble as I had expected. If anything, I felt stronger.

A part of me *had* gone with Seth, but a part of him had stayed behind. It salved the growing ache, warmed me, made me smile. I slipped Seth's ring onto my finger, turned my face to the sky, and waved farewell.

epilogue

I was still standing on the landing pad when the authorities arrived. They weren't just police like Frank had said, either. When Junior crawled out of the helicopter, he was followed by three men wearing dark suits and serious expressions. They introduced themselves as CIA agents.

I may have forgotten to mention to the agents, until well after they had come down to the Plantation House and interrogated Darlene, my dad, and me, that the Mulos had left the island. The agency was not happy. . . . Especially when Watts filed his report. He claimed I had tried to poison him.

I never did learn where the Mulos went after they left our island. All Frank could say was that he dropped them in the city.

The doctors said Dad should make a full recovery, but it will take some time. Until then, he can't work, and he can't travel. He spends his days at the beach. Darlene is running the resort until he gets better.

I'm still going to see Cami . . . or at least that's what Dad believes. As soon as she heard what I intended to do, Cami agreed to cover for me.

That paper Mrs. Mulo gave me? It was Mom's location.

She lives in Seattle.

I booked my flight today.

An Imprint of Penguin Group (USA) Inc.

For my girls

SLEUTH / SPEAK
Published by the Penguin Group
Penguin Group (USA) Inc., 345 Hudson Street, New York, New York 10014, U.S.A.
Penguin Group (Canada), 90 Eglinton Avenue East, Suite 700,
Toronto, Ontario, Canada M4P 2Y3 (a division of Pearson Penguin Canada Inc.)
Penguin Books Ltd, 80 Strand, London WC2R 0RL, England
Penguin Ireland, 25 St Stephen's Green, Dublin 2, Ireland (a division of Penguin Books Ltd)
Penguin Group (Australia), 250 Camberwell Road, Camberwell, Victoria 3124, Australia
(a division of Pearson Australia Group Pty Ltd)
Penguin Books India Pvt Ltd, 11 Community Centre,
Panchsheel Park, New Delhi - 110 017, India
Penguin Group (NZ), 67 Apollo Drive, Rosedale, North Shore 0632, New Zealand
(a division of Pearson New Zealand Ltd.)
Penguin Books (South Africa) (Pty) Ltd, 24 Sturdee Avenue,
Rosebank, Johannesburg 2196, South Africa

Registered Offices: Penguin Books Ltd, 80 Strand, London WC2R 0RL, England

Published by Speak, an imprint of Penguin Group (USA) Inc., 2008
This omnibus edition published by Speak, an imprint of Penguin Group (USA) Inc., 2010

1 3 5 7 9 10 8 6 4 2

CIP Data is available.

Speak ISBN 978-0-14-241118-6
This omnibus ISBN 978-0-14-241826-0

Printed in the United States of America

Acknowledgments

They say that being a writer is a solitary pursuit, but that just isn't so. The making of a book takes much more than just the efforts of the author; it takes an entire team of smart people working together. It has been my good fortune to work with the best of the best.

As always, special thanks to my family for their encouragement and for picking up the slack when I wander off into the writing zone. GUSH to my CPs: Jen, Ginger, Barb, Nicole, Julie, Kate, Karen, and Marsha.

Resounding thank-you to Diane Lutz, Christine Solberg, and Wendy Clark of the Greater Seattle RWA for sharing their experience and perspective and for having the patience to answer countless questions.

Words cannot adequately express my gratitude to the good folks at Puffin for their continued work and support. Huge, HUGE thanks to the sales team for spreading the love, to designers Theresa Evangelista and Linda McCarthy for giving me the best covers ever, and especially to my phenom editor Angelle Pilkington and to Grace Lee for their collective editorial genius. Working with you all has been a sincere pleasure!

Death by Latte

CHAPTER 1

I lied to my dad. That's how the whole thing started. I told him I was going to South Carolina to visit a friend, but instead I hopped a flight to Seattle. It made complete sense at the time, but being alone and far from home can make a huge difference in perspective. And lies have a strange way of catching up to you in ways you never imagined.

You have to understand my situation: I hadn't seen my mom in four years. She stayed behind when my dad left for the Pacific to open an exclusive island resort. He took me with him . . . and she let me go. She never came to visit. Not once. All I wanted was to see her again. I didn't intend for things to go so terribly wrong.

Looking back, I guess I should have known better; before we even touched down in Seattle, my stomach felt like it had been stuffed with broken glass. I suppose my body was trying to tell me what my head refused to accept—that sneaking off wasn't such a great idea.

By the time the taxi dropped me off in front of Pike Place Market, I was having serious second thoughts . . . but it was a little late for that then. All I could do was wait for the Market to open, find my mom, and hope she'd be happy to see me.

Oh, yeah. Did I mention that I hadn't told her I was coming?

That part is not my fault. I might have told her if I'd had the option, but I didn't have any way of contacting her. The only reason I even knew where to find her was that a mutual friend had let me in on the secret. But that's a whole other story.

My flight got into Seattle at eight that morning. The Market didn't open until ten. So even after the taxi ride, I had over an hour to wait. That hour passed excruciatingly slowly. It probably didn't help that I kept checking the glowing plate-shaped clock over the entrance every two minutes, but I couldn't help it. Now that the wait was almost over, each passing second was torture.

Delivery trucks came and went. Tarp-covered carts clattered over the bricks around me. Vendors called out greetings to one another as they hauled buckets of bright flowers and crates of vegetables and fish inside the arcade. *They* all seemed to move in real time, so why did the minutes tick by in slow motion?

I had to literally force myself to turn away from the clock. Obsessing wasn't going to do me any good. I had to find something—anything—to take my mind off the time or I'd to go crazy. Some of the shops across the street looked like they were open, so I wandered over to take a look.

Shop windows framed everything from fresh pastries to Native American art, but none of the displays really registered. Even the aroma of fresh coffee and frying dough from the coffee shops couldn't draw my attention. Physically I might have been looking in windows, but mentally I was still counting down minutes.

Finally, I noticed people filing through the main entrance. The doors were open. My stomach began to churn again. Now that the moment had arrived, I wasn't sure I was ready for it.

I hugged my arms and trudged back across the street. Just inside the entrance, people clustered four or five deep around a fish stand. They were all gawking at something, but I couldn't tell what. I worked my way through the crowd until I saw a worker in orange-and-black overalls in front of the long glass counter, his finger hooked through the gills of a huge silvery fish. He was talking to a lady in a floral sundress, projecting his voice like a stage actor.

"What time's your flight?" he asked.

"Three."

"Where do you live?"

"San Diego."

"Are you single?"

The crowd laughed and the sundress lady blushed prettily. The fish guy hefted the fish and flung it over his head. "One king salmon packed for California!"

The salmon flew through the air to where another worker behind the counter stood waiting with a sheet of brown paper. The fish slapped into his arms and he wrapped the paper around it in one fluid movement. "One king salmon packed for California!"

The first guy worked the crowd, posing for pictures, hawking the fish, joking with the customers. I watched for a couple of minutes, but I realized I was just avoiding the inevitable.

I eased behind a guy in a Mariners jersey, and as had become habit when I was anxious, my hand reached for the ring that hung on a chain around my neck. It had been only months since Seth Mulo gave me that ring, but it seemed like much longer. A lot had happened since then; my dad had gone in and out of the hospital, the CIA agents looking for Seth's family had invaded every possible sanctuary on the island, we had closed and then reopened the resort, and I had lied to my dad and flown two thousand miles to find my mom. Through it all, I could never shake that tingle-in-the-back sensation that I was being watched.

Just thinking about it made the hairs at the back of my neck prickle. I fought the urge to sneak a glance over my shoulder. With all the other doubts and misgivings in my head, the last thing I needed was to let paranoia crowd in among them. I tucked the ring under my shirt and turned from the fishmongers. I'd worry about the other stuff later. After I found my mom.

Unfortunately, I didn't have the slightest idea where

to begin looking for her. I didn't see a booth directory posted anywhere and the arcade corridor was a confusion of carts and booths and storefronts.

The closest stall belonged to a local jewelry artist, according to the banner that hung above his workspace. The center of the table had been draped in black velvet and held an impressive display of silver bracelets, charms, and chains. An elderly gentleman—the artist, I presume—sat behind the table, bent over the new piece he was crafting.

I approached hesitantly. "Excuse me."

He looked up, woolly eyebrows raised.

"I'm sorry to bother you, but do you know where Pike's Pottery is?"

The man scratched his beard with the silver tool he'd been working with. "Couldn't tell ya. Prob'ly down the hall or outside."

"They don't have a regular spot?"

"Naw. Most of us are whatcha call day-stallers. We get our space location assignments at morning roll call."

With that, he went back to his work. I mumbled my thanks and scanned the crowded arcade once again. I didn't understand exactly how the space thing worked, but I got the part that mattered: Pike's Pottery could be anywhere in the Market. I would have to look for it.

People of all sizes and shapes flowed into the arcade and down the corridor like a swift-rising river and I allowed myself to be swept along with the current, craning my neck to look at the booths as I passed each one.

Heavy perfume from incense and flower carts swirled about my head. Harmonica music drifted through the air. The produce guy across the hall laughed, his voice booming over the noise of the crowd. "Hey, you squeeze it, you buy it!"

Finally, on the other side of the corridor, I spotted a booth practically groaning under the weight of a collection of pots and bowls, vases and urns. A tall, dark-haired guy stood behind the table, absently dusting each piece. No banner advertised the name of the business, but I figured if it wasn't Pike's Pottery, at least the guy might be able to tell me where that booth was, assuming that he kept track of his competitors.

I had almost reached the booth when a woman carrying what looked like a very heavy cardboard box squeezed into the space behind the booth, nudging the man out of her way. My breath caught. Her hair was different from when I'd seen her last—shorter and maybe a little darker. The bohemian skirt and gauzy shirt were worlds away from the khakis and jeans she used to wear, and four years ago, she never would have been caught dead in all the drippy beads and chains hanging around her neck. But the rest of her looked the same. Ordinary. Average. She looked like me.

My feet stopped working. I couldn't move, so I just

stood there and let people bump past me as I stared at my mom. I swallowed against the huge lump that swelled in my throat. This was it. No turning back.

Smoothing my hair with a shaky hand, I forced myself to walk forward. Mom looked up as I approached the booth.

"How can I help . . ." Her words died and she blinked at me. "Aphra?" she whispered.

Everything I had intended to say when I first saw her vanished and all I could come up with was "Hi, Mom." For the briefest of moments, I saw something joyful flicker behind her eyes. It gave me hope. But then, right before my eyes, her face went blank. Truly. It's like she purposefully erased all expression until the only thing left was an empty canvas with no feeling, no warmth.

My heart tumbled right into my stomach. It's not like I'd expected her to go all misty and climb over the table to sweep me into her arms or anything, but it might have been nice if she could have at least pretended to be happy to see me.

Instead she just frowned. "What are you doing here?"

What did she *think* I was doing? "I came to see you."

The tall dark guy stepped up beside her and jerked his chin in my direction. "What's going on? Who's this?"

"This," Mom said, "is my daughter." Her tone was distant. Annoyed. I swallowed my confusion.

His eyes narrowed and he looked me over like I

might spread disease or something. "Your *kid*? She can't be here. Get rid of her."

My mouth hung open. *Get rid of me?* I couldn't believe he was being so blatantly rude. I waited for Mom to chew him out, but she just stood there looking at me with that stupid vacant expression on her face. "Aphra," she said evenly, "you need to leave."

"Leave? I just got here!"

Her eyebrow twitched, but otherwise she gave no indication that she had even heard what I said. "Joe?" Her eyes never left me. "Hand me the keys, would you?"

The guy slapped a set of keys into her hand and she stepped out from behind the stall, gesturing with her head. "Come with me."

I planted my feet and folded my arms. "I'm not going anywhere."

Still, no emotion registered on her face. She slipped her arm around my waist and leaned close, lowering her voice. "Aphra, this really is not the time or place."

"Well, I'm sorry," I whispered back, "but you haven't really given me a lot of other options, have you?"

Her calm expression flickered once again. What was that behind her veiled eyes? Amusement? Exasperation? "Come with me. We can talk outside."

At least that was something. I allowed her to steer me toward the wide portico, and I swear I could feel Joe's glare on my back the entire way.

Sunlight stabbed my eyes the moment we stepped through the door and I drew back, but Mom nudged me forward. I stumbled ahead, squinting in the harsh light. From what I could actually see in those moments before my eyes fully adjusted, the street had filled with the same bright jigsaw puzzle of vendor carts, stalls, and flower booths as inside the arcade. Outside, though, there was the added attraction of street entertainers. On one corner, a violinist offered an intricate, lush melody. On the other, a guy with a couple of spoons beat out the rhythm of the song against his thigh. We had to skirt around a cluster of people watching a man in a Technicolor vest twist long, skinny balloons into unlikely shapes.

Mom walked briskly, like she was late for a business meeting or something. I had to practically run to keep up with her. "Mom, I'm sorry I didn't call you first, but—"

She shot me a quick look and shook her head just enough for me to get the meaning. "Don't speak," she said in a low voice.

Mom didn't, either. Speak, that is. Not until we walked halfway down the street, where the crowd thinned out. "What are you doing here?" she finally asked. "How did you get here?"

The tone of her voice took me back to another time and place. When I was about ten, I had gotten hurt riding my Schwinn down a steep and rocky dirt-bike path that I had been forbidden to try until I was older. Mom tried to be stern with me when she found out what happened, but she couldn't quite hide her concern behind her words. My throat suddenly felt tight and achy. I took several steps before answering. "I flew."

"Aphra, I'm serious. How did you find me?" She glanced over her shoulder before adding, "The Smiths?"

"Ha." When Seth and his family had come to our resort, they had registered under the name of Smith. Since Mom was the one who had sent them to us, she was probably the author of that creative alias, but we both knew their name was Mulo.

"Mrs. Mulo told me where to find you," I whispered.

Mom's lips squashed into a straight line. "She should not have done that." Her pace quickened as she led me down a steep sidewalk to a parking area tucked beneath the raised freeway. We wove between parked cars and concrete support pillars, traffic whooshing overhead. She stopped next to a dirty white Econoline van, and pulled out the keys.

"Where are we going?" I asked.

She didn't even look up, but unlocked the passenger-side door and opened it. "To the airport. You can't stay here."

I took a step back. "No."

Whatever softness or concern I thought I had heard before vanished. "Excuse me?"

"I told you before; I'm not leaving."

"Aphra, you don't understand. I'm not asking—"

"No. *You* don't understand. You owe me, Mom. I've

waited four years to get some answers from you, and I'm not leaving until I do."

Mom signaled me to be quiet while a woman with a stroller passed by, and then she nudged me toward the van. "We're not going to have this conversation here."

I pulled away. I had waited too long to talk to her and spent a good chunk of my resort earnings to buy the plane ticket for the opportunity. There was no way I was going to let her send me home without an explanation. I just wouldn't go. What was she going to do? Carry me onto the *plane*? "We're not going to have the conversation at the airport, either," I said.

She gritted her teeth. "I see. Please get in."

I raised a brow at her forced civility and matched it with my own. "I'd prefer not to."

"We'll go someplace where we can talk."

I folded my arms and stared her down.

"You have my word," she said.

Once, her word might have meant something to me, but she was no longer the mom I used to know. I had no idea if her word was worth a thing anymore, but I really wanted to believe it was. Which is why I caved. I shrugged my backpack from my shoulders, swung it into the van, and then climbed in after it.

Inside, ceramic dust coated the cargo area and clung like microscopic barnacles to the front console and the seats. It smelled old and dry. The closing door behind me sounded like the bars of a prison cell clanging shut. That would have been a good time to cut my losses and go home. But, of course, I wasn't about to do that.

Mom climbed into her side and settled onto the seat, turning the key in the ignition and checking the rear-view. Her actions were all very calm and measured, but irritation was clearly written on her face. I folded my arms tight across my chest and I turned my own face to the window so she wouldn't see the angry tears gathering in my eyes.

I suppose I had known all along that my surprise appearance might not go over well. Mom had a life, after all, and I had interrupted it. But what did *she* have to be mad about? She's the one who left all those years ago. If anything, *I* should be the one pulling faces and acting all put out about things.

We drove in silence for what felt like a very long time. Mom didn't say anything, and I wasn't about to talk just to fill the void. I did steal glances at her, though. Her expression never changed.

"What did you want to talk about?" she finally asked.

I stared at her. "Are you kidding?"

She didn't reply.

I turned back to the window. She left the main road for a steep side street where she pulled over to the curb to park.

"Aphra, I'm sorry you're upset, but you can't just show up out of the blue like this. Not now. There are things you don't know . . ."

"But I *do* know." I swung to face her. "I know you were with the CIA. I know you left Dad and me to help protect the Mulos when the agency no longer would. I know you sent their family to stay with us because you thought it was the one place where no one would find them. But that's over now, Mom. They're gone and I'm here. It's my turn now."

She shook her head sadly. "That's just it, Aphra. It's *not* over. Not by a long shot. That's why I can't let you stay. It's not safe for you here."

I laughed bitterly. Not safe? How safe did she think it was sending the Mulos to our island with a paid assassin on their tail? And when I thought about everything I had done to get to Seattle—deceive my dad, ask my best friend Cami to lie for me, deplete my savings—my laughter nearly dissolved into tears.

"Aphra, I wish . . ." I could see the indecision in her eyes. There were things—obviously—she wasn't telling me and it looked like she was trying to decide whether she should.

"Do you know what happened when the Mulos got to the island?" I blurted.

Her face changed immediately and the expression became guarded, wary. "I know some."

"And you still don't know if you can trust me?" I didn't

intend for my voice to sound quite so small or nearly as pathetic, but the words had the intended effect.

"I trust you, Aphra," she said, "but I don't want you to get hurt."

It was a little late for that.

She must have read that thought because she turned in her seat to face me full on and took one of my hands in both of hers. She looked into my eyes, choosing her words very carefully. "Aphra, do you know *why* the Mulos were running?"

I nodded. The Mulos—Seth's family—had once been part of a sleeper cell. Seth's parents defected and offered to help the CIA in exchange for immunity.

"And me?"

"You . . ." I hesitated, lowering my voice, as if anyone could hear us in the van. "You were their contact with the Agency."

She gave me a quick nod. "So you understand the type of people I work with. This is no place for—"

"But I thought you quit."

Her guarded, blank expression returned. "I'm sorry?"

"Seth told me that you left the Agency four years ago." Which happened to be the same time she left my dad and me . . . but I figured it wouldn't be good timing to bring that up.

Her nostrils flared and she took several deep breaths before speaking. "What else did Seth tell you?"

I hesitated for a moment. I didn't mean to get Seth in

trouble—but why should she be angry if all he did was tell me the truth? "He said you suspected that one of the sleepers had infiltrated the Agency. And that when the CIA couldn't—or wouldn't—protect Seth's family, you helped them disappear. But now that they're safe, can't you—"

"Aphra, the Mulos are not the only family in the program who've been compromised. People came forward. They trusted the government. But someone gave them up. Those people must be protected until we can find the identity of the Mole's plant inside the Agency. That's what we've been doing here the past several months—following leads. And the closer we get, the more dangerous it becomes."

We? The guy at the market must be her partner, then. And the pottery business would be their cover. I leaned back against the seat, suddenly very tired. "You're still working for them, aren't you?"

Her voice sounded far away when she spoke. "It's complicated."

I shot her the hardest look I could muster. "Then why don't you uncomplicate it? Either you work for the CIA or you don't."

She searched my eyes for a long moment, hesitating, questioning. Finally, she said, "*Officially,* I quit. I cleared my desk and said my good-byes. But, yes, I still answer to the Agency. Our operation is funded by the Agency. My job is not done, Aphra."

I folded my hands into tight fists and stared, unseeing, out the window. What about her job as my mom?

"So you understand why you need to leave? It's much too dangerous for you here. I'll call your dad to meet you in Los Angeles or—"

"Dad can't fly."

Her brows lowered. "What?"

"The doctors won't let Dad travel until he's completely recovered."

"Recovered?"

"From the poison . . . and a minor infection from the tracheotomy. But that wasn't Dr. Mulo's fault. He wasn't exactly working in a sterile environment."

"Jack was poisoned?"

I frowned. "I thought you said you knew what happened on the island."

Her face took on a pinched look that I might have read as genuine concern if I hadn't been so mad at her. "My reports were apparently . . . less than complete."

"He almost died."

She blinked rapidly against the tears glistening in the corner of her eyes. "But he'll recover?"

"Yes."

Her voice cracked as she asked, "Who . . . ?"

"An assassin named Hisako. She was the one trying to kill the Mulos."

"Yes, I knew about her, but I don't understand—"

The cell phone in her pocket buzzed. She flipped it open and barked into the receiver. "What is it?"

As she listened, her expression grew even tighter. She glanced over at me and frowned. "I can't right now. I need to . . . No. Don't go anywhere. I'll be right there."

She snapped her phone shut. "Well, Aphra, it looks like you get your way for now. Something urgent has come up that requires my attention, so I'll need you to come with me. We can talk more tonight."

I sat up straighter, trying not to let my smile show. "Where are we going?" I asked. She didn't answer, but I didn't really care. She wasn't sending me away. Not yet. And I'd take any small victory I could get.

Chapter 2

I watched Seattle slip by, the gray-blue water of the sound on one side and the Space Needle rising above the skyline on the other. Ever since I had learned where my mom was living, I'd dreamed about how exciting it was going to be to see those very sights. But now the magic was gone. Everything outside the car windows was just a backdrop.

Mom didn't say a word as we drove. It looked like she was going to once or twice, but she held her tongue. And I held mine. There were so many questions I had to ask her, but I knew I wasn't going to get answers just then.

The road wound through business districts and eclectic neighborhoods before hugging the edge of a massive lake dotted with boats, their white sails puffed full. Under a steel-gray sky, an unseen breeze teased whitecaps on the water. I sat a little straighter, staring at the lake. Already, I missed the ocean back home so much it almost hurt. It was as if I needed to be near water to feel connected. Too soon, buildings and trees obscured the view of the lake, so that all I caught as we zipped past were flashes of blue.

Eventually the van slowed, the turn signal ticking rhythmically, and we turned onto a smaller side street.

"This is where we live," Mom said, gesturing with her chin toward an old four-story apartment building. The architecture was a strange mix of arches, columns, and porticos beneath a flat-top roof.

Mom cleared her throat. "We're . . . subletting, shall we say, while the owner of the apartment is on sabbatical, so we must be careful to maintain a low profile."

"Don't worry," I said. "I'll behave myself."

A wide driveway to one side of the building sloped downward and emptied into a shadowed parking garage beneath the building. A light flickered on as we entered the garage—it must have been on some kind of sensor—but it didn't do much to brighten up the place.

Before Mom had even pulled into her parking spot, a guy who looked to be in his early thirties, with close-cropped hair and horn-rim glasses, rushed toward the van. As we rolled to a stop, he peered into the windows with what I considered to be more than polite curiosity. I stared right back at him. Who was he? I could only guess by Mom's nonreaction at seeing him that she had expected to find the guy waiting there. He probably worked with her, too.

She calmly put the van into park and switched off the ignition while he, on the other hand, fidgeted like he was about to jump out of his skin. He looked like the uptight sort with pressed jeans and a starched oxford shirt buttoned all the way up to the collar. I couldn't see his feet from my vantage point inside the van, but

I could just imagine him wearing polished loafers and dark socks.

Mom told me to stay put and then climbed out to talk to the guy.

"What's going on?" I heard him say before she shut her door. "Where's Joe?"

She and the glasses guy had an animated conversation in front of the van that I couldn't hear. I debated rolling down the window a little so I could eavesdrop, and I might have except that Mom gestured toward the van and the guy's eyes followed her movement. He nodded and walked around to open my door.

"Well, hello." His soft Southern drawl honeyed the words. "It's such a pleasure to meet you."

I swear it was like he was talking to a preschooler. Made me want to hit him. Instead, I mumbled a greeting, hefted my backpack, and climbed out of the van.

He pressed a hand over his chest. "Oh, look at her. She's lovely. This girl is just the spittin' image of you, Nat."

Nat? My mom had always hated people to use that nickname instead of her given name, Natalie. She'd said it made her sound like an annoying insect. But she didn't show any reaction that it bothered her when this guy said it.

He snaked a gentle arm around my shoulder. "All right, darlin'. I s'pose we better go on inside. After that long flight, I'm sure you'll be wanting some rest."

I threw a glance back at my mom, but she was busy unloading a box from the back of the van and didn't look up.

Horn-Rim Glasses Guy guided me toward the stairwell. "I'm Stuart Hunt, by the way." He held out his hand and I automatically shook it, though it seemed like a silly gesture, seeing as his other hand was still draped over my shoulder.

"Aphra Connolly," I mumbled.

"I still can't get over it. Natalie's daughter. Here. It *is* quite a surprise."

He opened the door for me and ushered me inside. The stairwell was painted a vivid blue, and the landing was tiled in a cheerful mosaic pattern. I couldn't help but notice that the tiles themselves looked worn, though, and the grout was stained black and chipped out in several places. A vague odor of turpentine and stale cigarette smoke hung in the air.

"Resident artists," Stuart said, as if he could read my thoughts. "Lots of 'em. Natalie and Joe fit right in with their pottery." His lips pressed together as if hiding a smile. He glanced at my backpack. "I'm afraid it's a rather long climb—we're on the third floor and there's no elevator. May I help you with your . . . luggage?"

"No, thanks," I said quickly. "I've got it."

"Of course." He let the smile spread across his face. "An independent woman. Just like your mother."

I glanced back at Mom, who followed us carrying what

looked like a pretty heavy box. I wondered if Stuart's perception of her as independent kept him from offering to help her with it. I wondered if I should. Offer, I mean.

But then Stuart took my arm and guided me up the steps. "Is this your first time in Seattle?"

"Yes."

"Well, you'll just love it here. It's so . . . eclectic." He smiled, displaying impossibly white, cosmetically perfect teeth. Not that it surprised me. Everything about the guy was fastidious, from his perfectly trimmed hair to his perfectly trimmed fingernails.

When we reached the third-floor landing, he held the door open for me, and—almost as an afterthought, it looked like—for my mom. He ushered me across the hall to a polished wood door with a brass plate tacked in the middle of it that read 307.

"I think you'll be pleased to see where your mother resides," he said. He dug a key from his pocket to unlock the door. "It's actually large by Seattle standards, so we do feel rather fortunate to have found it." He grinned in a way that made me think fortune had little to do with it.

The place wasn't luxurious by any means. Not that I was being a snob, but it was a far cry from the resort—even the employees' quarters. But it was clean. Obsessively so. Even the couch cushions were symmetrically arranged. I eyed Stuart's proud smile and knew immediately who was responsible for that touch.

"It's very nice," I murmured.

"Why, thank you." He beamed. "But you haven't even seen the best part yet. Come on back. I'll show you."

"She doesn't need a tour, Stuart," Mom said.

"Nonsense." He ignored her and led me down a long hallway. "All the bedrooms are along this hall," he said. "Except for this here." He tapped the door and it gave a hollow thunk. "This is the commode . . . and a shower, in case you'd like to freshen up a bit." He eyed my travel-crumpled shorts and T-shirt with a pained expression. "But first"—he opened another door grandly to reveal a tiny room at the end of the hallway—"this is the study. It has a lake view. Come see."

I followed him out a set of sliding doors to a small overhang that he called the balcony. There wasn't even enough room out there to put a chair or anything. More accurately, it was the small landing of what looked like a fire escape. A narrow ladder to the side of the balcony stretched up past other balconies and down, I supposed, to the ground.

Stuart directed my attention once again. "You have to lean out a bit to see the water. See, look. Over there. That's Lake Union."

"That down there?" I pointed to the water I could see beyond the trees that stood behind the building.

"No, no. That's part of the Ballard locks. Those locks connect Lake Union to Salmon Bay and eventually the sound. Like a ship canal, you understand? But that . . ." He leaned even farther out and pointed toward the corner of the building. "*That* is Lake Union."

I appropriately "ahhed" at the small patch of grayish water. Really, I couldn't see enough of it to be truly impressed.

He stepped back, satisfied.

Just then, a gruff man's voice demanded, "What is *she* doing here?"

I jumped and spun around to find Joe in the doorway, glaring at me like I was the devil incarnate.

"I didn't have a chance yet to get her to the airport," Mom said.

"So you brought her *here*?"

She stared him down. "Not now, Joe."

Mom must have been his senior because he clamped his mouth shut, following orders. To a point. He may not have used words, but the look in his eyes spoke volumes. He was not happy.

She nodded toward the front room. "Let's get started."

Stuart bowed to me. Seriously. He actually bowed! "If you'll excuse me. Duty calls."

I looked to Mom, but she had already turned away and was following Joe down the hall. Stuart left the room and closed the door behind him. The signal was clear. I was to stay out of the way while they did whatever it was covert CIA agents did.

I shook my head. *Come see the view.* Yeah. Right. Get the kid to the back room where she won't be a bother was more like it. Stuart's Southern-gentleman act was effective, I'd give him that. I might have laughed at his clever manipulation if I wasn't just a little bit peeved. Okay, more than a little. I didn't like being duped.

I tiptoed over to the door, half expecting it to be locked, but the handle turned easily in my hand. Slowly, I cracked the door open just enough to see the three of them at the end of the narrow hallway, heads bent together around the kitchen table, an open laptop before them.

"Look at the coordinates," Stuart was saying. "This could be it."

"Verified?" Mom asked.

"Not yet. I can put a call in to—"

Mom laid a hand on his arm and he stopped. "Aphra," she said, "could you close the door, please?"

I pulled back, face burning. I clicked the door shut and stood staring at it. In that instant, I was a little kid again, caught spying on the grown-ups. I wasn't one of them. I didn't belong with them. I shook my head to clear it of that thought. I *did* belong with my mom. Didn't I? Just not at that moment.

I stood hugging my arms. The room began to feel very small. Confining. I paced. For the record, it took only four long strides to cover the entire length. Before long, I began to feel claustrophobic.

I pushed back out onto the little "balcony." At least I could breathe out there. Leaning out over the railing, I peered at the little patch of visible lake. It was hardly worth the effort. I folded my arms, resting my elbows on the railing, and blew out a breath. What was I supposed to do for the next however-long?

"Nice morning, huh?"

I had been leaning out to the right to see the lake and hadn't noticed that there was a guy on the next balcony to the left. He had a tall, lean frame and, judging by the smoothness of his face, couldn't have been much older than me. The sun-bleached tips of his tousled mocha hair seemed to catch the light when he moved. Dark eyebrows raised in question over deep brown eyes. He smiled and I swear it was like the sun had broken through the clouds.

I realized my mouth was hanging open and closed it. "I'm sorry," I managed. "I didn't realize anyone was out here."

His smile broadened. "No worries."

I stood there, feeling awkward and obvious, and ran my hand down the front of my shorts, smoothing out the wrinkles. Suddenly I wished that I had taken Stuart's suggestion to freshen up.

"I haven't seen you around before," he said. "Are you new?"

"Oh. I'm . . ." I shuffled my feet and reached for the comfort of the chain around my neck that held Seth's ring. "I'm just here visiting my mom."

"Well, welcome to the neighborhood." He stretched his arm across the space separating the balconies. "I'm Ryan, by the way."

I shook his hand. His grip was firm and his rough skin warm. I swallowed and pulled my hand back. Why was my mouth suddenly so dry? "I'm Aphra," I croaked.

"So, Aphra, how do you like Seattle?"

I said, "It's nice," and then groaned inside. What an insipid answer!

"How long will you be with us?"

"I—I'm not really sure."

He leaned casually against the railing. "I know what you mean. I'm a part-timer myself."

"Part-timer?"

"Yeah, I work the salmon season up in Ketchikan to pay for school. I only come down here to make deliveries."

"What school do you go to?"

He grinned. "UW Seattle, where else? Go Huskies!"

"Oh. So . . . do you take a boat to Ketchikan, or . . ."

His laugh danced in the air between us. "Are you kidding? No way. I fly." Then he glanced at the ladder and back at me. "Have you been up to the roof yet?"

I followed his gaze. "Um, no."

"You've got to go up there. Great view . . . although there's not much to see this morning; it's too overcast. On a clear day, we have a pretty spectacular view of Mount Ranier."

"I hope I can see it sometime." And I meant it, too. I hoped my mom would let me stay long enough.

"You can see the lake from up there. And my plane."

"Oh?"

"Yeah. Come on. I'll show you." He hoisted himself up onto the railing and then out onto the ladder in one smooth motion, pausing just a second to turn and look back down at me. "Do you need help?"

Was he kidding? I'd been rock climbing since I was ten. I'd even climbed a trellis or two. "I've got it."

I followed him up the ladder, pushing aside the little uneasy quells that said my mom wouldn't be happy to find me gone from the room. But if she was going to ignore me, what did she expect? Plus, come on. Like I wasn't going to follow this guy.

Ryan reached back from the top and offered his hand to help me up the last few rungs and onto the roof. This time I accepted his offer. He pulled me up, and it could just be wishful thinking, but I'm pretty sure he held on to my hand longer than was absolutely necessary.

I had to admit, the view was much more impressive from the roof than it had been from the balcony. Lake Union stretched out to one side, the water gray blue under the haze of clouds. "It's beautiful."

"Just wait until the clouds burn off," Ryan said. "You won't believe the view." He crossed to the far side of the roof and leaned against the half wall. I followed as if magnetically linked with him.

"There's my baby," he said, beckoning to me.

I was already right next to him, but I couldn't help it. I took another step forward. He leaned close, nearly touching his face to mine, and wrapped an arm around my shoulders. "Look down there, you see those docks?" He pointed down to the lake and the motion pulled me even closer. "The second one from the end. You see that plane?"

I did. Just the top of it.

"That's mine."

"Cool."

"Well, actually, it's my family's, but I fly it when I'm working."

He flashed another smile and my stomach flip-flopped. I pulled away and crossed to the other side of the roof. He followed, chatting easily about the joys of flying and how he'd gotten his pilot's license through the Civil Air Patrol when he was just sixteen. I hardly heard his words because of the alarm bells suddenly clanging inside my head.

I'm not quite sure why it took so long for me to come to my senses. Maybe because I was hungry for some normal conversation. Maybe because I was enjoying his proximity so much. But I knew my mom wouldn't be happy about me risking her cover, sneaking about and making contact with her neighbors—even polite, charming, and exceedingly good-looking neighbors.

I backed toward the ladder. "Um . . . I should probably go. It was nice meeting you."

"Yeah. You, too." He gave me one last dazzling smile. "I'll see you around."

I'll admit to being more than just a little disappointed that he stayed on the roof instead of climbing back down with me, but what did I expect? He probably thought I was a stupid little girl who had to get home before her mommy got mad. And he would be right.

After my rooftop encounter, there was no way I could stay confined in the tiny room. I grabbed my backpack and tapped on the door before opening it. Mom, Stuart, and Joe stared at me from the kitchen table.

"Excuse me," I said. "Would it bother you if I took a quick shower? I don't think I can stand these clothes a minute longer."

They exchanged glances. Stuart shrugged. Joe scowled. Finally, Mom gave me a brief nod. "Yes, of course. Go ahead."

I thanked them and padded down the hall to what Stuart had called the commode—a term I hadn't heard since my dad and I left South Carolina years before.

Even in the bathroom, Stuart's fixation with order was evident in the way the towels were folded over the bar and the rubber shower mat was aligned at right angles to the wall. More color-coordinated towels were stacked neatly, square in the center of the toilet tank, and a bottle of hand soap had been perfectly placed on the back corner of the sink.

I grabbed my clean clothes from my backpack and stripped out of my old ones, stuffing them into a plastic bag I had brought for that purpose. The chain holding Seth's ring came off next, and I zipped it securely into a little outer pocket of my backpack before stepping under the water.

I suppose I took a leisurely shower; I wasn't really keeping track. All I knew was that my options within the apartment were severely limited and I preferred the feel of warm water drizzling over my head to the claustrophobia of the back room. I didn't think I took *that* long, though, so I was more than a little bit taken aback when someone started pounding on the door. I still had to rinse my hair.

"Just a minute!" I called.

"Hurry up!"

I could tell by the cranky tone that it was Joe. I almost wanted to take longer just to spite him, but I knew that would have been childish. Satisfying, but childish. I don't know what I had done to make him dislike me so much, but it was clear he did. And, in turn, that didn't endear him to me.

Still, I wanted to keep the peace with my mom, so I hurried to finish my shower. I had barely turned off the water when he pounded again. What was his problem? I toweled off as quickly as I could and wiggled, still damp, into my clothes. All I could do with my hair was pull it back into a quick ponytail.

I opened the door and Joe nearly fell into the bathroom. He must have been leaning on it from the other side. I gasped and stepped back, but he grabbed my arm and yanked me out of the room. "About time," he growled, and pushed past me into the bathroom.

"Wait." I reached out to stop the door from closing. "Just let me get my—"

Slam!

I turned to complain to my mom, but she and Stuart stood at the kitchen counter now, furiously discussing something in low, agitated voices. I edged closer.

". . . every day in the same exact place," Stuart was saying. "I know when something has been moved."

Mom shook her head. "I understand, Stuart. But that doesn't mean—"

"No? Well look at this." Stuart turned the screen of his laptop toward her. "You know I monitor everything that comes in and out of this place, right? I even put tracking code in my own computer, which he must not have been counting on."

"What are you talking about?"

"This." Stuart tapped the screen. "It's Langley. He sent them a message last night."

It wasn't until that moment that Mom even noticed I was standing there. "Aphra, I'll be with you in a moment."

I gestured back toward the bathroom. "But my—"

Her look silenced me. I shuffled—as slowly as I could—down the hallway, but I didn't need to worry; she had already forgotten me. I leaned against the wall just out of her line of vision and listened.

"What did it say?" she whispered to Stuart.

"I don't know. It was encrypted and it will take me a while to work it out. But look . . . the same office, two days ago. And this"—I could hear him tap the computer screen—"last week. He's been in constant contact with someone in that office. Why? What isn't he telling us?"

Mom made a disbelieving sound. I don't know if she was denying it was true or if she just didn't want to accept it. "He could be talking with an old friend. Joe was with the Agency for over twenty years; he's got a lot of colleagues."

Stuart's voice sounded peeved. "Okay, if you say so. You're the boss."

"I'm sure it's fine," she assured him. I hadn't been around long enough to be the best judge, but to me, her confidence sounded forced.

Joe came out of the bathroom then, in as foul a mood as he'd entered. Mom and Stuart fell silent and didn't even respond while Joe griped and complained. Whatever it was the three of them had been discussing before, Joe was obviously not very happy about it.

"You two do what you want," he snapped. "I'm going back to the Market. In case you have forgotten, Natalie, we have a scheduled contact today. One of us should be there." With that, he grabbed the keys from the counter and slammed out the door.

Stuart shot a meaningful look at my mom, but she studiously ignored him. Despite her outward calm, though, I could practically feel the tension building, filling the room.

I realized once again that the timing of my visit had been supremely bad. But I couldn't have known. It wasn't my fault. At least, that's what I tried desperately to believe.

CHAPTER 3

After Joe slammed out of the apartment, no one moved or spoke for a full minute. Mom finally broke the silence. "I checked with the airlines," she said, glancing up at me. "There aren't any direct flights until six."

So she had been aware that I was still standing there. I wasn't sure whether to act chagrined or innocent. "Um, okay." A six-o'clock flight meant I wouldn't have to be to the airport until four-thirty or five. At least I'd get to spend part of the day with my mom.

Or not. Stuart moved his laptop closer to her. "That will give us just about enough time to go over these witness statements." He gave me an apologetic smile. "It'll only take a moment. You don't mind, do you, darlin'?"

Of course I minded. And I hoped Mom did, too. I waited for her to say something, but her eyes flicked over to whatever was on Stuart's screen and she didn't give me a second thought.

I grabbed my backpack from the bathroom and retreated to the study. I threw the backpack on a chair and paced back and forth, the frustration building inside me until I wanted to scream. But all that would probably accomplish was for me to get dropped at the airport early. I wasn't really mad at Stuart, although for someone who was so well mannered, it was a pretty insensitive move to interject himself and the work like that. But it was my mom I was truly upset with. We had only a little while before we had to get ready to go to the airport. She'd been gone for four years; couldn't she give me even a couple of hours?

And what was I supposed to do until she was ready for me? There was nothing to do in the room. It felt like a cage. A very small, very boring cage.

I pushed out the door to the balcony, but even that felt too confining. At least the sky had cleared.

That thought was quickly followed by the memory of Ryan saying how the view from the roof was so spectacular on clear days. And that thought was followed by the picture of him leaning close, pointing out his seaplane among the boats and planes at the docks. Heat crept up my face. I had to admit it would be pleasant seeing him again—if only to say good-bye. I wondered if he would still be up there.

It didn't take long to decide what I was going to do. I slipped back into the room and crossed to the door. I opened it a crack. Mom and Stuart were still busily discussing whatever it was she wanted me out of the room for. I closed the door quietly and depressed the lock. Just in case.

Back out on the balcony, I quickly climbed to the top before I could change my mind.

I have to admit I was disappointed to find the rooftop deserted. I sighed. At least the view was worth the climb. I turned slowly, drinking it in. It was just as Ryan had described, only better. On one side of the building and down from the locks lay the lake, the sun winking across the surface and changing the color from a slate gray to a deep cerulean blue. On the other, the white dome of Mount Rainier rose from beyond the city. I couldn't believe how close it looked.

"I *thought* that was you."

I jumped and spun around. "Oh! Ryan. Hi."

He gave me one of his easy grins and I couldn't help but smile back. He crossed the roof to stand next to me and leaned his elbows on the railing. "Turned out to be a perfect day, huh? One of only about sixty sunny days for the year."

"It's beautiful," I murmured. And it was. Beautiful, that is. But it wasn't perfect. Not by a long shot.

"Enjoy it while it lasts. We're supposed to get rain tomorrow."

My smile faded. Not because of the rain, but because if Mom had her way, I wouldn't be there to see it. "Oh."

"Yeah. I'm supposed to make a run in the morning, but I think I'll take off tonight before the weather gets here. After the Mariners game, of course."

"Of course."

"Ah. You a Mariners fan?"

"Uh . . ." I had never actually seen a baseball game in

my life, but that didn't stop me from saying, "Sure, whenever I'm in Seattle."

He laughed and I joined him, but my laugh sounded high-pitched and phony to my ears. What was I doing? I didn't even know this guy. Why was I flirting with him? He was in college and he flew a plane. I was just a child compared to him. And then, of course, there was Seth . . .

I quickly sobered. "I should go in. I just wanted to see this one more time."

He cocked his head and frowned. "I guess I'll see you around then."

"Yeah." I stepped a foot onto the ladder. "I'll see you."

He said good-bye and turned his back on me to wander back over to the railing. I climbed downward, feeling a little hurt and a lot stupid.

At least the distraction gave me time to think. I made a decision; I wasn't going to sit around in the room anymore—well, okay, since I had climbed to the roof and back, I really hadn't been sitting around, and I didn't intend to. If Mom had things to do, she could go ahead and do them. With me.

I swung my backpack up onto my shoulder and marched to the door, not being careful to open it quietly this time. I strode down the hall.

Stuart nudged her when I walked into the kitchen. She gave me a look—not really startled, but not altogether composed, either. "We don't have to leave for a few minutes, Aphra."

"I know." I settled into one of the kitchen chairs. "I got bored back there."

"Well, of course you did, darlin'," Stuart said, gushing. "I'm sorry; I wasn't thinking. Nat, perhaps we should finish this later. I think Aphra wants to spend some time with you."

He was right. About me wanting to spend time with my mom, I mean. But it still bugged me when he said it like I was some little baby wanting her mama. Not half as much as it bugged me the way Mom sighed and shut down her computer, though. She acted like it was some kind of chore that she had to figure out what to do with me until she could dump me at the airport.

She stood. "Are you hungry, Aphra? We could go grab something to eat before your flight."

"Sure," I said halfheartedly. Now I felt like a petulant little kid who was getting her way only because she'd thrown a tantrum.

"Well, grab your things. Let's—"

"Wait." Stuart held up a hand. "Nat, you better come look at this."

She crossed to his side of the counter and stood next to him, staring at his computer. "What is this?"

"This right here is Joe." He tapped the screen.

"You put a *tracking device* on the van?"

He looked insulted. "I put a tracking device on *all* the vehicles. How else would I know how to find you if something happened?"

"He's in the city. So what?"

"He said he was going to the Market. What's he doing on the other side of town?"

"Maybe he had errands. I don't see how this is any of your—"

"But he said he—"

"Let it go, Stuart. I'm going to take my daughter out now. Are you going to track *me*?"

Stuart sulked and went back to staring at the computer screen. He didn't even say good-bye when we left.

Well, no wonder Mom had grown moody; she worked with a couple of prima donnas. "I don't know how you can stand it," I said.

She paused, one hand on the stairwell door. "Stand what?"

"Stuart. And Joe. What's with them?"

She pursed her lips for a second and then ushered me down the stairs. "There's a lot you don't understand, Aphra."

"So you keep saying."

Mom paused and regarded me for a moment. "You're right. I think it's time you were enlightened. But not here. We'll talk in the car."

The garage light clicked on as soon as she opened the door. Compared to the bright colors and artistic touches inside the building, the garage felt sad and bleak. Just the perfect setting for a heartfelt mother–daughter talk, I thought dismally.

Mom cut across the garage, past a chain-link compound crowded with kayaks and locked-up bicycles, toward a small blue sedan parked in the corner. She pressed a button on her key fob and the horn chirped, lights flashed. That would be our ride, then.

I looked around the garage for the van, but I didn't see it. Joe must have taken it. Personally, I would have chosen the car if I were him, but I was more than happy to swap vehicles. As looks go, the car was about as unremarkable as the van, but it was obviously newer and probably more comfortable.

I opened the back door and threw my backpack onto the seat and then climbed into the front.

"Put your seat belt on," Mom said automatically. I almost laughed. Or would have, if I didn't feel so much like crying. Sad as it was, that was the first motherly thing she had said to me since I had gotten to Seattle—now that I was leaving.

She stuck the keys into the ignition, but she didn't start the engine. For a long moment she just sat, looking out over the steering wheel—at what, I don't know.

"Joe, Stuart, and I work together for a reason," Mom said, "but none of us chose the assignment." She traced the pattern of the leather grip on the steering wheel. "Each of us has a history with the Mole. I was in charge of protecting the woman who sent him to jail. Joe ran the task force that gathered evidence against him. Stuart hacked into an online crime ring the Mole had orchestrated while he was in prison."

When she raised her eyes to me, I was struck by the pain I saw in them. And scared.

"Once he escaped from prison, the Mole swore to take revenge, and he hit where it would hurt most. Joe lost his wife. Stuart's parents were murdered." She paused, letting the information sink in. "I am the only one who hasn't lost someone, Aphra, and I'd like to keep it that way. Do you understand why you need to stay far away from me? In the meantime, I can put up with a little surliness from the boys. They've earned the right to be moody."

She turned the key then, and the engine hummed to life. I couldn't say anything, but just stared at her as she carefully backed the car out of the spot. She might as well have backed over my chest. I wished that I could take my words back. I wished that I could play the day over and be a little more understanding. I wished that she had told me in the first place.

She shifted the car into drive and gave me a long look before pulling out of the garage. "I'm sorry that I had to keep this from you. I know you think I chose my job over you, but you are and always will be my first priority. Until we know where the Mole is hiding and who his operatives are within the Agency, I figured that the less you knew, the better. I thought it might keep you from becoming a target."

"Then why did you send the Mulos to our resort?" The words slipped out before I could stop them.

A small sigh escaped her lips, tinged with regret. "It was a bad call. I thought we had covered their tracks. I thought no one would find them."

"You didn't know," I murmured, anxious to salve the guilt I saw in her face.

"No, but I should have." She turned the corner and I realized we were passing the lake again, on our way back toward the city. "In my mind, you were still twelve. My little girl. I should have known better than to send a teenage boy to the island. And now . . ."

"Now what?"

"Now you're on the radar." She slid a sad look at me. "They'll watch you, hoping Seth will contact you. And now that you've left the island, they will want to know where you are going and why."

"Hold on. What are you talking about? Who's 'they'?"

"The Agency. And possibly . . . others."

"But . . ."

"Why do you think I stayed away all those years? I didn't want to draw attention to where you were."

"What about the cards? You sent me cards."

For the first time she smiled. Well, almost. Her lips curved upward, but her eyes were still sad. "I'm glad you got them. I never knew."

I decided not to tell her how Dad had kept them from

me and that I had only found where he had hidden them a couple of months ago. There's nothing either of us could do about that.

"What were the flowers on the back? Every one of them had a flower."

Her eyes misted as she looked at me. "You noticed them? Those were myosotis. You know, forget-me-nots? Corny, I know, but at the Swiss resort where your father and I honeymooned, the things grew everywhere. I loved them, but Jack said they were like weeds; you couldn't kill them. I . . . I wanted to give him a sign that I was still okay."

"And the postmarks?" I asked. "They were from all over the place."

"Yes. We've had to keep moving. Seattle has been our longest stopover, and we've only been here about four months. But we should probably move on now . . ."

She didn't say much else. She didn't have to; I could read the tension in her hunched-up shoulders and her death grip on the steering wheel.

I slid down in the seat, feeling like a complete idiot. All this time, the only one I had been thinking about was myself, worrying about how *I* felt, what *I* wanted. And now I had caused Mom more worry and compromised her operation. I should have listened to the part of me that said the Seattle trip wasn't a good idea. I should have stayed at home where I belonged.

•••

We were halfway to the airport when Mom's cell phone buzzed. She grabbed it from her pocket and flipped it open, glancing at the screen before answering. "Where are you?" Pause. "And you didn't think that it would be a good idea to tell me before you rushed off?" Pause. "No, I cannot come to your—" Her grip on the phone tightened. "What? No, tell me now." She listened and her face went white. "I understand," she said in a deliberately neutral voice. "I need to deliver the package and then I will meet you."

The package. Me. I was keeping her from doing her job. "Mom—"

She cut me off with a shake of her head. "Half hour. Maybe forty-five minutes." Pause. "Of course you can wait! Stay where you are."

I nudged her arm. "You can go *now*. I'm in no hurry."

She seemed to be considering it as she slid a glance at me, but then she shook her head and cupped her hand over the phone to whisper to me, "No. I need to get you out of here."

"Mom. I can wait in the car. Don't worry; I won't get in the way."

She hesitated only for a second, but that was enough. I understood a lot in that instant. I was a burden, an extra worry—and she didn't need any more of those.

"Really," I said. "Do what you need to do."

The relief on her face was clear. "I'll be right there,"

she said into the phone. She snapped it shut and swerved into the outside lane. We took the next exit and doubled back toward the city.

I pretended to be watching out the window, blinking fast to keep the tears in check. All I had hoped for and waited for these past years was to be with my mom. Unfortunately, my timing sucked. Maybe once she had found the answers she was looking for, there would be time for us. Until then, I needed to keep out of her hair.

I knew what I had to do. When Mom went looking for Joe, I would find my own way back to the airport.

I recognized the area near the Market as we drove toward the crowded parking lot under the freeway. Had I really just left there that morning? I saw the van parked next to one of the pillars. Joe must be close. Mom pulled into one of the last remaining vacant spots and switched off the engine. For a long while she just sat and stared out the windshield. Her frown told me she was unsure again.

"Go," I insisted. "I'll be fine."

She looked at me with unreadable eyes. I couldn't tell what it was that she was trying to hide. Regret, maybe? "Lock the doors," she said. "Stay low."

I assured her that I would. And I planned to. Stay low, that is. I just wouldn't be doing it inside the car.

She hadn't been gone more than a minute when a taxi rolled by, headed up the hill. I jumped from the car to flag it down, slamming the door behind me. Too late, I remembered the automatic locks. My backpack was inside the car. All my money, my ID, everything else was inside the car as well. I pounded my hand against the window and rattled the door handle. How could I have been so stupid?

I noticed some people a couple of rows down, casting curious looks in my direction. So much for laying low. I stopped pounding and stepped back. What I should not be doing was attracting attention.

Hugging my arms, I glanced around the parking lot. There were at least a dozen people walking through the lot, either coming or going. Obviously, I couldn't just stand around waiting for my mom to come back. They might think I was casing the lot to break into cars or something.

Maybe I could wait in the van. I rushed over and jiggled the door handles, just in case Joe had left it open. He hadn't.

There were plenty of shops nearby and I supposed I could hide out in one of them, but no matter where I went, I would eventually have to explain to my mom why I hadn't done as I had promised. I slumped against the van and looked down the street in the direction she had gone. I should probably hang out in one of the shops along that route so I could see her return. At least that way she wouldn't get back to the car and find me gone.

Then I saw her. Well, just her head, really, but she

had stopped only a block or so away with the cell phone pressed against one ear and her hand pressed against the other.

As if she could feel me looking at her, she glanced back at the parking lot. I ducked behind the van again, unable to shake the feeling that something was wrong. Besides me being locked out of the car, I mean. It was the way she was frowning, her brows in a worried bunch over her eyes. The whole time I had been with her, she'd been careful to keep her face impassive, completely expressionless. Either she'd let her guard down just then because she didn't think anyone was watching . . . or something was up.

When I dared peek around the van, I saw her hurrying down the sidewalk, away from me. On impulse, I decided to follow her. I knew I shouldn't. I knew she'd be mad, but I couldn't just sit there. Not after that look I'd seen on her face. I couldn't imagine what I could possibly do to help, but if she was in trouble, I had to give it a try.

I rushed to the street corner and pummeled the cross-walk button. The red hand kept flashing as she walked farther and farther away. I couldn't wait. I bolted across the street. A Nissan coming down the hill screeched to a stop, horn blaring. The driver yelled something at me, but I didn't have the patience to listen. I raced after my mom.

I lost her in the crowd by the end of the second block. She must have turned up a side street or gone into a store or something because one moment I saw the back of her head and the next she was gone. I planted my hands on my hips and tried to catch my breath as I turned in a slow circle, looking for any sign of her.

That's when I saw Joe. He was sitting at a little table in front of a sidewalk café, checking his watch and looking around as if he was waiting for someone.

So where was my mom?

A waiter in a long green apron stepped over to Joe and set an oversize cup on the table. Joe barely looked up. He checked his watch again and reached absently for the cup, raising it to his lips to take a sip. Abruptly, his expression changed. He made a bitter face and set the cup down so quickly that coffee and froth sloshed onto the white tablecloth. Frowning, he raised his fingers to wipe away the foam that clung to his upper lip and then stared at the residue. He sniffed his fingers, brows dropping tight and low. His frown deepened. With a quick glance back toward the café, he tried to stand, but dropped heavily back onto his chair.

The whole thing probably took only a couple seconds, but it played like a bad dream, everything unfolding in slow motion. He raised a hand to his throat, a mixture of confusion and anger crossing his face as his eyes bulged wide and his mouth hung open. And then he began to make choking noises.

Back home on the island, I had been certified as a lifeguard. My training taught me to react quickly and analyze later. Seeing Joe struggle to breathe kicked me into autopilot. If I had taken the time to think, I might not have run toward him. I might have considered that someone was trying to kill the guy and it would do well for me to lay low. But I wasn't thinking. I raced to where he had fallen onto the sidewalk and dropped to my knees beside him.

"Joe? Can you hear me?" He was still clawing at his neck and I had to hit his hands away so I could loosen his collar. "Are you getting any air?" I asked, fighting to keep my voice steady.

"The . . . latte . . ." he wheezed.

Well, at least he was breathing. I pressed my fingers to the side of his neck. His pulse was going crazy.

He grabbed my hand. "In . . . the . . ." His words were lost in a spasm of coughing. "The . . . list . . ."

"Try to relax."

"Cup . . . hold . . . c-c-up . . . ho-holder . . ." Suddenly his eyes rolled back and his head jerked like someone had yanked a string at the top of his skull. His grip squeezed like a vise around my hand. I yelped and pried my fingers free.

At the same moment a hand grabbed my shoulder. "Aphra!" Mom's voice hissed. "What are you doing here?"

"He's . . . he's . . ."

"You can't get mixed up in this!" She yanked me to my feet. "Get back to the car. Go!"

She gave me a push and I stumbled through the crowd of people who had begun to gather around Joe's table.

A lady plucked at my arm. "What happened? Do you know that man?"

I rubbed my sore fingers and looked back to where Mom had bent over Joe, her eyes pinched with concern. "No," I said flatly. "I've never seen him before."

CHAPTER 4

I knew I was supposed to leave, but I couldn't pull my eyes from Joe's body thrashing on the sidewalk. My mom grabbed his head to keep him from smacking it on the cement, but there wasn't much else she could do for him. Only the waiter and one other man stepped forward to see if they could help. Everyone else hovered at a safe distance, watching. They acted as if they were at a Saturday matinee or something.

Mom looked to the waiter. "He's seizing. Grab a tablecloth to cushion his head!" Then to the man, "You. Call 911!"

The man whipped a cell phone from his pocket and stabbed at the numbers while the waiter yanked a tablecloth free of the nearest table. He bunched it up and shoved it under Joe's head so that my mom could let go.

The lady standing next to me wrung her hands. "What's wrong? Shouldn't they put something in his mouth? Why aren't they helping him?"

I ignored her and stared straight ahead.

Just then Joe stopped convulsing. His body arched one last time and then he lay deathly still.

"Sir?" Mom leaned close, pressing two fingers against the side of his neck. "Sir, can you hear me?" I could see the answer pass over her face before she let it go blank again. "He needs some air!" she yelled at the crowd. "Clear out!"

A few people took a step back, but most of them were glued to their spots. There was no way they were leaving the show. Mom started CPR, even though I'm pretty sure she knew it wouldn't do any good. As she was starting chest compressions, Joe's head lolled to the side, his eyes open but empty. My stomach lurched and I looked away.

In the distance, a siren wailed. The sound sent a quiver of fear through my belly. I'm not sure why. I hadn't done anything wrong . . . unless you counted the part where I came to Seattle uninvited, interrupted the work my mom and her colleagues were doing, and wandered into a crime scene.

I backed away from the crowd. I should have listened to Mom when she told me to go. I should never have come in the first place.

"Hey, miss," a woman in the crowd called. "Miss! Where are you going?"

I didn't turn back but walked quickly away from the scene. I wanted to run, but if I had learned anything from watching Mom, it was to not draw attention to myself. I walked down the sidewalk, outwardly calm, and tried to adapt my mom's bland expression even though I was screaming inside.

It took such concentration to keep the emotion from

my face that I had gone a couple of blocks before I noticed a man on the other side of the street who seemed to be matching my stride, mirroring my movements. I probably wouldn't have noticed him at all except that I caught a reflection of him in a store window. He seemed to be staring straight at me. I paused and pretended to admire something inside the store so that I could get a better look at him, but he bent his blond head away from me and stooped to tie his shoelace.

He was definitely following me. Why? And then I thought about it. I had interrupted Joe's murder. I had touched him, spoken to him. Whoever killed him might think Joe had told me something I shouldn't know. Something worth killing for. The idea brought with it a cold panic that coiled around my throat so tightly I could hardly breathe.

What should I *do*? I couldn't lead the guy to the car. I couldn't go back to the café, either. I wanted to yell, to scream, but instead I made myself stroll casually past the next shop, a vacant smile plastered on my face. Meanwhile, my mind raced. Mom would have been more aware of her surroundings. She would have already mapped out an escape route. I would have to improvise.

I took quick note of the people around me: a couple of guys in shirtsleeves, a cluster of touristy-looking types talking in loud voices, a lady walking a big black dog. It wasn't likely that the guy would do anything in front of all those people, so maybe he was just watching me.

I stood at the crosswalk next to the shirtsleeve guys, waiting for the light to change. From the corner of my eye, I watched as the man waited at the crosswalk on his side of the road. The light turned green. I stepped down from the curb. Across the street, he did the same. I took a couple of steps forward, but as soon as the cars started moving through the intersection, I spun, jumped back onto the sidewalk, and ran for the nearest store.

I didn't stop to see if he was coming after me. I just hoped that he wouldn't try to cut through the traffic, and that I'd have a minute-or-so head start.

A hanging bell jangled when I yanked open the door, and I dashed into what looked like some kind of New Age gift boutique. Inside, a cloying smell of incense weighted the stagnant air. Racks of crystal jewelry, dream catchers, and bottles of essential oils lined one wall and a wrought-iron staircase ascended along the other. Breathy flute music played softly in the background. My footsteps creaked across the aged wooden floor, but the lady behind the counter didn't even look up. She licked her thumb and turned a page in the magazine she was reading.

I cleared my throat. "Excuse me. Do you have a restroom?"

She gave me a brief, bored glance and pointed to the stairs. "Captain Nemo's. Up the stairs on the left."

I thanked her and took the stairs two at a time. On the second floor, the glass front of Captain Nemo's pub dominated the left-hand wall. Through the soles of my feet, I could feel the vibration of the heavy bass music inside. The bar was crowded with what looked like an after-work crowd. I could probably lose myself in there.

But then I saw something better. At the end of the hallway stood an emergency exit. I ran for the door and slipped through it just as I heard the bell downstairs jangle again.

I cringed at every footfall as I rushed down the stairs, every movement echoing through the bare cement stairwell. Because of the way the building was situated at the bottom of a steep hill, the exterior exit was only half a flight down. I set my sights on the door and tried to tread as lightly as I could. I had nearly reached it when the door on the first floor burst open.

"Hey!" a man's voice yelled. "Stop!"

I didn't care about noise anymore. I crashed out the metal exterior door and into the alleyway behind the building. Garbage bins and empty boxes filled the alley. Something sour leaked from one of the bins and snaked along the downward slope toward the building. I recoiled from the stench and ran the other way.

I didn't have to turn around to know he was behind me. I heard the exterior door bang open before I even reached the end of the block. I turned and pounded down a faded wooden staircase and tore through a narrow alleyway between two tall buildings. Back on the sidewalk again, I wiped the expression from my face and jogged to the corner. From there, I cut up the street to a path that wound through a miniature park.

As I tore down the path, I caught the flash of red lights through the trees to my left. My feet slowed and then stumbled to a stop as I realized that the café lay just below the park. Through the branches, I could see the round tables with their crisp white tablecloths. An ambulance idled at the curb as two paramedics draped a sheet over a figure lying on the gurney. The waiter was talking to a policeman, who was writing things down in a notebook. There was no sign of Mom.

She must have slipped away. Which meant she was probably heading back to the car. Where she would look for me. And I wouldn't be there.

I needed to get back to the parking lot, but I needed to be sure I lost my tail first. How, I wasn't sure, but I didn't have time to think about it. From behind me came the sound of running feet. I spun and bolted up the park's grassy hill to the street above. When I reached the sidewalk, I banked right. At the bottom of the hill ran the raised freeway—my only familiar landmark. As long as I made sure I could see the freeway, I would be able to find my way back to the parking lot.

I ducked into the first doorway I came to and pressed my back against the wall, praying that the man hadn't seen which way I had gone. I held my breath, waiting, hoping, resisting a quick peek around the corner to see if he was coming. One moment passed, then another and another. It seemed logical that if he had seen where I'd gone, he would have passed the doorway by then. I made myself wait a little longer just to be sure. Nothing.

Cautiously, I pulled myself away from the wall and peered down the sidewalk. It was empty. I didn't celebrate too much, though. If he had followed the path through the park instead of cutting through the trees, it wouldn't take him long to discover I hadn't gone that way, and he might come looking for me.

At one end of the block, I saw a whole group of people crossing the street, laughing, talking. More than the usual neighborhood foot traffic. I figured it would be easier to lose myself in a crowd, so I chased after them. Once I was sure he wasn't following me anymore, I'd find my way back to the car. I just hoped my mom would still be there.

By the time I reached the corner, they were halfway up the hill. I ran to join them—which turned out to be much harder than I had imagined it would be because of the angle of the hill. By the time I reached the tail end of their group, I was wheezing like a smoker with asthma.

I watched the hill below me. Nothing. Perfect. Mingling with the other pedestrians, I crossed the street. I had no idea where they all were going, but I did know there was safety in numbers. As long as I was surrounded by people, my pursuer would likely keep his distance.

Faint strains of reggae music drifted down the sidewalk and grew louder as I walked. Bright banners in green, yellow, and red stretched above the road ahead. A lone balloon drifted up into the sky. Suddenly I understood why so many people were headed in one direction and why the prevailing mood was so light. There must be some kind of concert or festival going on. That meant lots of people. Perfect for getting lost.

It turned out that the "festival" was just an evening concert in another rather small park. It wasn't exactly packed with people, as I had hoped, but at least the concert had drawn a decent crowd. Dozens of people lay about on the grass, sleeping, picnicking, and soaking up the festive mood. Others danced to the music close to where the band was playing. At the far end of the park, two tall, carved totem poles framed a spectacular view of the sound.

I turned and scanned the streets behind me. Still no sign of the mysterious blond-haired man. I wanted to believe that I had ditched him, but that seemed too easy. More likely, he was hiding somewhere. Watching. A sense of dread rose up like a glacier wave, threatening to crash down on my head.

I turned in a circle, suddenly feeling very alone in the midst of all those people.

And then it began to register that the area I was in had a familiar feel to it. I looked back toward the sound. I could see the rise of the freeway, just beyond the edge of the hill. The parking area where we left the car was down there, which meant . . . I stepped up onto a low retaining wall and looked down the street. With a rush of relief, I recognized the vendor stalls on the street in front of Pike Place Market.

I jumped down onto the sidewalk and ran for the Market. I could lose myself much better in the larger crowd there. And once I knew for sure I wasn't being followed, I could find my way to the parking lot. For the first time that entire day, I actually felt optimistic.

My optimism crumbled just a little as I neared the market. Instead of the crowd I had hoped for, just a handful of shoppers and tourists lingered. Most of the stalls were closed and a lot of the merchants were already disassembling them and sweeping the bricks around them. The long shadows that stretched between the buildings gave the scene a forlorn air.

Head low and radar high, I wandered past the remaining stalls, peering into storefronts and alleyways, behind booths, and down the shadowed street. And then I stumbled to a stop.

I blinked and rubbed my eyes. Just ahead, near a red-and-gold popcorn cart . . . I must've been seeing things, and yet there he stood. Instead of board shorts and sandals, he wore jeans and a T-shirt. He turned his head and his dark glasses caught the last rays of the sun. I couldn't breathe.

Seth.

Bit by bit, everything else faded away, like in one of

those old movies where all the action stops and the camera focuses in on just one person. All I could do was stare at him. It had only been weeks, but already my memory of him paled in comparison with the real thing. I hadn't forgotten the sharp curve of his jaw or the way his dark hair fell around his face, but I was delighted all over again by the way my stomach went all bubbly just from seeing him.

I called out his name, but I don't think he heard me. My first impulse was to run to him, but I thought better of it. What if I was still being followed? The last thing I wanted to do was drag Seth into whatever was going on.

It wasn't easy, but I let him walk right past me and managed not to reach out to touch him. He had stopped once again, and scanned the remaining booths like he was looking for something. Or someone. Had he come to the Market to find my mom and Joe? Was *he* the contact Joe had spoken of? I was still in such shock from seeing him that I didn't even wonder why he was in Seattle or how he had gotten there. That would come later. All that mattered at that moment was figuring out how I was going to alert Seth without drawing attention to him.

I followed him through the Market at a distance, watching him but being careful not to fully look in his direction. The way he strolled from one booth to the next, you'd think he was just any other tourist. I didn't miss the tension in his shoulders, though, or how his hands dug deep into his pockets the way they did whenever he was nervous or upset.

Finally, he moved from the outside stalls toward the arcade. If I was going to catch him, that would be the place to do it, before anyone looking on from outside could catch up to us. I quickened my pace, sidestepping merchants and their carts and managing to reach the entrance to the building about the same time as Seth.

I gripped his arm just long enough to get his attention and then walked ahead of him, hoping he would get the message and follow me. He did. I felt him at my elbow as I rushed toward the stairs that led to the lower-level shops. His footsteps echoed close behind mine.

The hallway below was deserted. The "DownUnder" shops apparently closed earlier than the booths on the arcade level. Still, I didn't like the idea of standing out in the open, just in case. I paused at the bottom of the stairs, looking for somewhere secluded that we could talk. The place was disappointingly lacking in hideaway nooks. Seth took the lead then, grabbing my hand without a word and pulling me down the hall until we reached an empty side hallway with a bolted door at the end of it.

He turned to face me and I couldn't help myself; I literally jumped at him and threw my arms around his neck. He didn't return the hug. I pulled away, embarrassed and confused.

"Seth," I said in a small voice, "what is it?"

He wouldn't meet my eyes, but looked down the hall. "I'm glad I found you," he said without feeling. "You know that ring I gave you at the resort? I need it back." His voice was cold. Detached.

Was he kidding? I stared at him. "That's it? You're not even going to say hello?"

"I'm serious."

And he was, too. I could tell by the hardness of his face. The icy glint to his blue eyes. My heart fell. "I . . . don't understand."

Seth dug his hands into his pockets again. "It's simple. I. Need. The. Ring."

My head spun. First my mom and then Seth. How could this be happening? My hand instinctively went to the spot on my chest where the ring usually rested. It wasn't there. I'm sure my panic must have shown on my face because his frown deepened.

"What is it? What's wrong?"

"It's gone! I always wear it on a chain. Right here." I splayed my hand over my chest. "I never take it off." Then my eyes grew wide as I remembered. "Except . . ."

"Except what?" I didn't like the urgency in Seth's voice.

"Except when I shower. I put it in my backpack this afternoon and—"

"Where is it now?"

"The ring or the backpack?"

He clenched his jaw. "Both."

I groaned as I remembered. My backpack was locked in the car. The car was in the parking lot. Where my mom might be waiting. I stepped back. "We need to go."

Seth grabbed my arm. His nostrils flared as he took a deliberate, deep breath. "*I* need the ring."

I shook him off. "Look, you can't just waltz in here and start making demands. I don't know what you're doing here, or how you got here or—"

He blew out a breath. "It doesn't matter."

My eyes stung and I blinked hard so that I wouldn't cry in front of him. "It does matter! I thought I'd never see you again, and here you show up with no hello and no explanation and the only thing you can say is give you back your ring? How can you be so obtuse? You have no idea what this day has been like. I just saw a man die, Seth. I don't even know if my mom is all right . . ." The words trailed off as my throat grew too tight to talk.

Seth's face softened—genuine sorrow flickering in his eyes—but just as quickly, they went blank again. "Look, I'm sorry for whatever you've been through, Aphra, and my week's been hell, too. The thing is, that ring belongs to my dad. I should never have given it to you."

"Oh." I stared at my feet. Maybe he was trying to make it easier, but it wasn't working. On the island, Seth told me that his dad had given him the ring when he was young. Seth had worn it for years. Maybe his dad got upset when he found out Seth had given the ring away, but I doubted it. Not upset enough to send him all the way to Seattle to retrieve it, anyway. Besides, something else was bothering Seth. I could feel it. "Why did you really come here?"

"To find you . . ." he said. I looked up, hopeful, until he continued ". . . so I could get the ring back."

"Oh."

"Where is it?"

I told him quickly how I had left the ring in my backpack, how I had locked the backpack in my mom's car, and all the events that had transpired since. Even though he managed to keep his expression blasé and impassive, his eyes told another story. They looked genuinely sad about Joe's death, but hardened again when I mentioned the man who had been following me.

"Where is he now?"

"I don't know." I glanced back toward the main hallway. "I lost sight of him just before I reached the Market."

"Do you know where the car is from here?"

"Yes." At least I hoped I did.

Seth followed me back up the stairs to the main level. By that time, most of the booths on the arcade level were either closed or shutting down. A few people still clustered around the restaurants and the remaining produce stalls, but other than that, the hall was clearing out.

I noticed with a pang that the stall Mom and Joe had occupied that morning was still set up with all of their pottery. A knot rose painfully in my throat and I swallowed hard against it. “This way,” I managed to choke out. I pointed to the wide arcade doors.

We hadn’t taken more than two steps before I saw a familiar blond head among the stragglers outside. My stalker stood on the cobbled street, casually scanning the crowd—for my face, I realized.

I grabbed Seth’s arm to stop him and drew back behind the frame of an empty booth. The blond turned his head and an icy fist closed over my heart.

He was no random bad guy. He was a nightmare who had been haunting my dreams ever since he came to our island.

CHAPTER 5

I stood like a deer in the woods, afraid to move for fear it would attract a hunter's attention. Not that I could have moved if I'd wanted to. For several long, dreadful seconds, I was literally frozen in place. I couldn't even make myself speak, though I knew I should warn Seth.

All I could do was stare. How could it be? And yet there he was. The blond hair was new, but there was no mistaking the cold, dead eyes. The man outside was none other than Agent Watts of the CIA. But what was he doing there? Before my mind even formed the question, I knew the answer.

Earlier that summer, Watts had come to our island, chasing Seth and his family. I had no doubt that he was after Seth still . . . and I had led him right to his quarry. My head spun and fear roared in my ears. The whole day was like a bad dream that kept getting worse and worse.

As I looked at his predatory stance outside, it was hard to imagine that Watts had once been my mom's partner. Especially since their partnership had not engendered any loyalty as far as he was concerned. Where Mom had given up everything to protect the Mulos, Watts made it his mission to hunt them down. That I had stood in his way on the island had not helped matters. In fact, I'd made myself his sworn enemy when the herbs I had given him to make him sleep had some unpleasant side effects. He swore I had tried to poison him. At that moment I almost wished I had.

Seth's hand closed around my elbow and he leaned close. "What is it?"

His touch released me from my trance, but still I didn't move. "Watts," I whispered.

Seth didn't move, either, but his fingers tightened their grip, digging into my skin. "Where?"

I signaled with my eyes and Seth followed my gaze. At the same moment Watts raised his dull shark eyes and looked directly at us. His lips pulled back in what I swear was a snarl.

Seth spun and dragged me with him. We raced back to the stairs, bounding down two at a time. He grabbed my hand when we reached the lower level and drew me past the warren of shops behind the stairwell. We rattled on each door we passed, checking to see if any was open. I didn't expect any to be, so I was surprised when one metal door gave way. It led to what looked like a maintenance room, ladders, extension cords, and tools lining one wall and a control panel glowing with green and yellow lights on another. Seth herded me inside, closed the door behind us, and clicked the lock into place.

Except for the lights on the panel, it was pitch-black in

the room. I could barely make out the silhouette of Seth's head as he leaned close to me. "Where did you park?" he whispered.

"What?"

"The car! Where is it?"

I shook my head. "I don't know! I'm all turned around. We walked to it from the front of the Market this morning."

"Is it on a side street?"

"No. It was in a lot. Underneath the freeway."

"Close to the Market?"

"Yes. Just a couple blocks away. Down a steep hill. But I—"

Seth pressed his fingers to my lips. "Shhh!"

I heard it then, footsteps in the hallway outside. I groped for Seth's hand in the darkness and clung on to him, holding my breath. The footsteps drew nearer, slowed, and then stopped outside the door. I tensed, every muscle in my body coiled tight, ready to run. If only I had somewhere to run *to.*

The handle jiggled. The door rattled. I practically crushed Seth's hand.

And then the footsteps moved on. Still, I didn't dare move. Not for several minutes.

Finally, Seth whispered, "I think he's gone."

I realized I still had a death grip on his hand, so I slackened my grasp. I admit I had hoped he would hold on to mine, but he didn't. I swallowed my disappointment and let my hand fall to my side.

"There are stairs at the other end of the hall," I offered. "I saw them by the fish throwers' stall. If we can make it down there, and then out to the front of the arcade, I can find—"

"I think we can get to the parking lot from this level," Seth cut in. "There's a skywalk that leads straight there."

"Oh. How did you—"

"Last time I was here, your mom parked under the freeway. She took us across a walkway to get there."

"Where is the walkway?"

"I *think* it's down to our right."

"But you're not sure."

"Only one way to find out." Slowly, carefully, he opened the door. He checked the hallway and motioned for me to follow him.

Back out in the corridor, I felt exposed, a moving target. At any moment Watts could return. I didn't want to be around when he did.

A door at the end of the hall stood partway open, leading outside. We pushed through it and spilled out onto a wooden deck overlooking the street below and the sound beyond. From there, a covered walkway spanned from the Market to a bank of elevators across the street.

"Bingo," Seth said.

We ran across the walkway and crowded into the

elevator along with half a dozen closing-time shoppers loaded with parcels and oversize bags. My stomach churned as the doors slid shut and we rode downward. For all we knew, Watts could be waiting for us below.

I was such a wreck by the time we reached the lower level that I had to bite my tongue to keep from crying out when the door slid open. Fortunately, there was no sign of Watts as we stepped out into the parking lot. Still, I didn't believe we were home free. The shadows provided too many places to hide. He could be anywhere.

"Where's the car?" Seth asked.

I pointed to the far end of the lot. "There. Near the street."

Cautiously, we wove past cars and trucks, vans and motorcycles. We had almost reached the spot where my mom and I had parked when she burst out from between two parked cars. "Aphra! Where have you—" Her eyes grew wide when she saw who was with me. "Seth?"

"Hello, Mrs. Connolly."

Her voice dropped to a low whisper. "How did you get here?" Her eyes slid right and then left. "What are you doing out in the open?"

"Mom, I saw—"

She shushed me and unlocked the car with a beep of her remote. "Not now. Get in!" Grabbing my shoulder, she practically shoved me into the backseat. Seth scrambled in after me.

I started to reach up into the front seat to grab my

backpack when she opened the driver's door. "Aphra, stay where you are." Her voice sounded unnaturally calm. She slid into her seat and stabbed the keys into the ignition. "Both of you stay low and quiet until I tell you otherwise, understand?"

I dropped onto the seat and ducked down so that I couldn't see out—or be seen through—the window. Seth crouched next to me, draping an arm over my back. At first I was touched by his protectiveness, but as soon as we got out on the road, I could see he was just being practical. Hunched over as we were, it was hard to keep our balance. Whenever we went around a corner, we had to brace ourselves to keep from tipping over. I didn't really mind the turns, though, because when centripetal force pushed us together and I was pressed against him even for a moment, I felt safe.

Mom drove for several miles before she spoke, her voice tight and sharp. "How could you be so predictable, Seth? We've been monitoring the chatter at the Agency since you left the island, and you know what they say? Watch the girl and you'll find the boy. And you proved them right!" She shook her head, glaring at us through the rearview mirror. "I really thought you were smarter than this. The protocol exists to protect you."

"I understand. But . . . I didn't have a choice. Aphra has something of mine."

"What could possibly be important enough to risk the lives of everyone in this operation?"

His voice cracked. "A ring."

Mom strangled the steering wheel. "Explain."

"I . . . gave it to Aphra. My dad needs it."

Mom growled and yanked the car sharply to the left. I fell against Seth, but this time I didn't find any comfort in the contact. The hum of the tires sounded different, like the road's surface had changed. Sure enough, Mom slowed and the ride got bumpier. Finally, she swung the car in a wide arc, threw it into park, and killed the engine.

Trees loomed overhead and the sharp smell of pine filled the air. It looked like we were in some kind of nature park, with cedar-chip trails that led off into the shadowed wood.

Mom twisted around in her seat. "Aphra, where is Seth's ring?"

"It's in my backpack."

She hefted the pack and threw it over the seat back. It landed with a thud beside me. "Give it to him. And then, Seth, you are going to tell me what this is all about."

I sat up and zipped open the outside pouch. I felt inside. My stomach dropped. The pouch was empty.

Seth must have read the look on my face because he grabbed my backpack from me and shoved his hand inside the pouch. Finding it empty, he unzipped the bigger pouch and yanked out my toothbrush and toothpaste. My hairbrush dropped to the floor.

I tried to pull the pack away from him. "It was in the top one. That's the only place I ever put it."

He swatted away my hand and continued his search, dumping out my clothes and pawing through them.

I grabbed a wayward bra and stuffed it back into the pack. "Stop it! I said it wasn't there!"

"It has to be." He sifted through my things again. The desperation in his face scared me.

"Seth, what's going on?"

But he didn't answer. Instead, he wrenched open the door and bolted out of the car. I jumped out my side and raced after him. Mom ran after both of us.

Seth stomped back and forth, fists clenched so hard that the veins stood out on his arms. He kicked the wooden park bench that sat at the mouth of one trail and spun to face me. His face was livid and his eyes blue ice. "How could you lose that ring?"

I swallowed drily. I had never seen Seth angry before. It scared me. "I didn't lose it," I said weakly.

"Then where is it?"

"I don't know! Like I told you, I put it in my backpack when I took a shower this morning. I always put it right back on, but Joe pushed me out of the bathroom and—" A cold realization swept over me. "Joe! He must have taken it from my backpack."

"Why would he do that?" Seth's voice was approaching hysterical. "How would he even know it was there?"

Mom's voice was quiet. "He was searching her bag."

"He what?"

She bristled. "It was his job. Whenever we processed

people, he would go through their things. We had to be certain where their loyalties lay."

I stared at her. Great. My own mom didn't trust me.

"Don't give me that look, Aphra. I didn't authorize him to go through *your* bag."

"Authorize?" I asked. "Was he your subordinate, then?"

She rubbed a hand over her face. Suddenly she looked very tired. "He *was* my partner."

It sounded so plaintive, the way that she said that, and I wasn't sure if it was because Joe was gone, or because she suspected Stuart was right and Joe had been contacting the Agency behind her back.

"Did Joe say anything about the ring when he called you?" I asked.

"Not specifically. He did say there was something I needed to see and I had to meet him right away. But then . . ."

Seth sat heavily on the bench. "Someone got to him first."

"Suppose you tell me what's so important about this ring," Mom said. "Then maybe we can figure out why Joe would have wanted to take it."

Seth rolled his lips inward. "I can't."

"Seth, it's me! I've been with your family for years. If there's something wrong, I need to know about it."

He just glared at her. "You split us up. I didn't even know my dad wouldn't be meeting us until Mom and I got to Sydney."

She sighed. "We needed to make you harder to track. Splitting you up was the best option we had."

"Well, it didn't work. They found him."

Mom's mouth went slack. "When?"

"Couple of days ago. They want the ring, Natalie. If I don't get it for them within five days . . ."

The ground felt like it was tilting sideways. Last time I had seen Seth, we'd come face-to-face with an assassin who had been sent to silence Seth's family. Her black eyes and wicked smile still haunted my dreams. I could hardly breathe, remembering how she had tried to kill Seth and me. But the authorities had taken her into custody. Had she escaped? "Who has your dad, Seth?"

He didn't even look up. "I don't know. The Mole wants him dead. The CIA thinks he's a liability."

Mom's face tightened. From what she had told me, I knew what she must be thinking: the CIA didn't think he was a liability; the Mole's minions *within* the CIA thought he was a liability. Either way, something about the scenario the way Seth explained it didn't make sense.

"You said they're holding him," I said to Seth, "but if they want him dead, why didn't they just kill him when they found him?"

His head whipped up and I could have hit myself for causing the panic and grief I saw in his eyes.

"I . . . I'm sorry. That didn't come out right." I sat beside him and tried to take his hand, but he moved it away. I bit my lip and looked up to my mom for help.

"What Aphra was trying to ask—rather indelicately—was why the change in tactics? What makes them so interested in this ring that they would create a hostage situation to get it?"

A shadow passed over Seth's face. It was subtle, but it was there. He took a breath like he was going to say something and then he clamped his mouth shut. "I . . . I don't know why they want it," he said finally. "Dad never told me it was special. Not like that, anyway. I thought it was just an old class ring or something. I would never have given it away if I'd known . . ."

I felt like the biggest scum that had ever walked the earth. How could I lose the one thing Seth had entrusted me with? "Mom, think. Where could Joe have put it if he took it?"

She shook her head helplessly. "I wish I knew. Stuart's been monitoring the Agency daily and nothing has been said about a ring. None of this makes sense."

I agreed. "It *doesn't* make sense. If they—whoever they are—knew where Seth and his mom were, why wouldn't they just go after them? If Mr. Mulo told them Seth had the ring—"

"He never told them that I had it," Seth cut in. "They think my mom—"

"Whatever. My point is, if they knew where you were, why wouldn't they just come get it?"

"They didn't necessarily know where we were, even with the phone call. My mom and dad had international cell phones so they could keep in touch, and they never stayed on long enough for tracking."

Mom frowned. "Cell phones were not part of the plan."

"I guess they made it part of the plan."

"Are you sure they really have your dad?" I asked. "What if they're using this ring thing just to flush you out?"

Seth looked to the ground. His voice dropped to barely a whisper. "They . . . cut off his finger while they were on the phone. My mom heard him scream."

My stomach heaved and darkness crowded around the corners of my vision. I thought I was going to lose it right there, but I had to be strong . . . for Seth. At least that's what I told myself.

"I need the ring," Seth said firmly, "to keep my dad alive."

"Mom?" My throat was so tight I could hardly force out the words. "Where is Joe's body? What if he had the ring with him?"

"He didn't. I managed to gather all his personal effects before the paramedics arrived." Her voice grew even more distant. "It's protocol. There was no ring."

"Where could he have put it?"

"I don't know," she said. "If he didn't have it with him this morning, it must still be at the apartment."

Seth jumped to his feet. "Then what are we doing here? We have to go find it!"

• • •

None of us spoke as we drove back to the apartment building. There was nothing to say. We had to find the ring. Beyond that . . . I didn't want to think about it.

The first thing I noticed when we pulled into the garage was Stuart, wiping down the handles of the van. He must have driven it home earlier from the Market parking lot. I assumed he was wiping it clean of fingerprints. His or Joe's, I didn't know.

He rushed the car when he saw it was us. "Nat! Where have you *been*? I was about ready to clear out. I thought you might have—" His words died when his gaze slid to the backseat and he saw Seth. "Mulo?"

Seth dipped his head in greeting.

For the first time since I'd met him, Stuart seemed to be at a loss for words. He just stood there, staring at Seth. "When . . . ? How . . . ?"

Mom climbed from the car and filled Stuart in as much as she could. He listened silently, though I could see the agitation building as his face grew redder and the little muscle at the corner of his jaw tightened and twitched.

He removed his glasses and pinched the bridge of his nose. "So Aphra had this ring all along," he finally said when Mom was through.

I nodded. "Until this morning."

"We need to look for it," Seth put in.

"Here? Now?" Stuart was incredulous. "We don't have

time. We should already be gone as it is. As soon as the police identify Joe—"

"Joe has no identity," Mom cut in flatly. "He never existed."

"Right." Stuart crossed his arms. "Tell that to the people who saw him expire this morning. Tell it to the paramedics who—"

"Who will not know who he is."

"Our cover is blown, Natalie. People at the Market have seen you and Joe together for months. How long do you think it will be before they start asking questions?"

"We'll be quick," she said.

Stuart folded his arms and muttered, "This is not wise." Still, he followed us inside.

In a cluster, we clamored up the stairs and burst into the apartment. Mom led the way to Joe's small room. Right away I could tell it wouldn't be a simple search. Unlike Stuart, neatness was obviously not Joe's thing. A blanket lay in a puddle next to his bed. The pillow had fallen back against the wall. Papers littered the floor and clothes were scattered everywhere—on the bed, on the floor, draped over the lone chair, and tumbling out of an army duffel.

Among the four of us, we scoured every inch of that room. Twice. Seth even checked all the floorboards to make sure there were no hidey-holes anywhere. No luck.

"We'll search the entire apartment if we have to,"

Mom assured him. "If Joe took that ring, it has to be around somewhere."

I chewed the inside of my cheek, wondering why my mom would say such a thing. My gut told me she was wrong, and I had to believe she knew it, too. Joe left that morning shortly after he came out of the bathroom. That didn't really give him much time to hide anything in the apartment. And just because Mom didn't find the ring when she went through his "personal effects" at the coffee shop didn't mean he hadn't taken it with him. He could have hidden it anywhere along the way. Plus, he'd been gone for a good long while before he called to tell Mom where he would be. She had to wonder what he'd been doing all that time. On the other hand, none of this changed anything. Of course we had to look. Before we cleared out, we had to be certain the ring had not been left in the apartment.

Mom began handing out orders like a drill sergeant. "Aphra, check the bathroom; Seth, start going through the cupboards and drawers in the kitchen; I'll search the den; and Stuart, you take the front room."

I had to give Stuart credit; he set to work without question, flipping over his carefully positioned couch cushions. And even though he was the one who was antsy for us to clear out of the apartment, he pulled out all the stops searching the place. He even dug his hands through the soil of the potted plants. It didn't improve his mood, though. By the time we had finished searching the apartment, the stairwell, and the garage, day had turned to night outside. With each passing moment, Stuart was becoming more and more irritable.

"This is not protocol. We should have been gone a long time ago."

Mom shrugged him off. "It's better to leave after dark, anyway," she told him. He just tightened his lips and finished packing up his computers.

Seth was inconsolable. He paced in the corner, muttering, "What am I going to do?"

I tried to comfort him, but he just glared at me. "You're the one who lost the ring."

"I didn't lose it! It was taken from me."

"It wouldn't have been taken if you hadn't left it."

"I did *not* leave it!"

He folded his arms and turned away.

Mom was gathering her papers and arguing with Stuart. When she caught me watching, her face turned cold, almost hostile. I couldn't take it anymore. I had to get away from Mom, from Stuart, and especially from Seth.

No one even noticed when I slipped out the door and into the hallway. I wanted to scream. To punch something. To punch myself.

I never thought I'd say it, but I wanted to go home. If I were back on the island, I could pretend the whole trip never happened. I could pretend my mom wanted me to find her. I could pretend Seth liked me. I could pretend I didn't feel like the biggest loser on the face of the earth.

But pretending never made anything true. In reality I knew I could never go back. Not to the way things were. Too much had happened. I pushed through the door to the stairwell and ran blindly down the steps, not stopping until I spilled out into the garage. The lights flicked on—thanks to the stupid sensor over the door. I hugged my arms and sank down along the edge of the wall, waiting for them to click off again. It was hard enough to face the reality of the cold, stark garage, the overpowering smell of rubber, grease, and motor oil, and the fact that I had let a lot of people down. I didn't need the glare of the light highlighting my flaws.

A tear rolled down my cheek and I swiped it away. I had no right feeling sorry for myself when Mom had lost a partner and Seth's dad was being held hostage somewhere.

The lights had barely turned off when the door opened and they blazed on again. Seth's broad shoulders filled the doorway, but there was a posture of defeat to them, and in the hesitant way that he stepped through the opening. I turned my face away from him, scrubbing my hands over my eyes to hide the tears. The last thing I wanted was for him to see me crying.

The click of the heavy metal door closing echoed through the garage and I could hear Seth's footsteps on the rough concrete floor. "Aphra?" His voice sounded as if it had lost its edge, but I'd lost all faith in my ability to guess what he might be thinking. I didn't answer.

He took another step. "Aphra, I'm sorry. I didn't mean to blame you."

"But it's my fault." My voice sounded small. Pitiful.

He closed the distance between us and touched a tentative hand to my shoulder. "It's getting cold. I grabbed this from the apartment for you."

I looked up to see him holding out a Seahawks sweatshirt. His gesture made me feel even worse. I stood and took the sweatshirt from him, unable to look in his face. I dutifully slipped it on over my head and stood awkwardly, struggling for something to say.

"I'm so sorry, Seth." My voice cracked.

"You didn't know."

"What you must be going through . . ."

He dug his hands into the pockets of his jeans and hunched his shoulders. "They hurt my dad," he said. He sounded lost and frightened.

Tears filled my eyes once more, but I was no longer ashamed of them. They were for Seth, not for me. "I'm sorry," I whispered again. He held my gaze for a long while and then brushed a tear from my cheek with the back of his finger.

"Ah, jeez, Aphra." His voice was rough and husky. "I didn't mean to . . ." He took my hand hesitantly, almost shyly, and drew me to him. The garage lights flickered off and in the darkness I found the courage to wrap my arms around his waist. I laid my cheek against his chest, listening to the rhythm of his heart. He smelled like I remembered, felt like I remembered. I wanted to cry for real.

Because even though in that moment I finally had what I had wanted—to be with Seth, his arms around me—I realized with painful clarity that was not how it would always be. Seth and I would never end up together. We couldn't. If we stayed alive long enough to find the ring and save Seth's dad, the Mulos would have to run again. And if what my mom said was true, I would always act as a kind of divining rod that the bad guys could use to lead them to Seth. The only safe thing for us to do would be to stay apart.

I held him tighter, knowing that it might be the last time I ever would. We could have stood like that all night and I would have been happy. But I knew the clock was ticking. Mom and Stuart would be ready to clear out at any time. Whoever had killed Joe could be looking for us next. I had to set things right and then step out of Seth's life forever.

I pulled back, wiping my eyes. "We can't give up."

In the shadows, I couldn't read Seth's face. He didn't say anything, but his head moved. Maybe he was nodding in agreement. I didn't know.

With new determination, I pushed away and marched toward the door.

"What are you doing?"

"I'll find it for you, Seth. If I have to retrace Joe's steps from the moment he left the apartment, I'll find it."

"Don't be crazy. What are you going to do, walk to the city? Do you even know how to get there from here?"

"I'll . . . I'll take the car. I have a pretty good sense of direction. I can find the way."

He made an incredulous sound in his throat. "Right. You think your mom's going to just hand over her keys?"

"I wouldn't ask her."

"Aphra. Be real. Your mom and Stuart worked for the CIA. You're not going to be able to swipe anything without them knowing."

"Well, I can't just sit around and do nothing! It's making me crazy."

He stuffed his hands into his pockets again. "I know."

The pain in his voice deflated my bravado. I felt empty inside. Helpless. "Seth, I need you to know how sorry I am."

"I do know." His voice was gruff. "But it's my own fault. I didn't know the ring was such a big deal."

I edged closer until I could see the worry line his face as deeply as the shadows. "*Why* is it such a big deal, Seth? Why do they want it so much?"

He looked at me with an intensity I'd never seen in him before—like he wanted to tell me something, but he wasn't sure if he could.

I drew his hand from his pocket and clutched it in my own. "You can trust me, Seth."

He bobbed his head, but still didn't say anything for what felt like a very long time. Finally, he spoke in a low voice, barely a whisper. "The ring . . . contains a list."

"It *contains* a list? What kind of list? How?"

His hand slipped from mine. "I . . . can't say . . ."

That wasn't exactly the answer I was hoping for, but I knew better than to pursue it. Yet. "Seth, the people who are holding your dad . . . what do they want the ring for?"

"I don't know. I only heard one side of the phone call."

I swallowed, remembering what Seth had said about his mom having to hear his dad scream on the other end of the line. I couldn't even imagine the helplessness and horror she must have felt. "How is your mom dealing with all this?"

He shrugged and looked down at his feet.

"Why didn't she come with you?"

"She didn't know I was leaving."

"What?"

"I wasn't meant to hear the phone call. It came in the middle of the night. She probably thought I was asleep. All I could think was that it was my fault. I had given the ring away; I had to get it back."

I took his hand again. "We'll find it. If we have to—" I blinked. "Wait. A list! I almost forgot! Joe talked about a list, too. Right before he died."

Seth's eyes widened. "What? What did he say?"

"I'm not sure I remember it all. It didn't make sense to me at the time. Plus he didn't give me complete sentences, just random words. At least I thought they were random."

He tightened his fingers around mine. "Think, Aphra. What exactly did he say?"

I screwed my eyes shut tight, trying to remember. "Something about a list and a . . . a cup or something. I thought he was talking about his coffee cup. Like he knew he'd been poisoned. I watched him, Seth. I saw him take a drink and then he started jerking and fell to the ground and I ran to him and . . ." I tried to erase the image of his panicked face from my mind. "He could hardly take a breath."

"When did he tell you about the list?"

"He said 'the list is . . . '" I grasped at the air as if I could find the answer hanging there. "*In* something."

"In the cup?"

"Cup *holder*! That's what it was, a cup holder."

"What kind of cup holder? Like for takeout? What does that mean?"

"I don't know. He didn't have any cup holder with him."

"Are you sure he didn't say anything else?"

"I'm sure." I could barely stand under the weight of Seth's stare. It was like he was trying to *will* me into understanding exactly what Joe was talking about. But I didn't. Unless . . . "Wait. What if he was talking about the cup holder in the van? Maybe the ring is in there."

We raced to where the van was parked, but the door was locked. Seth cupped his hands around his eyes and peered through the window.

"Do you see anything?"

"No," he said. "It's too dark."

"We have to get the keys."

"Wait!"

I stopped midstep. "What? Why?"

"I don't want to alert Stuart and your mom." He glanced pointedly at the stairwell door. "If we find the ring, we don't say anything to them, okay?"

"I don't understand."

"We don't know who has my dad. I trust your mom, but . . ."

"But they're probably watching her."

"Right. And she said herself that there may be a leak in the Agency. It would be better for everyone if they think I'm going home empty-handed. At least until I can take care of my dad."

"Okay." I looked around the shadowed garage. "But how are we going to get into the van?"

"We need some wire."

We searched quickly among the shelves and castoffs scattered around the garage, but there was no wire to be found except for some flimsy, plastic-coated electric wire, and that wasn't what we wanted, according to Seth. "It needs to be sturdy enough to pull up the pin."

The words were familiar enough to me—I'd learned to pick household locks from our super back at the resort—but I couldn't envision the inside mechanics of a car door.

"Wait. I got it." Seth popped the arm off the windshield wiper. "It has a U-hook on the end. I can use that."

He slid the makeshift hook down between the window gasket and the window, fishing inside the door.

I folded my arms. "I don't even want to know where you learned to do this."

"I lived near Detroit," he said. Like that explained anything.

I glanced nervously at the stairwell. Any moment, Mom and Stuart could be ready to leave. I doubted either one of them would appreciate us messing with the van . . . or keeping whatever we discovered a secret. "Quickly!"

The lock clicked.

Seth climbed into the van and I pushed in behind him. We felt in the dark for the plastic cup holders. One of those insulated aluminum coffee cups sat in the hole closer to the driver's side. The little sipping spout was half open and I could smell the remains of Joe's coffee—bitter and black. I lifted it gingerly. It felt creepy handling his cup, but I had to check beneath it, just in case.

Nothing. The look on Seth's face told me he had found nothing in the other side, either. Another dead end.

I wasn't ready to give up yet. "What about . . . Could he have put the ring in the *car* before he went to the coffee shop?"

"Only one way to find out."

I jumped out of the van and ran to the car. Crossing my fingers, I grasped the handle. "It's open," I called softly.

I climbed into the car and felt for the cup holder. Unfortunately, this one slid out from the dash like a CD drive on a computer. It featured two holes cut into the molded plastic that cups could fit into. There was no room for a ring to be hidden behind the mechanism.

Seth peered in through the open door. "Well?"

"Nothing."

I could literally feel his disappointment, but what did he expect? It had been a dumb idea, anyway. If this ring was so valuable, there's no way Joe would have left it lying around in a cup holder where anyone could see it.

I froze. He *wouldn't* have wanted anyone to see it. He would have hidden it. "Back to the van! We've got to pull it out."

"What?"

"The cup holder. It's just molded plastic sunk in a hole in the console. He could have put the ring beneath it."

I didn't need to say anything more. We raced to the van and clawed at the edge of the cup holder until we were finally able to pry it up.

I felt around the vacant hole, checking for secret compartments or other covert stuff like that. Clearly the vehicles were standard issue, because there were no James Bond–type features anywhere.

Dejected, I fitted the cup-holder piece back into the hole. I grabbed the coffee cup from where it had fallen on the floor, dribbling coffee all over the floor mat. It rattled. I drew in a breath. A slosh I might expect, but a rattle?

I dumped the coffee out the door. It splattered on the garage floor.

"What are you doing?" Seth hissed.

"Hold on." Hands trembling, I unscrewed the lid and upended the cup. Out slid the ring, still attached to my chain.

"You got it," Seth breathed.

Just then, the lights flicked on. I blinked against the sudden glare and closed my fist around the ring.

"What's going on?" Mom marched across the garage, followed closely by Stuart. "What are you doing in there? Get out this instant."

Seth climbed out the passenger-side door and I climbed out the driver's side, slipping the ring into my pocket as I went.

"We were just searching the van," Seth explained.

"Well?" Stuart looked beyond me and into the van through the open door. "What did you find?"

I made my face go blank. "Nothing."

He pushed past me to see for himself and stepped right in the puddle of spilled coffee. He looked down.

I rushed to redirect his attention. "Um . . . what if he left it in the coffee shop? We should go back there and—"

"Absolutely not." The light danced on his glasses as he shook his head. "You don't think the police will have that place staked out?"

"But—"

"Too dangerous. Besides, I'm sure the Agency has scoured the place from top to bottom by now."

"Oh." I tried to look suitably disappointed as I shut the van door. "Just trying to help."

Stuart gave me a condescending pat on the arm. "And we appreciate it. We've really wasted enough time, Natalie. We need to move out now."

Mom gave a resigned sigh. "I am so sorry," she said to Seth. "We'll figure something out."

Seth hung his head like he was completely defeated. Even though I knew he was only acting, it broke my heart. "I understand," he managed.

Mom and Stuart headed back inside. At the door, Mom paused and turned back to us. "Be ready to leave in five."

I nodded, afraid to speak for fear I'd give something away. The moment she closed the door, Seth rushed to where I was standing.

"Where is it?" he whispered.

I pulled the chain from my pocket and held it out to him, the ring swinging like a pendulum.

He grabbed it and clutched it to his chest. "Yes!"

"So you still have time to help your dad, right?"

His smile faded. "I hope so."

"Can you call them? Tell them you're coming?"

"Not without tipping off everyone else."

"Who's everyone? Who else is after this ring, Seth?"

He wouldn't meet my eyes. "I don't know."

"I think you do. I also think you know *why* they're after it." It wasn't an accusation. Just a fact.

Finally, he looked at me. "The ring contains a very important list."

My stomach twisted. The list again. Is that why Joe was killed? "What kind of list are we talking about?"

"A list of names." Seth waited for that to sink in, and then added, "Sleepers."

I drew in a breath. The other members of his parents' sleeper cell! I thought of how I had been carrying that ring around for the last couple of months and my head felt light. But . . . I had never seen any lists. And it's not like there were a lot of hiding places in a ring. "How is that possible?"

"I'll show you." Seth held the ring up toward the light. "Look. The names are etched into the back of the stone."

I squinted at the ring, searching. "What? Those little scratches?"

"Yeah. You'd have to use a microscope or something to read it, but those little scratches could reveal the identity and alias of every sleeper agent in that organization."

"Wow."

"No kidding."

"Isn't your family's name on the—"

He held up his hand, signaling me to be quiet. "Did you hear that?"

I shook my head.

"Hold on." He handed me back the ring. "I thought I heard something." He crept toward the stairwell door and I followed close behind. We didn't find anything, but it was enough to shake us up.

I stuffed the ring into my pocket and took Seth's hand. "Wait for the lights to die," I whispered. "We'll head outside."

We stood next to the wall until the lights clicked off and then climbed up the ramp to the street, keeping close to the edge so that the sensors wouldn't pick up our movement and trip them on again. At street level, we had almost stepped into a puddle of light from the streetlamp when my attention was drawn to a car parked on the opposite side of the street. I wouldn't have noticed it had it not been for something glowing and red in the front seat of the car. It seemed to hover in the air, grow brighter red, then dull again. A cigarette. I pushed Seth deeper into the shadows. "Someone's in that car."

Sure enough, the red glowed bright one more time

before we heard the mechanical whir of the power window rolling down. The cigarette flipped from the car, drawing a red arc in the air. Seconds later, the stench of burning tobacco wafted toward us.

"What's he doing?" I whispered.

"You think someone's watching the apartment?"

"Could be."

Just then, the driver lit another cigarette, cupping his hand over the flame so that the glow illuminated his face. I sucked in a breath. Same blond hair, same cold eyes. I drew back against Seth.

"What is it?"

My blood ran cold just thinking about him.

"Watts."

CHAPTER 6

Seth swore. "What is Watts doing here?"

"What do you think?"

Grabbing my hand, Seth pulled me back into the garage. He drew me against him again, but not romantically this time. We were both terrified. At least I was terrified, and I figured Seth was, too, the way his heart was racing.

"We can't go out this way," he murmured.

"You think?"

He took my hand. "Come on. *This* we need to tell your mom and Stuart."

We felt our way back through the garage, not even worrying about the light this time. We ran up the stairs and burst into the apartment.

Stuart must have been right at the door when it flew open because he jumped back, swearing. "Watch it!"

"Watts is here," I blurted.

"What? Impossible."

"I saw him outside. He was—"

"You recognized him in the dark?"

"Yes!"

Stuart looked to Seth. "Did you see him?"

Seth nodded and Stuart's face grew serious. "Where?"

He turned and yelled over his shoulder, "Nat? We've got a problem."

Mom rushed over to where we were clustered near the door. "What is it?"

I told her how we had seen Watts sitting in the car in front of the apartment building.

"Was he alone?"

"I don't know. It was dark."

"I told you we should have cleared out long ago," Stuart muttered.

"Well, we're clearing out now. Out back toward the locks. Let's go."

"Where are we going to go?" I asked.

"To the lake. We have a boat."

"What? You never said anything about a boat before."

She shook her head. "There was no need. We only share what information is necessary."

How could I ask anything else after she said that? Maybe I didn't need more answers, anyway. If I thought about it, pieces began to fall into place on their own. I had assumed that the reason they had moved into that particular apartment building was simply that the apartment owner was gone on sabbatical, but they had purposely chosen a place on the waterfront.

It made sense that they would have a boat nearby, and an alternative escape route. According to Ryan, the locks connected Lake Union with the sound and eventually the ocean. This way, they weren't landlocked.

Mom led us down the slope to a path that wound along the locks to the lake. As we neared the first dock, she instructed us to slow down. "Act natural," she said.

Seth threw me a pained look and I raised my shoulders. So it was cliché. It also happened to be smart.

"Aphra? Hey, Aphra. Is that you?"

I jumped and turned around.

Ryan strode out of the shadows carrying a duffel bag. Sweat glistened along his hairline and he was breathing heavily, like he'd been running. "What a pleasant surprise to see you here. How's it going?"

I forced a smile. "Good. And you?"

"Good." His eyes strayed to Seth, then to Mom and Stuart in turn.

"So," I said, directing his attention back to me. "What are you up to tonight?"

"Heading out." He lifted the bag in evidence. "Game's over."

"Oh. Right. Who won?"

"Mariners by a run."

"Sounds like a good game."

"It was."

I could practically feel Mom's eyes boring into my back. I shifted uncomfortably. She would be wondering how I knew Ryan, and the answer wouldn't sound good. I snuck out of the apartment—not once but twice—discussed personal information with a stranger, and by so doing had compromised our clean escape. I had to get rid of Ryan without making it seem like that's what I was trying to do, since it might draw more attention to our presence on the docks.

I glanced up at the sky, where a handful of dark clouds blotted out the moon. "I better not keep you. It looks like rain."

"Naw, that's nothing."

"Well, *we* should get going," Mom cut in pleasantly. "Nice to meet you, Mister . . . ?"

"Anderson, ma'am. Ryan Anderson." He shifted his duffel to his left hand and extended his right. "I believe we're neighbors."

Mom's brows raised ever so slightly, but she maintained her smile. "Well, then. Perhaps we'll see you around."

"Yes, ma'am. Good night."

Ryan dipped his head in farewell and walked off down the path, gravel crunching beneath his feet.

I didn't want to look in my mom's face. Or Stuart's, or Seth's for that matter. I stared at the ground.

"Let's go," she said, voice grating.

We clomped down the dock to the last pier, where the boat—a small open utility boat with an outboard motor—was tied. Mom started undoing the moorings while Stuart reached down to start the motor.

Hot white light flashed. The air felt like it was being sucked from my lungs, and my head rang as if someone had clapped their hands over my ears. Hard. I don't remember falling, but the next thing I knew, I was sitting on the dock, head pounding. The boat was a mass of flames. Papers fluttered down all around us. It didn't—couldn't—register for a full second what had happened. I think I tried to scream, but my voice had lost its power. Mom lay crumpled around a pier like a broken doll. It probably saved her from being thrown into the water. I crawled over to her on my hands and knees.

"Mom! Mom!" She didn't respond. I twisted about in a panic, looking for Stuart. He'd know what to do. But Stuart was writhing on the deck, clutching his hand to his chest. Seth sat not far from where we were, shaking his head and looking dazed.

"Seth, are you all right?"

He nodded slowly, as if he wasn't quite sure.

"See if you can help Stuart!"

Seth swayed to his feet and stumbled over to where Stuart lay and I turned my attention back to my mom.

I felt along her neck for a pulse. I couldn't tell if the pounding I felt in my fingers was my own pulse or hers. "Mom! Can you hear me?"

She moaned and her head lolled to the side. I almost cried. At least she was alive. I checked her over quickly, looking for injuries. Even in the darkness, her face looked red, as if she were badly sunburned. Other than that, she seemed fine. No blood, no broken bones. The impact of the explosion could have knocked her out. Either from that, or slamming into the pier. The important thing was that she appeared to be otherwise unharmed.

I wished I could say the same for Stuart. Once I had made sure my mom was okay, I turned to help Seth. What I saw horrified me. Stuart's glasses tilted on his head, the right lens shattered. His face was black from the flash and he still cradled his left hand to his chest. His shirt was soaked in blood. Blackened, bloody stubs were all that was left of his ring and pinkie fingers.

My stomach heaved and I looked quickly away. I wanted to cry, but that wouldn't do us any good. The explosion may have alerted Watts. We had to get out of there. And then we had to get Stuart medical attention.

"Aphra! What happened?" Ryan ran down the dock toward us. "I saw the flash. It sounded like an explosion."

But before I could answer, headlights swung over the lip of the road back by the path. Watts's car. There was no time for explanations.

"Ryan! We need your help!" I jumped to my feet and grabbed his hand. "That guy is after us." He followed my gaze to where Watts—in a suit and tie now—jumped out of the car. "We need to get out of here!"

He hesitated for a second, but when he saw Mom lying on the pier and Stuart's injuries, he nodded gravely.

"The plane," he yelled. "I'm on the next dock over and already prepped to take off. Come on!"

He scooped my mom up from the dock like it was no

effort at all. “Help them,” he yelled, nodding to where Seth was trying to pull Stuart to his feet. “Let’s go!”

I grabbed Stuart’s good hand and slung his arm over my shoulder. Seth propped him up from the other side. I tried not to look at Stuart’s mangled hand or the blood or his wide-eyed stare. “It’s going to be okay,” I assured him. “We’re going to get you out of here.”

We had to practically drag Stuart to where Ryan’s plane bobbed gently in the water. The whole time I felt like a huge, lumbering target. I glanced back to see Watts running down the hill toward the path. “He’s coming!”

Ryan set my mom on her feet and motioned for me to hold her. Seth grabbed Stuart so that he wouldn’t fall over and I rushed to hold up my mom. She leaned heavily against me, moaning. At least she was coming to. Ryan clamored onto the landing skids and threw open the latch on the door. “Get in!”

I handed my mom back to him and climbed through the door. He passed her to me and I pulled her inside, propping her against the wall of the plane. When I poked my head back out the door, I saw that Watts had reached the path.

“Hurry! Hurry!”

Seth pushed Stuart forward, but Stuart twisted and strained in his arms.

“No,” he growled. “No!”

“Get in!” Ryan ordered.

“Nooooo.”

Seth wrestled Stuart onto the skid where Ryan was waiting to hand him up into the plane. Stuart must have been crazy with pain, the way he kept screaming and resisting, but among the three of us, we got him inside.

Ryan scrambled in after him and clanged the door shut behind him. He bolted up to the front, slid into one of the only two seats on the plane, and started throwing switches. The plane shuddered and vibrated as the engines roared to life and the propellers kicked in.

"Hold on!" Ryan yelled as the plane began to glide forward.

Hold on to what? We were crammed into an empty freight area, with nothing but a couple of cargo nets stretched floor to ceiling and a hand truck strapped to the wall. No jump seats. And more importantly, no seat belts.

I grabbed the securing straps for the cargo nets and tethered my mom and myself to the wall. Seth tried to do the same with Stuart, but Stuart kept swatting him away. Somewhere along the way he'd lost his glasses and he squinted fiercely, growling obscenities. Finally, Seth gave up and wrapped a strap around himself. Stuart curled into a ball in the corner, hand tucked up under his armpit.

Unsteadily, the plane jumped and skipped like a drunken albatross, wings dipping left then right before steadying and tilting upward, pulling us up into the air.

My ears popped as we climbed and my head still rang, but we'd made it. We were alive and together. That was all that mattered.

The plane steadied once we leveled off. I undid the straps and took a long look at Stuart. I was afraid he might go into shock—or that he already had. He seemed confused and disoriented and that wasn't a good sign.

"Ryan! Do you have a first-aid kit?"

He didn't answer. Probably couldn't hear me above the roar of the plane. I crawled to the back of his chair and saw that he was wearing headphones. I gestured at him to remove them. "Do you have a first-aid kit?" I yelled.

"In the corner!" He waved vaguely behind him. The plane wiggled when he took his hand off the controls and he quickly straightened it.

My stomach flipped and I fought a sudden wave of motion sickness. I'd never experienced it before, but our resort manager Darlene got motion sick nearly every time she climbed into our helicopter on the island. It didn't even have to be off the ground for her to start turning green. She always wore special motion-sickness bracelets to help her cope. I used to laugh at her for it, but now I struggled to remember what pressure points those bracelets hit because I really didn't have time to get sick. I slid to the floor of the plane, leaning up against the back of the chair as I felt along my wrist with two fingers, like a nurse taking a pulse.

Seth crawled over beside me.

"Are you okay?" he yelled.

"I'll be fine. Just a little sick to my stomach." I worked up a shaky smile. "Stay with my mom, will you? I'm going to try to help Stuart."

I crawled back to search for the kit.

In the back corner I found a white plastic first-aid box with a small red cross on the front. It didn't offer much more than a couple of rolls of gauze and some bandages, but at least that was enough for me to wrap Stuart's fingers. That is, if he'd let me. He was still hunched over, cradling his hand and mumbling to himself.

I approached him warily. "Can you let me see?" I shouted. "I want to help."

He just looked through me and shook his head like he was confused.

"Let me see your hand."

He held it out to me. "My finger . . ."

I hated to tell him it was fingers, plural. I just nodded sympathetically. "Can I wrap it?"

He grabbed my hand with his good one and looked at me with wild eyes. "The ring?"

"It's safe." I didn't realize I'd let that slip until the words left my mouth. I held my breath, but Stuart didn't respond at all. I pulled my hand from his grasp. "Let me help you," I yelled. His eyes went vacant as he offered me his hand.

Gingerly, I wrapped what remained of his fingers,

hoping that I was doing it right. Explosions and amputations were not items covered in lifeguard certification.

"Tuck it neatly," he told me.

I blinked at him. "Yeah, okay." At least he was beginning to sound more like his neat-freak self. That had to be a good sign.

I stayed with Stuart for a few moments, just to make sure he was lucid. For such a prissy guy on the outside, he was surprisingly tough when it mattered. He sat stone-faced, his bandaged hand in his lap, taking measured breaths. "Where are we going?" he asked.

"I—I'm not sure." I took a quick look at Ryan. All I had cared about was getting away from Watts. I hadn't even bothered to discuss a destination. "He works in Alaska. Maybe—"

Stuart narrowed his eyes. "We are *not* going to Alaska."

"I'll, um, go talk with him, okay? You going to be all right?"

But Stuart had already tuned me out. He stared vacantly at his hand, muttering to himself.

I crawled forward to talk to Ryan, but noticed that my mom was awake and watching me. I scrambled over to her.

"Hey. How are you feeling?"

She held a hand to her head. "I'm . . . fine. What happened? Where are we?"

"There was an explosion. Ryan helped us escape."

She frowned. "Ryan?"

"We saw him on the docks, remember? He's the guy that lives in your building."

"No, he doesn't."

"But . . . " I shifted uncomfortably. "I met him yesterday. He lives next door to you."

"We ran a check on every resident before we moved in. He was not one of them." Her eyes slid up to the front, where Ryan sat at the controls. "Where did you meet him?"

"On the balcony." My voice was so small it nearly got lost in the drone of the engines.

"Oh, Aphra," she scolded. "You know better than that."

I bit my lip. As much as she made me feel like a naughty six-year-old, she was right. I should know better. Especially after the thing with Hisako at our resort. People are not always what they seem. You can't trust someone you don't know. It's just that Ryan seemed so nice . . . *looked* so nice. Ugh! How could I be such an easy mark?

Stuart crawled over like a three-legged dog to join our huddle. "What is it?"

Mom didn't even have to say anything. Since she and Stuart had worked together, they were probably in tune enough that they were beyond words. She inclined her head toward Ryan and Stuart followed her gaze. He looked back to me. "Where is he taking us?"

"I don't know." He cupped his hand over his ear to illustrate that he couldn't hear me. Plus he probably wanted to make me admit it again, just to rub it in. He needn't have bothered. I knew full well what a complete idiot I'd been. If I had been paying attention, I might have noticed how convenient Ryan's appearance on the docks had been. And how quickly he showed up after the explosion . . . almost as if he knew it was going to happen. He could have planted the bomb himself, to entice us to climb into his plane. And I fell right into his trap. Mom would never have come aboard if she had been conscious. And Stuart . . . he tried to fight it, but we dragged him onto the plane anyway. I hung my head. "I'm sorry."

He regarded me for a moment, then turned to Mom. "I'm going to talk with him."

She shook her head. "Not yet. We haven't—"

"I won't *do* anything," he said. "Just talk. If I can get a reading from the instrument panel, at least we can guess where we're headed."

Seth leaned closer. "What are you guys talking about?" he shouted. I shook my head and pointed up to the cockpit. "What?" he repeated.

I opened my mouth, but I had no words to tell Seth how after everything he had done, after he had come all the way to Seattle to search for his father's ring, I had put him in a plane with someone who might very well want to take that ring away from him. I just shook my head and looked away.

Stuart was crawling unsteadily toward Ryan, which I wasn't convinced was the smartest idea. We had no idea how dangerous he was or who he worked for. My guess was the Mole, since Ryan had helped us escape from Watts, who was CIA. It didn't really matter, since we couldn't trust either one.

Stuart gripped the back of Ryan's seat and hauled himself up. In the shadows, I could make out Ryan's profile as his head turned . . . and Stuart's fist raised. What was he doing?

Seth looked to my mom. "What's happening?"

Before she could answer, the plane banked sharply to the left. Mom was still strapped down, but Seth and I tumbled hard against the wall. He grabbed the net with one arm and me with the other as the plane wobbled again. "What is going on?"

I wished I knew. It had looked to me like Stuart was about to attack Ryan. Maybe Ryan banked to throw Stuart off balance. If that was the case, then Ryan was done pretending to be nice. Whether I wanted to or not, I had to warn Seth. I pulled his head close to mine. "Ryan might be a—"

The plane lurched and dropped and my head smacked right into Seth's nose. He reared back and his arm slipped away from my waist. We banked right this time, the wing almost straight down, and I slid across the floor, slamming into the other wall. Pain shot through my shoulder. I managed to grab on to the securing strap with the other arm and pull myself up. In the cockpit area, Ryan and Stuart were fighting for control over the plane. Neither one was winning.

"We have to help!" I yelled to Seth.

He shook his head and stopped rubbing his sore nose long enough to pantomime that he couldn't hear. I let go of the net and started crawling toward him when I was thrown forward, crashing into the backs of the pilot seats. I tried to pull myself up when the plane climbed and sent me sprawling backward.

Seth grabbed my hand and pulled me back by him and my mom.

"Tie yourself in!" she yelled.

We wrapped the nets and the ties and anything else we could find around us as the plane bucked one last time. The propellers sputtered. The sound of the engines died. My stomach tumbled as the g-force pressed me back against the wall.

"Put your head between your knees!" Mom yelled. "Lock your hands behind your head like this!" She illustrated, lacing her fingers.

I followed her directions, trying to stay as calm as she appeared to be, but my hands shook and tears welled in my eyes.

"We're going to be okay," she yelled.

I nodded, even though I wasn't so sure.

She broke her crash position and gave me a rough hug. "I love you, Aphra," she said hoarsely. "No matter what happens, always remember that."

I hugged her back—for the first time in four years—just before we went down.

CHAPTER 7

The world spun first sideways, then upside down. I clung to the cargo netting, trying to focus only on Seth and my mom as my body slammed into the floor, the ceiling, the wall. If I was going to die, I wanted theirs to be the last faces I saw.

Suddenly we jumped as if we'd been swatted by a giant hand. The plane flipped. Tumbled. Dropped. There was a horrible screeching sound. Crashing. Shattering glass and tearing metal. And then . . . we stopped.

The smell of pine trees and rain and freshly shredded wood filled the plane. Cool air washed over my skin. I craned my neck to see a huge tree branch impaled through the windshield, illuminated by a faint blue light from the instrument panel. I couldn't see Ryan or Stuart.

"Mom?" I nudged her from the snarl of netting we were caught in. She coughed.

"Is she all right?" Seth's voice sounded very close, but I couldn't see him as I hung upside down in the cargo net. I reached back a hand and he brushed my fingers with his. "Are *you* okay?"

"Yeah." And I was. Except that all the blood was rushing to my head, making my eyes bulge and my lips ache.

My pulse throbbed in the bump on my scalp. "Help me get out of this." I started to pull my arm free of the net.

"Careful," Mom said, her voice weak. "There could be glass . . . sharp metal."

Inch by inch I lowered my body to the ceiling of the plane. I helped Mom out of her straps while Seth undid his.

My head was still spinning. "What happened?"

"The pontoons . . . " Mom said. "They must have slowed us down when we hit the trees."

"Hit trees," Seth repeated. He sounded dazed. "We crashed."

"Yes," Mom managed.

We sat still, letting it sink it. All around us it was eerily quiet.

"Where's Stuart?" I asked.

"I don't see him," Seth said softly.

I closed my eyes, imagining him thrown from the plane, his lifeless body lying broken and still on the forest floor. "What about . . . Ryan?"

Seth craned his neck to see around the seats. "He's still strapped in. It looks like there's blood on the glass in front of him. His head probably hit the windshield."

"Do you think he's dead?"

"I don't know."

We let that one sink in, too. And then Mom coughed. "We need . . . to get out. The forest can . . . be dry in August. Flammable. If the plane . . ."

She didn't need to say anything more. Seth sat up straight. "I'll check the door."

"Be careful!" I said. "The glass."

Seth slid, carefully, cautiously, inch by inch to the door. He pushed against it. "It's jammed."

"Try again," I urged.

Seth wrestled with the handle and pushed a shoulder against the door. It didn't budge. "Can we get out through the window? It's already broken."

I chewed my lip and looked to my mom for guidance, but she was quiet and I couldn't see her face very well in the shadows. "I don't know. The glass is pretty jagged. That's probably our last resort for an escape route." I crawled carefully toward him. "I'll help with the door. We're upside down, so the pressure points might be different. Let's try pushing from a different angle."

"I can't even get the handle to budge."

"We'll do it together."

We wrestled with the door until finally the latch gave way. The metal screeched as Seth pushed the door open.

It was unbelievably dark outside. "Where are we?" I whispered.

Seth shivered beside me. "I don't know. I can't see anything."

Which was true. The moon barely managed to break through the clouds overhead, let alone direct its weak light through the tall trees that surrounded us. The only things I could make out were tree trunks and the heavy, bone-chilling mist that drifted in through the cabin door.

It almost made me want to close the door again. Mom had said that the plane could start a fire, but I wasn't so sure. We hadn't set off any sparks yet. Maybe we were okay. Was I willing to risk our lives on a maybe, though? "We should check around the plane. Make sure there's no fuel leaks or anything."

"Maybe we should get your friend out of that chair first," Seth said, pointing to where Ryan dangled upside down from the pilot's seat.

I flinched at his word choice. Ryan was hardly my friend. Not that it really made a difference, but I didn't like the implication. Of course I had earned it.

Seth eyed the gash on Ryan's forehead and the blood that steadily drip, drip, dripped onto the ceiling. "Maybe we should check if he even has a pulse."

I reached up between the seats and felt for Ryan's neck. When I touched him, he moaned. I yanked my hand back. "He's alive."

Seth pulled a face as though disappointed. "Okay. Let's get him down out of that chair."

He reached beneath Ryan to support his weight as I undid the harness. Ryan slumped downward and I grabbed his legs to keep him from falling right on top of Seth.

His foot slipped away and swung down, crashing into the branches.

"Aaaah!" someone cried out.

"Seth! It's Stuart!" I dropped Ryan's legs and dug under the prickly pine branch. "He's wedged under here."

Seth lowered Ryan to the ceiling of the plane and hurried to my side. Together we worked Stuart loose and pulled him from under the branches. Even in the darkness I could tell he was pretty badly scratched up. But at least he was breathing on his own. Since he'd been in the front with no seat belt on when we crashed, that in itself was a miracle.

Everything I knew about first aid said that we should have put both of them on a stiff board before moving them, in case they had hurt their spines. Unfortunately, we had no boards.

I peered into the dark belly of the plane. "Let's take the nets down," I said to Seth. "We can use them to drag these guys clear of the control area so we can help them."

We unhooked the nets and laid a couple of them flat. Carefully, we slid Stuart onto the nets and dragged him to the rear of the plane and then did the same for Ryan.

"How is he?" Mom asked. She sounded groggy.

"He's alive," I told her. Beyond that, I didn't know. "How are you?"

"A little banged up, but fine." She crawled over to where Ryan lay. "Looks like he's lost a lot of blood."

"Head wounds bleed a lot," I said, straightening the nets. "They look a lot worse than they are." In fact, his head looked pretty bad, but I didn't want to think about what that might mean. The first-aid training I had received when I got my lifeguard certification back home only covered so much. "We should probably see if we can stop the bleeding. There was a first-aid kit in here somewhere . . ."

The light from the instrument panel didn't quite reach to the back of the plane, where I had left the kit—not that it would still be there after the way we'd been tossed about. "See if you can find it," I said to Mom. "Seth and I are going to check the plane outside to make sure we're not setting ourselves up to become a giant tiki torch."

Even in the shadows I didn't miss the way her brows raised as I was talking. Whatever. Maybe it was time she got a taste of what it felt like to have someone else tell her what to do.

Seth jumped down from the plane and reached back to help me down. I didn't really need the help, but I appreciated the gesture.

"I can hardly see anything out here," I said. "Can you?"

"Not much." He tightened his grip on my hand. "Where do you think we are?"

"I can't tell. Someplace with really big trees."

"Thanks, Sherlock."

"Maybe we're on a mountain. The ground's sloping pretty steep here. Plus it's cold. Much colder than it was in Seattle. So we're probably at a higher elevation."

"Not bad."

"I try."

"Well, let's get looking, since we can see so well."

We felt our way around the plane. Between the mist and the ground cover and the fact that there was no light to speak of, we pretty much had to. I fell more than once anyway, the ground was so uneven.

I wasn't exactly sure what aviation fuel smelled like, but I didn't smell anything that didn't seem to belong in the woods. As far as we could see, there were no sparks being thrown, there was no imminent danger of fire . . . especially since my feet were soggy just from walking around. I couldn't imagine how anything so damp could be tinder dry. Maybe Mom was mistaken. But I wasn't going to tell her that.

When we crawled back into the plane, Stuart was sitting up. He may have been leaning against the wall of the plane for support, but for someone who should by all rights be dead, leaning was remarkable progress.

"What did you find?" he asked. He practically grunted the words.

"Nothing exciting," I said. "How are you feeling?"

"I've been better."

I crawled across the floor. "Where do you hurt?"

His laugh was more of a horrible wheezing sound. "What are you going to do? Fix me?"

"Don't pay any attention to him," Mom said from the shadows. "He's in a lot of pain."

"What's wrong?"

"He may have broken some ribs. Or at the very least bruised them."

"Ouch," Seth said. "That's got to hurt."

Stuart wheezed the awful laugh again, but this time it ended in a spasm of coughing. That must have hurt even worse, judging by the little sobbing noises that followed.

"Isn't there anything we can do to help him?" I asked.

"Yes," Mom said. "We can get him to a doctor."

Ryan could use a doctor, too. And probably Mom. Since she had lost consciousness after the explosion, I worried that she might have a concussion. But first we had to find our way out of the woods. Literally.

"Mom? Do you know how to read the navigation system on one of these things?"

"Most likely. Yes."

"The lights are still on. Do you think . . . ?"

"Not a bad idea." She climbed up front and I followed her. She pressed some buttons and turned some knobs, but apparently whatever she hoped to accomplish didn't happen. She grumbled.

"What is it? What's wrong?"

She shook her head. "No luck. The navi's broken. So is the radio."

"So where *are* we?"

"We couldn't have gone far from Seattle," she said, maybe more to herself than to me, but I jumped on it anyway.

"That's what I was thinking. We couldn't have been in the air more than half an hour."

"True. But I had no orientation from the back of that plane. I can't even guess in which direction we were flying."

"Northeast," Stuart said weakly. "I saw . . . the instrument panel before we went down. We . . . were headed northeast."

"So we're—what? In the North Cascades?" Mom asked.

"That would be . . . my guess," he wheezed. "West side of . . . the pass, judging by the vegetation."

"Where was he taking us?" I wondered aloud.

"More importantly, who was waiting for us at the destination?" Mom cleared her throat. "Seth, the plane's locator device is flashing." She paused meaningfully. "It appears to be working fine."

Seth flinched. "So if Ryan's 'friends' were tracking the plane . . ."

Mom nodded slowly. "If we stay here, they would find us, yes."

"Then we need to get out of here!"

"Wait a second. Hold on." Stuart pushed himself up

on one elbow. "Where would we go? We have no idea where we *are*."

"We're in the mountains, right?" Seth said. "We head downhill and—"

"Downhill which way? We're in the Cascades, son. Mountains in all directions. With no clear sense of location, you could hike for days and end up in some valley *further away* from civilization than when you started."

Panic crossed Seth's face. He didn't have days to wander around in the wilderness. He had to get the ring to his dad. Immediately.

"We could wait till morning," I suggested. "Once we can see what's around us, it'll be easier to get our bearings."

Seth shook his head. "Whoever Ryan's working for isn't going to wait till morning to send someone to look for the plane."

Stuart scoffed. "They'd have to hike in."

"Unless they had a helicopter," I argued.

Mom cut in. "We *should* wait until morning. It's too dangerous to try and climb down in the dark. I've hiked up here before. Even in the light, the vegetation can be deceiving. The ground can drop off suddenly, and if you don't see where you're going, that can spell disaster. Besides, we'd be half frozen before sunrise. We can keep warmer inside the plane. If we hear anyone coming, we can hide before they reach the crash site."

"What?" Seth drew back. "No. We should at least try—"

"Seth, you were out there," Mom said. "Could you see where you were going?"

His shoulders slumped. "No."

"All right, then. We wait for sunrise."

We settled down in a huddle to keep warm. Even with the plane shut tight, the cold crept in, licking at my skin, sending shivers throughout my body. I was glad for the sweatshirt Seth had given me.

Before long, I could hear Stuart snoring softly. Even Seth's breathing settled into a slow, steady rhythm. As tired as I was, I couldn't make myself sleep. I shivered and snuggled closer to my mom. She'd been trying to act tough and in control, but I was worried about her. She'd been knocked out and then banged around pretty good. I couldn't help but notice that she had let me take the lead a couple of times since the crash. That wasn't like her. She could have a concussion. The climb down would not be easy for her.

With his injuries, it would be near to impossible for Stuart. I wondered if maybe there was an alternative to hiking down the mountain. Maybe we could hide and signal for help somehow—although I didn't know how we'd do that without alerting Ryan's friends.

Mom nudged me. "You should try to sleep," she whispered.

"You sleep. I'll take this watch."

"Hon, there's something I learned very early in this game. Sleep whenever you can because you never know when you'll have the chance again. You should get some rest. I'll keep an eye out. I got some sleep earlier."

"You passed out."

"I was resting, nonetheless."

I lay still for a moment, staring into the darkness. "What are we going to do about Ryan?" I whispered.

She didn't answer at first and I thought she had fallen asleep. "What do you mean?"

"When we go. We can't leave him here alone. He could die."

"Well, we can't carry him down the mountain. That would be impossible."

"But he's seriously injured."

"All the more reason not to move him."

"There could be wild animals."

"His people will come for him."

"And if they don't?"

I could feel her stiffen beside me. "Aphra, you have to learn to set priorities and stick with them, no matter the distraction. Sometimes you have to make tough decisions."

My throat felt hot and tight. I swallowed hard. I knew how it felt to be on the receiving end of those tough decisions. Her priority for the past four years had been to search for the Mole's minion. She had given up her family to do so. What did that make me? A distraction?

"Our priority is getting off this mountain," she said firmly. "We can't take him with us."

"I know." I lay silent, snuggling close to her. Beneath the mask of ceramic dust and sweat, she smelled just as I remembered, like white flowers in a meadow. Not exotic island flowers, but sturdy, reliable, mainland flowers. I closed my eyes, trying to store the moment for future memory. Once this was all over, who knew if I would ever see my mom again?

Chapter 8

I didn't think it was possible to sleep, but when I opened my eyes, the blackness had turned to gray. I sat up, stiff and cold. My body ached in places I didn't even know were possible. Mom was already awake, as was Stuart. They stood together by the plane's open door.

"It's time," she said. "We should get moving."

Seth had been sleeping beside me—a fact I wished I had realized earlier so that I could have enjoyed it. I nudged him. "Seth—"

He bolted upright, fists tight at his sides. His eyes were wild as he tried to focus on me, and for a moment I thought he really might take a swing at me. "What? What?"

I rubbed his arm—warily, keeping an eye on those fists. "It's morning. We can go now."

Panic crossed his face. I understood without having to ask; the clock was ticking. "What time is it?"

"About four," Mom said. "The sun won't be up for about an hour, but it's light enough to see."

He scrambled to his feet and reached back to help me up. I stood. Sort of. It was too tight in the plane to stand up all the way, so I sort of crouched and followed Seth to the open door.

I looked back one last time before jumping out. In the shadows, I couldn't be sure, but I swear Ryan was watching us leave.

Back home on the island, a rain-forest jungle hugs the back side of the resort. For years, I'd found solitude and solace hiking through the trees. Even so, the forest on the mountain that morning was anything but comforting. It was completely alien to me. Instead of the familiar palm trees and bamboo, I found myself surrounded by thick cedars and tall pines. The understory was so thick that we literally had to fight to get through it.

All around us, shrubs and pines grew so dense that I could barely see ten feet in any direction. Above, the tree cover filtered out the rising sun, and cast everything in shadow. Silence weighted the air. With the ghostly mist swirling around us, it was all too easy to imagine that we had fallen into a haunted wood from which we might never escape.

But we had to. Escape, that is. Seth was running out of time to at least let his dad's captors know he had the ring. We had to get down the mountain. Only the mountain wasn't going to make it easy. Beneath our feet, the ground bunched and fell away, both without warning. The brush looked like it was all about the same height, but beneath it, the ground could have a three-foot drop-off that we might not see until we had fallen and twisted an ankle or worse. And the entire time we hiked, I don't think we came upon a flat surface once. The ground sloped relentlessly downward. I could already feel my toes and heels begin to blister.

Stuart was a mess. He could barely see where he was going without his glasses, for one thing, and with all the blood he'd lost, he wore out easily. Seth practically had to carry him several times just so we could keep moving. So even though I wasn't feeling too great, I wasn't about to complain about blisters and sore feet. They were nothing compared to what Stuart had been through.

Mom and I led the way, clearing the path, each of us whacking back branches with lengths of metal we had pulled from the wreckage. It was hard work and the progress was slow. And it gave me blisters on my hands, to add to a growing list of discomforts I wouldn't complain about.

"We need to find a trail," Mom told me. "Even a deer trail would do. Someplace where the vegetation is worn down. We'll never make it out of here like this."

I agreed, but what could we do until we found such a trail? We kept whacking.

Finally, I had to ask. "How long will it take them?"

"Take who?"

"You said Ryan's people would come to find the wreck."

She hacked at a vine with her makeshift machete. "I don't know." The strain in her voice worried me. "I would assume they were tracking the flight from the moment we left the dock. They may well have been following us."

That left me with a new stab of panic. "So they'd know exactly where we went down. They could be here really soon."

"Yes."

"We have to move faster."

"Yes."

I attacked the brush with a vengeance.

"Nat," Stuart called weakly. "Could we rest for a moment, please?"

I glanced nervously over my shoulder. I wasn't at all sure we should stop. Not yet. We had been fighting our way through the brush for what seemed like hours, but had we covered enough ground to be safe?

But Mom agreed with Stuart. "Yes. Of course. Let's find a spot where we can sit."

We hiked a little farther before Seth spotted a fat log curving up from the mist. Stuart sank onto it with a sigh and leaned back against a tree. He closed his eyes. It was too shadowy to really get a look at his coloring, but the way he rasped in each breath, he *sounded* awful. I wasn't sure how long Stuart would be able to last, wandering around in the forest.

Mom sat next to him. She didn't say anything, just sat there. I wondered if she was thinking the same thing I was about his chances for survival.

Seth motioned to me and we walked a short distance

away, sitting together on a lichen-splotched boulder. "I can't carry him very much farther," he said in a low voice.

"I know. Mom and I can—"

"We should scout ahead and see if we can find a trail or a river or something that will make the hiking easier."

We walked slowly, counting paces and bending branches so that we could find our way back. It wasn't as complicated as it sounds, either, since there was really only one logical direction we could go. We followed the sloping ground downward.

After a while I began to notice more light shining through the tree branches. The trees themselves looked smaller, and spaced farther apart. The smells changed, too. Instead of just mold and damp pine, I caught a whiff of something else, fresh and clean, mingled with . . . I wrinkled my nose. Old fish.

"Do you hear it?" Seth said.

I stood still and listened. Sure enough, from somewhere not too far away came the distinct rush of water. A river.

We had to scout three different routes, but finally, we found our way to the riverbank. After the eerie darkness of the forest, the river was almost mystical, the way the predawn glow caught the water. It also felt like it was a few degrees cooler by the water.

I shivered.

Seth wrapped his arms around me and pulled me close. For the first time since the crash, I felt warm. I rested my head against his chest and let my eyes follow the rush of the river to the valley below. Against a backdrop of jagged, snowcapped peaks, dark, narrow pines rose from the mist, contrasted with splotches of golden yarrow. Under different circumstances, the scenery alone would have taken my breath away. But we weren't on some sightseeing trip. We were there because someone wanted Seth's dad's ring. Wanted it bad enough to kill for it. And, in Ryan's case, perhaps to die for it.

I drew the ring from my pocket and placed it in Seth's hand. "Everything's going to be all right."

He worked his jaw. "It has to be."

I tightened my arms around his waist. For the sake of Seth's dad, I knew we had to find a way to get the ring through to him. But I also knew that as soon as we did, Seth and I would have to say good-bye.

"We should get back," I whispered, even though part of me wanted to stay there forever.

Stuart didn't look much better when we returned to where he was resting. His face was pale except for two bright pink spots, high on his cheeks. Dark circles shadowed his eyes. I wasn't sure how much farther he would be able to go.

"We found a river," I said. "We can follow it."

"Near?" Mom asked.

"Not far. How's Stuart?"

"I'm fine," Stuart said. As if to prove it, he pushed himself up from the log, although he grunted from the effort. He squinted up at the angle of the sun in the small patches of sky we could see through the trees. "It's getting late. We should get moving."

It took twice as long to reach the river with my mom and Stuart as it had when just Seth and I were hiking. By the time we reached the edge of the forest, the sun had swung high in the sky and the last of the mist had burned away.

"We thought maybe we should follow the river," Seth said. "It will be easier to walk out here. Less undergrowth to crawl over." Which was true, but it was also rockier. We'd be climbing more than walking and I wasn't sure how much of that Stuart would be able to take.

Mom had another concern. "We'd also be more visible."

"If we hear a plane or anything, we can run into the trees," Seth assured her. It seemed to make the most sense.

The route proved to be easier, but Stuart still tired quickly. Before long, he had to stop and rest again.

I pulled Mom aside. "How much further do you think we have to go? Stuart lost a lot of blood last night. His ribs must be killing him. And I'm afraid his hand is going to get infected." The gauze that I had wrapped it with was black with dried blood and dirt. We probably should have taken it off altogether, but he was being very protective of his hand. He didn't want anyone to touch it. Besides, I wasn't entirely sure I wanted to look at those fingers again, so I really hadn't tried to pursue the issue.

"We've got to keep his strength up," Mom said. "Wild huckleberries grow in this area. Thimbleberries, too. Maybe we should take a moment to gather some lunch."

The berries grew on long, tangled brambles that left our hands scratched and raw from picking them. Stuart was too weak to be of much help, so Mom and Seth and I gathered what we could and then sat on the rocks with him to eat them.

When we were done—which didn't take long—Seth picked up a small stone and threw it toward the river. "Do you suppose they found him yet?"

"Ryan?" Stuart daintily dabbed the corner of his lips with a grubby finger. "I don't know. I'd think we would have heard the helicopter."

I looked up. "How do you know they'd bring a helicopter?"

"Think about it. They're not going to land a plane up here. We don't know where the nearest roads may be. A helicopter would be the quickest way to the accident site."

"Then why wouldn't they have come last night? If they didn't have to hike in, why would they wait?"

He shrugged. "Maybe that tracking device *wasn't* working," he said blandly. "They may not have been able to see the wreckage until it was light."

"Who do you think he works for?" Seth asked. "The CIA?"

I glanced at Mom. If Ryan was CIA, wouldn't she know it? Besides, Watts was CIA and Ryan had helped us get away from him. But Mom didn't let on that she knew anything.

"He's one of *them*," Stuart said bitterly, and I could only assume he was talking about the Mole and his minions. I know it wasn't really a big reveal—it was the only other alternative—but seeing the look of panic that crossed Seth's face, I wished that Stuart had learned, like my mom, to keep his thoughts to himself.

CHAPTER 9

We heard the helicopter for the first time when the sun hung directly overhead. I almost didn't hear the *thwap-thwap-thwap* of the rotors at all because it was lost in the noise of my mom and me chopping through the brush. Plus the sound was so familiar—I'd heard it almost daily on the island—that it almost didn't register until it was too late.

It was Seth who picked it up first. He froze in his tracks and grabbed my arm. "Wait. What was that?"

"What?"

"That sound?"

I heard it then. "Mom. Listen!"

She stopped her blade midswing and gave me a quizzical look. But then she heard it; I could see the understanding dawn on her face. "Helicopter," she said. "Get down!"

We crouched in the brush and waited for the sound to go away.

We continued our hike in a state of heightened alert. Every noise, every shadow, sent us scurrying back into the tangled underbrush and the trees. But as the afternoon wore on, we began to be less vigilant. Plus, by then we were exhausted. The route we were trying to follow was very nearly impassable. With the exception of the short, fitful rest in the plane, we hadn't slept. And berries can provide only so much energy.

I was becoming clumsy in my fatigue, tripping over my own feet, not to mention the vegetation. My mind was a jumble; I didn't seem to be able to clear my head, but I couldn't quite pin down one thought and stick with it, either.

I was aware enough to be worried about Stuart, though. If I was a mess, Stuart—with his blood loss and bruised ribs—was even worse. He kept muttering things that didn't make sense—although I admit I was beyond trying to figure him out—and was starting to become irritable with Seth when all Seth was doing was trying to help him keep up.

We had all become draggy and unaware when the sound returned.

We'd come to the edge of a steep drop when we heard it, distant at first, but definitely drawing closer. In a cluster, we stumbled into the woods, tripping over vines, getting snagged on the brambles, fighting in vain to make our tired bodies move faster. Once again, we hid in the brush at the base of a huge tree, but this time, we saw the beast.

It was like a scene from an action movie. We huddled in the bushes, barely daring to breathe, when suddenly a black helicopter rose from beyond the hill, the wash of its rotors reaching all the way back to where we crouched, stirring the foliage around us.

The tinted cockpit glass seemed to stare at us like huge, rounded bug's eyes. I'm not sure how long it hovered there—it felt like a long time, but was probably only seconds—before it banked sharply and flew away.

Believe me, that eerie encounter was enough to wake us up. My own awareness returned with a vengeance until I thought I would jump out of my skin at every sound.

"They saw us," Seth said. "We have to get out of here."

"We have no way of knowing what they saw," Mom countered, but I could tell by the way she tensed up that she knew he was right.

"They'll be expecting us to follow the river," Stuart put in. "We need to move deeper into the forest."

"But we can't *move* in the forest," Seth said. "We've got to get out of here!"

I left them to argue and hurried back over to the top of the hill. I thought I had seen something and I wanted to be sure.

Mom followed me. "What is it?"

"Down there," I said, pointing. I wasn't sure she saw it at first, but then her eyebrows rose. From a clearing at the bottom of the hill, a couple of thin plumes of smoke rose, curling in the air.

"Campers," she said.

"Campers," I agreed. "They could be our ticket out of here."

• • •

To ease Stuart's mind, we took the hard way down, through the woods. I tried to help him as much as possible so Seth wouldn't end up having to carry him again. Still, Seth did most of the heavy lifting, and by the time we reached the bottom of the hill, he was shaking with fatigue.

"You should rest," Mom told him. "You, too, Stuart. Aphra and I will scout ahead."

Seth didn't even argue, and that worried me.

"We'll be right back," I assured him.

We hiked back toward the river.

"You have a plan, I take it?" Mom asked.

"A plan?"

"Right. Talk me through your thought process."

I blinked at her. Since when did she want to hear what I thought? "Okay . . . the way I figure it is that these campers had to get in somehow. They either hiked, drove, or rafted. I don't think they would have hiked, so that leaves driving or rafting, so—"

"Why don't you think they hiked?"

I stopped and looked at her. Was she serious? "Well, because *we* have been hiking all day, *without* schlepping along camping equipment, and it has not been enjoyable. I can't imagine anyone choosing to put themselves through that."

"Maybe they know the trails."

"All right. Fine. Let's say hiking is a possibility, too. Still, there could be a truck . . ."

"And if there is? What would we do, ask for the keys?"

I shook my head. "Wow. You're really supportive."

"I just want to know if you've thought it out."

"Well, I haven't, okay? I've had just about as much time to work this out as you have. Do *you* have any great plans you'd like to share?"

"Don't be snide, Aphra. It doesn't become you."

"Well, I'm sorry. When I get attacked, that's how I react." I stomped ahead of her.

"Who's attacking you?"

I spun around. "Do you *hear* yourself? All this questioning, criticizing. What do *you* call that?"

"Is that what you think this is?"

"Um, hello. Yeah. You treat me like a little kid who doesn't know what to think."

"When I saw you last, you *were* a little kid."

"Well, I've changed since then. But not as much as you have."

She actually looked stung, as if she had no idea. "What are you talking about?"

"Oh, come on." I eyed her up and down. "You're not the same person at all. We used to have fun together. Life was a big adventure. Now I don't even know you anymore. You've become this uptight, pinch-lipped government *agent*."

She bristled. "Aphra, don't be unfair."

"Unfair? That's pretty funny coming from you. You

made me think you and I were a team and then you *left*. Now all I want is a little support, and you can't even give me that."

"I do support you," she said, voice softening, "but this is not a game, Aphra. You need to be sure in your actions. Decisive. That's why I'm challenging you, to make you stronger. To be the smart and tough young woman I raised you to be."

"Raised?" I stepped back. "How could you raise me when you were never there?"

I wished I could take the words back when I saw the tears in her eyes, but I was too hurt to tell her that. I folded my arms and turned away.

She approached me slowly, reached out tentatively, rubbed my arm gently. "I'm so sorry, Aphra. I . . . I should have been there for you. I hope you understand I just wanted to protect you."

"And I wanted a mom."

"I'm here now."

I wiped a stray tear from my cheek. The anger had passed like a summer storm and all I felt now was regret. "I'm sorry for messing things up."

"Oh, no, no." She pulled me into her arms. "You haven't messed up, Aphra. I handled things all wrong."

"But if it wasn't for me—"

"If it wasn't for you, I'd have nothing to fight for. If it wasn't for you, I'd have given up long ago."

I think we both cried ourselves out, standing by the

river. If given a choice, I don't think I would have chosen the route I'd taken, but in the end, I'd do it again without hesitation. I had found what I'd been looking for. I found my mom.

CHAPTER 10

After we had dried our eyes, Mom and I scoped out the origin of the smoke I had seen from atop the hill. Sure enough, downriver we found a campsite. We didn't get too close, just near enough to see the tents and campfire through the trees. Then we hiked back double time to where Seth and Stuart were resting. I waited for Mom to tell them about our discovery, but she looked to me and nodded, giving me the lead.

"We think we might be able to locate some transportation," I began.

Seth's eyes lit up. It was the first encouraging thing he'd heard all day. "Where?"

"We don't *know* that we'll find anything," I said, "but there are some campers down the river. We figure they might have a car or a raft . . ."

Stuart shook his head. "No. We shouldn't be involving civilians. This could get dangerous."

I couldn't help it. I laughed right in his face. Was he kidding? It *could* get dangerous? We'd passed the realm of possibility and landed smack in the middle of absolute certainty about twenty hours ago. Had he not looked at his hand lately?

"We won't involve the people," Mom said firmly.

"Only the transportation." She raised a hand to stop my protest. "*If* they happen to possess any."

Seth, of course, was more than ready to take the gamble. Stuart kept mumbling and complaining the entire time. If it wasn't for the need to cut him some slack for being injured and all, I would've liked to slap him. As it was, I had to settle for tuning him out.

By the time we neared the camp, long shadows stretched out from the trees and the chill had returned to the air. Shivering, I tried to pick up the pace as much as I could, considering Stuart's inability to keep up. I just figured that the faster we moved, the warmer we'd be. Plus, the quicker we found a way out of there, the sooner we could put the whole thing behind us.

Wood smoke hovered with the gathering mist, and the smell of roasting meat made my stomach rumble.

"What if we just told these people that we needed help?" Seth whispered. "Wouldn't that be easier?"

Mom shook her head. "There would be too many questions we couldn't answer. The fewer explanations needed, the better."

I liked Seth's idea of asking for help, especially if we could share the fire and the food, but Mom was right. Plus I knew from personal experience that a person could be placed in deadly trouble by getting involved. We couldn't impose that danger on anyone.

Men's voices carried through the evening air, and we skirted the perimeter of their camp, keeping out of their way. I spotted four of them on the other side of some green domelike tents, sitting around a campfire, drinking and laughing. Since we didn't see any cars or even tire tracks, we continued on to the river, hoping for a boat.

Sure enough, up on the rocky bank sat two kayaks. My heart dropped. Two. I'd been hoping for a raft or something on which we could all ride out together. With two, we'd have to split up.

As I'd expected, Mom suggested that she and I ride together, leaving Seth once again to take care of Stuart's deficiencies. Between his injured hand and aching ribs, there was no way Stuart could paddle a kayak with any effectiveness, so Seth would have to do enough paddling for both of them.

"It shouldn't be difficult since we will be following the river downstream," Mom assured him. "You sit in the back so you can do the steering."

"I know," Seth said. "I've been kayaking before."

"So have I," I put in—as if it were relevant.

I'd actually only been sea kayaking, and never tandem. Plus these kayaks were built a little differently from what I was used to—wider and a bit shorter, without the upswept bow of the island kayaks. But a kayak was a kayak, I figured. How hard could it be?

While the guys slid their kayak into the water, Mom held ours steady so that I could climb to my seat. I settled down into the cockpit and readied my paddle. She pushed away from the shore before slipping into her own seat.

I held my paddle just above the water until she gave the signal. She counted until we found a rhythm and then instinct took over. I dug deep, pushing the water behind us as fast as I could in order to catch up with Seth and Stuart. The kayak cut through the water like an arrow, racing over the dips and swells. Before long, my arms burned and my shoulders tightened, but I tried not to think about it. Even though my body craved rest, my mind still yelled, *Go! Go!* Cold mountain air snaked across the bow, rippling the fabric of my shirt, blowing back my hair and raising goose bumps on my skin, but all I could think about was getting down the river, away from locator beacons and helicopters. We couldn't paddle fast enough.

I heard rough water as we came toward a bend in the river. That couldn't be good. I tensed and called behind me, "Mom?"

"I hear it."

"What do we do?"

By now, I could see the froth kicking up in the river ahead of us. Each stroke brought us closer. My hands gripped the paddle so hard that I swore I was going to go right through the wood. "Mom?!"

"We'll ride it out! I'll do the steering," she shouted. "You just tell me if you see any major obstacles."

The current pulled us downstream and I soon found that I was using the paddle more for keeping upright than for actual paddling. Icy water sprayed in my face and drenched my hair and clothes. My fingers throbbed from the cold.

I tried to navigate through the worst of it, yelling back to Mom, "Right! Left!" but still we hit rocks under the water, teeth-jarring hits that sent us reeling to the side or shot us into the air, only to slap back down onto the surface to be drenched all over again.

I blinked away water, shivering so hard that my back ached. My arms felt heavy. My head felt thick. That could be why I wasn't quick enough to tell my mom about the huge boulder sticking up from the water until we were right upon it. I did manage to scream, but not until the bow cracked against the boulder, rebounding and spinning us completely around.

Mom fought for control, but we were shooting down the rapids backward. There's not much she could have done. I'm not sure exactly what happened next, but my guess is that the stern hit another rock. Only this time instead of spinning the kayak, it sent it end over end. I shot up in the air. The paddle flew from my hands, but I barely spared it a thought, because I was headed face-first into the river. I pushed free of the cockpit and splashed down ahead of the kayak.

Freezing water closed over me.

My first instinct was to try to swim against the current,

but I did remember from preparing for the whitewater trip—you know, the one with Mom that never happened all those years ago—that if you were thrown from a boat, you were supposed to sit back, try to ride the current feetfirst, and cross your arms against your chest. This rule, of course, presupposed that you were wearing a life vest to keep your head above the water, and maybe a helmet to keep from cracking your skull on a rock. I kept going under and getting a mouthful of water every time I went down. I lost track of Mom and the other kayak. All I could think about was finding the next breath of air and not smashing into anything. That was plenty. Once the river calmed down, I could worry about little things like hypothermia and being stranded alone in the woods.

More than once, my feet smacked into underwater rocks and I was thrown out of position and had to fight to maintain the posture. It was during one of these fights that I hit my tailbone on a rock. Pain flared up my spine and down both legs. I could hardly move. My head dragged under the waves. Water shot up my nose. I gagged and coughed, fighting to keep my head up.

Finally, we came to a bend in the river and the water quieted just a bit. The current was still strong, but at least I was able to gain some control.

I turned around. Where was Mom? All I could see was dark water, swirling, frothing.

"Aphra! Over here!" Stuart and Seth stood knee-deep in the water, making big arm gestures and yelling at me to swim to shore. Their kayak lay on the rocky bank. Apparently they had managed to avoid getting tossed into the water.

Seth cupped his hands around his mouth and yelled something to me, but his voice was lost in the roar of the river.

"Where's my mom?" I yelled.

He shouted something else and pointed.

I almost missed seeing her float by me. Her hand flailed above the water, but in the darkness it almost looked like a jumping fish. But then I saw her face surface. She gasped for air and went under again.

"Mom!"

The current pulled her away from me and I had to swim after her. In the cold, my arms and legs were weighted. It felt like I was swimming through sludge. Frozen, moving sludge. "Mom! Mom!"

Her head popped to the surface a yard or so ahead of me. It took almost all the energy I had left to reach her. I grabbed the back of her shirt. In her panic, she grasped at me and pulled us both under. I fought to get free and pulled away, almost losing her in the current again.

"Relax!" I yelled. "Hold still!"

Never before had I been so grateful for my lifeguard training. I didn't have to think about it; instinct took over. I pushed her so that she was floating on her back and hooked an arm around her torso. With every ounce of strength I had left, I swam with the other arm for the shore. As hard as I pulled, though, I didn't even seem to be moving. The current sucked at us both, carrying us farther downstream.

Seth yelled and splashed through the water, running along the shore to keep up with us. I kept my focus on him and swam harder. He jumped into the water as I got closer and swam out to meet us. Together, we dragged Mom in.

She coughed and gagged, but at least she was breathing on her own. We staggered onto the shore, shivering, legs wobbling. Even though we were out of the water, I knew we weren't home free. The sun had dipped behind the mountains, taking with it what warmth it had provided. We were wet. We were cold. We were lost. We were in big trouble.

"A-Aphra," Mom said between shivers. "I had n-no idea you c-could do that."

"Look!" Stuart cried, pointing downstream. "Lights!"

There were lights, and a lot of them. Maybe a town? I guessed they were about a mile away. I just hoped we could make it that far.

We never got a chance to find out.

Before we had gone ten yards, a black truck crested the hill above us, its bright headlights sweeping down on us and capturing us like some kind of freeze ray.

"You're a hard crew to find," a man's voice called out. "We'd about given you up for dead."

CHAPTER 11

It was over. There was no place to run except back into the river, and that hadn't worked out so well the first time. I grasped Mom on one side and Seth on the other and waited for the inevitable.

The man trotted down the hill toward us, his dark shape backlit by the headlights behind him. "Don! They're soaking wet! We need more blankets!"

I tried to focus on him, but he shined a flashlight in my eyes and I couldn't see anything but white light. "Pupils responsive!" he yelled, and wrapped a heavy, coarse blanket around me.

"You're lucky we saw you," he said as he moved on to Mom. "We had just about called off the search for the night."

"What?"

"The search. We've had crews out all day looking for you. You must have seen them. They spotted you this afternoon, but by the time they called in your location and got bodies up there, you were gone."

Spotted us . . . the helicopters . . .

Ranger Don—I assumed they were both rangers since they were dressed in matching uniforms like overgrown

Boy Scouts—harrumphed. "What were you trying to do, anyway? Get yourself killed?"

"It's a good thing those anglers radioed when their kayaks went missing. Least we knew to check the river."

"The crash site," I said. "Did you find—"

"Let's get you back to the station and your bodies warmed up and then we can talk."

"Station?"

"The ranger station. The quicker we get there, the quicker you can get dry."

Mom and Stuart sat on opposite ends of the middle bench seat in the rangers' SUV, and just behind them, Seth and I huddled together in the far back. Once we weren't moving, the shivering set in for real and we needed each other's body heat, even if there wasn't much to go around.

The whole scenario had a very surreal feel to it; one minute we're fighting our way through the wilderness and the next we're riding along all warm and comfortable on a cushy seat with Bach on the radio. Well, maybe not *completely* comfortable—the SUV bumped and bounced over the rocky terrain, throwing us around pretty good in the back. That, plus the itchy wool blankets they had given us smelled like wet farm animals and . . . well, it seemed strange to be worried about such mundane comforts when just a short while ago I wasn't even convinced we were going to make it down the mountain alive.

When we reached the ranger station, Ranger Don and the first ranger, whose name I never did get, ushered us up the wooden stairs and inside, clucking over us like a couple of old hens. It wasn't until the door closed behind us that I noticed the blond man in the dark suit seated behind the desk.

"Thank God," he said. "We've been looking all over for you."

My face went numb as Watts's cold eyes swept over us.

"They were down by the river, sir," Ranger Don reported. "Just as you predicted."

Watts stood. He planted his hand at his waist, pushing back his jacket enough that his shoulder holster was plainly visible. You know, just in case we forgot who was in control. "Thank you for your outstanding effort today, gentlemen. We couldn't have done it without you." Then, turning to us, "We have some dry clothing and blankets in the next room. And I understand you're in need of medical attention."

"We're fine," I blurted, even though Stuart seriously needed a doctor for his hand. It made me sound like a petulant little kindergartner, but I couldn't stand the way Watts was acting all benevolent.

"I'm glad to hear that," Ryan said from the doorway. "I was worried about you."

My breath caught. I should have known. His head was bandaged and he wore a dark suit and tie similar to the one Watts had on. So, Stuart had been wrong; Ryan was CIA after all. And Stuart had been wrong about leaving Agent Ryan behind at the crash site, too. If we'd taken him with us, he wouldn't have been able to alert Watts about our condition or our whereabouts. Of course we wouldn't have made it very far trying to carry Ryan as well as Stuart, either, so I don't know what choice we had, but it made me feel better to be angry at Stuart, so I wasn't going to analyze it too closely.

"Ladies, you may have the room first," Ryan said, bowing his head in our direction. "Please change quickly. The men should get out of their wet things as soon as possible."

My legs shook so badly that I could hardly follow Mom into the back room. As if practically freezing outside wasn't enough, just being in the same room with Watts again made my blood run cold. I wanted to scream. My mind went back to the chase after Joe died—had that only been a day and a half ago? Watts *had* been following me. He followed me to the apartment. He was following me still. Would I ever be free from him?

I couldn't believe that everyone else was being so calm! Well, maybe I could understand Ranger Don and the other ranger. They probably didn't even know what was going on. I doubt Watts and Ryan announced that they were from the CIA, that they'd killed Joe, and that the rest of us were probably expendable, too. But what was Mom thinking? She hardly even blinked as we passed Ryan in the short hallway leading to the small back room. Were we just going to blithely allow them to herd us wherever they wanted us to go? We had to get out of there. Seth's dad was depending on it.

In the room was a pile of gray sweatpants and sweatshirts folded on a chair. On top of that sat two plastic Fruit of the Loom packages. I picked one of them up and recoiled. Underwear. One set of women's, one set of men's. I didn't know what was creepier, the thought of putting on underwear that one of those guys out there had bought or going commando under the sweats. I reasoned that the underwear was in a sealed package and the sweats were not, so I'd go with the extra layer. I ripped open the package and gingerly removed a pair, passing the others to Mom. The sweats were all men's size large, so they were huge on us, but at least they were warm.

"What now?" I asked in a small voice as I pulled the sweatshirt over my head.

Mom raised a finger to her lips and looked to the door. Of course. We couldn't talk in there. We couldn't talk anywhere near Watts or Ryan. Somehow we had to figure out a way to communicate, because I didn't intend to go down without a fight.

I pushed up the sleeves and rolled the pant legs so that I wouldn't trip on them and hurried out to the other room. I noticed that Stuart's hand had been freshly bandaged, but he still looked miserable. Seth caught my eye as I entered the room, and then glanced down at his hand. It was curled into a tight fist. I wasn't sure what he was trying to tell me. To fight? I slid a glance at Watts, who had apparently been watching me.

"I hope you found everything you needed," he said smoothly.

"Almost," I said, probably not anywhere near as smoothly, though I was trying to keep my voice steady. "You wouldn't happen to have any shoes and socks up here, would you? My feet are freezing."

He almost didn't bother to hide his smile. Of course they wouldn't give us shoes and socks. Barefoot, we were less of a flight risk. "Please forgive the oversight. We'll find you appropriate footwear when we get to town."

Somehow, I didn't find that comforting.

Mom came out of the room behind me. I couldn't help but think how appropriate it was that our matching gray sweats looked like prison issue.

"Stuart, Seth, why don't you go put on your dry clothes now that the ladies are done," Watts said. I could practically *see* the smirk in his voice.

Seth looked at me again, eyes boring into me, willing me to understand. I caught the movement of his fist once more, before he dropped it to his side.

His fist. The ring. Of course. He'd have no place to hide it while he was changing. I blinked and made myself look away. I didn't make eye contact with him at all as he followed Stuart to the back room, but I managed to stand just close enough that he bumped into me as he passed. He pressed the ring into my hand. I slipped it onto my thumb and made a fist around it, letting the long sleeve of the sweatshirt fall down over my fingers.

The first ranger offered Mom and me some hot coffee. "It'd do good to raise your core temperature."

I snorted and looked over at Watts. No way was I drinking any coffee he'd been anywhere around. Not after seeing what had happened to Joe. I shook my head no.

Finally, once everyone was dressed and warmed and Stuart's vital signs had been checked, Watts announced our departure.

"Gentlemen, thank you again," he said to the rangers. "You have done us a great service today."

They way the two of them beamed, I had to wonder what kind of story Watts and Ryan had told them. As I watched the exchange and their innocent reaction to it, I began to think that they might just be our best allies in this situation. They didn't know what Ryan and Watts were up to. Okay, I didn't know what Ryan and Watts were up to, either, but I knew it wasn't good. If I could just remove the blinders from their eyes, they might be willing to help us escape.

The one thing I couldn't do was leave that ranger

station. Once we were alone with the CIA boys, how would Seth ever get away? He was running out of time.

Watts opened the door. I looked desperately to the naive park rangers, screaming in my head, *Don't let them take us!* They were not tuned in to my telepathy.

What else could I do? I clutched my stomach and doubled over. "Ugn!"

Mom wrapped an arm around my waist. "Aphra, what is it?"

"I don't feel so good," I said weakly. "I . . . need to use the restroom."

Watts rolled his eyes, but how could he refuse me in front of the rangers? He nodded—as if I had been asking his permission!—and pointed out the door to the loo. I hurried inside and locked it behind me.

The bathroom was a dismal little space that looked as if it had seen better days. I curled my toes in disgust at the feel of the cool, somewhat damp tiles beneath my bare feet. I didn't even want to think of the kinds of diseases I could get from direct skin contact. The floor was cracked and yellowed—by age, I hoped—and the toilet in the corner leaned a bit to the left. The single bulb hanging from the ceiling cast an ocher pall over it all.

Worst of all, the place seriously stank of old plumbing and stale pee. I considered cracking open the window, but I didn't want Watts and Ryan to think I was trying to sneak out and come barging in on me. I wasn't going to. Sneak out, that is. Even though I would have loved to put as much distance between Watts and myself as humanly possible, I wasn't going to leave my mom and Seth. Okay, or Stuart, either, even though he had really started to grate on me. I just couldn't do it. Besides, if I did run away, where would I run *to*? No, I would stay put, but I had to find a way to leave a message for the rangers.

I turned in a slow circle, looking for something—anything—I could use to write with, but the bathroom was as depressingly bare as it was filthy. The only decor besides the sink and toilet was an empty paper-towel dispenser, a cracked mirror, and a framed portrait of Smokey the Bear. I am not kidding.

Nothing to write on. Nothing to write with. I chewed the inside of my cheek. There had to be *something* I could do. I looked at the mirror again. A spiderweb of cracks fanned out from the corner as if something—a head or a fist or similar—had smacked it. All I needed was one sliver. Maybe I could scratch a message on the wall or something.

I picked at the edge of the mirror with my fingernails, trying to pry up a piece of glass. It was one of those old drugstore numbers, glued to a cardboard backing, which not only shadowed the reflection just a bit, but also made it supremely hard to pull off a shard without destroying your fingernails. Finally, I was able to work a piece loose.

Someone banged on the door. "Are you all right in there?"

I couldn't tell whose voice it was. "Um, yes. I'll be right out." I flushed the toilet for effect.

It didn't work. The banging continued.

"Hold on!" I started to scratch at the wall with the broken piece of mirror, but barely made a letter before the doorknob rattled. I spun away from my SOS, curling my fist around the shard from the broken mirror.

The door swung open and Ryan crowded through the doorway. His gaze flicked past me to the wall. If he noticed my pathetic scratches, it didn't show in his bland expression. "We need to be going now," he said. He steered me out to the porch, where the others were waiting.

Seth shot me a look, eyes wide and questioning. I gave him the slightest shake of my head. I would say that I was trying to act normal, but normal left the building the minute I'd set foot in Seattle. The best I could do was to not fidget so that I wouldn't draw attention to the glass in my hand.

"Let's move," Watts growled. He yanked my mom's arm, pulling her down the porch steps.

Seth jumped forward to defend her, but Stuart held him back with his good hand. He shook his head, pantomiming a gun with his finger, cocking it with his thumb.

Ryan prodded Seth and Stuart forward. I managed to

hang back long enough to tug on Ranger Don's sleeve. "Help us. Please," I said in a low voice.

"That's all right, little lady. It was our pleasure," he said.

"No. I mean, we need—"

Ryan returned to my side and slid a hand around my elbow. "Come, Aphra. Let's not keep Agent Watts waiting."

Watts made my mom sit with him in the front seat of a black Escalade. He put Seth, Stuart, and me—in that order—in the middle seat and Ryan behind us, again with a great show of his gun.

The result was that we couldn't talk to one another without one of them knowing. I stared out the window, watching the moonlit mountain scenery slip by. Someday, I thought, I'd like to come back and visit the Cascades when I could actually enjoy it. If I lived that long.

My fingers throbbed from picking at the glass. A fat lot of good that had done. I ran my thumb over the sharp edge of the sliver of mirror in my hand, trying to come up with a better idea. Outside, the mist had turned to a fine rain, making the road and the trees and the plants around us shine in the weak moonlight.

"Where are you taking us?" Mom asked, her voice nearly lost in the hum of the tires and the *squee-squee-squee* of the windshield wipers.

Watts's eyes never left the road. "Does it matter?"

I exchanged a glance with Seth. Of course it mattered. Why wouldn't it matter?

"You can't go back to your apartment, as I'm sure you know," Watts continued. "That has been sterilized."

Mom didn't say anything.

"You could always publicly return to the Agency, you know. You and I made a good team."

I blanched at the thought.

Mom's voice was monotone. "A rogue agent has no team."

"You're not a rogue, Natalie." He gave her a sideways glance and smiled. It made my stomach turn. "Ooh. You meant *me*. Valuable lesson, Natalie; learn to play the game."

She pressed her lips together and turned her head so that I couldn't see her face anymore.

Watts chuckled and drummed his fingers on the steering wheel. I closed my hand around the glass until it bit into my skin. How I wanted to rake it across his face and wipe that smirk from his lips!

Seth caught my eye and made a face like he was asking me what we should do. I made the same questioning face back. What *could* we do? There were more of us, but they had the gun. Maybe two, if Ryan was packing, which he probably was now that he was all suited up and official. Plus Stuart didn't really count for our side because he was on the injured-reserve list. So we had three against two plus the guns. Not good odds, but something told me that our odds would become even worse once we got to wherever we were going. If we were to have any chance of escaping, we had to take it before we reached our destination.

We couldn't signal Mom to be a part of whatever we might do, which meant it was up to Seth and me. I slid the hand holding the glass shard forward and opened my palm just enough to show him. Problem was, in the shadows, I don't think he saw it. At least if he did, he didn't show any reaction, which I suppose was very clever, but it didn't help me much. I looked down at my hand then back up again like he'd done with the ring. Down and up, down and up. *Come on, Seth, get the message.*

He gave me an exasperated, wide-eyed stare as if to say, *Yeah, I got it. So what are we going to do with it?*

Heck if I knew.

And we never got a chance to find out, because all of a sudden Stuart snatched the glass shard from my hand, and in one fluid movement he swung his good hand back, slicing Ryan across the cheek, as he slammed the elbow of his other arm against the back of Watts's head, knocking him out cold. Watts swerved into the oncoming lane. Twin spots of light raced toward the car. A horn blasted. Mom reached over and jerked the steering wheel the other way. We smashed into the guardrail and rebounded, spinning almost a complete three-sixty before coming to a stop. Watts's head came to rest on the steering-wheel horn, provoking a sustained, three-toned wail.

"Grab his gun," Stuart yelled, pointing back at Ryan. But Ryan wasn't incapacitated. He was angry. He reached for his gun before Seth or I could grab it.

"I wouldn't do that if I were you," Stuart said. In his hand he held Watts's gun, and pointed it right at Ryan's head.

Chapter 12

"Hands where I can see them," Stuart ordered. "Seth, grab his gun."

"Seth, don't do it," Ryan growled.

"The gun, Seth!"

Seth hesitated, but finally reached back and took Ryan's gun from its holster.

"You don't know what you're doing, kid."

Seth tightened his grip on the gun. He couldn't quite bring himself to point it at anyone, though, or to put his finger on the trigger, I noticed.

"Okay, now everyone out of the car," Stuart ordered.

No problem there. I couldn't get out of Watts's car fast enough. The ground was cold and wet and the gravel bit into my bare feet, but I didn't care. I finally felt like I could breathe again.

Seth climbed from the car as Stuart held the gun on Ryan.

Without taking his eyes off Ryan, Stuart motioned with his bandaged hand to Seth. "Lemme see that thing. Is it even loaded?"

Seth furrowed his brows, turning the gun over in his hands. Stuart snatched it with his three good fingers. "Worthless!" He threw it to the other side of the road, where it skittered across the asphalt. The wheel of a passing car caught the gun and twirled it on the road like some macabre game of spin the bottle. The muzzle slowly came to a stop—pointed back at us.

Mom jumped out and ran to my side. "Are you all right? What was that? What's happening?"

"It's okay. I'm fine," I assured her.

Stuart made Watts and Ryan get out of the SUV with their hands clasped behind their heads. He ordered them to kneel on the wet road while Seth frisked them to make sure they weren't carrying any other weapons. If I didn't thoroughly dislike Watts, I might have felt sorry for the guy. He looked so confused . . . and chagrined for having been overcome in front of both his former and current partners—by a guy with one good hand, no less.

Once he was sure they didn't have any weapons, Stuart allowed them to stand.

"Why the hell'd you hit me?" Watts demanded, rubbing the back of his head.

"Effect," Stuart said. "Get the ring."

My head spun. They were *together*?

Watts stepped up to Seth and stuck out his hand. "Give me the ring, kid."

Mom gasped. "You! Both of you! How could you, you dirty—"

"Ah, ah, ah." Stuart pointed the gun at her. "Watch that temper, Nat."

Watts poked his finger in Seth's chest. "The ring!" he demanded.

Seth didn't even flinch. "I don't have it."

"Of course you have it," Stuart snapped. "Your little girlfriend here told me all about it."

Seth shot me a disbelieving look and I shook my head wildly. I wanted to deny telling Stuart about the ring, but that seemingly insignificant moment on the plane came back to me all too clearly.

"You knew the kid had the ring all this time?" Watts sniped. "Why didn't you just take it and save us all this trouble?"

"I needed them to get me off the mountain," Stuart said simply.

"Stuart." Mom's voice shook. "Why are you doing this?"

He laughed humorlessly. "Well, it's like my daddy used to say: 'Son, keep your friends close and your enemies closer.'"

"Enemies? But . . . we're on the same side."

Stuart laughed and I have to say, it was about the ugliest sound I've ever heard. "Well, you got that wrong."

"But . . . why?"

"You were getting too close. I joined you and Joe to keep an eye on you, Nat."

"We were right, then. The Mole had someone inside the Agency."

"No, you were wrong. The Mole has *several* someones."

"And you are one of them."

"Bingo."

"But how could you?" Mom exclaimed. "What about Joe? Did you kill him?"

Stuart laughed again. The sound made my stomach turn. "Not personally, no."

Mom looked stung. "Damian?" she said, calling Watts by his first name. "*You* killed him?"

"I got bills to pay, Natalie. I'm gonna give my services to the highest bidder."

"But why? Why Joe? Why not—"

Stuart laughed humorlessly. "He found something, Nat. A list of names on that ring of young Romeo's here. That's why he wanted you to meet him. He discovered a name on the ring that I could not afford to have revealed. Mine."

The confusion lingered in her eyes. "Your name was on that list? You mean . . . you're a sleeper? But . . . your parents!"

"Yes, that was a nice touch, wasn't it? Their deaths went a long way toward convincing the Agency to embrace me. Who better to trust than some poor kid whose parents were killed by the Bad Guy?"

"What are you saying? You killed your own parents?"

"They defected. *They* chose their demise."

I stared at him in horror. Suddenly he wasn't the annoying and pathetic nerd anymore. He was a monster. And if he was the kind of person who would kill his own parents, we were in deep trouble.

The monster turned to Seth. "Give the man the ring, kid."

"I. Don't. Have. It."

Stuart was not amused. He gave Watts a look and then nodded at me. Watts grabbed my arm and yanked me forward. Stuart shoved the cold gun barrel against my scalp and drew the hammer back with a click. "One more time, kid. Where's the—"

"Don't shoot!" I cried. "He really doesn't have it! I swear."

"Start talking." He pressed the metal harder and harder into my skin until I winced.

"He gave it to me. Before the river. H-he didn't have any pockets and I did, so he gave it to me to hold!"

Stuart raised a brow and looked at Seth. "Is that true?"

Lie, Seth. Lie!

"Yeah, I gave it to her."

"Well," Stuart drawled. "Isn't that nice." He lowered the gun. "Aphra, sweetheart, I need you to give me the ring."

"I—I don't have it anymore."

Watts grabbed a handful of my hair and yanked my head back. As if that wasn't painful enough, Stuart jammed the gun against my cheek. "I'm going to ask you one last time—"

"Stop! Stop this!" Mom jumped toward me. "You leave her alone!"

Watts backhanded her and sent her sprawling onto the pavement. She tried to get up and he kicked her down again. She lay still. Rage poured out of me. I didn't even think of the consequences. I wrenched away from Watts's grip and jumped on him like a cat on fire, clawing, biting, spitting. He threw me to the ground, but I got some pretty good licks in first.

Watts pulled back his foot to kick me, too. I rolled to the side, drawing my legs up and covering my head with my hands. Then something exploded. Watts dropped to the ground, screaming and holding his knee. Blood oozed from between his fingers.

"Oh, be quiet." Stuart sneered and lowered the gun. "One thing I cannot abide is a man who loses control." He held up his bandaged hand with the missing fingers. "I'd say we're even now."

Leaving Watts to whimper on the ground, Stuart turned to me again. "You see, Aphra? I'm losing my patience. Please give me the ring."

"I swear, I don't have it. I lost it when I got tossed from the kayak!"

"Oh, really." He pointed the gun straight at Seth. "I'm through playing games. You have until the count of three to tell me the truth. One . . ."

"Wait!" I scrambled to my feet.

Seth looked at me with wild eyes, shaking his head no. I knew he was afraid to lose the ring for fear of losing his dad, but the way I saw it, if Seth was dead, his dad would be dead, too.

"No, please!" I pleaded. "It's at the bottom of the river, Stuart! If I could give it to you, I would—"

"Two . . ."

"Wait! I'm sorry! I'm sorry! I have it!"

Seth's shoulders slumped.

"Please," I cried. "Don't hurt him." I pulled the sweat-shirt sleeve back and slid the ring slowly from my thumb.

"Aphra, no," Seth whispered.

I couldn't look at him, couldn't bear to see the defeat on his face. I kept my eyes on Stuart and held the ring out to him. He took the ring in his bandaged hand. Looked down.

That was all I needed. I kicked up and out and caught him square in the stomach. Not that I have a powerful roundhouse or anything, but with his hurt ribs, it was enough to make him stumble backward, off balance. Ryan flew at him and grabbed Stuart's injured hand, twisting his arm behind his back until he dropped to his knees. The gun clattered to the road. Ryan kicked it away.

"Down on the ground!" he yelled, twisting Stuart's arm higher. He forced Stuart facedown onto the concrete.

Seth jumped in then, peeling Stuart's fingers back one by one until he let go of the ring.

"Aphra!" Mom yelled.

I had been so intent on the fight that I hadn't noticed Watts drag himself toward Stuart's discarded gun. I pounced on the gun and scooped it up. It felt cold and awkward and *wrong* in my hand. Trembling, I gripped it tight and pointed the barrel at Watts. "Stop right there," I warned.

He didn't stop, but lunged for my ankle. I danced away. "Stop! Now!"

He crawled forward on his elbows.

I aimed the gun at the ground near Watts's head and squeezed the trigger. The gun kicked so hard, I could feel the pain all the way up my arm. The gravel sprayed up in front of his face. He stopped.

Mom pushed up from the ground and limped over to where I stood, ears still ringing from the gunshot. She nudged Watts with her foot. "Valuable lesson, Damian. Don't mess with my daughter."

Ryan took control of the scene. It was weird to watch him in his agent's role. I preferred the image of laid-back college student.

While Mom held the gun on Stuart and Watts, Ryan grabbed some plastic zip-tie handcuffs from the SUV.

With Seth's help, he trussed them up like Sunday chickens and hauled them to the side of the road.

He asked me to retrieve his service revolver from where Stuart had tossed it. I brought it back to him gingerly. Despite what Stuart had said to cover for throwing the gun away, I was pretty sure it was loaded. I'd had enough of loaded guns for one night.

"Here you go," I said.

"Thanks, Aphra. I owe you one."

I shrugged and stepped back.

He snapped the gun into his shoulder holster. "I'm sorry about Seth's dad," he said.

"How did you—never mind. I don't want to know."

"That's probably best."

I looked at my hands. "I'm sorry we left you in the plane."

"It was a good call. You did what you had to do."

"It wasn't easy."

"None of it was. But you did good." He looked over to where Mom was talking with Seth. "Ever thought about following in your mom's footsteps and joining the Agency?"

"Not on your life."

He chuckled. "You know, I'm going to have to call for an ambulance."

"Okay."

"And because a weapon was discharged, there will be an investigation. I'll need to call for backup."

"Uh-huh . . . oh!" If he called for backup and Seth was still there . . .

He laid a gentle hand on my arm. "You know, Aphra, they can give me a ride, if you want to take off."

It took me a moment to understand his meaning. "So you don't need us to wait around until your . . . ride gets here?"

"No. I have things under control—thanks to you. Go on. Get going before I change my mind. Watts left the keys in the ignition."

"I don't understand. We can take the Escalade?"

"It's yours."

"You don't even want the ring?"

He shrugged. "Me, personally? No. It's not my style. The Agency? Well, I'm sure they'd like to look at it. But I think young Mulo over there needs it more than they do."

"You're letting us go."

"I'm giving you a head start."

I didn't know what to say. I gave him a quick hug. "Thank you, Ryan. I mean it."

"Hey, they told me to watch over you. Keep you safe. I'm just doing my job."

CHAPTER
13

We drove down the mountain in silence. In some areas, the mist was so thick that Mom had to slow the SUV to a crawl until we passed through it. She gripped the steering wheel during those times in a white-knuckled stranglehold. The glow from the dashboard lights illuminated her frown and the tenseness of her jaw. Time was running out. Every minute that passed was another minute Seth's dad was held captive.

About halfway down the mountain, an ambulance passed us going the other way, lights flashing, siren blaring. "They'll send the backup next," I murmured.

Mom glanced at me and then back at the road. "What?"

"Backup," I repeated. "He said he was going to call for an ambulance and backup."

She nodded, but didn't say anything for several miles. Finally, she spoke. "How long did you know?"

I furrowed my brows. "About?"

"Ryan. How did you know we could trust him?"

"I still don't know that we can. Maybe he handed off Stuart and Watts and he's on his way down the hill to get us right now."

She nodded. "He has a job to do." She stared straight

ahead, her mouth set in a grim line. "But I'm sorry you've had to learn not to trust."

"So am I." I closed my eyes and leaned my head against the seat back.

Ryan's words echoed in my head. *They told me to watch over you.*

There's a thin line between suspicion and paranoia and I hate to think I may have crossed it, but the more I thought about it, the more suspicious I became. The vehicle we were driving belonged to—and had been equipped by—the Agency. An Agency man had suggested we take it. Why?

It could be that he felt bad for the things that had happened. It could be that he was letting us go out of the goodness of his heart, but I didn't believe it. It was likely bugged. And there was no doubt in my mind that we were driving around in a huge tracking device.

Maybe Ryan sent us away—in his vehicle—because he wanted to see what we would say and where we would go. Maybe we weren't the endgame. Maybe we were pawns. Which meant we had to ditch the SUV. Fast.

My eyes flew open and I bolted upright. "I need to go," I said. "The first rest stop. It's an emergency."

Mom shot me a look. "Are you feeling all right? You want me to pull over now?" The concern in her voice almost made me want to cry.

"I'll be fine until the next rest area," I assured her. "But hurry."

We couldn't reach the rest stop quickly enough. I fidgeted more and more as each mile marker whizzed by. Mom kept giving me anxious glances and I'm sure she thought the worst.

"If you want me to pull over . . ."

"Rest stop, one mile," Seth called from the backseat.

Mom looked relieved. Not nearly as relieved as I was... or would be once we got rid of the Escalade.

The turn signal tapped a staccato rhythm as she pulled off the road and into the parking area. She switched off the engine.

"Why don't we all go," I suggested, "so we won't have to stop again."

Mom gave me a strange look, but thankfully she didn't argue. Seth, however, didn't seem to get the message. He made no move to open his door until I twisted around in my seat and gave him the evil eye.

When he got out I grabbed his arm and pulled him clear of the SUV. He followed, but hesitantly. I'm sure he thought I'd lost my mind. "What is going on?"

"It may be nothing." I glanced back at the Escalade. "It's just that back at the apartment Stuart said he tracked everything, like it was standard procedure. Then, of course, there was that tracker on the plane. And then when Ryan gave us the keys . . ."

Mom nodded grimly. "I wondered about that."

"So what are we going to *do*?" Seth asked.

I folded my arms. "We're going to get another ride."

• • •

Mom did the asking. We figured she'd seem more legitimate than a couple of teenagers, but still, I was amazed at how easy it was for her to swap cars.

She approached a guy who had stopped to buy a Coke from the vending machine. He was dressed in jeans and hiking boots, and wearing a North Face jacket. From where we were standing, I could see a large backpack in the back of his Jeep.

I couldn't hear exactly what Mom said, but it didn't take long for her to convince the hiker guy to trade vehicles with us. Even though it had been my idea, his response baffled me. I mean, he had to wonder why she would want to exchange a loaded, top-of-the-line Escalade—albeit with some bumper damage from the guardrail—for a rusted out, dented, plastic-for-windows Jeep. Normal people don't do things like that. Plus in our matching gray sweats and bare feet, we looked like escaped convicts or something. Wouldn't he at least consider that the Escalade might be stolen? But no, he didn't even balk.

"You're on," he said, pulling his Jeep key off of a jangling key ring.

"Where are you headed?" Mom asked—a little too casually, I thought.

"Up the pass."

"You going to hike the backcountry?" she asked.

He looked at her like she was an idiot. "Um, yeah." He stopped just short of adding, "Duh."

Perfect.

Mom and I stood together and watched him drive off. I hoped he enjoyed himself before the Agency caught up with him and demanded their property back.

We quickly inspected his Jeep. Mom was pleased to find that the gas tank was nearly full. That meant we wouldn't have to stop for gas for a long time. Which was a good thing, considering that we had no money. I found his registration paper in the glove box.

"He's from Bridgeport. Where's that?"

"About eighty miles from here. It's on the way to Spokane."

"We're going to Spokane?"

She bent to check the tire pressure. "I can access funds there."

The finality in her voice didn't invite questions, although I did wonder just how far-reaching that undercover operation she had been working in was. I had thought it was just her, Joe, and Stuart, but she must have contacts elsewhere. How else was she going access anything without the benefit of identification? I realized anew that there was a lot about my mom's life that I didn't understand.

"You're sure he can reclaim his Jeep?" I asked her for the tenth time.

"We'll leave it in a tow-away zone. They'll impound it and send him notification."

With that, Mom climbed into the driver's seat and

fastened her seat belt. I hesitated. "Do you mind if I ride in the back with Seth?"

She glanced back to where Seth was settling onto the small backseat. I could read all sorts of caution in her eyes and I understood her reserve; she didn't want me to get hurt. But she and I both knew it was already too late for that. She sighed. "Fine. For now."

I climbed into the back and Seth pulled me close to him. We were together. That was all that mattered for the moment.

Mom turned the key in the ignition. After two tries the Jeep's engine roared to life. We rattled out of the rest stop—in the opposite direction from the Escalade.

Conversation was impossible inside the Jeep. The wind whistled through the flimsy windows and flapped the canvas roof. But I didn't really want to talk, anyway. The only thing Seth and I had left to say was good-bye and I wasn't ready for that yet.

We reached Bridgeport about one in the morning. It was a sleepy little town, snuggled up to the Columbia River. I knew that only because we had been driving alongside the river for several miles, and because a sign at the entrance to town proclaimed Bridgeport "Gateway to the Mighty Columbia River." The whole town was only about six blocks deep and maybe a couple dozen blocks long.

"Forget a tow-away zone," I said. "Everyone in town will probably recognize the guy's Jeep on sight."

"Yes," Mom agreed. "It does pose a problem."

"A problem? This makes it easier for him."

"For him, yes." Mom tapped her fingers on the steering wheel as we drove slowly down the street. "But it's going to make our borrowing another car unnoticed more of a challenge."

"Maybe we should keep going," Seth put in. "Ditch the Jeep in the next town over."

Mom shook her head. "Wouldn't do much good. There's nothing but small towns for at least another hour. Our hiking friend could have been picked up by now, and if so, we can't afford to stay with his vehicle even one moment longer."

We trawled the town along the waterfront until Mom saw what she was looking for. "Out-of-state plates," she said, pointing to a Toyota pickup that looked like it had seen better days. "It'll be snug for a while, but it will have to do."

I, of course, didn't mind being snug. I wasn't too crazy about the stale cigarette smell in the truck, but I was beyond being picky. We left Bridgeport—and the Jeep—behind and turned east toward Spokane.

Remembering my mom's advice, I snuggled close and rested my head on Seth's shoulder. We had a two-hour drive ahead of us, and after that, who knew when we could sleep? Wrapped in his arms, I closed my eyes and allowed myself to dream.

•••

I woke to the glow of a Denny's sign. We were parked on the outer edge of the parking lot and Seth was shaking my shoulder. "Time to wake up."

Mom handed me a pair of cheap tennis shoes, the Wal-mart price tag still attached. "We're dumping the truck here. It's just a short walk to the hotel."

I tore off the tag and slipped the shoes onto my feet. I was too tired to question when she had bought them. *How* she had bought them. Had she already "accessed" her funds? In the morning I would look for answers, but for the time being, all I wanted to think about was a hot shower and a warm bed. And the fact that Seth would be with me a little while longer.

Seth and I waited on a bench in front of the hotel while my mom went inside to register. Neither of us said anything for a long while.

He picked up my hand, turned it over in his. I hadn't paid attention until then to exactly how filthy my hands were, with dirt caked black under my fingernails like a mechanic's. Blistered from bushwhacking. Unattractive. But Seth didn't seem to notice. He threaded his fingers through mine and looked into my eyes.

"I'll have to go soon," he said. "And then . . ."

I knew without hearing the words. Once Seth's dad was safe, the Mulos would move on. Seth would become someone else. He could not risk contacting me again.

"I wish it were different," he said.

"So do I." My throat was so tight, I could barely get the words out.

"Where . . ." His voice cracked. He cleared his throat and tried again. "Where will you go from here?"

I frowned. "I haven't really thought about it. I'm not sure if I can go home. Not until this is over." I didn't even know what "this" was, or if it would ever be over, but the words sounded right at the time.

"I'll think of you," he said.

I dropped my eyes so he wouldn't see the tears welling up in them. "I'll think of you, too," I whispered.

Mom came out of the lobby then, the tiredness etched deep in the lines of her face. I looked up at her, questioning. "Did you get a room?"

She didn't answer me. In fact, she didn't even look at me. "Seth," she said. "I need you to come with me for a moment."

Seth stood, and I jumped up beside him. I tightened my grip on his hand. I didn't like the sound of her voice. "Mom, what is it?"

She looked at me with sad eyes. "It will be easier this way."

I heard the car pull into the parking lot, heard it crunch over the gravel as it came nearer, but still I didn't want to believe it.

Seth pulled me close one last time. I clung to him, my tears soaking the shoulder of his sweatshirt, darkening the fabric. He stroked my back, my hair. His lips found mine and he kissed me deeply.

Behind him the car's engine idled. A man's voice said, "Seth. It's time."

Seth started to pull away, but I clung to him tighter.

He pulled my arms loose. "I have to go now," he whispered.

I wiped my eyes and tried to smile at him. "Say hi to your dad for me."

"Aphra—"

"No!" I stepped back. "Don't say it. I'm not ready for good-bye."

He brushed my lips with his one last time before he got into the car. And then he was gone.

Mom slipped her arm around my waist and stood with me. I laid my head on her shoulder. We didn't talk. We didn't have to. We watched the car drive away until its red taillights faded into the darkness.

EPILOGUE

My name is Marissa Vaterlaus and I'm about to begin the new semester at an exclusive boarding school in southern France. At least that's what it says on my visa.

According to the computer, I checked into a posh New York hotel three weeks ago for one last shopping fling before hitting the books. In actuality, I didn't become Marissa until today. This afternoon, in fact. I needed to remain Aphra Connolly long enough to send my dad a card. On the back I drew a picture of two forget-me-nots, intertwined. I hoped he'd understand.

It was a dangerous gamble, sending the message. The Mole seriously wanted Aphra dead and making contact of any sort gave him a location of origin to trace. But I couldn't let Aphra go without some kind of good-bye to her father.

Especially since she may never see him again.

I'll meet my mother in Paris tomorrow.

We have a lot of catching up to do.

An Imprint of Penguin Group (USA) Inc.

For Nin

SLEUTH / SPEAK
Published by the Penguin Group
Penguin Group (USA) Inc., 345 Hudson Street, New York, New York 10014, U.S.A.
Penguin Group (Canada), 90 Eglinton Avenue East, Suite 700,
Toronto, Ontario, Canada M4P 2Y3 (a division of Pearson Penguin Canada Inc.)
Penguin Books Ltd, 80 Strand, London WC2R 0RL, England
Penguin Ireland, 25 St Stephen's Green, Dublin 2, Ireland (a division of Penguin Books Ltd)
Penguin Group (Australia), 250 Camberwell Road, Camberwell, Victoria 3124, Australia
(a division of Pearson Australia Group Pty Ltd)
Penguin Books India Pvt Ltd, 11 Community Centre,
Panchsheel Park, New Delhi - 110 017, India
Penguin Group (NZ), 67 Apollo Drive, Rosedale, North Shore 0632, New Zealand
(a division of Pearson New Zealand Ltd)
Penguin Books (South Africa) (Pty) Ltd, 24 Sturdee Avenue,
Rosebank, Johannesburg 2196, South Africa

Registered Offices: Penguin Books Ltd, 80 Strand, London WC2R 0RL, England

Published by Speak, an imprint of Penguin Group (USA) Inc., 2009.
This omnibus edition published by Speak, an imprint of Penguin Group (USA) Inc., 2010

1 3 5 7 9 10 8 6 4 2

LIBRARY OF CONGRESS CATALOGING-IN-PUBLICATION DATA
Gerber, Linda C.
Death by denim / Linda Gerber.—Sleuth ed.
p. cm.
Summary: Sixteen-year-old Aphra and her mother, a CIA agent, are hiding in France after having been given new identities, but they must go on the run again when their location is discovered by a dangerous criminal.
ISBN 978-0-14-241119-3 (pbk. : alk. paper) [1. Spies—Fiction. 2. Criminals—Fiction 3. France—Fiction. 4. Italy—Fiction.] I. Title.
PZ7.G293567Def 2009
[Fic]—dc22
2008041322

Speak ISBN 978-0-14-241119-3
This omnibus ISBN 978-0-14-241826-0

Printed in the United States of America

Acknowledgments

The writing of this book was made possible by the encouragement and support of my family who continue to be my number-one cheerleaders. Thanks, guys!

Also, special thanks to my CPs, Jen, Ginger, Barb, Nicole, Julie, Kate, Karen, and Marsha for their wisdom and patience, and to Davide and Natalie Lorenzi, Jonathan Neve, and Ammi-Joan Paquette for their generous language and translation help.

As always, I am indebted to the fantastic team at Puffin for bringing the book to life. Heartfelt thanks to Angelle Pilkington (welcome to the new addition!), Grace Lee (best of luck with nursing!), and Kristin Gilson (I appreciate the 11th hour save!) for their editorial genius, and to designers Theresa Evangelista and Linda McCarthy for their brilliant cover designs. It's been my sincere pleasure to work with the best people in the business!

DEATH BY DENIM

CHAPTER 1

I knew it was just a matter of time before they caught up with us. Knew it every morning as I kissed my mother good-bye and walked out the door. Knew it every afternoon as I rode my bike home from the school in Lyon, France, where I had enrolled under a counterfeit name. Knew it every minute of every day, so it shouldn't have hit me with such a jolt when I noticed the man following me. But it did.

Part of the shock, I suppose, was the realization that I'd seen him before. Despite all the rules and techniques my mom had tried to drill into my head since we'd slipped underground, his presence hadn't more than grazed my consciousness before. Looking back, I recognized how often he'd been in shadows or hovering around the periphery of my attention. It wasn't until he grew bold and walked right past me, though, that all the other sightings registered in my head. Then everything fell into place—*thunk, thunk, thunk, thunk*—like bars in a cage locking tight.

We'd been out to dinner, my mom and I. It was a beautiful evening with the first promise of summer riding on the breeze, and a sky so clear above us that the stars shone like a million tiny lanterns. We strolled along the Rhône River on our way home, watching the barges glide past, the reflection of their lights stretching across the inky water like shimmering tentacles.

I let my mind wander; I imagined those barges following the river until eventually it emptied into the open sea. How long would it take them to sail from ocean to ocean and finally reach the island I used to call home?

Like before, I was so preoccupied that the man's presence barely registered. He'd been leaning against the stone retaining wall, smoking. Watching us, I know now. As we neared, he pushed away from the wall and dropped his cigarette, grinding it out with the toe of a snakeskin boot. I'm not sure if it was the movement or the boot that drew my attention. All I know is that I was suddenly very aware of him striding toward us.

As I'd been taught, I made a quick catalog of his features without letting my eyes fully rest on his face. He stood a full head taller than me, broad-shouldered but thin almost to the point of being lanky. Even in the darkness, I could see the leathery texture of his skin, like he'd spent a lot of time in the wind and sun. He reminded me of the kind of rugged outdoorsy types they featured in those old Marlboro cigarette ads.

Mom must have felt me stiffen next to her as he neared because she slipped her arm through mine to propel me forward. "Keep walking," she whispered. She didn't have to remind me, though; I knew the drill. *Head up, no eye contact. Just. Act. Casual.*

I patted her hand and laughed as if she'd said something really clever. Okay, so maybe the pat and the laugh were overkill, but I had to do *something* to mask the pounding in my chest and the weird catch in my throat as I drew each breath.

The man brushed past me, so close that the sleeve of his denim shirt touched my arm and I could smell the sharp burnt-roofing-tar stench on his breath. The vibration of his snakeskin boots striking the stones so close to my feet seemed to echo *run, run, RUN!* But even then, I didn't know exactly why.

It took several steps for the dark, smoky stink to register in my head as familiar. And the boots. I'd seen them before. That's when it all came flooding back. That's when I knew.

We'd been found.

To be honest, I was surprised we lasted as long as we did. Despite my very real-looking fake passport and student visa, I had been sure from the moment my mom and I arrived in France that everyone we met must know we were imposters. We kept to ourselves at home and I didn't make friends at school, but no one seemed to notice. I was one of the few students who wasn't boarding there as well and, from the talk I heard in the hallways, they just thought I was a stuck-up American.

By the time we passed the half year mark without incident, I had dared to believe that we might be safe after all. We lived a quiet expat life, me going to a real school instead of taking online classes, and my mom acting like a normal mother instead of a CIA agent. I think we both liked the role-playing reality so much that we wanted it to be true. Little by little, despite the constant training to be vigilant, we began to slip into our faux identities. We began to relax.

Maybe that's why they waited so long to hunt for us. They must have known that once our guard was down, we'd be easier to catch. Exactly who "they" were, I couldn't say, except that they worked for a man called The Mole. He was the leader of a sleeper cell who had turned to organized crime to fund his operation. Both my mom and I had gotten in his way at one point or another, and the man held a grudge.

The Mole and his minions remained faceless to me, which made them all the more terrifying; I never knew who to trust. Plus, I had seen what those minions could do. Twice I had watched people die because of them—first a woman named Bianca on our island back home and then Joe, my mom's CIA partner, in Seattle.

All I could think as the man's footsteps echoed behind me was that the past had caught up with us. It was starting all over again. And I could be next.

Mom's fingers pressed into my skin. "Up," she whispered, steering me toward the stairs that led to street level. We climbed slowly, casually, even as panic swelled in my chest, urging me to move faster.

As we reached the top of the stairs, I could see a nightclub about half a block to the left, music and patrons filling the street in front of it. I grabbed my mom and tried to drag her toward the safety of lights and people. It was all I could do not to break into a run, but she held me back.

"What's the matter?" she asked in a low voice. "Who was that man?"

"I don't know who he is but I think he—" My throat constricted, pinching off the words. I had to take a breath and start again. "I think he's following us."

Her brows shot up. "You've seen him before?"

She didn't have to voice the reprimand behind her words; I knew I should have been more aware. I nodded miserably.

She pressed her lips together and nodded. That was enough for the moment, but I knew I would have to explain once it was over. "Let's go."

Even in the balmy night air, my stomach had turned to ice. I focused on the lights of the club and tried not to think about the man behind us. I could feel Mom close behind me and that gave me some comfort, but I still felt as if I had a huge bull's-eye painted between my shoulders.

As we got closer to the club, the music thrummed so loud that I could literally feel the beat. I had to yell to be heard as I pushed my way through the crowd to the open door. *"Pardon. Pardon. Excuse-moi."*

Once inside, I paused to get my bearings. It was one of the rules Mom had drilled into me: *Know where the exits are at all times.* The problem was, the inside of the club was darker than the night outside, with a confusion of colored lights flashing, twirling, pulsing to the music. I could barely make out the silhouette of chairs and tables and people, let alone the layout of the building. A stairway just inside the door led up to a balcony that overlooked the main room of the club, but I knew better than to take the stairs. *Don't escape up.* It wouldn't do us any good to get trapped on a roof with no way down.

Mom pressed close against my back and pointed toward the rear of the club. I squinted through the darkness and relief flooded over me as I spotted a door beyond the bar. An exit. We wound our way around tables and past a crowded dance floor, the dancers jerking like silent film actors underneath the strobe lights.

Suddenly, a man's hand grabbed mine and twirled me onto the floor. I reacted on instinct, all those months of self-defense training with my mom switching into autopilot. I yanked my arm up and out, breaking the hold, while at the same time stomping with my heel as hard as I could. It wasn't until that moment that I realized the man before me was not my pursuer at all, but a much younger guy with brown eyes that widened in surprise—and then pain—as my foot slammed down onto his insole.

"Oh!" I cried. *"Je suis désolée!"* But I didn't have

time for much more of an apology than that. My mom whisked me away before I could do anything else to draw unwanted attention.

I could hear the dancer guy behind us swearing loudly in French, telling anyone who would listen that I was crazy and that all he had wanted to do was dance with me. I didn't have time to feel bad about it. Besides, it was his own fault. He should have asked first.

Still, Mom couldn't resist pressing her cheek close to mine and whispering, "Assess the situation *before* you act!"

"I know," I muttered. "I know."

We reached the back door without further incident and pushed out into a dark alley behind the club. Dirt and age had yellowed the bare bulb above the door so that its weak light barely managed to reach the bottom of the stoop. Shadows swallowed the empty crates and garbage cans beyond. Carefully, we picked our way down the alley to where it intersected the street.

"Now," Mom said, "why don't you tell me what—"

"Shh!" I grabbed her arm and pulled her deeper into the shadows, sniffing the air like a bloodhound. My nose filled with the same raw, burning odor I had noticed when the Marlboro Man passed us by the river. "Do you smell that?"

She frowned. "What?" For a moment I wondered if I had been imagining things, but then her lips parted for a quick intake of breath and her eyes grew wide. "French cigarettes," she whispered. "Cheap ones. Perhaps even hand rolled. Those can be more pungent."

Side by side, we peered around the corner of the building. Sure enough, Marlboro Man stood not more than three feet away from us, sucking on his cheap cigarette, watching the entrance. I was right; he *had* been following us.

"Come on," Mom whispered, and pulled me back down the alley. We slipped down a side street and broke into a full-on run. Looking back, I'm pretty sure my mom had a destination in mind, but all I was thinking about was getting away.

We had gone maybe three or four blocks when Mom slowed to a brisk walk. She scanned the street and then stooped to pick up a loose rock. I thought maybe she was going to try to use it to clobber the Marlboro Man if he came after us, but then we came to a chrome-and-glass phone booth, its flickering fluorescent light casting reverse shadows along the brick sidewalk.

"Keep an eye out," Mom said, and opened the door to the booth. She stepped inside and swung the rock upward, shattering the light.

I jumped at the sound, but I have to admit I was grateful for the resulting cover of darkness.

Inside the booth, Mom picked up the receiver and punched in a number. I inched forward and nudged the edge of the door with my toe so that it wasn't closed all the way. The call connected and I could hear the burr of the phone ringing on the other end of the line. A man's voice answered.

"C'est moi," Mom said softly. It's me.

All I heard from the receiver for a long moment was silence, and then the man spoke again. I couldn't make out the words, but there was no mistaking the tone of the voice—low and urgent.

Mom listened quietly and then nodded, as if the man—whoever he was—could see her head move. *"Oui."* She paused again. *"Je comprends."* And then she hung up.

I jumped back as she replaced the receiver, even though I was pretty sure she knew I'd been listening. Before turning to face me, she straightened her sagging posture, and then pushed through the door and started walking. "We have to go."

It took half a second for her words to register. She didn't mean go, as in get away from the phone booth; she meant go, as in clear out. Leave town. Immediately. And, though we had been prepared all along for that eventual probability, I suddenly felt lost.

"Our bags . . ."

"We can't go back for them," Mom said, already walking away. I had to run to keep up with her.

A weight settled on my chest as I realized we were going to abandon the Lyon apartment we had lived in for the past seven months. It's not like we had a lot of memories there, just trappings of our fake lives, but since we'd left everything else behind when we slipped underground, those trappings were all I had. Leaving everything behind was like losing myself all over again.

I started making a mental list of the things I would miss. There wasn't much; we had made a point of not gathering things that could be used to identify us. We kept no journals, took no photos, we didn't have an answering machine because we had no phone. But . . . my heart sank. We had each kept a small bag with a change of clothes, a little bit of cash and extra copies of our fake identification next to the door in the apartment, in case we needed to leave in a hurry. Even those would be lost. Not that our fake IDs would do us any good now that we'd been found, but it felt like the last thread tying me to the past had been severed.

"What now?" I asked. I hated how small and lost my voice sounded.

Mom didn't even slow her step. "That man on the phone was my contact with the Paris Station. He'll make new arrangements for us."

The CIA's Paris office? I tried not to let my surprise—and concern—show. When we left the States, my mom had taken care of all the details herself because The Mole's minions had infiltrated the Agency and she wasn't sure who she could trust.

My silence must have given away my thoughts,

because she nudged me with her shoulder. "Hey. Don't worry." She tried to sound light and upbeat. "Lévêque will take care of us. We'll meet with him first thing in the morning. Everything will be fine." She gave me a smile that I'm sure was supposed to convey confidence, but after so much time together I was getting to know her too well. I'd come to recognize the little twitch at the corner of her mouth as a sign that she was worried.

She reached for my hand like I was a little kid. "Come, now. The last train to Paris leaves at ten so we'll have to hurry."

Hand in hand we sprinted for the station, arriving out of breath just moments before the train was supposed to leave. The ticket windows were closed so we had to buy our tickets from the machines. It felt like forever that Mom was feeding coins into the slot and another eternity for the machine to print and spit out our tickets. We grabbed them and raced through the turnstile, reaching the train car just as the warning chimes sounded, signaling that the doors were about to close.

The train had already started to move by the time we settled into our seats. I leaned back against the upholstery, silently saying my good-byes to Lyon. Then I noticed Mom's grip on the armrest tighten and I followed her gaze out the window.

Marlboro Man was running onto the platform. Late. Too late. I smiled at his failure . . . until it hit me. My ticket. I flipped it over and my heart dropped. Ours was an express train. No stops between Lyon and Paris. He may have missed us, but he would know exactly where we were headed. And when we would get there.

One glance at Mom and I knew she was thinking the same thing.

We were in trouble.

CHAPTER 2

I hugged my arms, eyes darting around the train car like an animal trapped in a moving cage. No, I didn't know for sure that the Marlboro guy worked for The Mole, but it was a pretty safe bet. No one else was looking for my mom and me. No one that I knew about, anyway. So if Marlboro found us, The Mole had found us. The very thought made my insides curdle.

I leaned close to Mom. "Do you think that guy has connections in Paris?" I whispered.

"I don't know."

"But he could."

She looked at me, the expression completely dissolving from her face. "Yes, he could."

I sank back in my seat. That's what I was afraid of. Now that he knew where we were headed, if Marlboro Man had colleagues in Paris, all it would take was a phone call and they could have the station surrounded by the time we got there. Or he could be waiting for us himself. Either scenario made me feel faint.

"Maybe he didn't see us get on the train," I said. But I knew he had; I could tell by the look I'd seen on his face that he knew we'd slipped through his fingers.

Mom didn't answer, but stared straight ahead, tapping her fingers on the armrest. Trying to figure out how we were going to get off the train undetected, I imagined. I hoped she would be able to come up with something, and quickly.

Me, I couldn't think of a thing, which worried me because I was usually pretty good about thinking on my feet. But then again, I hadn't clued in to being followed by the Marlboro guy, had I? It's like when I left my name behind, I lost the thinking part of me as well. I didn't know how to be me, but someone else. I was having an identity crisis, and I'd been running for only seven months. I couldn't imagine how the people who were forever uprooted by the Witness Protection Program maintained their sanity.

As soon as that thought came into my head I tried to push it out again. Because I knew what would follow, and thinking about him hurt too much. "Him" would be Seth Mulo. Seth's family was also on the run from The Mole. The difference was that Seth had been running most of his life.

When he was very young, Seth's parents defected from The Mole's sleeper organization and turned to the U.S. government for asylum. Eventually, the CIA assigned my mom to protect them. She sent Seth and his parents to hide at my dad's island resort where she thought they would be safe. She was wrong. The Mole sent an assassin to kill Seth's parents and naturally, I got caught up in the drama. Together, Seth and I spoiled The Mole's party—which was one of the reasons he wanted us dead.

I stared out at the French countryside, rolling the word *us* around and around in my head. Sadly, with Seth and I, there was no more *us*. We were too dangerous to each other to stay together. The Mole had used me to find Seth in Seattle and I wasn't willing to take the chance again. No, the only solution was for Seth and I to stay far away from each other. That wouldn't stop me from longing for him, though.

Too soon the two-hour ride had passed. I felt the momentum of the train slowing and I had to pull my thoughts from Seth. Lights dotted the landscape, increasing in number as we rolled into the city. We were almost there. I could feel the panic rising like an ice-cold blush.

I tried to act cool, but I'm sure Mom could see the way I was trembling as I turned to her and whispered. "What do we do now?"

She looked at me for a long moment and simply said, "It will be all right." But the corner of her mouth twitched when she said it—and she wasn't even smiling.

The train pulled up to the platform, creaking and groaning to a stop. My stomach twisted. How were we going to get out of the station without getting caught? There weren't many people on the train, so it's not likely we could blend with the crowd. Plus it was after midnight by then, so the station itself wasn't all that crowded. I thought about sneaking out the wrong side of the train and hiding along the tracks, but I was afraid those tracks could be electrified.

"What do we do?" I asked again.

She raised her eyes to meet mine. "I'm going to be sick."

"What?"

She pulled me close and lowered her voice to a whisper. "I'm going to pretend to be sick. Get up and walk toward the exit. I'll be right behind you. Before we get off the train, I'm going to faint. If we're lucky, they'll take us into the station office to make sure I'm all right."

"But . . ." One of the cardinal rules of being on the run was to not draw attention to yourself. Fainting on the train was sure to attract attention. On the other hand, there weren't many people around, so our exposure would be limited. And really? What alternative did we have?

We stood.

"Oh, and one more thing," Mom whispered. "We're French."

At once I understood why she would be the one fainting; Mom and I could both speak French fluently, but my accent was better. When I was just a kid, she had enrolled me in all sorts of language classes because—according to her—I had a gift with languages. She said if you teach a kid a foreign language when they're young enough, they can learn to speak without an accent. The result was that I could speak several languages like a native and a lot more at least conversationally. French was one of the native languages. So I was going to be the mouthpiece. I hoped I was up to it. I straightened. *"Oui, Maman,"* I murmured.

I strolled down the aisle as she said, trying not to look tense as I waited to hear the thud of her dropping to the ground behind me.

I was almost to the door when it happened—only when she fell, it was more like a crash than a thud. Even though I had been expecting her to faint, the noise truly startled me. Which I suppose was good, because when I whirled around to see if she was okay, my reaction was genuine.

"Maman!" I cried. *"Maman!"* She lay sprawled between the seats, her face completely slack. I bent over her and tugged on her hand—as if that would have done any good had she truly fainted. She moaned and rolled her head to the side. I dropped her hand, eyes widening in shock. Something dark and wet matted her hair to the side of her skull. Blood?

The conductor appeared out of nowhere, asking if everything was all right. I turned my eyes to him numbly, not sure what to say. We were supposed to be acting, but the blood was most definitely real. *"Ma mère est blessée,"* I said. It was the truth. My mother was hurt.

He whipped a walkie-talkie from his belt to call for

assistance and then turned his attention back to me. *"Qu'est-ce qui s'est passé?"* he asked. What happened?

Again, I could truthfully say I didn't know. I could guess; she'd probably hit her head when she fell. Beyond that, I wasn't sure. Had she planned it to make her faint seem more convincing?

Another man in a train uniform arrived, carrying a first aid kit. He set it on one of the seats and helped the conductor sit Mom up. She moaned again and blinked her eyes, but held her head fairly steady. I sighed with relief.

"Vous allez bien?" the second guy asked her. Are you all right?

She nodded weakly and allowed him to dab at her head to clean it up. Either she was a really good actress or she was a little dazed to see the amount of blood on the gauze when he pulled it away. I thought she might faint again, for real this time.

Another official-looking person crowded into the aisle behind us. She wore a pinched expression and held a clipboard in her hands. Bingo. Damage control. She would be the one responsible to make sure that the station had no liability for mom's injury.

The gauze guy finished cleaning up the wound, which turned out to be rather small, even though it had bled a lot. He offered to bandage it, but Mom declined. She'd do just as well just holding a compress to her head until it stopped bleeding, she said.

I turned to the clipboard lady and asked if there was someplace my mother could rest.

She was only too willing to comply. *"Absolument,"* she said. Absolutely.

Clipboard Lady showed us into a windowless office crowded with a desk and a couple of chairs. She said that Mom could rest there as long as she needed.

"Merci." I lowered Mom onto one of the chairs. Still holding the gauze pad to her head, she drooped forward until her head rested on the desk.

The lady hovered for a moment. Could she call someone for us? A doctor, perhaps? Did we need anything to eat? To drink? I politely told her no to everything. Mom just needed to rest. Finally, satisfied she had done her duty, the clipboard lady left the room, closing the door behind her.

Mom immediately sat up. "Is she gone?"

I folded my arms. "You scared me half to death."

"Yes, well." She dabbed gingerly at her head. "I didn't quite intend to split my head open, but it was effective, don't you think?"

"Does it hurt?"

"I've had worse. At least the drama gave us a place to hole up for a few hours."

"Hours? When do we meet with whatshisname?"

She threw her bloodied gauze into the trash can. "We won't see him until the café opens at six."

"What café?"

But she was through answering questions. She leaned back in her chair and closed her eyes. "Let's just take advantage of the room while we have it. Get some rest."

Was she kidding? "I'm not tired."

She opened one eye to look at me. "Sleep when you can—" she began, but I finished the mantra for her.

"Because you never know when you might sleep next. I know. But I'm really not tired."

"Suit yourself." She closed her eye again. Soon her breathing fell into a gentle rhythm.

I dropped onto the chair opposite the desk and watched her. It amazed me how she could switch gears like that. Plus, we had no idea if Marlboro or his friends were waiting for us outside the office. How could she be so relaxed? But then again, it *was* late. The more I fought it, the heavier my eyelids became.

The next thing I knew, Mom was shaking my shoulder and whispering my name. "Aphra."

My name, and not the fake one I had been using for the past seven months. For half a heartbeat, I thought I was home and the whole undercover thing had been one long, very bad dream. But then I realized I was still in the station office and reality came flooding back. I shook the sleep from my head. "Time to go?"

She tucked a strand of hair behind my ear. "I'm afraid so."

A quick glance at the clock on the wall told me it was past four. Two more hours until we met Lévêque. I stood. "Let's go."

We hiked to the Metro and rode the night trains all over the city until dawn. I'm afraid I was too tired to get much out of our Paris tour, but I didn't fall asleep again; the Metro wasn't quite as comfortable—or secure—as the office had been. We kept a careful watch out, in case we were being followed, but we never saw anything to make us suspicious. Still, I wasn't convinced that the Marlboro guy would give up so easily.

Finally, just past five-thirty, we got off the Metro at the Louvre-Rivoli station. Even though I knew from the name of the station that we would be next to the Louvre, I wasn't prepared for the wonder I felt as we emerged from the underground to find the museum right in front of us. The sun was about to make its morning debut so the sky was just lightening from purple to mauve, a blushing backdrop for the architecture. The early morning glow reflected softly off the glass pyramid in the courtyard. The effect was quite literally breathtaking.

I forgot all about Marlboro and gawked like a tourist as we walked past the courtyard, beyond the museum and to Tuileries Park, which stretched out behind the Louvre. I had never seen anything like it in my life. I was used to the wild beauty of the island, but the Tuileries was formal, structured, symmetrical. "It's beautiful," I breathed.

"Wait until you see the gardens," Mom said. From the pride in her voice, you'd think she landscaped the place herself. She took me by the hand and led me down the wide paths to the gardens in the center of the park. Standing in the midst of flowers and statues and sculpted shrubberies, I almost believed that we were just sightseeing, until Mom took me by the shoulders and pointed me toward one end of the park.

"Take a moment to orient yourself," she said. "If we get separated, I want you to know where you are."

I nodded, quickly sobered by the thought.

"You see down there?" she continued, pointing. "That is the Obelisk on the Place de la Concorde down the Champs Élysées. At the end of the boulevard there is the Arc de Triomphe. And this way"—she turned me to face in the opposite direction—"is the Carousel. It's like a mini Arc de Triomphe."

"Why do they call it a carousel?"

"Aphra, pay attention. You need to understand the layout of the city in case—"

"We *won't* get separated," I said. She had given me a similar spiel in Lyon, but we'd never been separated there.

"Where we are standing," she continued pointedly, "is the geographic center of the city. There are twenty districts, all laid out in a sort of clockwise spiral from here. We are in district one. If we are ever separated—"

"But we won't—"

She held up her hand to stop me. "If we *are*, I need you to go to Saint-Lazare Station. It's in the eighth district. There is a glass dome in front of the station, and an enclosed phone booth under the dome. That is our meeting place, do you understand?"

I nodded.

"Good." She smiled cheerily. "Now, shall we go get some breakfast?"

I couldn't believe she could think about *food* after all that talk about being separated, but then I quickly remembered. We were meeting Monsieur Lévêque at a café. *"Oui,"* I said quickly. "That sounds good."

I was happy to find that the café in question was a little outdoor restaurant situated right there in the park. We sat at one of the corner tables, facing outward. *Always sit with your back to the wall.*

We had barely settled into our chairs when a tall, elegantly dressed gentleman with a newspaper tucked under his arm took the table right next to ours. He reminded me of the cultured Frenchman in the old *South Pacific* movie Mom and I used to watch back when she lived with my dad and me. He laid his newspaper on the table and summoned the waiter.

"Bonjour monsieur," the waiter greeted him. *"Vous désirez?"*

"Un café serré, s'il vous plait." He ordered his coffee in a very nice baritone voice, and the waiter scurried off.

As the man waited, he unfurled the paper and began

to read. That is, he unfurled *most* of the paper. One section he laid carefully on the table, just at his elbow. His coffee arrived, he sipped delicately for a few moments, then stood and walked briskly away, leaving his newspaper folded neatly on the table.

I was about to comment on the fact when my mom stood abruptly as well. *"Bon. Allons-y,"* she said. Let's go. As she passed the man's table, she swept up the newspaper and tucked it under her arm. Smooth. Natural.

A drop! I couldn't help a flush of pleasure to realize that the cultured Frenchman must be our contact, Lévêque. It was about all I could do to contain myself as Mom and I strolled back through the park toward the Louvre. I was dying to know what was in that newspaper. Our new identities? Money? Instructions?

Finally, Mom motioned to an empty park bench and we sat. She laid the newspaper on the bench beside her. My hands itched with a longing to grab it, open it.

"Aphra," Mom said at length, "how badly do you want to see what's inside that newspaper?"

"Um, very badly?"

"I'm aware of that. Do you know how I know?"

I shook my head.

"The agitation is written all over your face, your body language. If you'd have had the chance, you would have opened the paper long before now, am I correct?"

"I suppose."

"And what do you suppose would have happened

if the paper contained sensitive information? What if someone were watching?"

I stared at her like she was speaking a foreign language. . . . One I *hadn't* learned.

"You do recall that we were being followed in Lyon, yes? Control is very important, honey. Never let your emotions dictate your actions."

"I understand," I mumbled, feeling about two feet tall.

"Now," she reached for the paper, calmly, slowly. "Let's see what the news has in store for us today."

CHAPTER
3

I was disappointed when we found no secret messages folded into the paper. No money, no maps. Nothing I would have expected. But if Mom was similarly let down, she didn't show it. She scanned the print on the front page, as composed as ever. Almost in afterthought, or so it appeared, she handed me the other section of the paper. "Here, why don't you read this one?"

I took the paper, mentally shaking my head. Duh. Our message wasn't folded up inside the paper, it was *in* the paper. Clever. "What am I looking for?" I whispered.

Her eyes never left the page. "We'll know when we find it."

I'm proud to say I was the one who spotted the notation. Actually, it was just a number, written in red ink with a fine, slanted script: *0900*. I found it above an article about Jim Morrison's grave, which lay in a famous cemetery just outside the city.

"This is an interesting article," I said. "Take a look."

She glanced at the paper I held before her and murmured, "Mm-hmm," and then turned back to the section she was reading. I deflated. Maybe the number wasn't significant after all. But then Mom folded her portion of the paper and stood. *"Etes-vous prête à partir?"* Are you ready to go?

I tried not to smile too big. *"Oui, je suis prête."*

We arrived at the cemetery a little bit early. The notation had indicated nine A.M., written in military time. We probably got there around eight-thirty. Even then, we had taken our time getting there; it was only a few miles away from where we'd been. In the end, though, there wasn't a whole lot we could do to waste time that early in the morning.

The sun had barely risen farther in the sky, but the temperature kept climbing. And the humidity. I had watched the clouds gathering overhead and hoped they would cool things down, but they just seemed to hold the moisture in the air.

We wandered through the monuments and gravestones waiting for him, feeling hot and sticky. After having spent the night on the train and slept in the station office without the benefit of a toothbrush or a change of clothes, I was starting to feel pretty rank. All I wanted was to make the contact and go find a nice, cool shower somewhere.

I got half my wish. The clouds dropped lower and then opened up, pouring down rain as if we were standing under a spigot. We ran for the cover of the trees, though we were already soaked through. Then, just as abruptly as it had begun, the rain stopped, though I didn't trust the remaining clouds. Still, no sign of Lévêque.

I was just beginning to think that we had misinterpreted the message when finally I saw him. M. Lévêque, all suave in a designer summer-weight trench coat, strolling along the path toward us. And at least *he* was smart enough to be carrying an umbrella. He stopped just a few headstones down from where we waited and stood, as if paying his respects to the unknown dead. Mom inched nearer to him, but she didn't look in his direction.

"I'm glad to see you're safe," he said in a low voice. His accent was not French.

Mom barely nodded, keeping her eyes downcast.

"Where have you been?" he continued. "You disappeared off the map. Didn't tell anyone where you were, what you were doing . . ."

She bent and straightened the shriveled stems of long-dead roses at her feet. "We were in Lyon," she said simply. "I thought it best we keep to ourselves for a while."

"We can't protect you if we don't know where you are, Natalie."

"I understand. Do you have our new cover?"

"Not yet. There have been some . . . delays."

Her posture went rigid. "What kind of delays?"

"Funding, documents. I'm sorry. We'll meet this afternoon on the running path at the Bois de Boulogne. I hope to have some news for you then." He turned to leave, but called over his shoulder. "I've left you some things with Joan of Arc."

And with that, he strode away. Mom watched him leave, her face completely blank. "Go get the umbrella," she said.

"What umbrella?"

She gestured with her eyes and I followed her gaze to see M. Lévêque pause at the cemetery exit. He folded his umbrella and hung it by its hook handle on the gate as he peeled off his raincoat. He folded the coat neatly over his arm then ambled away from the cemetery without a backward glance.

I ran and grabbed the umbrella, pretending to call out to him in case anyone was watching. *"Monsieur!"* But of course, he kept walking. I tucked the umbrella under my arm. I could feel the crinkle of paper. Money. Or more instructions.

When I returned, Mom was not waiting where I had left her. My first impulse was to run down the path looking for her, but I knew that was irrational. *Don't let your emotions rule your actions,* Mom said. I fought the urge and stayed where I was until she returned, carrying two shopping bags—one in each hand.

"What are—"

"Walk," she said.

I turned and strolled out of the cemetery with her as if it was the most natural thing in the world to have picked up an umbrella and bags in a graveyard.

We didn't open the bags until we were safely checked in to a nearby hotel and locked in our room. Mom looked inside the first bag and threw it to me. "This one's yours," she said.

I opened it like a kid at Christmas. "What is this?" I held up a running shoe.

She pulled out a new pair of running pants and held them against herself for size. "You heard him. We need to meet on the running paths this afternoon."

Whatever. I was just happy to have clean, dry clothes to change into. I tossed aside my soaking-wet Vans and slipped my feet into my new Pumas. They fit perfectly. M. Lévêque was my new best friend.

If only I had known our friendship would turn out to be so short lived.

Since we didn't have to meet M. Lévêque until late that afternoon, Mom mandated that we use some of the time we had to kill by taking a nap. I knew she was big on the rest-when-you-can thing, so I didn't argue, but I knew I wouldn't be able to sleep this time.

I lay on the bed and stared at the ceiling, wondering who I would be in my new life. I doubted we would stay in France; that cover had been blown. I hoped it would be somewhere near the ocean. Somewhere like home. The thought summoned images of my dad back on our island. A deep sadness settled on my chest as it always did when I thought about him. He would be so worried about me. I hoped my note had at least brought him some comfort.

As they often did, my thoughts then drifted back to Seth Mulo. Where was he? Was he still safe? The last time I'd seen him, he was leaving to deliver a ring The Mole wanted in exchange for Seth's dad. I could still feel his arms around me before they came for him. I never even said good-bye; I couldn't make myself form the words. Now I worried that I would never get the chance.

The CIA was supposed to be with Seth on that mission, protecting him, that much I knew, but nothing else. Whenever I asked my mom about him, she would assure me he was safe, but that's about all she would tell me. The last time I asked, she took my hand, but her grip was not gentle and mom-like and comforting. The pressure of her fingers felt like a warning. "We've talked about this," she said evenly. "Seth is safe now. Let him go."

I pulled my hand away. How easy she made it sound. *Let him go.* Like he was some carnival balloon on a string that I could just let loose and forget once he had floated away.

She didn't understand.

Seth and I shared a bond that Mom with all her agent smarts should have anticipated when she sent him to our island. He was sensitive and smart and made me feel special when I was with him. And more than that, we understood each other. We had been through hell and back together. How could she ask me to turn my back on that?

A familiar ache swelled in my throat, and my chest felt at once heavy and hollow. I didn't want to admit it, but maybe my mom was right. Seth was gone. For his safety, as well as our own, I could never see him again. Thinking about him all the time was like slow torture. Whether I liked it or not, I had to let go of his memory.

I pushed off of the bed and padded into the bathroom, where I took a long, hot shower, washed my hair, and had a good, long cry. I hoped that it would get easier as time went by.

Mom woke when I came out of the bathroom and headed in for a shower of her own. By the time we were both dressed in our new clothes, my stomach was starting to growl. We hadn't eaten since dinner the night before and that seemed like a long, long time ago.

I sat at the desk, thumbing through the guest services book the hotel had left in our room. "Can we order room service?" I asked. "I'm starving."

Mom paused from combing out her wet hair. "I saw a patisserie on the corner this morning. Why don't we go grab something?"

"Is that okay?"

She picked up the room card and the roll of euros

Lévêque had left for us and stuffed them both in her pocket. "Sure. We can cut through the hotel lobby to minimize exposure."

I tossed the amenities book aside and bounced off the bed. "How long until we have to meet at the park?"

"Not until after he gets off work at five. Another couple of hours. We have time." She opened the door and stepped aside. "After you."

I was feeling a little better since my cry in the shower. Not much, but a little. I wondered if it showed, this monumental decision I'd made. Would Mom notice? I caught a glimpse of myself in the elevator mirror as we rode down to the lobby. As far as I could see, I looked exactly the same—only in more expensive clothes. You know, the kind that real athletes wear: a layered racer tank and matching shorts, both made from that lightweight fabric that's supposed to wick the moisture away from your skin. At least that was different. I suppose that was the best I could expect.

In the lobby, we had just started walking to the door when the desk clerk called after Mom.

"Pardon, Madame." He waved an envelope at her. *"Il y a un message pour vous."*

The smile froze on her face. She thanked him, and accepted the message with about as much enthusiasm as she might have taken a vial of toxin. She turned it over to read the front and that little muscle at the side of her lips started twitching again.

"Quand est-il arrivé?" she asked. When did it arrive?

The clerk started speaking rapid-fire French, apologizing like he thought he was in trouble. He said that he had just begun his shift a short time ago and didn't know when it had arrived, only that it was there when he got in. *"Je ne sais pas,"* he kept saying, *"je ne sais pas."*

Mom managed a smile and thanked the clerk, assuring him that all was well. But I could tell she was shaken. She tucked the envelope into her pocket and suggested we use the restroom before we left for our day about town. If I hadn't already guessed something was up, I knew then; we weren't headed "about town." We were just going to the patisserie next door. We detoured to the ladies' room, where she locked the door and leaned up against it. Gingerly, she tore open the envelope and read the note inside. For the first time I could remember, she let her blank facade slip. Her eyes grew wide and her lips turned down, parting just enough to draw in a gasp. She stole a quick glance at her watch.

"What is it?" I asked.

"I need to go. Alone." She pushed the door open to one of the stalls and started ripping the note into tiny pieces, letting them drop into the toilet. "Do you remember our meeting place?"

I stared at her. "I don't understand. Isn't that only for if we became separated?"

"We will be. But only for a short while." She flushed

the note away and turned to face me, but she couldn't meet my eyes. My stomach felt hollow. This was not my usual in-control mom.

"What is it?"

She just shook her head and raked her fingers through her still-damp hair. I couldn't help but notice the way her fingers were trembling. That's when I got really scared.

"Mom . . ."

She grasped my hand. "Wait for me at the phone booth under the glass dome at the Saint-Lazare station. And if you don't see me within—"

"I'm coming with you."

She shook her head. "Not this time."

"Why? What's wrong, Mom?"

"Aphra, I need to ask you to trust me on this. I'll tell you eveything as soon as I can, but now is not the time. I'm sorry."

"How long will you be?"

Ignoring my question, she pulled the money from her pocket and peeled off four large bills. "Put these away. Wait for me at Saint-Lazare. If I am not there in two hours, go to the U.S. consulate."

I was genuinely scared by then. "What's going on? What was in that note?"

Finally, Mom gave in. "It was from Gérard Lévêque," she said in a low voice. "He says we must leave Paris immediately. I'm to meet him for instructions." She kissed me on the forehead. "Wait for me at Saint-Lazare. I love you."

And then she was gone.

If ever I needed a signal that she still thought of me as her little girl, that kiss was it. And as much as the gesture made me feel all warm and fuzzy inside, I didn't want her to see me as a helpless little girl just then. I needed her to believe in me. Maybe that's why I chose to do what I did.

I waited for a few seconds and then eased out of the ladies' room to follow her. I know I had promised that I would wait at Saint-Lazare, but I couldn't leave her. Like she said that morning, when a person lets her emotions think for her, that's when she gets into trouble. Well, the way she had reacted, I knew the note had evoked an emotional response that wasn't allowing her to think rationally.

The desk clerk barely glanced up as I ran from the lobby, which was a good thing because I'm sure my face would have betrayed too much. I tried to hide the worry as I jogged down the street toward the Metro, but I'm not sure I succeeded.

I hid behind the station sign, watching my mom pace up and down the platform, waiting for the train. I felt naked. Exposed. Because I could think of only one reason Lévêque would warn us to leave Paris. The Mole had found us again.

When the train arrived, I slipped onto the car next

to the one my mom took. I positioned myself behind a large man in a *Les Bleus* T-shirt and watched her through the sliding door.

Every time we made a stop and more people pushed on board, my chest grew tighter and tighter until I could barely breathe. And each time the doors slid closed, it felt like a snare snapping shut, over and over again.

Mom got off the train at the Esplanade de la Défense station. She jogged along a gravel path that followed the contours of the Seine until she had to stop for traffic at the intersection of a large bridge. On the other side of the bridge stretched a huge wooded park.

I ducked and hid in the bushes along the path until the route was clear, and then eased out into the foot traffic, following her down a wide path that led through the trees.

If she hadn't been distracted, there's no way I could have gotten away with following her without her knowing. It just served as further proof that she was not herself. She *needed* me.

As parks go, the one I followed her through that day was beyond beautiful. The running path wound past lakes and miniature waterfalls, and was canopied by tall oak trees that must have been hundreds of years old. Sometime in its history, the park must have been part of an estate; an elegant mansion stood at one end of the property, surrounded by an ornate fence. I imagined the running paths had once been meant for horses.

I kept a close eye on my mom's bouncing head several strides ahead of me, pulling farther and farther ahead with every step. She wasn't jogging; she was flat-out running. It would have been easier to keep up with her if the park wasn't such a popular destination. The track was clogged with runners and cyclists and people simply out for a lovely summer stroll. Of course, I'm sure that's why Lévêque had chosen that particular park to meet. Among the throngs of other joggers, they would practically be invisible as they ran side by side, sharing information. But it made it harder for me to keep my distance, still keeping her in sight without being obvious about it.

When we rounded a curve in the path, I had to slow for a woman with a jogging stroller and then again for some guy running with his dog. A group of older men were walking four abreast, and I had to slow my stride again to wait for an opening so I could get past them. Still, I managed to keep pace.

But then a group of little kids dressed in matching outfits ambled onto the path, herded by a pinched-faced teacher. Boys and girls alike wore crisp, white tunics over navy blue shorts, with round straw hats on their heads that had little ribbons dangling down the back. They were cute, but in my way. When I slowed down to avoid running them over, Mom pulled even farther ahead. I veered to the left of the group and tried to pass them, but one little boy dropped the toy boat he was carrying and stooped right in front of me to pick it up.

I stumbled to a stop. The teacher jumped forward to pull him out of my way, gushing apologies. *"Pardon, mademoiselle! Désolé."*

"Ne t'en fais pas," I murmured. It's okay. But it wasn't quite, because when I looked up, my mom was gone. I flew down the path, feeling like that little kindergartner again. Only this time it was worse because my mind slipped back to the last time I had lost my mom in a crowd. That incident had ended with me watching her partner die.

The logical part of my brain knew it was highly unlikely for the same thing to happen again. Still, I half expected to round the bend and find M. Lévêque sitting at one of the park's small, round tables, reading his newspaper, reaching for his coffee the way her partner, Joe, had done . . . right before he keeled over from being poisoned.

I shook my head to chase the thought away. The only thing I needed to be worried about was finding my mom. It seemed unreal to me that I could have lost her so quickly. I had been distracted for only a moment.

And then her voice echoed in my head, so urgent, reminding me to go to the station.

I drew in a shaky breath, a weight settling on my chest. Maybe I wasn't so sneaky after all. She had probably seen me following her and ditched me. But why? What was it about this meeting that was so different from this morning? I thought of how she had been so shaken when she read the note. This meeting with M. Lévêque must be dangerous if she didn't want me there, but if it was too dangerous for me, it would be just as dangerous for her.

Suddenly, I was unsure of what to do. Should I try to find her? She might need help. I started down the path again, but stopped before I had gone three steps. I could just imagine what she would say if I went against following the procedure she had taken such pains to spell out to me. Especially if by doing so, I messed up whatever it was she was planning. She had made it very clear she wanted me to go to the station and wait for her there.

Mom had always said to trust my instincts . . . but what if my instincts told me two completely different things?

In the end, I decided to go to Saint-Lazare as I had promised. She had made it clear that she didn't want me with her. I slogged back to the Metro, defeated. On the map outside the gate, I was able to find Gare Saint-Lazare and determine the route I should go. I pulled one of the bills from my pocket and bought a ticket, slipping through the turnstile before I could change my mind.

The platform was crowded with commuters in suits and ties, parents with fidgeting children, tourist-types in Bermuda shorts thumbing through guidebooks, and what looked like an entire rugby team. They were all talking, laughing, acting as though it were any other normal day. I tried to blend in with them, but I'm not sure how well I succeeded in adapting their casual postures and worry-free expressions.

From down the track, I could see the headlights of the train approaching. I stole one last glance back toward the park, half hoping to see Mom jogging toward the Metro. That's when I saw him. He was standing at the entrance to the Metro, smoking one of his foul cigarettes. The Marlboro Man. My breath caught. It couldn't be a coincidence. Could it?

Just then, he turned his head and looked toward the platform. I jumped behind one of the support pillars, heart hammering. I didn't know if he saw me, but I wasn't going to wait to find out.

A train rolled to a stop on the tracks behind me and the doors opened with a hydraulic hiss. I jumped into the crowd of commuters and pushed my way onto the nearest car. When I looked back at where he had been standing, I couldn't see him anymore. Where had he gone?

And why wasn't the train moving? Cold sweat prickled across the back of my neck. Any second, I expected to see Marlboro stroll up onto the platform and corner me on the train. I looked around frantically, searching for an alternate exit.

Fortunately, I didn't need it. The doors slid shut and the train began to move. I gripped the handrail to keep my balance and leaned against the door, resting my forehead on the cool glass as I watched the station slip away.

As the train picked up speed I studied the route map on the LED display above the door. There were eight stops before I had to transfer trains at the Champs Élysées station. Only two more stops from there to Saint-Lazare. If I figured an average of about three minutes between stops, that meant at least half an hour before I reached our meeting place. Half an hour that my mom could be in trouble.

But I tried not to think about that. I tried not to think about anything as the train rolled through station after station. People got off, more people got on. I avoided looking at any of them directly. I felt like I had a huge neon sign above my head flashing the words *Scared American*.

Located as it was in the heart of the city, the station at Champs Élysées was much more crowded than the one at la Défense had been. I'm not really used to crowds. Logically, I knew that it should be easier to lose myself in the mob at the station, but it only made me feel more conspicuous. And as I searched for the right track for the train to Saint-Lazare, I couldn't shake the feeling that I was being watched. I spun around, fully expecting to find Marlboro Man lurking in one of the corners.

My mom would have been disappointed if she could have seen my lack of cool. My first time away from her in Paris and I was completely falling apart. I forced a deep breath—not the best idea in a Paris Metro station, believe me—and tried to release some of the tension as I blew it out again. It didn't work. The best I could manage was to keep my face blank and try to blend in by walking to the next track like I had some kind of purpose.

Before I got to the platform, a garbled French voice announced over the loudspeaker the arrival of the train. At least that's what I think it said. It was too distorted to understand, but I could see *something* approaching, so I ran to meet it.

It wasn't until the train pulled up to the platform that I was able to read the destination sign by the train's sliding doors. It wasn't the one I wanted. I glanced up at the huge digital board on the wall to look for line thirteen. It took me a moment to find it. Which might be why I didn't see him step up behind me.

He touched my arm. "Excuse me."

Automatically, my head whipped around—not only because he spoke in English when I would have expected French, but because I recognized the voice. I could quite literally feel the blood drain from my face, and it felt like it had been replaced by ice water.

"Ryan?" I managed to whisper. I'd last seen CIA Agent Ryan Anderson in the Cascades in Washington State. What was he doing in Paris? Did it have anything to do with my mom's meeting with Lévêque in the park? I began to open my mouth, but he shook his head just enough to signal me that I should hold my tongue.

What came next happened so suddenly that even now as I look back, it catches me by surprise. The chimes on the platform gave the closing-door warning. Just before they slid shut, Ryan grabbed my arm and dragged me onto the train.

"I'm sorry," he said, "but there's been a change of plans."

CHAPTER
4

I tried to wrench away from him, but Ryan kept a firm grip on my arm, just above the elbow. I don't know if he intended it or not, but his thumb hit a pressure point when he squeezed and it really hurt.

On a seat nearby, a gray-haired gentleman with horn-rim glasses lowered the paper he was reading to give me a questioning look. He raised his brows as if to ask if I was all right. For a very brief moment, I considered shouting that I was not, in fact, all right, but then my mom's words swirled through my head. *Assess the situation. Act, don't react.*

I didn't know why Ryan was there. I didn't know how he had found me. Most of all, I didn't know if he had anything to do with my mom's disappearance in the park. The one thing I *did* know was that until I knew the answers to those questions, it would be better for me to keep my mouth shut.

I gave the man what I hoped was a reassuring smile—one that would not only convey my appreciation for his concern, but would give him confidence that I was in control of the situation. Only I wasn't. In control, I mean. My legs shook so badly that I very nearly sank to the floor. I had to bite my tongue to hold back the questions threatening to tumble out of my mouth.

I stole a glance at Ryan's face. Like my mom, he had the annoying ability to maintain a completely blank expression. But his eyes . . . I dropped my gaze quickly. The warm velvet brown of his eyes might have made me feel protected and safe . . . except for the fact that he had found me in Paris, where my mom and I were supposed to be completely incognito.

The man with the newspaper seemed to sense my unease and gave me one last grandfatherly glance. For his benefit and to preserve the illusion I was trying to create, I leaned into Ryan and rested my head on his shoulder. That must have taken Ryan completely by surprise because he flinched, muscles tensing before he caught himself and forced them to relax. The man didn't seem to notice the reaction, though. He went back to his newspaper, apparently satisfied that all was well.

The train slowed, and I stumbled forward. Ryan caught me with one arm and set me back on my feet. It was my turn to flinch, because he didn't let go of me after I'd recovered, but pulled me closer. He brushed my hair back from my ear and leaned in close so that his head nearly touched mine.

"This is our stop," he whispered. His warm breath feathered against my neck, a not unpleasant sensation, I had to admit. He straightened as the train rolled to a stop and let his arm slide down so that his hand rested firmly at the small of my back. Not in a romantic way, but not really detached, either, just kind of . . . protective.

The doors slid open and he guided me forward. Once we were off the train, he grabbed my hand and picked up the pace as he pulled me through the crowd. I realized too late that I had forgotten rule number one. I hadn't been paying attention to the route on the train and I didn't recognize the platform we were on at all—the lay-out and posters on the curving wall didn't seem familiar. I twisted my head around to see the station sign, but it didn't do me any good; I didn't recognize the name. I had no idea where we were.

Near the exit gate, the crowd knotted and snarled before feeding through the cage-like revolving door turnstile one by one. Ryan's grip on my hand tightened and I noticed the way his jaw tensed and flexed. I could guess what he was thinking: Only one of us could go through the turnstile at a time. If I went through first, I could bolt the moment I got to the other side. If he went through first, I could turn around and run the other way. But neither scenario would do me much good.

I gave his hand a squeeze to let him know I wasn't going anywhere. I still didn't know what was going on, but my gut told me that Ryan was on my side, even if I didn't always agree with his methods. Besides, I was smart enough to realize that if I took off as soon as he released me, he'd only come after me. A chase through the subway was not the best plan for keeping a low profile. Plus, where would I run *to*? I didn't know the area. He had nothing to worry about. Yet.

Ryan let go of my hand when we reached street level and slipped his arm around my waist. He leaned close again. "Try to look a little less miserable," he said in a low voice. "People are beginning to stare."

"Why don't you tell me what's going on," I whispered back, "and then maybe I'll *be* a little less miserable."

He smiled at that, but whether it was real or for show, I hadn't the slightest idea.

I tried to get my bearings as we walked. Judging from the boutiques and small cafés, we were in one of the older quarters, but I hadn't been in Paris long enough to know which one. Buildings with ornate detailing sprouted up directly from the narrow cobblestone streets—no sidewalks, no landscaping. The streets themselves wound and curved until I was completely turned around. Of course, maybe that's what Ryan was counting on.

Finally, he stopped in front of the recessed entryway of one of the buildings. He gave me a quick once-over and then said, "Keep your head down."

I did as I was told, but not before sneaking a quick peek at the entry in question. As with the windows above, the door was framed by elaborate molding that arched dramatically across the top. Along the right side of the door was a call box with a row of black buttons labeled with gold numbers. Above the box, a security camera pointed downward, presumably so that apartment owners could see who was ringing before they let them in. Which would be why Ryan wanted me to lower my head.

The door buzzed and Ryan opened it. He stood to the side and nodded toward the interior. "After you."

Cast in shadow, the hallway inside looked like a prison cell. I hesitated.

"Aphra," Ryan said. It sounded like a warning.

I stood my ground. "No. Not until you tell me what's going on."

For an instant a shadow passed over his face, just before the blank expression took over again. "We'll talk about it inside, you have my word." He swept a quick glance up the street. "Not here."

"I just want to know what's—"

Before I could react, his hand whipped out and grabbed my arm. He dragged me forward until our faces were literally centimeters from each other. This time, the sensation I got from his close proximity was far from pleasant. "Natalie is waiting for you," he said through gritted teeth.

Why hadn't he said so in the first place? A rush of relief swept over me and I allowed him to pull me inside. The door slammed heavily behind us.

The building didn't have an elevator so we took the stairs. It was only a couple of flights up, Ryan told me as we climbed.

"We're borrowing an apartment," he explained. "Very temporarily."

I nodded grimly, remembering how Mom and her partners had been "subletting" her place back in Seattle. Not for the first time, I wondered what happened to the owners when the Agency needed a place to set up shop.

In the hallway upstairs, cooking smells mingled with old-building mustiness and stale cigarette smoke. Ryan led the way down a long hallway lined on either side by dark, narrow doors. It was eerily silent except for a faint baby's cry and the distant sound of someone practicing an intricate run on a piano. We stopped at a door with a brass 29 tacked beneath a matching peephole.

Ryan gave the door three sharp knocks, paused, and then knocked twice more. From inside came the sound of hurried footsteps and then the metallic click of locks being drawn.

The door cracked open an inch or two and then closed again. Another metallic sound—a security chain, I guessed—and then the door swung open. To my disappointment, it wasn't my mom who stood there, but a tall redheaded woman in a stark black business-type suit. The look on her face was far from welcoming, but she motioned us inside, anyway.

"What took so long?" she snapped as she reset the series of locks on the door.

"She'd already gotten on the train," Ryan said.

"Where's my mom?" I asked.

"Aphra?"

I spun to find Mom crowding into the small entryway. She reached out for me and gathered me into her arms, holding me so tightly that I could barely breathe.

When she let me go, I turned to Ryan. "Now will you please tell me what's going on?"

He exchanged a meaningful look with the red-haired lady. "I think we'd better sit down," he said.

The redhead ushered us all into a tiny kitchen equipped with the smallest appliances I'd ever seen. Seriously. You couldn't even fit a cookie sheet into the oven and the fridge looked like one of those little cube things you might put in a dorm room. The stainless-steel sink was about the size of something you'd find on an airplane, complete with a leaky faucet.

We settled onto uncomfortable metal filigree chairs around a small glass-topped table. Ryan clasped his hands as if he was about to pray and rested them on the table in front of him. He took a deep breath and inclined his head toward the redhead.

"This is Agent Janine Caraday." He spoke directly to me. I supposed the introductions had already been made to my mom. "She works with the Paris Station."

I nodded, confused. I thought no one at the Paris Station besides Lévêque knew we were there.

"She was hoping you and your mom could be of some assistance."

"With what, exactly?"

"Lévêque sent me a message this morning," Caraday said. "He arranged a meeting, but then he never showed."

I looked to my mom, frowning. How much were we supposed to let on and to whom? "Lévêque? I'm not sure I—"

"Your mother has already confirmed that he was your contact," Caraday cut in.

Was? I didn't like the sound of that. "What happened? Where is he?"

Ryan answered, almost apologetically. "Lévêque is dead."

I felt like a hole opened beneath my chair. The blackness sucked and pulled at me. I flicked a look at Mom, and the grief on her face told me that she had accepted the news. I didn't. I couldn't. "What? No. He can't be. He was . . . He wanted to meet with us. We just got his note and—"

Mom held up her hand to silence me and asked in a soft voice, "How did it happen? When?"

"They found him in the river this morning," Ryan said.

The room tilted and I grasped the table for balance. We had just *been* with Lévêque that morning. He must have been killed right after he left us. I thought back to my premonition in the park and imagined Lévêque once again, sitting at a quiet table, sipping his coffee. This couldn't be happening. Not again.

“We need your help,” Agent Caraday said.

It was a little late for help. At least for Lévêque. Besides, what could we possibly do? They already seemed to know more than we did.

“We believe his death is connected to his contact with you,” she continued. “He . . .” Her voice broke and she let her gaze stray to the window. She pressed her lips together. Hard. Finally, she spoke again. “Forgive me. Gérard Lévêque was a friend.”

“I’m very sorry,” my mom said gently. “He was a good man.”

“Yes, he was,” Caraday’s voice wasn’t soft and mournful anymore. She practically bit off each word.

Mom leaned forward, laying her hands on the table. “He sent an urgent note to the hotel this morning, asking me to meet him. I didn’t receive the note for several hours after it arrived. And now . . .” Her words trailed off and it took her a moment to find them again. “What can we do to help?”

Caraday didn’t hesitate. She stood and retrieved a boxy leather attaché case and brought it to the table. From the case, she withdrew three plastic evidence bags and laid them on the glass.

“These were found on his body.” She pushed forward a bag that contained deep blue strips of cloth that showed white in the frayed edges. Denim. “His hands and feet were bound with this. The same fabric was used as a gag.”

I stared at the bag, my stomach turning. The edges of the plastic were foggy with condensation. The denim was still wet. They must have collected the samples right after they pulled him from the river.

And it was about to get worse.

Caraday picked up another bag and removed about a dozen Polaroid photos. She fanned them onto the table and selected one that showed a close-up of a man's wrist. The skin was gray except for a shadowed ribbon of purple punctuated by claret-colored scrapes. "These ligature marks indicate signs of struggle. Notice how the skin is rubbed raw here and here."

She tapped the photo to indicate where we were supposed to look, but I couldn't make myself focus on the picture at all.

"Here you will see the image from a computed tomography that shows sediment in his paranasal sinuses. We also found frothy liquid in his airway and fluid in his ears, all indicative of drowning."

That meant Lévêque had been alive when his killer threw him into the river. Bile rose in my throat and I had to swallow hard to keep it down.

"You can see indications of struggle here," she continued, pulling out a partial headshot of Lévêque, only you wouldn't know it was him because the face was all puffy and ashen and the mouth was distorted, pulled into a perpetual grimace by a band of cloth stretched tight like a horse's bit. "It appears he tried to bite through the cloth, but was unsuccessful. At first we assumed that the gag was simply that, a gag, but when we removed it, we found this."

She slid the third baggie forward. It contained another piece of cloth, this one white—perhaps a handkerchief. Someone had written on it with black marker. "We're hoping you can tell us what it means."

My mom glanced up. "What is it?"

"A note we found stuffed in his mouth," Caraday said matter-of-factly.

I could feel the blood drain from my face as my head went light.

Ryan slid a worried look to Caraday. "Maybe we shouldn't do this with her in the room."

His concern comforted and riled me at the same time. I wasn't a baby. I had seen the effects of murder before. But this . . . I couldn't shake the awful feeling that Lévêque had died solely because he had met with us that morning. Otherwise, why would Caraday be talking to us?

Ryan gave me what I thought was an encouraging nod. "If you want to wait in the other room . . ."

"No. I'm fine. Thanks." I straightened in my seat, mimicking Caraday's detachment. "What does the note say?" My voice shook only a little.

Caraday smoothed the edges of the plastic bag and read aloud: "*The fourth will find where they hide deliver the children lest he should ride 07060800.*"

I scrunched my brows in confusion. "What does it mean?"

Ryan shifted on his chair and looked to my mom. "We were hoping you could tell us."

I glanced at Mom. She was studying the note with a perplexed look on her face.

"Clearly the note is a warning meant for you," Caraday said impatiently. "You notice that Lévêque was not killed near his home or workplace, but near the park where you were supposed to meet."

"I don't understand. . . ." Mom said.

"Someone knew your plans! And they wanted us to know they knew. Every detail of the murder was planned to send a message. We even ran tests on the fabric. Vintage Italian denim. *Cimosati* selvedge. Used in the Parades collection last season."

"Where was it manufactured?" The strain in Mom's voice caught my attention. I turned to stare at her. Though her face revealed nothing, her hands were clasped so tightly together in her lap that her knuckles were turning white.

Caraday didn't miss a beat. "Northern Italy. Lombardy region. Lakeside town by the name of Varese, just north of Milan. But the mill's been closed for years."

Mom closed her eyes for a long moment and drew a deep breath before speaking. "I know what the note means."

CHAPTER 5

We all sat silent; the only sound in the room was the steady *drip, drip, drip* of the leaky faucet. Mom stood up and broke away from the table, pacing across the room. She turned to face us. "The Mulo family have recently . . . relocated to Varese," she said, her voice hollow.

I blinked at her, not wanting to comprehend the significance of that statement. If every detail of Lévêque's murder had been planned to send a message, then using fabric made in the very city where the Mulos were hiding meant only one thing. They, also, had been found.

Caraday nodded slowly, turning the new information over in her head. She watched my mom with interest. "What do you make of the note?"

"Nothing that you haven't already thought of, I'm sure."

"Perhaps," Caraday said, "but I'd like to hear your interpretation."

Mom folded her arms and shrugged. "'The fourth' refers to the fourth horseman of the apocalypse, as described in the Book of Revelation. 'I looked and there before was a pale horse,'" she quoted. "'Its rider was named Death.'"

A shiver passed through me at those words, but Caraday only nodded. "And the numbers?"

"The numbers indicate a date and time. July sixth at 0800 military time—eight o'clock in the morning. Our deadline, perhaps."

"Who are 'the children'?"

I didn't want to hear the words, because I knew exactly who the children were, but it didn't stop me from holding my breath as I waited for Mom's answer.

"My daughter," Mom said miserably, "and the Mulos' son, Seth."

"What does it mean, 'deliver the children'?" Ryan asked. "Deliver them from death?"

"I don't think it means *deliver* in the biblical sense," Mom said, her voice dead. "It means *deliver them,* as in give them up."

"So a threat is implied," Caraday mused.

I snorted. *"Implied?"*

Her expression didn't change. "He wants Aphra and Seth."

"He?" I asked. "You know who did this?"

Caraday and Ryan exchanged a look. Sort of a how-much-do-we-tell-the-kid kind of thing that made my blood boil.

"Tell me," I demanded, although I was afraid I already knew the answer.

"Aphra," Mom said, shaking her head. I could see on her face that she knew the answer, too.

"No. I want to hear it."

Caraday cleared her throat. "We had wondered if The Mole was involved, and now . . . Well, this has confirmed our fears. It makes perfect sense."

"No," I shot back. "It makes no sense at all. If The Mole knew where my mom and I were, why did he have to kill Lévêque? Why not just come after us? And what's with the note? If he knows where the Mulos are, what does he need us for?"

"He *doesn't* know where the Mulos are," Caraday said. "Our intelligence sources tell us that he is still searching. He has identified the city, but so far the Mulos have managed to stay hidden. Even our operatives haven't been able to find them."

Mom bristled. "You have people *looking* for them?"

"For protection only," Caraday soothed. "Once we discovered that The Mole was gathering his forces, we knew he must be closing in."

"So he's baiting us," Mom murmured, sinking back onto the chair. "He wants us to lead him to the Mulos."

"No," Caraday said, "He wants *your daughter* to lead him to the Mulos."

Mom flinched, but she didn't deny it.

"Why me?" I asked.

Caraday shrugged. "The Mole has a psychopathic profile. No remorse. No conscience. Manipulative. Callous. Pathologically egocentric. You and the Mulo boy have vexed him ever since you captured his assassin on your island."

I closed my eyes, trying to blot out the memory. A Japanese assassin named Hisako had followed Seth's family to our island. She was the one who had killed Bianca. She had nearly killed my dad. Seth and I were only doing what we had to do to protect our families. Besides, Hisako had come after us, not the other way around.

"We . . . didn't mean to 'vex' anyone," I said weakly.

"Add to that the insult of unmasking his two top men within the Agency," Caraday continued, "and he wants more than just revenge. He wants satisfaction."

I felt like a giant hand had closed around my chest. I couldn't breathe. The Mole wanted Seth and me dead. And then he would kill Seth's family. And probably my mom. The hand squeezed. I'd seen what The Mole could do . . . or rather, what his minions could do. And although I had known since the showdown with his henchmen in the Cascades that I was on his hit list, it had never seemed completely real to me. Not even while Mom and I floated around France, as invisible as ghosts. But now I knew he knew where I was and suddenly it became very real. Undeniably so.

But why give us a month's warning?

Then it struck me. "Wait! You got the date wrong."

"What?"

"The dates. You said 0706, right? They write the day first here, not the month."

Caraday's eyes widened. "Of course. He didn't mean July sixth, he meant June seventh."

"What day is it?" I asked.

"June sixth," Ryan said.

Cold fear snaked down my back. I turned to my mom. "Do the Mulos have a phone? Can we call them?"

She shook her head. "No phones," she said quietly. "Too dangerous."

"Then we have to go warn them!"

"I'm glad to hear you say that"—Caraday leaned across the table and took my hand—"because we have a plan that will help us do just that."

My brows slid downward. "You already have a plan? But you just found out where—"

She waved my question away. "As soon as we ran the tests on the fabric, we knew that Varese was significant. A signal. And now"—she nodded to my mom—"we understand why. Our suspicion has been confirmed. A special team has been gathering, ready for my word. With you on board—"

Mom drew an indignant breath. "You're not suggesting that *Aphra* go to Varese!"

Caraday leaned back in her chair. "That's exactly what I'm suggesting. The Mole won't be able to resist. And as soon as he reveals himself—" She slammed her hand onto the table.

"Oh, no. You will not use my daughter as bait."

"She'll be safe." She fixed my mom with a challenging look. "Just as safe as young Mulo was when you dangled him in front of The Mole's men in Cardiff."

"What?" I looked from Caraday to my mom. "What is she talking about?"

Mom shook her head. "Nothing. It doesn't have anything to do with—"

"Your mother," Caraday interrupted, "instructed Seth Mulo to draw his father's captors from the house when he delivered that ring so that the Agency could capture them. Sounds like bait to me."

I leaned away from my mom. "You *what*?"

"I wasn't in charge of the operation," she protested.

"But you are the one the boy trusted. You told him what to do," Caraday insisted.

I turned to my mom. "Tell me. What happened when Seth returned the ring?"

She didn't speak for a long moment.

"I can tell you," Caraday said.

"No, I will." Mom shifted in her seat. "When Joe found the ring," she said, speaking of her dead partner in Seattle, "he had it scanned to retrieve the list of names etched into the stone. That's how he was able to identify Stuart as a member of The Mole's cell." Stuart had been her other partner, a double agent. I could see the hurt of his betrayal still in her eyes. He had nearly killed us both. In that moment, I understood her reluctance to tell me what I wanted to know. She was trying to protect me. What she didn't understand was that not knowing what had happened to Seth hurt worse than anything The Mole or any of his minions could do to me.

"So what happened then?" I prodded.

"We couldn't let them know we had discovered the secret of the ring; it was the only reason they were keeping Victor Mulo alive—as a trade to get the ring back. But we knew, based on their track record, that they would probably kill him once they had the ring, so we had to take steps to prevent that."

"It would have been an awful death," Caraday put in. "He had crossed his former comrades. They have a special hatred for traitors."

Mom shot her a withering look and Ryan coughed. "A little too much information," he said.

Caraday slid him a sideways glance. "She's old enough to handle the truth, don't you think? She's seen enough of it already."

She was right. I folded my arms and looked back to Mom. "What did you do to prevent it?"

"We knew that they would consider it a coup to kill two Mulos, so . . ." She ran her hand through her hair. "We did arrange for Seth to make the drop. But he was heavily covered. We knew they would come after him, and we were ready when they did. He wasn't harmed at all."

I stared at her, seeing her in a much different light.

She looked like a complete stranger to me. "I can't believe you'd allow that. I thought your job was to *protect* Seth and his family."

"He *was* protected." She reached for my hand but I pulled it away. "An entire team of highly trained specialists were with him."

"Just like a team will be with Aphra when she goes to Varese," Caraday said.

"She's not *going* to Varese," my mom shot back.

I pushed away from the table. "Stop. Just, stop!" I ran from the kitchen but the apartment was so small I didn't really have anywhere to go. I paced in the tiny front room, ready to burst.

I heard a chair scrape against the kitchen floor and then Caraday's voice said, "I'm sorry. I shouldn't have dropped this on you like that. I should apologize to your daughter."

I folded my arms and waited for her to appear in the doorway.

She entered the living room tentatively. "This has been a lot for one day, hasn't it?"

I raised my chin. "You think?"

She took a step toward me. "Look, Aphra. I'm sorry. I know this isn't easy for you."

That was putting it mildly.

"You have to understand, I—"

"You were right."

She threw a quick glance over her shoulder to the

kitchen and then lowered her voice so my mom wouldn't hear. "Excuse me?"

"You've got to bring him in," I said. "As long as he's out there . . ." I gestured vaguely out the French doors and past the balcony. Out to where I knew The Mole and his minions watched and waited. "Until The Mole is captured, this will never end."

Caraday quickly covered the remaining distance between us and took my hand. "We can talk about this later," she whispered. She glanced over her shoulder again. "Your mother . . ."

I nodded. Mom didn't need to know.

Agent Caraday returned to the kitchen to smooth things over with my mom. I edged closer to the door to eavesdrop. I'll give Caraday this much, she was one hell of a smooth talker. She had my mom placated inside of ten minutes, without directly lying. She assured Mom that she understood her concerns and conceded that if she had a daughter, she would probably want to be as careful. Once Mom had calmed down, they moved on to more talk about the forensic evidence they had gathered from Lévêque's body. *That* I didn't want to hear.

I wandered back to the window and stared out over the rooftops. Shadows stretched long in the late afternoon sunlight, softened by the haze of heat as if filtered through a lens.

"You hungry?"

I jumped and turned around to find Ryan standing behind me, offering a baguette sandwich. I shook my head. Despite my earlier hunger, all that talk about Lévêque's death had ruined my appetite.

"Take it." Ryan pushed it toward me. "You should always eat when you can. You never know—"

"Not you, too."

"What?"

"The mantras. That's all I ever hear from my mom. Eat when you can, sleep when you can, never jump into a conveniently waiting taxi . . ."

"She's teaching you well." He took my hand and slapped the sandwich into it. "Eat."

I sighed and took a bite to appease him. Bread and cheese never tasted better. I didn't stop until I had eaten the whole thing. "There," I said. "Are you happy?"

His mouth twisted into a smile. "Very."

"Did you know him well?"

His smile faded. "Who, Lévêque? No, I worked with him only a few times."

"So why are you here?"

"The same reason you are."

"Why is that?"

"To end this thing."

"Ah." I turned away from him and stared out the window again. I didn't know what to say to that. I wasn't sure I wanted to tell Ryan what Caraday and I had talked about. I hugged my arms. "You know what? I'm kind of tired. Can you tell my mom I'm going to lie down for a while?"

"Sure." He turned to leave the room.

"And Ryan? Thanks for the sandwich."

His smile returned. "You got it. Sweet dreams."

I curled up on the end of the sofa and I really did try to sleep. Mom should have been pleased that I was following her advice. I'd take whatever sleep I could get because once Caraday told me what she had planned, I knew it probably would be my last sleep for a long, long time.

The problem was, I was powerless to quiet the debate raging in my head. Past experience had taught me not to trust anyone and here I was considering going against my mom and putting my life in the hands of someone I didn't know. Caraday did appear to be very much involved with the investigation of Lévêque's murder, and it looked like my mom trusted her, but I'd learned long ago that appearances were not always what they seemed.

The biggest factor pushing me toward Caraday's plan was the fact that it was exactly what my mom would have done if I had been any other pawn, and not her daughter. By her own—albeit reluctant—admission, she had dangled Seth in front of The Mole's minions when they freed Seth's dad, and the operation had been a success. Apparently, this was a page right out of my mom's playbook. And now that the opportunity had come to use it against The Mole, she was allowing her emotions to cloud her judgment.

Well, I couldn't do that. I wanted my life back. And I wanted Seth to have his. The Mole had to be stopped, and if it took me squirming on the hook to catch him, that's what I would do.

I screwed my eyes shut tight and counted backward. Not from one hundred. Oh, no. My mind was much too distracted for that. I started at five hundred. I think I got down to about twenty-three before I drifted off.

When I awoke, the sky outside had turned a dusky purple. I scrubbed my hands over my eyes and tried to remember what I had dreamed. *If* I had dreamed. I wasn't sure. All I knew was that I woke with a feeling of urgency. I had to help Seth, and I had to do it immediately. I stood and padded back toward the kitchen for a drink of water. A shadowed figure stepped out from the doorway.

"It's time," Caraday said.

I nodded and drained my glass. Without a word, I followed her out the door and down the apartment building stairs. Once we had slipped outside into the balmy night air, she whispered her instructions.

"You will take the overnight train to Varese." She held out a small piece of paper. "Here is the Mulos' last known address."

"How did you get it?" I asked.

"Your mother. She doesn't know you are doing this. Are you still okay with that?"

I straightened my shoulders and nodded.

Caraday tucked the paper into my hand. "You must

memorize this address and then destroy the note, do you understand?"

Again, I nodded, my fist closing around the paper.

"The Mole will know you are coming," Caraday said softly. "He will be following you, but don't worry; he wants you and the Mulo boy together. You will reach his family unharmed. Once you are there and The Mole emerges, our operatives will take over." She handed me an envelope containing a train ticket and a small stack of Euros.

I pulled out the train ticket and stuck the envelope in the waistband of my running shorts, pulling the hem of my shirt down to cover it.

"Your train leaves for Varese in less than an hour," she whispered. "Go now."

"My mom—"

"She's sleeping. Go."

I slipped out into the shadowed streets, my heart tripping crazily. I'm sure part of that was adrenaline, but a whole lot had to do with the fact that I had no idea what I was about to get myself into.

Hurrying through the darkened street, my heart sped up even more. I wasn't sure I could find my way back to the train station in the daylight, let alone at night. I bit my lip, eyeing the shadowed doorways and alleyways, and prayed I wouldn't get lost.

For once I was glad for Mom's nagging about being aware of my surroundings because as I worked my way backward through the streets I began to recognize the boutiques and cafés Ryan and I had passed earlier that day. I also heard traffic noises just outside the quiet of the neighborhood so I knew I was headed in the right direction.

But then I heard another noise. At first I thought it was the echo of my own footsteps because the cadence matched mine exactly. I had to skip a step to avoid stepping onto a storm grate, but the footstep behind me fell without the interruption.

I thought of how I had seen Marlboro Man at the entrance to the Metro and my mouth went dry. Had he followed me? I didn't waste the time to turn around and find out, but tore down the street like my hair was on fire. I turned one corner and then another trying to shake him, but it wasn't working. I needed lights, people, attention. I slipped through a narrow alleyway and came out near a busy intersection and cut across the street. Cars swerved and honked angrily, but I didn't have time to worry about them. The Metro station lay dead ahead but not close enough; I could hear feet pounding the pavement behind me. Gaining ground.

Suddenly, a man on a bicycle swerved right in front of me, ringing his bell furiously. I reared back and jumped out of the way just in time to avoid the collision. The person behind me wasn't so lucky.

I heard the crash and the bike going down, but I wasn't about to stop to take a look. I leaped down the stairs to the Metro two at a time and pulled the ticket Caraday had given me from my pocket. When I tried to use it to release the turnstile, though, the turnstile didn't budge. I cursed under my breath. It was a long-distance train ticket and didn't work for the Metro. I shot a panicked look back at the stairs and then jumped over the machine.

A lady inside the ticket booth yelled something to me, but I couldn't stop to listen. I tore down another set of stairs to where a huge route schedule was posted on the wall. I paused long enough to find my train and platform number. My heart sank. There were ten minutes before the next train. What was I supposed to do for ten minutes? Where was I supposed to hide?

I spun around, looking for someplace—anyplace—but there was nothing, not even a bathroom to duck in to. All I saw were a handful of pay toilet booths, and I had no change.

It was well past rush hour, so only a few people milled about, waiting for the train—no crowd to get lost in. Even worse, I realized, the platform itself was a dead end. No escape routes. I was trapped.

By then I was in full panic mode. I spun around to head back to the main platform and ran smack into Ryan. He was breathing heavily and his face glistened with sweat.

He caught me as I stumbled backward. "We'll need to work on your evasion technique."

My hands curled into fists. "That was *you* chasing

after me? Why didn't you just tell me? I about had a heart attack."

"You didn't exactly hang around long enough for me to tell you anything."

"Ever heard of calling after me?"

"Would you have stopped?"

"No. Why are you following me, anyway?"

"To make sure you were safe."

I thought about me dodging cars on the boulevard and I wanted to hit him. "Go back home, Ryan. You're not going to stop me."

"Stop you from what?"

"Oh, come on. I know what you're doing."

He raised his chin, challenging. "And what is that?"

"You found out where I'm going and you came to take me back to my mom."

"Of course not," he said. "I'm coming with you."

"What? No." What was I, twelve? I didn't need him to hold my hand. "I can do this myself."

"So you know where to find your boyfriend?"

I don't know why that made me mad, but it did. Maybe because I knew it could never be true. "He's not my boyfriend," I said darkly.

Ryan started to reply, but his voice was drowned out by an incomprehensible voice coming over the loudspeakers. He cocked his head as he listened and then pointed his chin toward a long line of cars rumbling into the station. "This is our train."

"*My* train," I corrected.

"I'm coming with you."

"No, you're not."

He grabbed my shoulders and pulled me close so that his face was within inches of mine. "It's my job to protect you," he said in a low voice. "I'm coming with you."

CHAPTER 6

I stared him down. This was not the first time Ryan had told me he had been assigned to watch over me. When we were in the Cascades, he'd said the same thing. What was he, my permanent guardian? I wasn't sure if I liked the idea or resented it. In any case, it made arguing with him pointless. I had little alternative but to give in. At least for the moment. "Fine," I grumbled.

Ryan ushered me onto the train and steered me toward a couple of vacant seats. The weight of his hand on my back felt at once comforting and confining.

As soon we sat, he grabbed my hand, intertwining his fingers with mine. My eyes grew wide and I quickly tried to pull my hand away, but that only made him tighten his grip. Again I pulled and once again his fingers tightened. It was like getting caught in one of those Chinese finger traps you get at cheap arcades. Anyone looking on would think we were just two lovers holding hands, but I knew there was nothing romantic intended; Ryan had tethered me to him as surely as if he had locked handcuffs onto both our wrists. His smug smile made me want to fight. I wasn't as weak as he seemed to assume. On the other hand, any action I took would cause a scene and my mission would be over before it began. I sighed and let my hand go limp.

It wasn't until we transferred trains in Gare de Lyon that I realized Caraday had booked a private compartment for the overnight trip to Varese.

Ryan grinned like a little kid. He plopped down on one bench seat and stretched out his legs, resting his feet on the opposite bench. "Perfect." He tucked his hands behind his head. "Maybe we can catch a few Z's on the way."

That left me with no other option than to take the seat next to Ryan.

Suddenly, I didn't know what to do with myself. I folded and unfolded my hands in my lap, crossed and uncrossed my legs. Finally, I hugged my arms and stared out the window—anything to avoid looking him in the face. Several hours of awkwardness alone in a dark, enclosed space with Ryan was not exactly what I had in mind when I signed up for the assignment. I would have preferred to make the ride alone.

He must have misinterpreted my unease because he reached across the empty space between us and placed his hand on my knee. "You okay with this?"

I stared at his hand, a wave of heat spreading across my face. "What do you mean?"

"What they're having you do. You can still back out, you know."

"Oh." I dragged my eyes away from his hand on my knee and searched his face. Was he saying I was a coward? "I won't back out."

"I didn't think you would."

"You understand why I have to do this, then."

He cocked his head and gave me a solemn once-over. "Yeah. 'Cause you're your mother's daughter."

I frowned, hugging my arms even tighter.

"What? You don't think so?"

I shrugged. "I know I'm her daughter."

"But?"

"But I'm not sure what that means."

"It means that this is in your blood."

"This what? What are you talking about?"

Ryan spread his hands. "This. The life. You can't leave well enough alone. You have to know what makes things tick . . . and then you have to do something about it. Just like your mom."

I wanted to deny what he was saying was true, but it had been my inability to leave well enough alone that got me mixed up with the Mulos in the first place, and I'm sure Ryan knew that. He probably had a file on me somewhere if he was supposed to be my bodyguard or whatever. He would know that when the Mulos came to our island, I couldn't rest until I discovered who they really were and what they were up to. And by the time I found that out, I was neck deep in intrigue and it was impossible to walk away.

"Is it in *your* blood?" I asked.

He grinned, his teeth flashing white in the darkness. "Hell, yeah."

I latched on to his enthusiasm, hoping to steer the conversation away from me. "Runs in your family?"

His smile faltered. "Yes," he said after a moment, "yes, it does."

I realized that I must have struck a nerve, but I didn't know what I should do about it—stay clear or keep pressing. I didn't have to decide, though, because he took the initiative. "It's not always black and white," he said. "Sometimes you can pursue one dream only at the expense of another."

"I'm not sure I—"

"Your mom is fiercely proud of you, Aphra. She must have really trusted that you were ready to find your way, or she wouldn't have let the job's call take over."

I blinked. How had he done that? He switched from his nerve to mine so smoothly I never saw it coming. Well, I wasn't going to play into his hands. I steered back into safe territory.

"Why did you follow me to Paris?" I asked.

He didn't hesitate. "To keep an eye on you."

"So you didn't trust my mom to keep me safe?"

"Listen, Aphra." His voice grew serious. "When that ring of Mulo's revealed the list of The Mole's associates, we were able to capture most of them. But a handful, including The Mole, just went further underground.

Until we can account for every name on that list, you are my responsibility."

That was sobering enough to keep me quiet for a moment, but then I had to ask, "So you don't think what I'm doing, going to Varese and all, is dangerous?"

"On the contrary. I think it's very dangerous. That's why I'm riding along."

"Oh." I let that sink in for a moment, but it didn't compute. "So you're supposed to be protecting me, but you don't mind if I do something that might get me hurt."

"Oh, I mind," Ryan said. "But I wasn't joking when I told you I thought you'd be an asset to the Agency. You need to have the experience of an op to see what it's all about." He grinned again. "Then you'll be hooked."

I gave him half a nod. What he didn't understand was a lot. He really thought it was going to help me to think that my mom was willing to leave me and my dad because being an agent was just too thrilling to give up? Maybe that was his incentive for sticking with it, but I would never believe it was hers. I couldn't.

I turned from him and closed my eyes. His words chanted in my head with the rhythm of the wheels on the tracks: *You'll be hooked, you'll be hooked, you'll be hooked.* No, he didn't understand me at all.

I woke sometime after midnight. The sway of the train had changed; we were slowing down. With a jolt

I realized I was leaning against Ryan's shoulder and I quickly sat up. "Are we there?"

"No. We've only just crossed the border."

"Maybe they need to check our passports."

"They don't do that within the EU. Once you're in, you can travel anywhere." He checked his watch and peered out the window. "We shouldn't be stopping. Sit still. I'm going to check and see what has happened."

Ryan ducked out into the aisle and I rushed to the doorway to watch him go. At the end of the car, a man in a conductor uniform stood talking on a two-way radio and gesturing wildly with his free hand. Ryan didn't even talk to the guy; he just stood there and listened, and then he came back to report to me. He ushered me back inside the compartment.

"You're not going to believe this; the train ahead of us hit a cow and several cars derailed."

"No way. A cow?"

"That's what the man said. Line's closed from here to Omegna until they can clear it off."

"How long will that take?"

"Emergency crews have been summoned, he says, but no telling how long it will be until they arrive."

"So what do we do?" I tried to sound calm, but inside the panic was rising again. The whole operation could be thrown off if I wasn't on my mark by morning. Caraday had said that The Mole hadn't found the Mulos *yet*, but I didn't doubt that he would, and that he would hurt Seth's family if I wasn't there as the sacrificial lamb.

"First thing we do is clear the train. They're ordering everyone off."

There was nothing to be done but to join the rest of the grumbling passengers in our car filing down the narrow aisle and out the door. A uniformed train worker stood on the platform, directing people into the station. If his haggard face and drooping posture were any indication, he was as tired as we were and just as irritated by the inconvenience.

Apparently, the station itself was not prepared to accommodate travelers in the middle of the night. The lights were on, but nothing was open—not the ticket booths or the stationmaster's office or any of the small shops that lined the perimeter. The only place to go was into a small lobby area, where there weren't nearly enough chairs for everyone to sit.

I wasn't worried about the seating arrangements, though. I kept glancing at the huge round clock on the far wall, calculating and recalculating how much time we had left before showtime. Impatience buzzed through me. I paced. The room was too small, too crowded. I was suffocating. And I had to get to Varese.

Ryan wandered over to the ticket counter and grabbed a train schedule printout. He brought it over to me and we scanned it together, looking for an alternate route or some other alternative that would get us to Varese on time.

And then I smelled it. The strange sour stench I noticed every time I caught the Marlboro Man following me. My heart lodged in my chest like a chunk of ice. I turned slowly, scanning the crowd. I couldn't see him, but I knew he was there.

I grabbed Ryan's hand. "We need to get out of here," I hissed. "Now."

He leaned close, a sleepy smile on his lips, but I saw the way his eyes became sharp, alert. "What is it?" he whispered.

I didn't have time for explanations. "We need to *go*," I insisted.

To his credit, Ryan didn't press me again, but quickly steered me toward the tall wooden doors at the front of the station. I don't know what made me turn my head. Premonition, maybe? All I know is that just as I reached for the metal bar handle of the door, I felt an uncomfortable tingle at the back of my neck and glanced behind me.

The room went black—or so it seemed. All I could see for that awful moment was the angry face of the Marlboro Man as he fixed his cold eyes on me. Ryan must have noticed him, too, because he tightened his grip on my hand and yanked me with him as he pushed through the door and out into the night. It didn't occur to me at the time to wonder if Ryan recognized the man or why he would have been alarmed to see him.

Ryan slowed for a heartbeat as he turned his head left

and then right, assessing the escape routes, I figured, since he pulled me to the right and down a short flight of stone steps and into the shadows. Behind us, I heard the door bang open again. I didn't have to look back to know it would be Marlboro Man, but looking was the immediate reaction to the banging door. Sure enough, it was him. And he was carrying a gun. Suddenly, my back felt like an open target. It spurred me to run even faster, to push my stride longer to keep up with Ryan so I wouldn't slow him down.

Ahead to one side lay a huge open field, backed by a deep stand of trees. On the other side, a two-lane road wound down a hill, presumably into the town, lit at regular intervals by the soft glow of streetlights and fading away into the gathering mist. Either route would leave us vulnerable, exposed, but at least the field was cloaked in darkness, and if we made it across the field alive, we might be able to hide in the trees. I pulled on Ryan's hand this time, veering into the field. He adjusted his course without question. I wondered if it was because he trusted my instincts or because he had the same idea himself.

We bounded through the field, high-stepping over the rows of some kind of vining crop. Weak moonlight skittered ahead of us, along straight, narrow rows of stubby vegetation that caught on our feet and threatened to trip us if we weren't careful where we stepped. By the time we were halfway across the field, my muscles felt like burning rubber, and my chest was a hot, tight vise, forbidding me to catch my breath.

I could hear heavy footsteps crashing through the field behind us. We were close, so close to the cover of the trees, but close wasn't going to cut it. I wondered who Marlboro would try to take down first. Probably Ryan. I would be easier to catch. But the guy never fired a shot. Maybe he preferred to do his work at close range.

When we reached the safety of the tree trunks, I could have cheered, but I knew I had to save my breath. The chase was not nearly over. Ryan took the lead again, dodging around trees, trailing me behind him like a child's toy. Moonlight filtered through the leaves above us, casting Rorschach shadows on the ground, and camouflaging the terrain so that we couldn't tell if we were about to trip on a rock or step into a hole. I twisted my ankle more than once and nearly fell on my face, but Ryan held me up. Ryan kept me going.

The moonlight faded as we pushed deeper into the woods, and at first I thought it was because the trees were so much thicker, but as it grew darker and darker, I glanced up to see that heavy clouds had swept across the sky, blotting out the moon and whatever light it might have offered. Which was good because it meant we would be hidden in the darkness, but not so great because it was getting to the point that we could barely see three feet in front of us.

From behind—I couldn't tell how close—came a

sharp crack as if someone had stepped on a very large twig. I tugged on Ryan's hand to signal him to stop. We pressed our backs up against a tree trunk and waited. I wanted to gulp in great rasps of air, but I forced myself to breathe silently, easy in, easy out, until I thought I would choke. There wasn't much I could do about my thundering heartbeat, though. I closed my eyes, wincing with every *ba-bump*, quite sure that Marlboro Man would have had to be deaf not to hear it.

I heard him pass by. I didn't dare turn my head to visually verify it was him, but I didn't really have to. I could smell—the burnt-tar stench, now mixed with pungent BO. That was enough for me.

Ryan shifted so that his body was shielding mine against the tree and he stood there, pressed up against me, until Marlboro Man was long gone and his odor faded away. It made me feel, if not exactly safe, at least protected. Grudgingly, I had to admit that I was actually glad that Ryan had insisted on coming along. I would have preferred it to be Seth pressing me up against the tree, but that was a thought for another time. Our only concern at the moment was getting out of the woods undetected and finding our way to Varese.

Suddenly, Ryan was gone from me. He sprang into the darkness and I heard scuffling to my left. Someone grunted. It didn't sound like Ryan. And then I heard a heavy thud and the ground vibrated beneath my feet.

Ryan returned, out of breath. "Let's go. Quickly." He took my hand again.

"Is he . . . ?"

"He's out, for the moment."

"What about his gun?"

Ryan grinned as he held the weapon up so it could catch the faint moonlight. "No worries," he said, and tucked the gun into the back of his waistband underneath his shirt. He led the way through the trees double-time. I had to practically run to keep up with him, but I wasn't going to argue. I kept thinking that Marlboro Man could wake up at any moment and when he did, he'd be plenty angry. I didn't want to be anywhere in the vicinity when that happened.

Eventually, the trees thinned and spilled out of the woods near a paved road. Not the same road we had seen that led into town, I guessed, since this one was flat and straight, whereas the other had curved away from the station.

"What now?" I whispered.

"We keep moving."

"How close are we to Varese? Can we take a taxi?"

He snorted. "We're not that close."

"Can we take one to the next station? Beyond the cow on the tracks?"

He nodded. "That's the idea. We just need to figure out how to get there."

"There was a taxi stand back at the station. . . ."

"No good," he said. "Our friend back there could be waiting for us."

"The city center, then. It can't be far from the station, can it? Do you think this road connects with the other one?"

Ryan hitched his hands on his hips and peered through the darkness. "Only one way to find out."

We followed the road, walking on the pavement because it was easier than navigating the uneven ground. A breeze had picked up and I, in just the tank and shorts, started to shiver. Not horribly, but enough that Ryan noticed.

"Here. Take this," Ryan said. He peeled off his jacket and draped it over my shoulders. I tried to give it back—I was beginning to feel just a little too much like a damsel in distress—but he glowered at me. "Put it on."

I figured it probably wasn't worth the argument, so I slipped my arms into the sleeves. Just then, two beams of light swept toward us down the road.

Ryan grabbed me and pulled me off to the side. "Stay low," he warned. "We don't know who it might be."

I ducked low as he was doing until the lights drew nearer and a delivery truck came into focus. "A ride!" I jumped up and waved my arms madly to flag it down. The truck passed slowly, but then rolled to a stop just a few yards ahead of us, the red taillights glowing like hot coals. I ran toward them.

"Wait!" Ryan yelled after me. "Be careful!"

But I had already reached the cab. The trucker powered down his window and asked if we needed a lift. *"Volete un passaggio?"*

"Sì, fantastico. Grazie!" I said. Yes, please!

Ryan was at my side before I could reach the door handle. He grabbed my arm. "What do you think you're doing?"

I pulled away from him. "I'm going to Varese. Are you coming?"

The driver leaned toward the passenger seat and said in English, "I don't go to Varese. But I can take you as far as Cassano Magnago, *sì*?"

I didn't know where Cassano Magnago was, but it must have been on the way to Varese if the driver said he could take us "as far as." And it would be farther away from Marlboro Man than we were at the moment. *"Sì,"* I said, and climbed up to the cab. *"Grazie."*

Ryan made an exasperated growling sound, but he climbed up behind me just the same.

The cab of the truck had obviously not been designed for three passengers and the fit was tight. Still, our driver appeared to be very pleased to have company for the long, dark drive ahead. He shoved a couple of notebooks and paper bags that had been sitting next to him underneath the seat and brushed the bench free of any crumbs there might have been—though it's not likely he could have seen them in the dark.

"I am Salvatore," he said, touching a meaty hand to his chest.

"*Buona sera*, Salvatore," I replied. "I'm Donna and this is John. Thank you so much for offering us a ride."

"Ah, Donna!" He grinned broadly, gold tooth catching the light from the dash. "An Italian name, yes?"

I nodded slowly, settling onto the seat. "Uh . . . yes. Of course. I am named for my grandmother who lives in Varese."

"Wonderful, wonderful," Salvatore exclaimed. "You are American?"

"Canadian," I said, giving him a winning smile.

Ryan slammed the door shut behind himself, and Salvatore released the emergency brake. "I have been to Canada once." As tight as we were in the cab, I was practically straddling the gearshift, but it didn't seem to bother Salvatore. He ground the gears into first. "Many years ago. I see the Niagara Falls."

Ryan fell easily into our fictional personas. "My cousin lives near Niagara Falls," he said. "Plays for the Bills."

"*American* football?" Salvatore sounded genuinely mortified.

"He's big," Ryan said, "but he doesn't have the speed to play regular football."

"*Sì, certo, certo,*" Salvatore mused. "One must have speed for the football."

"I hope to see Inter Milan play while we are here," Ryan said.

That was all Salvatore needed to hear. He launched into a lengthy description of the soccer team's strengths and weaknesses. I had no idea what he was talking about, but Ryan seemed to be getting into it.

Between the drone of their voices, the darkness outside, and the hum of the tires on the road, I began to feel drowsy. I fought it; even though I didn't know when I might sleep next, we were in a stranger's truck and I knew I should stay alert. But then I figured that Ryan was alert enough for the both of us and I let my eyelids shut longer and longer each time I blinked. I kept drifting in and out of their conversation. By the time I heard the gears shift down as the truck slowed, I was nearly catatonic.

Salvatore pulled over to the side of the road. "Only five kilometers that way you will find the Cassano Magnago station," he said as we climbed down from the cab.

"Thank you very much. *Grazie!*"

We stood and waved as he pulled back onto the main road. My brain was so tired I couldn't even think straight.

"Five kilometers . . ." I asked sleepily. "That's how far again?"

"Just over three miles," Ryan said.

"Then we better get walking."

The first thing I noticed as we crunched along the lonely road was that the dark clouds overhead seemed to be lower than they had been before. The second thing I noticed was that on this road, unlike the larger road we had just left, no streetlights lit the way. We literally had to stumble along through the dark.

And then it began to rain. The drops started out small and tentative as if they were scoping out the countryside before planning an assault with the bigger artillery. Sure enough, they grew bolder. Like the rain at the cemetery, big, fat drops soaked through our clothes and splashed up from the ground at our feet.

Ryan pointed to what looked to be a farming shed about one city block down the road. "Come on!"

I didn't need any more encouragement than that. He grabbed my hand and we ran through the rain to the shed, only to find it closed up tight, with a padlock hanging from the door.

"Hold on." Ryan pulled out the gun.

"Wait! Don't *shoot* it." I tried to grab his arm, but he shook me off.

"We'll leave some money for repairs," he said, and pointed the gun at the door. He fired and the lock fell open. Rolling the door back, he shooed me inside.

I couldn't really see much of the place, but I could smell it. Fresh dirt, old hay, and very possibly natural fertilizer gave the place a pungent, very farm-y odor. Once my eyes adjusted, I could see a tractor with a miniature flatbed attached to it sitting in the middle of the shed. Stacks of hay bales lined one wall and an array of farm implements hung on the other.

I had to admit that I was glad Ryan had destroyed the lock so that we could duck inside. Not more than a minute after we did, the sky ripped open and water poured down in solid sheets. With the rain, the temperature dropped even more and sucked away what little heat I had left in my body. I shivered so hard my teeth chattered and my back ached.

Ryan stood in the doorway, his tall figure silhouetted black against the lesser black of the storm. "Why don't you lie down and get some rest?" He said. "I'll keep watch."

Again, my sense of feminism bristled. I could stand watch just as well as he could. But I was tired. So very, very tired. And then there was my mom's voice echoing in my head. *Sleep when you can. Sleep when you can.*

I let my eyes stray to the hay bales and considered that it wouldn't hurt to close my eyes, just for a moment. Then I would trade places with Ryan and let him sleep. It seemed like an equitable arrangement to my tired mind. I drew Ryan's jacket around me and curled up on the hay and before I knew it, I was out.

CHAPTER 7

I saw Seth in my dreams. I was sitting on the shore, watching the waves curl inland when he emerged from the sea like Poseidon's warrior, sun glistening across his chest and on his wet, slicked-back hair. He strolled toward me purposefully. Water dripped from the hem of his board shorts, pooling at his feet, bringing the ocean with him.

He dropped to the sand beside me and pulled me into his arms. I snuggled up to him, curving my arm around his neck to draw him closer. He brushed the hair from my face and whispered my name.

"Aphra."

But the voice wasn't his.

All too soon I remembered where I was. Where *we* were. *Ryan, not Seth,* I thought, disappointed.

Ryan's fingers whispered across my cheek as he brushed back a stray strand of hair. "Aphra, are you awake?"

I'm not sure why I didn't answer him. I think it was something in his voice, like he was checking not to see if I was awake, but to make sure that I was asleep. I lay deathly still and waited to see why. Silence roared in my ears. And then Ryan's footsteps creaked across the floor of the shed, moving away from me. The rollers softly protested when he opened the door. I heard the gravel crunch beneath his feet as he stepped outside.

I sat up, feeling like a heavy stone had just been dropped square in the middle of my chest. From outside the shed I heard the low register of Ryan's voice. He was talking to someone. Talking in a furtive, don't-let-the-girl-hear kind of way.

I leaned forward, straining to make out the words. What was he saying? Who was he talking to? I stared at the pale shaft of moonlight spilling across the floor from where the door had not completely shut. *The rain must have moved on*, I thought absently.

And then I caught the urgent tone of Ryan's voice. I didn't like the way it sounded. Slowly, carefully, I scooted to the edge of the hay bales and pushed myself to my feet. I tiptoed across the wooden floor and hovered just inside the door.

". . . lucky to even find a signal. Yeah. We're near Cassano Magnago, probably another hour or so to Varese." He listened. "What? Are you ser— No, I know what you're saying. Right. Yeah, she's sleeping. . . . No, I'm not going to tell her. She'll come along; she trusts me. . . . Right. We'll see you in Milan."

His phone snapped shut and I backed away from the crack in the door. I leaped for the bales just as I heard the door squeak open. Squeezing my eyes shut, I tried to pretend I was sleeping, but what I really wanted to do was to scream. I couldn't believe that just hours before, I had felt safe and secure with Ryan, when all along he'd been lying to me. What wasn't he going to tell me? That we were diverting to Milan? The secretive tone of his voice played over in my head and I could have slugged him. *She trusts me. . . .* Yeah, right. Not anymore.

Ryan's footsteps drew nearer. He sat down beside me.

"Aphra," he called softly.

It was all I could do not to rear up and slap him in the face. Instead I rolled over and squinted up at him. "Hnnnh?"

"It's stopped raining."

I sat up, smoothing back my hair. "What time is it?"

"Six o'clock."

"Six?" I hadn't realized I had slept that long. I bolted off the bale of hay. "What time is the train?"

"Relax. We're not far from the station. We still have about a half hour."

Sure. If we wanted to catch the train to Milan. I pulled off Ryan's jacket and shoved it at him. "Here. Thanks for letting me use it."

He blinked at me. "Uh, okay. You sure you don't need it anymore?"

I headed for the door. "I'm positive."

He was right; the station wasn't far at all. Just down the road, past the hay fields and over a gentle rise. In the early morning light and with the mist left from the rain, the farmland we were hiking through looked like a pastoral painting. But I was much too angry to enjoy the scenery. He lied to me. He *was lying* to me. My mom was right; you can't trust anyone.

We'd only been walking for maybe fifteen minutes before I could see the tracks curve ahead and not long after that, the hipped roof of the station.

I did a lot of thinking in those fifteen minutes, and although I ended up with more questions than answers, one thing I knew for sure was that there was no way I was going to Milan. Not with the remaining threat against Seth and his family. I could only assume Ryan had been talking to the Agency, and no matter what they said, I wasn't going to abandon the Mulos.

How I was going to escape from Ryan was another matter. He wasn't going to let me just walk away. I thought of how he'd chased me the night before and I knew I wasn't going to outrun him, either. He'd said I needed to work on my evasion technique. Fine. That's exactly what I'd do.

As Ryan bought our tickets, I studied the schedule on the wall. It was six twenty-two. The train to Milan headed south from track four in six minutes. The train we *should* be taking curved north to Porto Ceresio, stopping in Varese. It left in twelve minutes. What made him think I would be stupid enough not to know the difference? Because I trusted him? Wrong.

I pretended not to notice the destination clearly posted next to the door and allowed him to lead me onto the deception train.

We found two empty seats together and Ryan stepped aside so I could take the one by the window. Or, more likely, so that he could box me in. I closed my eyes, resting my head against the back of the seat.

"You still tired?" Ryan asked.

"*Sì.*" I answered, without looking at him. Tired of being lied to.

Soon, the voice on the train's intercom announced our imminent departure. I stood. "Excuse me," I said.

Ryan glanced up, startled. "Where are you going?"

I gave him a pained look. "I need to . . . you know." I jerked my head toward the restrooms at the end of the car.

"Oh."

I climbed over him and hurried down the aisle, feeling his eyes on my back the entire time. I glanced at my watch. The train should leave in less than a minute. I reached the doors to the bathroom. Thirty seconds. Paused. Twenty seconds. I kept walking to the vestibule. Ten seconds. Ryan bolted out of his chair and started charging down the aisle toward me. The chime sounded overhead. Five seconds. I slipped out the doors just before they closed.

Standing on the platform, I watched as the train sighed and shuddered forward. Inside, Ryan slammed his fist against the window, yelling something I couldn't understand.

I cupped my hand to my ear and mouthed, "I can't hear you." The car passed and Ryan was gone.

According to what the schedule had said, I had six minutes before the train for Varese departed. I scurried into the station and bought a non-reserved ticket to Varese and then rushed back to track number one where the train idled, its engine harnessed and humming. Passing up the line of reserved-seating cars, I found one with a non-reserved sign toward the rear of the train and climbed on board.

There were only five other people scattered throughout the car. Three of them were sleeping—one snoring loudly—one man was reading the newspaper, and a guy with a huge backpack in the seat next to him was holding his cell phone in both hands, thumbs moving at lightning speed. None of them looked up.

I chose a seat two rows back from the snorer—far enough away that I had a little space, but close enough that I wouldn't stand out as the lone person if anyone glanced into the car.

It wasn't until the train had left the station that I started having second thoughts about ditching Ryan. Once the adrenaline wore off, I had to admit that I didn't actually know what I was going to do once I reached Varese. Besides find Seth, I mean. But being bait didn't seem like such a smart idea if there were no longer a trap. If the Agency had withdrawn its support—which I had to assume was true since Ryan was supposed to divert me to Milan—then we would be on our own.

What I didn't understand was *why* they would have diverted. When Caraday had spoken to me, she'd sounded so intent on carrying out the mission. Like it was as personal to her as it was to me. I couldn't imagine her changing her mind in less than six hours. Unless . . . I flopped back against my seat and groaned. My mom. She probably pitched a fit when she found out where I had gone. I could just see her demanding that they yank me from the job. I didn't know what kind of pull she had with the Agency, but given her top secret status, it was probably substantial.

I had one of those heart-dragging, gut-sinking feelings you get when you're waiting for the next shoe to drop. I was going to be in major trouble when she caught up with me. But how could that be worse than not doing anything and knowing that I would never have a normal life? Even if the Agency happened to warn the Mulos this time, unless they caught The Mole, the cycle would just continue again and again and again. Couldn't they see that by now?

All they had to do was look at how he had chased the Mulos over the years. Everywhere they had run, the Mole had come after them. He found them in California and Michigan, he found them on our island, he found them when they split up and now he'd found them in Italy.

What would stop him from finding them again? Or finding my mom and me?

Plus there was the way he had managed to infiltrate their own Agency. Weren't they the least bit worried about that? He had been able to embed a spy in my mom's operation in Seattle and he'd known exactly where we were in Paris. There was no reason to believe he would quit stalking any of us . . . unless he was caught.

Caraday was right; to catch The Mole, the Agency had to flush him out. Why weren't they doing that?

I probably would have dwelled on that particular point a bit longer, but my attention was drawn to the conductor in his dark blue suit, making his way through the car, punching tickets with a distinct *kachink, kachink*. I fidgeted and waited until he reached my seat and asked for my ticket.

"Il biglietto, per favore, signorina."

I handed it to him and he started to punch it, but then he stopped. He looked at me, then at my ticket, then at me again.

"You are English?" he said with a heavy accent.

My stomach dropped. Had Ryan alerted the train already? How was that possible? They were going to stop me. They were going to make me get off. They—

"Mi dispiace," the conductor said. "I am sorry, but this ticket goes to Varese."

"Yes," I said, not comprehending. "That's where I'm going."

"But this train come *from* Varese. We stop next in Vergiate."

"No." I felt like I'd just been dropped into a bad dream. Air rushed in my ears. I could barely feel my hand clutching the ticket. "But the sign said—"

"Mi dispiace," he repeated. "But no worry. There will be a train in Vergiate to take you to Varese."

I thanked him and slouched down in my seat, fighting back tears of frustration. How could I have done something so idiotic? Now there was no way I'd make it to Varese by eight A.M. as The Mole demanded. I stared out the window at the scenery—like a movie set rolling past—my stomach cranking tighter and tighter with every turn of the wheel until I thought I was going to be sick.

When we stopped in Vergiate, I slogged off the train and then watched in miserable frustration as it screeched and shuddered and rolled away from the station. The schedule board showed two trains headed to Varese—one in ten minutes and one in an hour.

I ran inside and bought a ticket from the machine to cover the ride from Vergiate to Cassano Magnago. From there, I could use my original ticket to get to Varese. I felt supremely stupid that I had to get myself back to where I had started from before I could move forward. By now it was already after seven. Because of my stupid mistake, I would never reach Varese on time. I don't know what The Mole planned to do if Seth and I weren't "delivered" by his eight A.M. deadline, but based on his track record, I didn't want to find out. Of course, I didn't exactly want to find out what he would do if he got a hold of us, either.

I paced, checking my watch every two minutes, and tried to formulate some kind of plan of action for when I caught up with the Mulos at the address Caraday had given me. The whole idea was to ensnare The Mole. Maybe if we led them on a chase to Milan . . . And then it hit me. Milan. Ryan would never dare show up there without me. He knew me. As soon as I stepped off that train, he had to know what I was planning to do. The first chance he got, I had no doubt Ryan would sound the alarm and come after me. By going on to Varese, I was essentially forcing their hand. Regardless of what my mom wanted, we would carry on with the operation as planned. At least that's what I hoped would happen.

There was one small hitch in my imagined scenario: Ryan could not have known that I would have gotten on a train headed in the opposite direction. They would have no idea where I was or when I was arriving in Varese. Or if I *was* arriving in Varese. My heart sank. I might have to go it alone after all.

Finally, an announcement echoed through the passenger concourse. I couldn't quite hear all the words, but I think it was saying that my train had just arrived. I rushed out to the platform. The train was there, but so were a whole lot of people, lined up at each car, waiting to board. Rush hour. I joined the queue at one of the back cars—I had bought an unreserved seat again, in case a name or identification was required to make a reservation. Suddenly, I wished that I had taken the chance and selected a seat.

By the time I entered the car, it was almost completely full. Ours was not the first stop on the line, and the train must have already been crowded. I scanned the seats as I wandered through the car, but I wasn't able to find one to myself. Worse, all the aisle seats had been taken so I'd be boxed in, no matter where I sat.

I ended up choosing a seat near the rear of the car so that if I had to leave in a hurry, at least I'd be near an exit. On the downside, my seatmate, a burly guy with oiled hair and several heavy gold chains around his neck, seemed to be watching me, waiting for me to meet his gaze. I turned as far from him as I could without being blatantly rude. No need to give him a reason to remember me. One of the advantages of the window seat, I supposed, was that I could pretend to be engrossed in the scenery—even if we were just sitting at the station.

As it was, sitting at the station gave me too much time to think. And my thoughts kept slipping back to Ryan, no matter how I tried to divert them. Two opposing images flashed through my head. The first was Ryan, shielding me by the tree, handing me his jacket, brushing the hair from my face when he thought I was asleep. But then there was the other image—Ryan outside the shed, pressing the cell phone to his ear, telling the Agency how he was going to trick me into going to Milan. I didn't know how both images could be the same person.

Meanwhile, more than an hour away, Seth and his parents were in danger and if the stupid train didn't start moving soon, I was going to be too late to do anything about it.

Finally, we dragged slowly and sluggishly forward before picking up speed and leaving the station behind. Outside, the early-morning sun had painted the sky a salmon pink and gilded the clouds left over from the night's rain. The train wound its way around a blue-gray lake, the waves blushing in reflection of the sky. If the circumstances had been different, I might have appreciated the beauty of it. As it was, the lake stood in the way of Seth, and all I wanted was to put it behind me.

CHAPTER 8

The train sighed into Varese just after eight in the morning. A full hour later than I planned to have met the Mulos. In the vestibule, I danced from foot to foot and waited for the doors to release. The second they hissed open, I jumped forward like a sprinter out of the gate.

I ran, weaving through commuters and tourists, students and working men. The acoustics of the tile floors and the granite walls of the passenger concourse magnified and jumbled their voices until it sounded like a loud, echoing henhouse.

At each turn, I half expected Ryan to step out and demand to know what I was doing. When I didn't see him, I was at once relieved and disappointed. But I didn't have time to worry about him. I had to get to the Mulos' apartment.

In the front of the station, a group of cabbies clustered together, smoking and laughing. One of them—a stout man in a leather vest and matching ivy-style cap, glanced over at me as I rushed outside. He threw his cigarette down and ground it out with the toe of his boot.

"Taxi, signorina?" he asked.

"Sì, grazie!" To my ears, my voice came out high-

pitched and shrill. I took a deep breath before giving him the address. *"Ho fretta,"* I added. I'm in a hurry.

He hurried to open the door of his boxy white car and bustled me into the back. I had barely gotten both legs inside when he slammed the door behind me.

Jumping into the driver's seat, he set the meter running, then shot away from the curb so fast that the force of it threw me backward. I sprawled across the seat, gripping the door handle as we whipped through the winding streets. All I saw of the city was a blur of white buildings with terra-cotta roofs, deep green vegetation, bright flowers in window boxes, and laundry waving on the lines overhead.

Finally, the taxi screeched to a stop and the driver announced we had arrived. I peered out the window at a three-story apartment building, square and squat with a shallow, hipped roof.

"Grazie," I said shakily. I handed him a twenty-euro bill for a six-fifty fare, but I wasn't about to hang around for the change. I jumped from the cab and ran for the entrance.

Unfortunately, the entry to this building, like the apartment back in Paris, was controlled by a panel of buttons, each labeled with a surname, presumably of the person or family who lived in the apartment. No numbers. How was anyone supposed to find a specific apartment that way? I ran my finger down the list of names. Not that I had imagined I would see the name Mulo, but

I had hoped for something overly common like Smith, or, since we were in Italy, Rossi. No such luck.

The only thing I could think of to do was to buzz each apartment in turn until I hit the right one. With luck, there wouldn't be anything like a three-tries-you're-out feature in the control box.

I buzzed the first one. No response, so I buzzed the next button down. The intercom at the base of the box crackled.

A woman's voice demanded to know who was there.

"Elena?" I asked.

She snapped that I had the wrong house.

I hit button number three. Again, no response. Just as I was about to buzz the next one down, a lanky guy in too-tight spandex shorts pushed out the door, shouldering a sleek racing bicycle. *"Permesso,"* he said. Excuse me.

"Non importa," I assured him, and stepped aside, holding the door for him. And then I let myself into the building.

As soon as he left, I tore up the stairs to the second floor and searched the numbers on the doors until I came to 2C. When I saw it, my heart twisted in my chest. The door to the apartment stood partially open.

A cold sense of foreboding slithered down my back and I flattened myself against the wall. I'm not sure how long I stood there, holding my breath, listening for sounds from inside the apartment, but it felt like a long,

long time. Only when I didn't hear anything did I dare to slide cautiously toward the door.

With the toe of my shoe, I pushed the door open just a little bit farther and peeked inside. I didn't see any movement.

"Hello?" I called softly.

No answer. I pushed the door open even wider and took a tentative step inside. And then I knew. The Mulos had already gone. It looked like they left in a hurry, too. In the small kitchenette to my right, dishes still sat in the sink. Some of the drawers were pulled partially open. To my left, a magazine lay open on a glass-topped coffee table in front of a sleek leather couch, a half-empty glass of water on a coaster beside it.

Tears blurred my vision and I wiped them away with the back of my hand. I was too late. The knowledge left me dead and hollow inside. I turned to leave the apartment when I caught a flash of silver on the floor next to the couch. I bent to pick it up. A knot tightened in my throat as it dangled from my fingers. I recognized it at once; it was the chain I had worn to hold Seth's ring. The clasp had broken. I wondered when that had happened. How it had happened.

"Ferma!" A deep voice behind me ordered. Halt.

I jumped and spun around. A tall man in a dark wool suit and narrow tie stood in the doorway, his black eyes fixed on me as if he'd just found a cockroach skittering along the floor. *"Cosa sta facendo?"* he demanded. What are you doing?

My mind raced. What could I say? Definitely not that I knew the people who had lived in the apartment. Then he might ask me who they were. *"Mi scusi,"* I apologized. *"Ho visto la porta aperta. . . ."* The door was open. . . .

He strode forward so that he hovered over me, his expression, if possible, soured even more than before. "You are American?"

I nodded, mouth too dry to speak.

He fished a leather wallet decorated with a brass shield from his pocket and waved it at me. "I am police. You cannot be here."

"I'm sorry. I'll leave." I tried to move past him, but he blocked my way.

"No. You are looting. For this, I must arrest you."

My eyes grew wide as I followed his pointed glare to the chain I held in my hand. "Oh, no! I wasn't stealing this. It's—"

"I advise you to say nothing further. You may call your consulate from the station. They will arrange the lawyer."

I shook my head. That was one thing I couldn't do. Not unless I wanted the consulate to find out that the person on my passport didn't exist. "Look, I seriously was not loo—"

He pulled a pair of handcuffs from his pocket. "Turn around."

I shrank back. No. This was all wrong. "Could I please see that badge again?"

"Turn around. Now." He pushed back his suit coat enough that I could see a pistol in the holster at his belt.

I stared at the gun. I wasn't exactly familiar with the Italian police procedure, but the arrest scenario didn't feel right. Something was definitely off. I didn't believe for a moment that he was a real policeman. But that only made things worse for me. It meant that he wouldn't have to play by the rules. I turned slowly, keeping my hands where he could see them. He already looked pretty agitated and I didn't want to give him any reason to reach for that gun. He yanked first one hand and then the other behind my back and snapped the cold, metal cuffs onto my wrists, squeezing them so that they clicked small enough to pinch. I bit my lips to keep from crying out. But when he yanked the chain from my hand, I couldn't help it.

"Save your breath, *signorina*," he said, and grabbed my arm to spin me around. "We go now."

I could hear doors open and caught a few curious neighbors gawking from their *appartamenti* as he marched me down the stairs and through the tiled entry. I kept my head down as we went, not out of shame, but to hide my face so that the black-eyed "policeman" wouldn't see how my eyes darted from door to door, searching for a familiar face, for an escape route, for anything that would get me out of the mess I had gotten myself into.

He marched me out to the street where a sleek silver car waited at the curb, its domed blue light spinning in flashing circles from the dashboard. More neighbors huddled in a curious cluster on the sidewalk, watching and whispering at a safe distance.

The fake policeman yelled at them to go back to their business. *"Tornate ai vostri affari!"* He opened the door of the car and then pushed me forward, grabbing my skull like a bowling ball so that I wouldn't smack my head on the top of the door frame—as if I didn't have the intelligence to duck. His fingers dug into my scalp and I flinched, which must have made him think I was trying to break away from him because he pushed me even harder and the force of it made me stumble. I fell forward so that only the top part of my body made it onto the seat, my legs sprawled out behind me.

"Get up," Black Eyes ordered. But since my hands were cuffed behind my back, it's not like I could push myself up. I struggled to find my balance, let alone the momentum to rise to my feet. Impatient with my slow response, he grabbed one of my arms and yanked it back even harder. New pain ripped through my shoulders.

"Aaaah!"

"I said up!" he growled.

"Aspetti!" a voice from out of the crowd shouted. Wait! It must have startled Black Eyes because his grip on my arm slipped. I dropped to my knees on the pavement with another burst of pain and twisted around just in

time to see a tall figure break away from the crowd. I blinked quickly.

Seth?

Behind him, a hand reached out to pull him back. Pale skin. Short, dark hair. Seth's mom, Elena. Her eyes grew wide and her lips formed one word—'No!' Seth pulled away from her and she threw a frantic glance behind her. I followed its path, but from my low vantage point, I couldn't see much more than the top half of his head. Still, I knew it was Seth's dad, Victor, Elena was looking toward, pleading with her eyes. He didn't move.

Seth approached the police car slowly, holding his hands in plain sight. *"C'è uno sbaglio,"* he said. There has been a mistake.

The policeman turned with amazing speed and drew his pistol, leveling it at Seth's head. "The mistake," he said, "is yours."

CHAPTER 9

I didn't know whether to laugh or cry. Seth was safe! Or at least he had been until he had the pistol pointed at him. I tried to push myself up, but I slipped and landed right back on my knees. Loose gravel on the cobblestones bit into my skin, but I didn't care. Seth was alive. That was all that mattered.

My chest literally felt like it was swelling as I stared at him, I was so happy. His skin had taken on a sepia tone since I'd seen him last, like he'd spent a lot of time in the sun. And his dark hair had gotten longer, the ends curling against his collar and wisping over his ears. His eyes were the same intense blue, though, and still had the power to make me feel warm all over.

I wanted to call out to him, but I knew better. He could be going under another alias, so it wouldn't be smart to use his name. I bit my tongue and watched helplessly as Black Eyes took an aggressive step toward him. He motioned with his gun for Seth to move forward.

"Hands on your head," he ordered.

Seth clasped his hands and rested them on the top of his head as he had been told. His blue eyes locked with mine as he walked toward the car. He was acting much calmer than I felt. When he got close enough, he reached down to help me up.

"Leave her, Romeo."

Seth ignored the guy and hooked a hand under my arm. I had just about gotten my feet under me when Black Eyes slammed his pistol against the back of Seth's skull. Seth crumpled and we both went down. I fell sideways against the car so that my arms pulled back at an odd angle and the metal of the handcuffs cut into my skin. Seth tried to push himself up, but swayed and collapsed again. I had to clamp my mouth shut to keep from screaming his name.

The man, who I can genuinely say I hated by then, prodded Seth with his foot. "You will listen when I speak to you," he said. *"Capisci?"*

A murmuring rose around us. Men in their shirtsleeves grumbled and shuffled their feet. Mamas in aprons and head scarves watched with wide eyes and whispered behind their hands. But no one moved to stop what was happening. I no longer saw Elena or Victor. I wondered—I hoped—that they had gone to get help.

The policeman turned his black eyes on the crowd. *"Non c'è niente da vedere!"* he shouted. There is nothing to see here! He ordered them back to their homes. Seth he left lying on the cobblestones. He stepped over him like he was a sack of trash and grabbed me by both arms to drag me to my feet. "Get in the car," he ordered.

I considered resisting but I was afraid that if I made him angrier, he would take it out on Seth. I climbed awkwardly into the backseat while Black Eyes made Seth kneel on the road and place his hands on his head once more. Then he took each hand in turn and twisted it behind Seth's back, snapping on another pair of handcuffs.

"In," he said, pointing to the car. Seth struggled to his feet and then climbed into the back with me.

I wanted to throw my arms around him, but even if my hands hadn't been bound and I could actually reach for him, I knew I wouldn't do it. I pretended not to even recognize him as Seth settled onto the seat. Black Eyes hmmphed and slammed the door shut.

As the man walked around the car to the driver's seat, I looked to Seth and hissed, "What is going on?"

"I could ask you the same thing," he whispered. "What are you doing here?"

"I came to warn—"

Seth cut me off with a shake of his head as the front door opened. The policeman slid into his seat and started the engine. Then he turned to glance at the backseat and smiled. It was the most sickening smile I'd ever seen in my life.

Seth and I couldn't speak as we rode along. Even though there was a Plexiglas partition between the front and backseats, a little circle of small holes had been drilled through it, so it was not a soundproof barrier. I didn't even dare to look at Seth too closely because I could see the policeman's eyes in his rearview mirror as he drove, and he was watching us. I did slide my foot across the floor so that it was touching Seth's, and Seth pressed his leg against mine, but that was as much communication as we dared.

While Seth sat stoically beside me, my heart was doing ninety and my hands were slick with sweat. I needed to take a cue from his example and not let Black Eyes know that I was terrified. He seemed like the kind of man who would feed on my fears like a shark with blood in the water.

I stared out the window, trying to keep my mind occupied, but it didn't do much good. The passing landscape barely registered. I did notice obliquely a long stand of spear-shaped cypress trees at the edge of a green field, and the thought occurred to me that we were no longer in the city, but that's about as far as the thought process went. I was too busy worrying about how Seth's parents would know where we had gone. Wondering if Ryan had managed to rouse Agency support. Watching for any signs of imminent help.

In the front seat, Black Eyes began to hum. I didn't even recognize what the song was, but I immediately hated the sound. My stomach twisted as I considered who he could be. My guess was that he worked for The Mole.

I stole a glance at Seth and he met my eye for just the briefest of moments before he quickly looked away again. For that instant, a connection passed between us, powerful and real. He was afraid as well; I could feel it. But I could also feel that he was even more determined we would get out of this thing together. I shifted on the seat, moving closer to him, and felt tentatively behind me. My fingers found his and we hooked them together, drawing strength from each other.

It wasn't until I noticed that we were entering some kind of industrial area that I realized I hadn't been paying much attention to our location. I had been too focused on what was inside the car to spare much thought for what was outside. By the time I snapped to and remembered what my mom had taught me, too much distance had passed for me to get my bearings.

I twisted around in my seat to check out the back window. All I could see were the red-tiled roofs in the distance and what looked like a lake far over to one side of the road. The plants and trees in the open spaces looked wild and untamed.

"Where are we?" I whispered to Seth.

He shrugged and shook his head. Not good. He didn't know, either.

The policeman eased the car up to a closed gate. He inched forward until it slowly opened. Either the gate was on some kind of motion sensor—which wouldn't provide the greatest security—or he had a remote in the car, or maybe someone inside opened the gate. Only there didn't appear to be anyone inside. The place looked completely deserted as we drove along the short drive to the empty parking lot.

"The weekend," Seth whispered. "They must be closed."

I had no idea who "they" might be, but I had a feeling, judging from the weeds pushing up through the cracks in the parking lot and the broken windows in the building before us that the weekend had little to do with the desertion.

"What is this place?" I whispered. The building was maybe as long as two or three football fields with high, multipaned windows and a couple of smokestacks poking up from the rear. The bricks were black with soot and ivy snaked unchecked up the sides of the building. The tall letters on the side of the whitewashed walls proclaimed the business name to be GIORDANO.

He circled the car around one side toward a loading area with a long concrete dock with four distinct bays. Parked on the blacktop surrounding the dock were several cars and a couple of black SUVs. So the place wasn't deserted after all. In fact, as our car inched forward into one of the empty bays, a trio of men with guns materialized from behind double swinging doors and watched us with interest. I looked to Seth and could tell by the way he stiffened in his seat that he had seen them, too.

Black Eyes killed the engine and stepped out of the car, slamming the door behind him. He climbed up onto the dock and carried on a long conversation with the men with guns. I couldn't hear a word they were saying, but with all the effusive gesturing of hands and dark glances into the car where Seth and I waited, I could only guess that they were talking about us.

Finally, one of the men disappeared back through the swinging doors. When he returned, a cold seed of fear sank deep into my gut. He had not come back alone; trailing close behind was none other than the Marlboro Man. He shook our fake policeman's hand and together they approached the car. I sat frozen in my seat, unable to do anything but watch in terror as they drew nearer.

"That man," I whispered to Seth, but that was all I could say before the door opened. I hadn't realized how stuffy it had become in the backseat until a cool rush of air filled the space. I took a deep breath and gave Seth's fingers one last squeeze before he was pulled from the car.

I scooted toward the open door to follow him out when Black Eyes stopped me. "Not so quick, eh, *signorina*?"

All I could do was watch helplessly as he led Seth away. A cold sweat washed over me. I wanted to run after him, or at the very least demand to know where they were taking him, but I knew I shouldn't say a word.

When he had disappeared through the swinging doors, Marlboro bent down to peer at me through the open door. He smiled, showing teeth that had been stained a sickening brownish yellow.

"Allora, signorina," he said. "You will come with me."

He reached inside the car and grabbed my arm, dragging me from the seat. Once again, I was struck by the bitter, burnt-tar-and-farm-refuse smell about him. I turned my head away from him so that I could breathe as he pushed me toward the crumbling concrete stairs leading up to the dock.

"Where are we going?" I demanded. He just grunted and propelled me up the stairs and across the loading dock to the double swinging doors.

I tried again. "Where's my friend?"

"Silenzio!" he barked, and pushed me through the doors.

Inside was some kind of interior loading area. Several wooden pallets lay scattered about, some still bearing bales of mildewing cotton. Stacked against the wall were dusty bolts of an indigo fabric. Denim, I realized with a jolt.

The room tilted and my head buzzed as if a million insects had been set loose in my brain. Denim. Caraday said it had been manufactured in Varese—that the textile mill had been closed for years. My eyes widened in terror as I looked around at the dilapidated fixtures in the room. If I had any doubts before, I now knew who had orchestrated my false arrest.

My stomach heaved as I realized that I was likely standing in the very mill that produced the denim used to bind and gag Lévêque before he was thrown into the river.

"This way." Marlboro yanked on my arm, indicating a long hallway crowded with wide, square rolling carts, all empty. A pungent odor hung in the air. Nothing terrible, just very strong. I wasn't sure what it was, but something about it smelled familiar. Like the scent that comes from ironing a cotton shirt. But mixed with the hot cotton smell and Marlboro's bitter stench was something much heavier. I guessed it might be the indigo dye they used on the denim, but I had no idea if I was right.

From the hallway, I could see a cavernous room, like an elephant graveyard full of old looms, some of them with cones of thread still attached.

He led me down a narrow corridor, the fluorescent lights overhead flickering a pale, sickly light. At the end of the corridor, he stopped in front of a black metal door and pulled a set of keys from his pocket. He unlocked the door and swung it wide.

"In," he said.

I peered inside the dark room. The heavy smell was even stronger in there. "What is this place?" I asked.

"You will have answers soon enough," he said, and pushed me through the door.

I stumbled inside and he slammed the door shut behind me. Except for a narrow sliver of light that bled in from the corridor, the room was entirely dark. I have a thing about the dark. Have had ever since Seth and I got stuck in a cave on the island and we had to literally feel our way out. Plus, there had been bats. I shuddered at the memory. I don't like not knowing where I am or what could be sharing the space with me. Logically, I knew there were probably no bats in the room, but there could be other vermin. Vermin that at any moment could jump on me and gnaw at my fingers . . .

I closed my eyes and made myself take several deep breaths, trying to let the tension out each time I exhaled. It didn't really work, as far as the releasing tension thing went, but it did help me to think a little more rationally. It wasn't going to do me any good to stand around in the dark freaking out. I slid one foot forward, and then the other, feeling my way along the floor until I found the wall. With my hands still behind my back, the only way I could feel for a light switch was to run my shoulder along the wall, so that's what I did. I started by feeling around the door first, and when that didn't yield any results, I searched farther out.

I'd made it halfway around the room with no success when suddenly the lights flicked on and the door opened behind me. I blinked against the sudden brightness and spun around. Marlboro had returned and he was not alone.

Next to him, with thick arms folded across an even thicker chest, stood a stocky woman wearing a tight, black business suit. "*Cosa sta facendo?*" she demanded. What you are doing?

I met her stare and squared my shoulders. "Looking for the light switch."

"It is in the hall. When we want you to have light, we will let you know." Her words were clipped, disdainful. I wondered what Marlboro had told her. "You will come here." She indicated a spot on the floor directly in front of her.

I crossed the room hesitantly. It's not like I had much choice. What was I going to do? Run away? To where? The loading dock with the gunmen?

"I must search for weapons," she informed me.

It took a full second to register what she meant. She was going to search *me* for weapons. That's why Marlboro brought a woman. I suppose I should have been grateful for that gesture of propriety, but I backed away. "Oh. No. I don't have any—"

"Stand still," she ordered.

I held my breath as she patted her hands along my arms and legs, and then along my sides.

"What is this?" she asked as her stubby fingers found the envelope tucked into the waistband of my shorts.

"Travel money," I said honestly.

She grabbed the envelope and turned it over in her hands, her face showing new interest. Her mouth twisted into a self-satisfied smile. *"Grazie,"* she said, and stuffed it inside her blouse. To Marlboro Man she proclaimed, "No weapons," and she marched through the door.

He waited until she had gone and then gave me an exaggerated bow. "You will come with me."

"Where are we going?" I asked.

"Enough." He grabbed my arm, his stench like a cloud that engulfed me. I wondered what it was in the tobacco the guy smoked that smelled so bad.

He led me back down the hallway into a huge room. I guessed it was the main section of the mill. The ceiling was probably three times as high as in the other room, crisscrossed with metal walkways above the work area. A row of windows, offices, I presumed, looked out over the workspace like skyboxes at an arena. I imagined bosses, stern as prison guards, watching from those windows, or strolling the walkways, making sure that the employees wove their quota of fabric.

From somewhere in those offices, strangely, I could hear strains of classical music. It seemed out of place in the shambles of the broken-down mill.

We rounded the corner of one of the huge loom machines to see Seth standing beside Black Eyes, presumably waiting for us. Seth looked up at me and gave me an encouraging smile, even though he had to know as well as I did that our situation wasn't good. It was all I could do to keep from running to him. That I wouldn't have been able to throw my arms around him didn't matter. I would have figured something out. As it was, though, I kept my distance, giving him a polite nod. There would be time for talking—and hugging—later. At least I hoped.

Seth and I were led up a set of rickety metal stairs to the walkways above. The angle of the stairs was steep and the stairway narrow—only one person wide—so we ascended in single file. As we climbed higher, I was able to get a bird's-eye view of the room below. Amid the machines, I could see several men and an occasional woman or two standing around, talking, watching us, working with some kind of wire—though I'm not sure what they would be doing since the mill was obviously defunct.

At the top of the stairs, Black Eyes motioned for us to stop. "You will stay here," he said, and left us with Marlboro Man as he ambled across the walkway and tapped on one of the office doors. He cracked open the door, spoke to someone inside for a moment, and then strolled back to where we stood.

"We will wait," he announced.

Marlboro reached into his pocket and pulled out a crumpled box of cigarettes and began to shake one loose.

"Idiota!" Black Eyes spat, knocking the package from his hands. He gestured with his eyes to the area below. Marlboro clenched his jaw and bent to retrieve his scattered smokes. Some of them rolled through the little spaces between the metal flooring and tumbled to the machines below and he cursed under his breath.

"Now," Black Eyes said to Seth and me, "you will come this way."

He led us across the walkway to one of the office doors

and rapped sharply. Without waiting for an answer, he opened the door and ushered us inside.

To my surprise, a gentleman sat in the corner of the room, playing a cello. I felt like I had stumbled into a dream. The man didn't look up, but continued playing his piece, eyes closed, swaying with the swing of his bow. The fingers of his other hand danced over the frets, pausing here and there, wavering to create vibrato. It was a beautiful performance. So why did it make me feel so uneasy? I glanced at Seth to see if he shared my apprehension and what I saw sent a slice of fear through my chest.

Seth's face had gone completely white. Even his lips had drained of color. He stared, wide-eyed, at the man with the cello, like he knew him. Like he was terrified of him.

Finally, the music ended, the last melancholy note hanging in the air before fading away. Only then did the man look up and smile. I was wrong about Black Eyes having the creepiest smile I'd ever seen. This guy upped the creepiness factor about a thousand percent. "Hello, Aphra," he oozed. His accent held a distinct Eastern European flavor. "So nice to finally meet you."

"I . . . I'm afraid I don't . . ." I looked to Seth again.

"Oh, yes. How rude. Mikhael, you haven't introduced me to your little friend."

At first I thought he was talking to Black Eyes, calling

him Mikhael, but then I remembered—Mikhael had been Seth's given name before his family had been forced into hiding. He told me once that he had been Seth so long that he preferred his new name to the old one. But if this man knew the old one . . . Suddenly, I felt like I needed to puke.

The cellist tsked. "I'm sorry, my dear. It appears Mikhael has forgotten his manners. I am Dominik Lucien Brezeanu, but you may have heard me called by my simpler name: The Mole."

CHAPTER 10

The Mole smiled his wicked smile and watched me like he was hoping for a reaction. I tried not to give him one, though I'm sure he could see the fear written on my face. I just stared at him, thinking that this distinguished-looking gentleman with his close-cropped silver hair and pale blue eyes was not at all what I had imagined when I pictured what The Mole might look like. I had imagined him as some kind of mob boss figure, wearing gold chains and smoking oversize cigars. But I guess evil is more effective if it comes wrapped in an attractive cover.

"It is a pleasant surprise to find you here," he said. "After this morning, I had quite given up meeting you. When my . . . associates dropped in to pay a visit to young Mikhael's family, they were rather dismayed to find that they had already left the premises. Warned off by the Agency, were you?"

He directed his question to Seth, but Seth stared straight ahead as if no one had spoken. That made The Mole chuckle. "He's a stubborn one," he said to me, "but we'll soon break him of that."

The thought of how The Mole or his minions might try to break Seth made my knees wobble. I could have crumpled to the floor right then, only I was pretty sure that would have been just what The Mole wanted. I took a cue from Seth and focused my eyes on a crack in the plaster behind The Mole's head.

The Mole chuckled. "So much like your mother," he said. "Pity, that."

I couldn't help it. My gaze snapped right back to where he was sitting.

"I didn't realize you had accepted my invitation," he continued, methodically loosening the strings on his cello before laying it in its case. "I'm afraid I already released the horseman."

The room spun. The horseman . . . the fourth horseman . . . death. "What are you saying?" I asked.

"The message was quite clear," he said. "Either she would deliver you children to me, or she would die."

My stomach heaved. The words of the macabre message danced mockingly in my head. *Deliver the children lest he should ride.* I assumed—I think we all assumed—the note was a threat against the Mulos. It never occurred to me that if he didn't get his way, the monster would go after my mom.

"But, I'm *here*," I said weakly.

"Ah, yes." He closed the cello case and fastened the latches. "But not by the specified hour. And if my sources are correct, had it been up to your mother, you would not be here at all."

I stared at him. How could he possibly know that?

Maybe he didn't. Maybe he just knew that any mother with half a brain wouldn't say, "Oh, you want me to give up my kid? Sure. Here you go."

"She will learn," the Mole continued. "You will all learn—you myopic capitalists with your unmitigated arrogance. You will be brought to your knees soon enough."

"What does that have to do with my mom?"

"It has to do with your mother," he drawled, "because she works for the most corrupt government in the world. She has pledged her allegiance to an administration of money-grubbing plutocrats who have commodified the entire culture. She supports a monopoly of global wealth and power. She forgets what your government has done to our country. How their sanctions starved our children, how—"

"Give me a break," I muttered. "She got in your way, that's all."

Seth gave me a warning nudge. "Aphra . . ." he said under his breath.

"Ah, yes. You see? He is learning. He knows that it was *his* family who set us on the path that has led us here today. His parents who betrayed their fellow comrades in favor of baseball, hot dogs, apple pie, and an SUV. But they sowed the seeds of their own destruction, boy. My years in federal prison were the best education America had to offer."

The Mole plucked a scarlet cashmere scarf from the

side of his stool and draped it around his neck. "It's true, I would not have chosen my own incarceration, but those years proved to be most valuable. I learned to navigate the underground, to connect with the power of international organized crime. Prison could not subdue me; it only extended my reach. Now I have comrades all over the world. Signore Labruzzo here is part of that extended family."

Black Eyes—Labruzzo—inclined his head.

"I have your parents to thank for the wealth of connections, Mikhael. I discovered an entire world of criminals in federal prison, all looking for a little . . . direction." He studied his impeccably manicured nails and added in a bored tone, "Despite whatever personal benefit I may have gained, however, your parents betrayed me, and traitors must be punished."

Seth's jaw tightened, but he didn't speak.

The Mole, unmoved, looked to me instead. "And your mother must pay for her involvement in their corruption. Had the American government not resorted to deceitful tactics to obtain their treasonous accusations, we would not find ourselves in this situation today."

I clamped my own jaw tight and breathed hard through my nose. I was not going to let him goad me into talking back, even though I'd like to tell him a thing or two. But it wouldn't do any good. You can't reason with insanity.

"You must understand," he continued, "I abhor

violence, but there are times when a big stick is more effective than a soft word. Your parents killed twenty years of progress toward bringing down American dominance. They destroyed the cell I so painstakingly pulled together and nurtured over the years. So I find it a fitting addition to my statement that I destroy their creations." He spread his hands as if to encompass Seth and me.

"What statement could you possibly make?" Seth spat.

The Mole cocked his head, his mouth twisting as if amused. "My colleagues have been scattered. Many have been captured. But the work will go forth. My statement"—he paused for effect—"is to show that I will not be hobbled."

I didn't want to ask. I truly didn't want to hear the answer, but I had to know. "What have you done with my mom?"

"I have done nothing with her." His lips split in an oily smile. "Yet."

He was lucky that my hands were still stuck behind my back or I would have clawed his eyes out. I gritted my teeth. "Where is she?"

"Your mother is on her way to rescue her daughter."

"But she doesn't know where I am."

He arched a brow over one pale eye. "Why, certainly she does. The Agency is not exclusive in the use of bait."

My mouth went dry. "I—I don't understand."

"It's quite simple. Since you would not go to her in Milan, she is coming to you."

Icy fear licked the back of my neck until my hairs stood on end. I knew I was playing his game, but I had to ask. "How did you know I was supposed to go to Milan?"

His cold smile made my stomach turn. "I have my sources. Close, reliable sources." He winked and I thought I'd lose it right there.

What did he mean, "close sources"? Close to him or close to my mom? Who even knew? Ryan would never have given me up. And then my heart sank. Caraday. I remembered the way she whispered her instructions to me, how she said my mom was sleeping when I left.... That should have raised a huge red flag, had I stopped long enough to think about it. There's no way Mom would have gone to sleep unless she knew that the Mulos were safe. So either she already had a plan in play or Caraday had been lying to me. Or both.

"And my mom and dad?" Seth asked, though I'm sure he would rather not have heard the answer.

"Yes," The Mole said in his saccharine voice. "They have received an invitation as well."

He crossed his long legs and brushed imaginary lint from his trousers, signaling the end of his interest in our conversation. "Labruzzo, we must finalize the preparations. Kindly show our guests to their new accommodations."

Labruzzo bowed as if he were a manservant.

"Oh, and Labruzzo, one more thing. Please explain what will happen when the Mulos and Signora Connolly arrive for their children, would you?"

Labruzzo's lips lifted. He fixed me with his black eyes. "Boom," he said.

My legs shook as we crossed back over the metal walkway. I had to breathe through my nose, afraid that if I opened my mouth, I'd scream. The workers down below, the wires, suddenly it made horrible sense to me; they were rigging the textile mill with explosives.

I could barely climb down the stairs, but Labruzzo had no patience for my being slow and growled at me to hurry up. He marched us through the machine room and down a wide corridor lined with the same square bins I had seen earlier near the loading dock.

In front of a battered wooden door, he stopped, jangling the keys on a large brass ring until he found the one to undo the lock.

The door swung open to reveal a room that was only about ten feet square. Even more carts crowded the room, these overflowing with what looked to be cast-off fabric and scraps, all heaped in the corners and spilling out onto the floor. Bits of plastic and paper, old pins and thread spools littered the floor. The tall windows on the far side of the room were caked with grime and only let in a weak, yellowish light. In the small space, the strange smell was even stronger than in the open space of the factory.

"In," Labruzzo ordered.

I drew back. If he was trying to kill us with chemical fumes, he might not be far off.

Labruzzo grabbed my shoulder and gave me a vicious shove. I stumbled into the room, slipped on a piece of fabric and fell to the floor. Pain shot through my elbow and up my arm.

"Aphra!" Seth rushed to where I lay amid the trash and dropped to his knees, but there wasn't much he could do to help me.

The door clicked shut behind us, followed by a metallic clunk. Probably Labruzzo setting the lock again. At least Seth and I were together. And, for the first time since I first saw him in Varese, we were alone. It should have been our "moment." We should have been able to hold each other and comfort each other and tell each other that everything was going to be all right, even though it wasn't. By keeping us cuffed, The Mole had even taken that away from us.

Frustration and anger swelled inside with edges so sharp it brought tears to my eyes.

"Hey," Seth whispered. "What's wrong?"

I rolled onto my side so that I could at least look up at him. He leaned over me, his eyes—his beautiful blue eyes—so filled with tenderness and concern that I cried even more.

"Are you hurt?"

I could only shake my head.

"Then what's the matter?"

"I want to hug you and I can't," I choked out.

"Hold on a sec." He let himself topple over so that he was lying on the ground facing me and then wriggled like a worm so that we were face-to-face. His voice went husky. "I want to hug you, too," he said. That made me cry again, only happier this time.

"Hey, shhh . . ." he said, and rubbed his cheek against mine. His warm skin felt sandpapery and soft at the same time. I closed my eyes and nuzzled against him like a cat, breathing in the smell of him—an earthy blend of lime and soap.

"I've missed you so much," I whispered.

"You have no idea." He pulled back so he could see my face. "I've been going crazy. No one would tell me where you were."

"Me, neither."

"Where *were* you?"

"Lyon and then Paris."

"Only a few hours away. No wonder they wouldn't tell me. I would have found you."

"I would have found you."

"You did find me."

I smiled. "Oh, yeah."

We lay there looking at each other for several heartbeats, and then Seth leaned close and brushed his lips against mine. A wave of champagne bubbles burst open in my stomach, my head, my heart. I stretched my neck to reach him again, and he kissed me, deeper, longer. For those brief minutes, I forgot my pain and my fear. All I knew was that Seth was there with me. I nestled my cheek in the hollow between his shoulder and his neck.

And then I opened my eyes.

I had found Seth—and because of that, he was lying on the floor of an abandoned factory, manacled and marked for death. I swallowed hard against the ache in my throat. If what The Mole had said was true, my mom had set an alternate plan in play to get the Mulos to safety. If it hadn't been for me, they might have gotten away.

"Why did you come forward?" I moaned.

Seth pulled back and looked at me incredulously. "What?"

"When Labruzzo arrested me," I said. "He was making a show of it, trying to flush you out." Just like Caraday said we were going to do with the Mole. The irony only made it hurt worse. "Why didn't you stay hidden?"

Seth shifted so that he was angled toward me. "Aphra, look at me."

I raised my face to him again. His brows dipped low. "I would never let anything happen to you," he said. "I stepped out of the crowd because it was not possible for me to stand by and watch you be hurt."

"But . . . you could have gotten away. You could have been free."

He shook his head. "No, Aphra," he said softly, "I will never be free of you."

His cobalt eyes held mine and for that moment, everything else melted away until it was just Seth and me and that was all I needed. It didn't matter what awaited us or how we were going to get out of it. For that little time I could believe that everything was going to be all right.

I was wrong.

Chapter 11

I could have lain there with Seth for hours, but our aching shoulders and the urgency of the situation wouldn't allow it. We needed to get out of the textile mill and warn our parents. With some difficulty, we pushed to our feet and stood together, trying to figure out a plan, trying to understand what had happened with each other to lead us to that spot.

"What happened this morning?" I asked him. "Before I got there."

Seth glanced back at the door, and then leaned close to tell me. "We were eating breakfast when a telegram was delivered. It was kind of a shock, since no one was supposed to know where we were."

"What did it say?"

"It was the message we dreaded getting for years, 'Send the books.'"

"I don't understand what that means."

"It's code. We had to learn the code before we went into hiding. If we get a message that says to 'pack the books,' we're supposed to make preparations to leave town. Pack a few things, maybe withdraw some money from the bank, but sit tight and watch and be on high alert. But if the message says to 'send the books,' that means to get out immediately."

"Oh." So the Agency *had* come to warn the Mulos. I should have trusted that they would, but I had to be sure. "Where did you go?"

"Nata—your mom had rented an apartment one building over. That was our safe place. She rented it with her own money so that no one would know about it. She figured that if we ran after someone discovered where we were hiding, they would never think to look so close."

That sounded like my mom. Be prepared. Trust no one. "If they didn't know about the apartment, where did the Agency think you were going to go when you got the 'books' message?"

He shrugged. "I hadn't really thought about that. All I know is that when we got the message, we had to clear out and go to the safe place and wait for instructions."

"So . . . once you got there, you were supposed to stay in the safe apartment, right? What made you come outside?"

Seth lifted one shoulder. "We could see the street from the window. That was something else your mom insisted on. So . . ." He let his gaze drop. "The police car caught my attention. I mean, he'd left his lights flashing so I figured something was up. I watched and when I saw him bringing you out of the building . . ." He looked up at me, face sincere and open. "I snapped. I ran out of the apartment and my mom ran after me. She tried to make me stop. And my dad followed her." His shoulders sagged. "They've probably been going crazy, trying to figure out where the police car would have taken us. I wonder how The Mole gave them the message where to find us?"

"He probably didn't have to. My mom would have gone to them immediately. They're probably all together." Which meant Caraday was probably with them and they didn't know she was in league with The Mole. A fresh surge of panic gripped me and I pulled my wrists against the handcuffs. "We've got to get these things off."

"Wait. Can you pick the locks?"

"Me?" I laughed. Well, not really a full-out laugh, but one of those "yeah, right" guffaws. "I've never even *seen* a set of handcuffs up close before now."

"But you have picked locks."

"Not these kind of locks." Back at the resort, I'd learned the basics of lock picking from our super, but we're talking about doors and cupboards. Handcuffs? No way.

"The concept is pretty much the same, though, right?" Seth persisted.

I chewed on my lip. I didn't share Seth's confidence, but it's not like we had a whole lot of other options. I might as well give it a try. There was only one problem. "What am I going to use as a pick?"

Seth scanned the room. "There's got to be something we can use in here. Let's look through the bins."

Without the use of our hands, even that simple task proved to be difficult. We had to turn around backward to dump the bins and then sift through the fabric scraps with our feet. It wasn't a very effective way to look for any object small enough to fit into a handcuff lock. Besides, if we happened to find something, how were we supposed to pick it up?

"This is going to take forever," I said.

"Let's split up." Seth pointed to the back corner of the room with his chin. "You take that corner and I'll take the other and we'll meet in the middle."

"I hope we're not still going at it long enough to reach the middle," I grumbled. Still, I slogged through the trash to my corner of the room and started looking.

We worked in silence for maybe five minutes when suddenly Seth jumped back from the bin he was about to overturn. "Holy crap!"

I spun around, expecting to see Labruzzo holding a gun on us or something. The look on Seth's face as he stared into the bin was equally as chilling.

"Aphra . . . you'd better come over here."

The tone of Seth's voice grabbed my insides and twisted them tight. "What is it? What's wrong?"

He shook his head, brows pinching together. "I think it's that guy . . . the agent from Seattle."

"What?" I rushed over to where Seth stood. There, half buried in rags, lay Ryan, his face slack and pale except for umber streaks of dried blood across his forehead and down one cheek. "No," I whispered. When I ditched him, Ryan had been on his way to meet my mom. If they found him . . . I stumbled backward, darkness creeping into the corners of my vision.

"Aphra? Are you all right?"

My lips parted but I couldn't find my voice.

"You think he's dead?" Seth's words sounded far away.

"I . . . I don't know." The way he lay crumpled in the bin, I couldn't tell if Ryan was breathing or not—and I couldn't check for a pulse with my hands stuck behind my back. I raised my eyes to meet Seth's. "Help me get him out of there."

Together, we carefully tipped the bin on its side. Ryan gasped in pain as he rolled out onto the floor. I let out a breath. At least he was alive. But I could now see the gash on the side of his head. That must have been where all the blood on his face had come from. Brighter, crimson blood matted his hair and soaked the collar of his shirt. He was still bleeding.

As if he could feel us staring at him, Ryan slowly raised his lids. His eyes rolled in their sockets until he finally managed to focus them on me. "Hey," he said. His voice barely registered above a whisper.

I bent over him. "How are you doing?"

He drew in a serrated breath. "Been . . . better."

Seeing him struggle to form the words made my heart lurch. "Shhh. Just lie still. We're going to get us out of here."

Ryan closed his eyes again, but his lips curved just enough to make me think he was trying to smile. He started to nod his head, but then winced and lay still again.

"That cut looks bad," Seth whispered.

"He'll be okay," I said automatically. I hoped it was true. It looked as though he'd been hit pretty hard on the head. He could have a concussion. Judging from his coloring and the amount of red soaked into his shirt and the rags around his head, he'd probably lost a lot of blood.

My wrists already ached where the edges of the metal cut into them, but I twisted and pulled my hands in frustration, trying to work the cuffs off. Trussed up as I was, there was nothing I could do to help Ryan. I couldn't wrap his wound. I couldn't make him more comfortable. I couldn't do anything. He drew in a deep breath and held it, wincing again when he let it out. I pulled against the cuffs even harder.

Seth bumped me with his shoulder. "Aphra, stop. Your skin's raw as it is."

When I looked up at him, I wanted to cry. In part because I felt so helpless, but also because of the concern and confusion I could read on his face.

"I've got to help him," I said. "This . . . this is all my fault."

Seth shook his head. "No. Don't start blaming yourself for—"

"But it's true. At first he was set to come with me to Varese but then I heard him talking on the phone. He was going to try and get me to go to Milan, so I ditched him. Then he had no choice but to come after me. If I hadn't been so stubborn—"

"I'm *glad* you were," Seth said. "If you hadn't been, I might never have seen you again."

I blinked back tears. "But I led them right to you! This is what The Mole wanted all along. I played right into his hands."

"Aphra. Stop it." Seth's voice became hard. "He used you, yeah. But what if you hadn't come? My family would have run again, but we would never have been free. He would never stop hunting us."

"I know." I thought of my frustration in Paris and I couldn't even imagine how sick of running Seth must be. "That's why I had to come."

His eyebrow cocked upward. "And here I thought you came to see me."

I allowed myself a smile at his attempt to make light of the situation. "That, too."

At my feet, Ryan moaned again. My smile faded. No matter what Seth said, I couldn't shake the feeling that Ryan wouldn't be lying on the floor if it wasn't for me.

When I stepped off the train to Milan, it was a pretty good guess he'd caught the next train to Varese to find me. If he hadn't come after me . . .

If he hadn't come after me, he would have shown up in Milan empty-handed. Knowing Ryan, he wasn't going to do that. Which meant he would have had to call someone to explain why we weren't coming. I sucked in a breath.

"What is it?" Seth asked.

"Someone knew where he'd be."

"What are you talking about?"

I dropped to my knees next to Ryan and nudged him. "Did you tell them you were coming back for me?"

He cracked an eye open again and tried to lift his head. "I . . . don't know what—"

"I heard the phone call. I know you were supposed to divert me to Milan."

His face went slack again. "Oh."

Seth's eyes flicked from me to Ryan and back again, confused, questioning. I turned away from him; I didn't want to explain about the shed.

"Did you tell them I got off the train?"

With some effort, Ryan nodded.

"So they knew that you were going to follow me."

He nodded again. "They said they would find us here."

I groaned.

"Wait. It could be a good thing," Seth said. "We need more numbers on our side. Maybe if—"

"No. Don't you get it?" My voice rose with my frustration, and Ryan shushed me. I stood so that Seth could hear my whisper. "It's just like The Mole said. He knew they were coming. Caraday must have told him. And she probably said where The Mole could find Ryan, too."

"No," Ryan said. "Not Caraday. She—"

"She gave us up!" My stomach twisted with anger. Seth was right; it wasn't my fault that we were there. The whole thing was one big setup. No matter what I did or didn't do, The Mole would have his endgame. He said that he'd released the horseman because Mom had not sent me to Varese as he had demanded, but that wasn't exactly the truth. I had come on my own. I had delivered myself. That should have changed the outcome, but it hadn't. It just changed the venue.

Behind my back, my hands curled into tight, angry fists. My mom was racing into a trap. Seth's mom and dad as well. Ryan lay bleeding on the floor with Seth and me manacled so we couldn't help him. I had reached my boiling point. The Mole had taken as much from me as I was going to allow.

From the moment my mom had become involved in helping the Mulos, The Mole had had a hold over our lives. I thought of all those years on the island, me believing that my mom hadn't come with us because she didn't want to when in reality, she was protecting us. She knew how ruthless The Mole could be. As long as he was after her, she'd had to stay away from us. The Mole had stolen four years from my family.

And what about Seth's? The Mulos had been on the run since Seth was in grade school. The Mole had chased them, taunted them, tried to kill them.

Like he had tried to kill my dad. My fingernails dug into the palms of my hands. Like he *had* killed Bianca. And Joe. And Lévêque, and I didn't even know how many others.

I thought of The Mole's smug smile as he hid like a coward in his little room above the working floor. He probably never did any of the dirty work himself. He just sat in the shadows, orchestrating, plucking strings. Well, I wasn't going to be played anymore.

"No more talk," I said. "Let's keep looking for something to get the cuffs off."

"Grab one of those . . . U pins," Ryan suggested.

The little silver pins were scattered across the floor. No doubt they'd been used to secure bolts of cloth. I couldn't believe that I hadn't thought of using one of them before. It's just that with those sharp points . . .

Ryan must have sensed my hesitation. "They're perfect," he assured me. "You just . . . break one in half. Use the . . . bent part as your pick."

Seth slid me a look. "Will that work?"

I couldn't help but laugh. "We've got a CIA operative telling us to use a pin and you're asking *me* if it will work?"

"I was just checking."

"Yeah," I conceded. "I think it will work."

We sat on the floor, each one of us feeling behind our backs blindly, fingers skittering over the trash in search of a pin. You'd think it would be easy, but it wasn't. Finally, Ryan had to push himself up onto one elbow to give us directions.

"A little more . . . left. Closer to you. Almost. Right there."

"Got it!" Seth whispered.

"Good." Ryan lay back down. "Break it in half at . . . the base so you have a . . . little hook on the end. Aphra, you move closer to him so he can reach your cuffs."

It wasn't easy, but I scooted backward so that my shoulders were touching Seth's. He reached out and found my fingers with his.

"Feel for . . . the round part of . . . the keyhole," Ryan said.

Behind me, I could feel Seth's head shake. "Aphra should do it—she's picked locks before."

Ryan raised his brows at me, lips pressing together like he was trying not to smile.

"Nothing illegal," I said.

He let the smile break free then, but it quickly turned to a wince. He sucked in a deep breath and let it out slowly. He didn't look good. We had to get him some help. Quickly.

I stretched my hand out and felt for Seth's. "Hand me

the pick. Carefully. I'll try." I stretched my fingers out to take the pick, but our behind-the-back coordination was not great. It dropped with a little *klink!* onto the floor. Seth tensed. I could literally feel his frustration building.

"It's okay," I assured him. "Just give me the other piece."

Slowly and painstakingly, we managed to transfer the piece of U pin from his hand to mine.

"Okay, I've got it." I said. "Now what?"

"Feel for the . . . keyhole," Ryan said. "It's round with . . . a little line coming from it."

I fingered the warm metal of Seth's cuff until I found the hole. "Yes, I've got it."

"Insert the hooked end into the hole . . . about one o'clock."

I fumbled with the pick to fit it into the circle part of the hole and felt around the mechanism. Like Seth had guessed, the feel was similar to other locks I had picked back at the resort, just much, much smaller. I pushed and twisted and pulled the pick and nothing happened. Again and again and again I tried until my hands grew slick with sweat. The sharp end of the pin-pick poked my fingers and the metal cuffs chafed against my wrists. Meanwhile, Ryan was losing more blood. Getting weaker.

"It's no use," I cried. "I can't do it."

Seth curled his fingers up around mine. "It's okay. Just relax. You can do this."

Warmth spread upward from my fingers and swelled in my chest. I know it sounds sappy, but if Seth had so much faith in me, I wasn't going to let him down. I closed my eyes and felt for the latch with the pick again. Once, twice, three times. Finally, I felt it move. "I . . . I think I got it."

But nothing happened.

"Why won't it open?"

Ryan blew out a long breath. "It's probably double-locked."

"What?" Panic squeezed my throat like a fist. "What does that mean?"

"Calm down." Ryan's voice dropped and he shot a glance at the door. "It's nothing to worry about. Double-locked cuffs . . . have a kind of a bolt that keeps the ratchet from moving. You've managed . . . to release one. The second will be easier."

Easy. Sure. Now if I could only make my heart stop racing around my chest and keep the sweat from soaking through my shirt.

"Aphra, look at me." Ryan's eyes met mine, steady, sure. "All you have to . . . do is find the narrow straight part that . . . runs upward from the circle."

I nodded, clamping my jaw tight, and jiggled the pin until it slid into the secondary slot. Ryan was right about it being easier; I got it after only four tries. With a click and a metallic scrape, the handcuff swung open on its hinge.

"Yes! Thank you!" Seth whispered. He twisted around and drew me into a backward hug, the handcuff swinging from his left wrist.

New pain shot through my shoulders from the pressure and I shied away. "Watch the arms!"

He drew back. "I'm sorry. I wasn't thinking."

"It's okay. I'm just a little . . ."

My voice trailed off as I caught sight of Ryan. He had dropped back into the rags, face sweaty and pale. He gave me a weak smile.

"Seth." I pointed to Ryan with my chin. "His head."

Seth touched the handcuffs on my wrists. "Will you be all right for a few more minutes?"

I forced a smile of my own and tried to ignore the throbbing ache in my shoulders. "I'm fine. Take care of Ryan."

Handcuff swaying, Seth quickly sorted through lengths of cloth on the floor until he found a piece long enough and clean enough to wrap around Ryan's head to try and stop the bleeding. He had just finished tying the knot when he stiffened, head cocked like a Labrador.

"What is it?" I whispered.

"Do you hear that?"

Without waiting for an answer, Seth jumped up and tiptoed to the door. He pressed his ear against the worn paint and listened.

"It sounds like they're leaving."

I struggled to my feet and ran over to the door. Sure enough, I could hear muffled voices, fading footsteps, car engines revving up, doors closing. They were scuttling out of the factory like rats abandoning the ship. Which could mean only one thing.

We were running out of time.

Chapter
12

Seth turned to me, dark brows drawn low. "We've got to get out of here."

"You think?"

"Give me the pin so I can get those cuffs off you."

The pin. It had been in my hand when I rushed to meet Seth at the door. My stomach tumbled right down to my knees. "I dropped it."

Panic and irritation clouded his face, but he drew a deep breath, like he was sucking in calm. "It's okay. It's okay." I wasn't sure if he was assuring me, or himself. "We'll make another one." He scanned the floor for more U pins.

"Seth," I said, my voice small. "We have to stop them."

He halted his search and stared at me as understanding dawned. If The Mole's people were leaving, that meant that the endgame was near. It meant that my mom and his parents were getting closer. And when they came looking for us . . .

Seth must have been thinking the same thing. "But how would they find this place? We're out in the middle of nowhere."

I shook my head at the irony. The Mole was using us

as bait, which was exactly what my mom hadn't allowed me to be. "I'm sure he left plenty of bread crumbs for them to follow. Besides"—I gave Ryan a sharp look—"I'm guessing we're on GPS."

Ryan raised his eyes to meet mine. He held my gaze for a long time before he nodded miserably.

"Wait." Seth shook his head in confusion. "What?"

"I should have figured it out earlier," I said. "The Agency does like its techno toys." Back in Seattle, one of my mom's old partners had boasted about putting tracking devices in everything.

Seth threw a sharp look at Ryan. "He's got a tracker on him?"

"Either that, or I do," I said.

Ryan closed his eyes. "How . . . did you know?"

I took a deep breath before speaking. Until that moment I hadn't been sure, but all the pieces were fitting into place. "You wouldn't believe the rules I had to follow with my mom," I said. "No phones, no e-mails, no friends. Keep to yourself, watch your back, don't draw attention to yourself. We should have been invisible. But somehow you knew exactly where to find us."

"Lévêque . . . could have told us you . . . were meeting in the park," Ryan countered.

"True. But you didn't find me in the park. You were waiting in the train station. Lévêque couldn't have told you I was going to go there. He was . . . dead." My voice caught on that last word.

"My job is to protect you. I had . . . to know where you were. . . ."

I took a step closer and stared him down. "Where is it? My wristwatch? No, it would be too easy for me to leave behind. My earrings maybe?" And then my breath caught. "My shoes."

Ryan hesitated and then he nodded.

I closed my eyes, shaking my head as I thought of how easily Lévêque had gotten us to take the shoes. How excited I had been to have them. "You embedded something in the shoes so you could follow me."

"Your mom, too," he said sheepishly. "We were afraid she would take you and go into hiding again and we wouldn't know where you were to protect you."

"You're such an idiot."

Seth stared at my Pumas, his fists tightening again. "They're going to follow your *shoes* to find us?"

"Yeah," I replied. "Ironic, isn't it? Caraday probably tipped off The Mole about the GPS and from that moment on, we were walking targets."

Ryan just shook his head. Not like he was denying it, I don't think, but like he couldn't believe it had happened. He looked so bewildered that I almost felt sorry for him. Not Seth, though. He rounded on Ryan, injuries or no.

"What were you thinking? Did it never occur to you that The Mole could use your own technology to track her as well?"

"He shouldn't have known. Shouldn't have . . ." Ryan leaned his head back against the rags and closed his eyes.

"What I don't get," Seth said, "is why they left Anderson here alive." He glanced at me. "I can see if he needed to follow you to find out where my family was, but what did they need him for? After he passed along the bugged shoes, why didn't they take him out right there?"

My mouth dropped open. "Nice, Seth. Real nice."

"No, he has a point," Ryan said weakly. "This . . ." He let his gaze wander around the room. "The entire thing is a game. Remember what . . . Caraday told you. The Mole is a psychopath. We all . . . crossed him one way or another. He's gathering us . . . together. To punish us."

A metallic taste spread through my mouth. I felt like I was going to throw up. It was a game. A game! My mom, Seth's parents . . . racing to save us, but running straight into a trap. So he could have his amusement. So he could have his revenge. He was so sick, watching us like rats in a cage. Arranging every little detail. Every little detail . . .

I groaned. "She must still be wearing her shoes."

"She what?"

"Her shoes. Her shoes! The GPS things! They're tracking my mom. That's how they know where she is. And if they're clearing out, it means she's close. And when she gets here . . ."

Seth's eyes met mine. "Boom."

•••

Seth was right about his not having the touch to pick locks. Even with Ryan patiently instructing him, he couldn't get that first lock. "I'm sorry," he kept saying. "I'm sorry."

"It's okay," I told him. "Really. I know how hard it is."

But that didn't make him feel any better. Especially when Ryan reached out to me weakly and said, "Come here. Let me try."

I couldn't see Seth's face because he was behind me, but I heard the little disappointed huff as he dropped his hand. I caught Ryan's eye and gave him a slight shake of my head. "No, Seth. You almost had it," I said. "Give it one more shot."

Ryan pressed his lips together, nodding as if he understood. I wasn't sure I did. Understand what I was doing, I mean. Since we didn't have a lot of time to mess around with, letting Ryan undo the handcuffs would have been the smart thing to do. But something told me that Seth needed to be the one to do it. I had to go with my gut on that one.

Finally, I heard a tiny *click*. He'd gotten the first lock. "The second one is easier," I assured him. "Much—"

"Shhh!" Ryan hissed. "Seth, down! Put your hands behind your back."

I could feel Seth's hesitation, but only for a heartbeat. He dropped to the floor just as the door swung open. Labruzzo's tall frame filled the doorway.

"Ah. You found him," he said.

I followed his line of sight to where Ryan lay, eyes closed, on the pile of scraps. When neither Seth nor I responded, Labruzzo grunted and took a couple more steps into the room. "You, *signorina*," he said, pointing to me. "You come with me."

A rush of icy fear swept through my veins. "Where are we going?"

"You'll see soon enough."

"I'll go," Seth said. I twisted around to see him rising to his knees.

"It's the girl I need," Labruzzo said. His oily voice slid over my skin and made me want to retch.

"She's not going," Seth said.

Labruzzo just laughed. "I don't remember asking your permission, Romeo." He grabbed my arm and yanked me to my feet. I bit my lip to keep from crying out from the pain.

"She's not well," Seth said, now standing.

I took his cue and feigned a cough. All that accomplished is that Labruzzo's grip tightened, his fingers digging into my skin like talons. "I don't really care." He pulled me closer to him.

I thought I might puke all over his shiny black policeman's shoes. One thing I knew; there was no way I was going to let him take me out of that room even if he dragged me. Which gave me an idea. I went limp. Because he had such a tight grip on my arm, my dead weight pulled him off balance.

That was all Seth needed. He jumped forward and swung his arm with the handcuffs still attached and caught Labruzzo right in the face. Unfortunately, handcuffs, even at a high rate of velocity, have only so much force. The impact didn't take Labruzzo down as much as I wished it had. It did, however, catch him off guard and he dropped me like dirty laundry as his hand slapped to the welt on his face. He snarled in pain and anger.

I had fallen to my knees so that I was facing away from him, but I could feel him close behind me. And I knew that it was only a matter of nanoseconds before he recovered from the shock of the handcuff whip. And then he would go for his gun. I didn't even think—because if I did, I might have hesitated, considering what I was aiming for. Like a slingshot, I swung forward and then threw all my weight into a back-of-the-head head butt to his groin.

The air whooshed out of him like a punctured tire. He doubled over and I rolled to the side so that he wouldn't fall on me. But he didn't fall at all. Stumble, yes. Curse a blue streak, yes, but hit the ground, no. All we'd succeeded in doing was to make him very angry. As I had feared, his hand immediately went for the gun at his waist.

Dead, cold fear swept over me. All I could think at that instant was that Labruzzo was going to kill Seth. I didn't care what came after. A low growl escaped my lips, so feral that it surprised even me. Labruzzo's head turned just as I kicked out at him. He danced away, leveling his gun at me.

The distraction was enough for Seth to swing his handcuff nunchuks again, this time clocking Labruzzo across the top of his head. Labruzzo roared and swung the gun toward Seth. I coiled my legs back again. I knew I had only one more shot at him and if I missed, Labruzzo would probably kill us both. I kicked out with every ounce of anger, pain, and fear I had bottled up inside and my foot connected with his knee with a sickening *thunk*.

Labruzzo fell to the ground, bellowing like a wounded bull. The gun tumbled from his fingertips and before he could reach for it, Seth snatched it from the ground.

"Down!" Seth yelled, brandishing the pistol with chilling disregard for someone who had not even been able to handle a gun just a few short months ago. But he didn't have to worry; Labruzzo's eyes rolled back and he passed out.

"Good work," Ryan said.

Seth's head shot up, as if he had forgotten Ryan was there.

"Get Aphra's cuffs off. We have to . . . get out of here."

Seth looked at me like he was in shock. Now that the action was over, the gun trembled in his hand. His fearlessness had been a bluff.

"The hard part's over," I assured him. "The second lock is easy."

His face crumpled. "I lost the pick," he said.

I could have laughed if he wasn't so serious about it. "That isn't the first one we've lost. Just make another one."

"But hurry," Ryan put in.

I shot Ryan a look to let him know he wasn't helping. He shrugged as if to say "what?" but I didn't miss the shadow of a smile on his lips.

Seth made his pick and to his credit, he was able to open up the cuff on the first try. I sighed with relief as I brought my arms forward, rolling my shoulders to relieve the tension. An angry red band circled my wrist where the cuff had been. I rubbed at the soreness with my other hand.

"Undo Mulo's other one," Ryan said.

I glanced down to where Labruzzo lay moaning on the floor. "Maybe we should just get out of here."

"We don't want . . . to leave him loose."

He had a point. I eyed Labruzzo again, wondering if I should just check him for keys. That would be much easier than fiddling around with an improvised tool. But he wasn't completely out and I wasn't about to get close to him by myself until his hands were good and secured. "Seth, hand me that pick."

It was much easier picking the lock when I could actually see what I was doing, but still it took several tries before I was able to pop that elusive first lock. By the time Seth was completely free of the handcuffs, Labruzzo was starting to stir.

Seth grabbed one of his arms. "Help me get him over by the pipes."

I hesitated, but he gave me another one of his earnest looks. "I won't let him touch you."

Together we dragged Labruzzo across the floor. Seth snapped a cuff around one hairy wrist and then fed the chain behind the pipe before twisting Labruzzo's other hand back and cuffing that one, too.

"Get his . . . keys," Ryan said. "And cell phone . . . if he's got one."

I reached forward to check Labruzzo's front pocket, but Seth stopped me. "I'll do it," he said.

By the time he had been relieved of his personal property, Labruzzo was starting to come to. He opened his eyes slowly, painfully. When the understanding of his predicament registered on his face, he rattled his handcuffs against the pipe. *"Porca miseria!"* he cursed.

"Yeah, that's right," I assured him. "You are a miserable pig."

Seth pulled my arm. "Come on, let's go. We'll have to help your friend over there."

I didn't miss Seth's sour expression at the mention of Ryan, even though it lasted for only a fraction of a second. "Wait." I turned back to Labruzzo. "Where are they?"

He didn't say anything, but his black eyes fixed me with a stare so cold I felt like I needed a jacket.

I shook off a shiver and bent so that I was eye level with him. "This place is wired, right? So where are the explosives?"

He raised his chin and made a big show of clamping his mouth shut.

"Fine." I stood. "Your decision. Hope you can live with it when we're gone and it's just you and the explosives."

He stared straight ahead and pretended not to hear me. Idiot. I turned to Seth. "Let's get out of here."

CHAPTER
13

Seth and I each took one of Ryan's arms and slung them around our shoulders and practically carried him from the room. He barely had the strength to stand, let alone walk. I noticed with a sick twist in my stomach that the rough bandage around his head was completely soaked through. No wonder he was so weak; he was still losing a lot of blood.

"What now?" Seth asked.

"We have Labruzzo's keys," I said. "I think we should get out of here. But should we call someone first? Tell them what's going on?"

"With . . . Labruzzo's phone? No." Ryan said it with such incredulity that I felt really stupid. I had already considered the possibility that his phone was tapped or traceable or whatever you call it, but it's not like I was talking about carrying on a personal conversation. Just a simple "hi, don't come to the textile mill because it's going to blow up" sounded good. But I had to defer to Ryan's judgment. He was the operative, not me.

We had made it as far as the loading dock before Seth drew to a halt. "Wait. What about your shoes?'

"My what?"

"Your shoes. You know, the tracking things. You leave here with them on, The Mole can see wherever we're going."

I pulled them off like they were on fire, but then I realized that if I left a locating device at the factory, my mom would follow the signal to find me, which is exactly what The Mole wanted her to do. Seth was right, though; I couldn't take them with us, either. I stared down at my shoes. All that time I'd been running around in them and I had never even guessed that I was being tracked by the CIA, let alone by The Mole and his minions. "Can we just . . . turn it off?" I said to Ryan. "The GPS thing, I mean."

"There is . . . no off."

"Then we'll smash it or something. Which shoe's it in?"

"Both."

"Where are they? Can I pull them out and—"

Ryan winced. "They're . . . built into the . . . sole."

Of course. Leave it to the CIA to make things complicated. I took a deep breath and let it out my nose before I spoke. "Fine." I chucked one shoe across the loading dock. "We'll split them up at least. We can dump the other one somewhere down the road. Maybe the confusion will be enough to keep Mom from bringing the rescue squad here until we can warn them. Let's go."

I helped Seth half guide, half carry Ryan down the

concrete steps to Labruzzo's car. Ryan leaned heavily against me as Seth jangled the keys, trying and rejecting them one by one in the car door. "It's not here."

I peered over his shoulder. "What's not?"

"The key to his car."

"But . . . he used his keys to drive us here."

"Maybe he has another set."

Ryan was getting heavier. I don't know if he was starting to sag more or if I was just getting tired, but whatever the case, he needed to get help quickly. We needed Labruzzo's car.

"Can you hot-wire it?" I asked Seth.

"What makes you think I can hot-wire cars?"

"I don't know. Because you lived in Detroit?" I said, repeating the explanation he had given me in Seattle when I questioned how he knew how to break into a car.

"Sorry, I flunked Auto Heist 101."

I almost didn't want to ask, but I did, anyway. "So what do we do now?"

Seth sighed and looked back toward the loading dock. "I'll go see if he has another set of keys."

"What? No. Not alone." I turned to Ryan to ask if he'd be all right if I ran back inside with Seth, but Ryan's face had gone slack. His eyes were closed. "Oh, crap. Seth, help me!"

Seth climbed up onto the loading dock and wrestled one of the bales of cotton free from a pallet and heaved it so that it landed just feet from the car. It burst open on impact, sending tangles of stale cotton in all directions. He jumped down after it and piled enough of it together that we could lay Ryan down in relative comfort.

He took my hand but after only a few steps he stopped and looked deeply into my eyes. "I need you to know," he said, "no matter what happens, I'm glad you found me again."

I squeezed his hand. "So am I," I whispered.

He nodded, like that made everything all right. "Let's do this."

We crept back up the stairs to the dock and through the swinging doors. I clung to Seth's hand, dreading the necessity of looking into Labruzzo's black eyes again, worrying with every step that the place was going to go up like a Roman candle. Since I had abandoned my shoes, I had to be extra careful to watch for stray pins, for which I was almost grateful. It was a good distraction from the growing fear rising like a tidal wave above me.

When we reached the refuse room door, Seth glanced at me once more. His reassuring smile warmed me completely through. He pushed the door open and in an instant the warmth evaporated.

The wave came crashing down. An empty pair of cuffs lay on the floor near the pipes. Labruzzo was gone.

The seriousness of our situation came to me in stages. My first reaction was completely visceral. My mouth went dry and my heart raced. A cold sweat prickled from the back of my skull down the length of my spine. Labruzzo was loose and he was angry. I thought of Ryan lying alone and defenseless outside. Next came the terrible realization that my GPS Pumas were on the loading dock, beckoning my mom and Seth's parents and anyone else foolish enough to come help us. And the building was a ticking time bomb.

"What do we do now?" I whispered.

"We get out of here," Seth whispered back. We retraced our steps. Desperation clawed its way up my back. Where would we get out *to*? The factory was out in the proverbial boonies. We had no transportation. And, since I hadn't been paying attention as we made the drive from the city, I wasn't even sure where we *were.*

But all those worries came to an end as we turned the corner toward the loading dock. Because they were eclipsed with a much greater concern.

"I'm very disappointed in you," The Mole said, aiming a much nastier-looking pistol at us than the smaller version Labruzzo had carried.

Labruzzo himself stood just behind The Mole, sneering at us like a playground snitch. One of his eyes had completely swollen shut, which made him look even more menacing, if that was possible.

"Perhaps you didn't understand your role in my soiree this afternoon," The Mole drawled. "Your presence is required to make it a truly memorable occasion."

I just stared at him, mind racing. If he was able to appear so quickly after we had escaped the refuse room, he must have been close. Close enough to see us on the loading dock—unless Labruzzo had a way to summon him without the cell phone. And if he was standing there trying to impress us with his genteel speaking manner, then he must not be too concerned about the explosives going off. Which meant that either we had plenty of time before the factory was set to blow or perhaps that the explosion would be set off remotely.

The second thing that struck me was that The Mole was the one physically standing there in front of us, holding the gun. In the past, he was simply the one pulling the strings, leaving the dirty work to his minions. But now they appeared to be gone and he was the one with his finger on the trigger. Aside from Labruzzo, The Mole was confronting us alone. Marlboro Man wasn't even there to back him up. Maybe Ryan and Caraday were right; The Mole was psychotic. Everything else he might pawn off to his minions, but killing us—*that* he wanted to do himself.

Finally, it hit me that The Mole hadn't said anything about Ryan. Cold fear washed over me as I thought how we had left Ryan passed out and helpless. I slid a quick peek at Labruzzo's car and though I could see tufts of cotton stirring in the breeze, there was no sign of Ryan.

I opened my mouth to ask about him, but then swallowed my questions with my fear. I would wait. Watch.

If the Mole had done something to Ryan, he wouldn't be able to help boasting about it. If not, the last thing I wanted to do was alert The Mole to the fact that Ryan was no longer where we had left him.

Just then, The Mole's pocket beeped. He drew out a BlackBerry and glanced down at it. "Ah. Our guests are arriving."

I couldn't help myself. "Guests?" My mom. Seth's parents. I felt sick inside.

The Mole ignored me. "Signore Labruzzo, if you would."

Labruzzo stepped forward, my Pumas dangling from his fingers. He had tied the shoelaces together and he draped them over my shoulders like a derby winner's roses.

"Come with me," he said.

Seth's grip on my hand tightened. "She's not going anywhere."

The Mole's lips split into a sickening smile. "And what do you suppose you are going to do about it?"

Wrong question to ask. In one fluid movement, Seth yanked my hand, pulling me behind him, and swung a kick to catch The Mole in the gut. "Run!" he yelled.

I hesitated. Because in that instant, two things happened—The Mole dropped both his gun and his BlackBerry and reached for Seth with his bare hands, growling like a rabid wolf, and Labruzzo jumped forward to help his boss. What Labruzzo did not do was draw a gun, which told me that he was unarmed. The gun we had taken from him must have been his only weapon.

I whipped the shoes from around my neck and swung them with everything I had at Labruzzo's head. One shoe caught Labruzzo just above the ear. He turned and snarled at me, but I had already followed through with the first swing and brought the shoes around a second time. Before he could lunge at me, the shoe hit him smack in the face. This time he was quick enough to reach up and grab the shoes before I had a chance to swing them around again, but while his attention was on yanking the shoes from my hands, I kicked my knee up and caught him in the soft center of his solar plexus. He folded like a snuffed cigarette, bending forward just enough for me to smash both hands down on the back of his head.

Labruzzo dropped to one knee, but he wasn't done fighting. He grabbed my leg and tackled me as he went down. I fell hard on my behind, and Labruzzo grunted his satisfaction. Unlucky for him, I didn't have time to waste with him. Next to us, The Mole had grabbed Seth by the throat. Seth was swinging and landing what looked like some pretty good blows, but The Mole's grip only grew stronger. I didn't even think about it; I coiled my free leg up and let loose, kicking Labruzzo square in the temple. He dropped like a rock, body draping over my leg. I kicked him again to get loose and then scrambled on all fours away from him.

By then, The Mole had Seth in a headlock. I lunged for the gun, but The Mole must have seen me going for it because he kicked the gun and it flew off the loading dock in a black metallic arc. I could hear it clatter on the driveway below. I would have gone after it, but Seth's face was beginning to turn purple. He clawed at The Mole's arm, horrible gagging sounds escaping his lips.

"Stop where you are or I break his neck!" The Mole screamed at me.

I froze.

"Now stand up. Slowly."

I did as I was told.

"Very good," The Mole said. "Please place your hands on your head."

Seth locked eyes with me. "Run," he mouthed. "Now."

I didn't know what to do. Would The Mole hurt Seth if I bolted? Would he *not* hurt Seth if I stayed where I was and did everything he told me to? The answer to the second question was no. The Mole was all about hurting Seth and me as much as possible. Which meant that I didn't have much incentive to stand there taking orders. But I didn't want to leave Seth at The Mole's mercy, either. I had to give The Mole a good reason to abandon Seth and come after me.

I stepped backward and my foot hit the BlackBerry. The contact was like a bolt of lightning shooting through me. I knew exactly what I needed to do.

CHAPTER 14

In that instant, everything began falling into place in my mind, like pieces to a puzzle. Labruzzo kept us locked up in that room so that the GPS in my shoes would bring my mom to the factory, but he sat down at the end of the hall so that he could make a quick getaway when my mom and her entourage arrived. The Mole hung around, watching, waiting for the perfect moment to detonate his explosives. He would want to watch, that was certain, so he would be using a remote electronic device. Like a BlackBerry.

I stooped down and swept up the phone, stuffing it into my shorts pocket, and then spun and ran back through the doors into the factory.

It took only a second to see that I was right. I didn't stop to look back, but I could hear The Mole toss Seth aside and come after me.

I rushed into the huge room with all the looms. The Mole's heavy footsteps rang out behind me. I dodged between the machines, in and out of the shadows, deeper and deeper into the mill.

"Stop," he yelled.

Ha. He wasn't even gaining on me. One of the distinct

disadvantages of having other people take care of your business, I suppose. He should have been more active.

And I should have been more careful. I wasn't watching the ground ahead of me. In the next instant, white-hot pain slashed through my foot. I fell hard to my knees and twisted around to see a shard of metal about the size of the BlackBerry I had stolen sticking out of the bottom of my foot. My stomach lurched and I had to swallow hard to keep from throwing up. Running through an abandoned factory without shoes . . . not smart.

I didn't even want to look at the thing, let alone touch it, but I knew the metal would have to come out. Breathing deeply, I gripped the shard with shaking fingers and pulled.

"Aaagh!" The cry ripped straight up from the center of my gut before I could stop it. I pressed my lips together, but it was too late. I'd given away my location. I could hear The Mole's footsteps slow and change direction.

Dropping the metal shard, I dragged myself behind one of the looms. The Mole must have seen that I had gone down, because he quit running. I could hear him, kicking through the debris on the factory floor, making his way to my hiding spot.

I pulled my knees close to my chest and pressed my back flat against the side of the loom, but it didn't matter how invisible I tried to make myself; a smear of blood trailed behind me, marking my position. All I could do was listen to the heavy scrape of his shoes drawing nearer. I held my breath, hoping he would pass me by.

He didn't.

The Mole stepped around the corner of the loom, grinning down at me like a demonic jack-o'-lantern. "Hello, my dear."

I scrambled to the side, hoping to crawl under the loom to get away, but he stopped me, stomping hard on my leg. I screamed in pain.

"Give it to me," he said.

"Give what to you?"

"You know exactly what." He held out his hand. When I didn't move to give his BlackBerry to him, he ground his heel into my leg. I cried out again.

"This is not a game, little girl," he said. "Where is it?" His face contorted in rage.

"I don't have it," I said.

The heel pressed down, down.

"I threw it away while I was running!"

Grind.

I howled.

"Give. Me. The. Phone."

But there was no way I was going to do that.

He stomped down and I heard my own bone snap. Pain rolled like thunder up my leg, followed quickly by a wave of nausea.

"I don't have it!" I screamed. Of course, he and I both knew it was only a matter of him bending down to take it from the pocket of my shorts. But after what I'd done to Labruzzo out on the dock, maybe he didn't want to get that close.

He raised his foot again.

"I wouldn't do that if I were you."

"Back away from the girl, Brezeanu."

I twisted around to see both Seth and Ryan, side by side, guns leveled at The Mole. He froze where he stood, but only for a moment.

"You will die for this," he growled at me, and then dived behind one of the looms.

Seth looked torn. His muscles coiled taut and his eyes darted back and forth, watching for movement. I understood exactly what he was feeling. It had to end. As long as The Mole was alive, we would never be safe. But Seth wasn't a killer. He might be able to hunt The Mole down. He might even be able to pull the trigger, but then he'd be as haunted the rest of his life as he would be if The Mole were still on his trail.

Ryan must have sensed it, too. "Get her outside," he barked. Like he was giving an order. Like Seth didn't have a choice.

Seth hesitated for only a moment more. Then he stuffed the gun into his waistband and stooped down to scoop me up in his arms.

Over his shoulder, I locked eyes with Ryan. "Thank you," I mouthed.

He nodded brusquely—a motion that caused

considerable pain, judging from the way his jaw clenched in reaction to it—and then turned his attention back to finding The Mole.

We had taken only a few steps when The Mole's words rang out like the voice of God, nowhere and everywhere all at once. "You think it's over?"

Seth spun, searching the shadows. I buried my face in his shoulder to keep from crying out from the movement.

Ryan raised his gun with both hands, though I could tell he had no clear target.

"You amateurs! You nothings!" From the disdain in his voice, I could practically see the sneer on The Mole's face. "You think I wouldn't have planned a fail-safe? You think you're home free because you stole a *phone*?" He laughed. Not the wicked, confident laugh of a master criminal, but the shrill cackle of a madman.

I clung to Seth. "He's insane," I whispered.

Seth didn't say a word, but held me tighter, cupping the back of my head as if he could protect me.

Ryan backed to where we were standing. "This place is wired like Times Square at Christmas. Get her out," he whispered to Seth. "Now!"

Seth turned toward the docks and I watched over his shoulder as Ryan crept down the rows of looms, gun raised and ready. And then a shadow moved, just out of my range of vision. I gasped and gripped Seth's shoulders.

"What is it?"

A dark figure leaped from behind a loom and rushed toward the staircase. Ryan spun and fired, but the shot went wide. The Mole clambered up the metal stairs, Ryan close behind. My eyes snapped up to the window of the room where we had first seen the Mole that morning. His sanctuary. His lair. The fail-safe! That's where it would be.

"Ryan!" I screamed. "The room!"

At the sound of my voice, The Mole turned his head, slowing him down just enough for Ryan to dive for his ankles. The Mole crashed to the walkway, flailing his feet. Ryan grabbed one of his legs and held on to it like a bucking bronco. He shot an angry look to where we still stood in the room below.

"Mulo! Get her out of here!"

"No!" I cried. I tried to wriggle out of Seth's arms. "Help him!"

"Mulo!" Ryan yelled.

Seth's arms tightened around me and he ran down the corridor to the loading dock exit. We pushed through the swinging doors and he drew up short. Bright headlights lit the dock, punctuated by red and blue flashes from half a dozen police cars. The muzzles of several guns immediately pointed toward us, clicked and ready, and a confusion of voices ordered us in both Italian and

English to freeze before Mrs. Mulo's voice rose above them all. "Seth!"

The guns lowered. From out of the glaring lights, Victor and Elena Mulo rushed forward, arms outstretched. My mom wasn't far behind.

And then a shot ripped through the air and chaos broke out on the docks again. Seth dropped to the ground, and I tumbled from his arms, fresh pain shooting up my leg.

"Secure the perimeter!" someone yelled.

"It came from inside!" another voice answered.

The burnt-tar smell filled my nose and for a moment I thought I must be imagining things until I lifted my head to see a pair of snakeskin boots. I screamed and pushed myself backward until I realized that Marlboro Man was lying facedown on the dock, his hands tied with plastic handcuffs behind his back. His face was turned away from me. But right next to him lay Labruzzo, trussed like a Thanksgiving turkey. He glared at me with his good eye and mouthed, "You're dead."

That's when I passed out.

I was only vaguely aware of what happened next. I heard a voice cry, "Get them down from there!" I could feel myself being carried and coddled. I recognized my mom's voice, but I didn't know what she was saying to me.

I caught only a few of the words that were flying around

me. "... still in there." "... a lot of blood." "... without alerting the local authorities." "... broken leg." "... in the van." I was aware of hands. Hands prodding, comforting, tying my leg to a splint. Dressing the wound on my foot. Reaching into the pocket of my shorts.

My eyes flew open. Caraday. I grabbed her hand. "No! Don't you touch it!"

Mom was at my side in an instant. "Aphra, what is it? Are you all right?"

I could only stare at Caraday, who stared back at me with wild green eyes. "She's working for him!" I cried. "Don't let her have it!"

Caraday shook her head and exchanged a worried glance with my mom. "I think she's delirious."

"No! I know—"

"Honey, relax," Mom pressed my head back down. She didn't believe me.

I struggled against her. "Where's Ryan? He can—"

Caraday spoke to someone behind me. Someone I couldn't see. "Can't you give her something?"

"No." I struggled against her grip. "No! Don't ... you understand? Caraday ..." I lost the rest of my statement in a haze of pain.

Caraday's voice was gentle, so gentle. "It's going to be all right, Aphra. It's over. You did it."

I pushed her away again. "Seth!" I yelled. "Seth!"

"She's going to hurt herself," I heard Caraday's voice say. Where did my mom go? Where was Seth?

Hands came at me. Held me down. I felt a sharp prick and then my arm was flooded with warmth, followed by a disconcerting numbness.

Someone reached into my pocket and took the BlackBerry and I was powerless to stop them. I think I cried, but I'm not sure.

"Go!" I tried to warn everyone, but my mouth could barely form the words. "We need to get out of—"

But the rest of the sentence was blown away in the force of an explosion so strong, it sucked the air straight from my lungs. I gripped someone's hand—I hoped it was my mom's—and prayed we would get out alive.

Chapter 15

The first thing I saw when I woke was my leg, wrapped in plaster, and suspended from a series of pulleys and cables above the bed. It hurt too much to turn my head, but I took in as much of my surroundings as I could with my eyes. Railing on the bed. Pink plastic pitcher and a cup with a bendy straw on the nightstand. Weak sunlight filtering through Pepto-Bismol–pink curtains, the rest of the room stark, white. A hospital. Mom slept in a chair in the corner, her mouth hanging open as if in silent protest.

The events leading up to the hospital came back to me in small pieces, not necessarily in order. The Mole playing his cello. The Mole crushing my leg. Ryan's head. Seth cradling me in his arms. Caraday reaching for the BlackBerry. Labruzzo looking up at me with his one good eye. *Boom.*

Mom woke with a start, as if she could hear my thoughts. She saw that I was awake and rushed to my side. Her hands had been wrapped in gauze, but she stroked my hair with the backs of her fingers. "How are you doing?"

I tried to speak, but my throat felt raw. The words came out in a hoarse whisper. "I'm sorry for leaving, Mom."

Her smile trembled. "You did what you felt you needed to do," she said. I noticed that she didn't say I was right to sneak away from her.

"Where's Seth?"

"He'll be in shortly. He didn't want to leave until he said—"

"Leave?"

She stroked my hair again. "The Mulos . . . were never here, you understand?"

It hurt too much to shake my head, so I just stared at her.

"There will be an inquiry. We don't want them to be part of that process."

"What happened?"

"Agent Caraday recovered a BlackBerry that we believe belonged to The Mole."

"Where is it?"

"It was destroyed in the explosion."

That part I remembered. That would be why Mom's hands were bandaged. Why my throat was so raw. "She tried to blow us up," I said.

"What are you talking about?"

"The Mole. She worked—"

"You're tired. We can talk about this la—"

"Where is she?" I demanded.

"She's in the ICU," Mom said finally. "She's had a rough time of it."

"Serves her right."

"Aphra!" The softness left Mom's voice. "Why would you say such a thing?"

"She was trying to kill us."

Mom's eyes flashed. "Agent Caraday was trying to *save* you. That device you were so carefully guarding was a bomb. You owe her your life."

"But she—"

"I know." Mom cut me off. "She sent you to Varese against my wishes. I was none too pleased with her about that. But the minute she found out Lévêque had been leaking information to The Mole, she told me everything. She called Ryan and tried to stop you and when she couldn't—"

"Wait. Lévêque?" My stomach flipped upside down. "*He* was working for The Mole?" The world I thought I knew was suddenly thrown into negative images—black gone white, and white, black. Nothing made sense anymore. I shook my head. "But . . . he's dead."

"An unfortunate result of his association."

"But . . . why? Why would they kill one of their own?"

Mom shook her head. "These kind of people, life holds no value to them. Lévêque must have outlived his usefulness."

I sank back into the pillows. Lévêque deserved what he got, didn't he? So why did it make me feel so sad?

"What about Ryan? Did he get out? Is he—"

"Don't worry. He sustained some burns and a nasty concussion, but he'll recover."

"And The Mole? Did you find him? Did he—"

She nodded gravely. "He's dead."

"So it's over," I breathed.

She stroked my hair back with the tips of her fingers. "Yes, Aphra. It's finally over."

"Scusate, signora." A nurse in colorful scrubs stood in the doorway. "There is a phone call for you."

Mom stood. "I'll be back." She bent to kiss my forehead before she left the room, just like she used to do when I was a little girl. "Rest now," she said. A lump rose in my throat and I didn't trust myself to say anything, so I just listened as the *clack, clack, clack* of her heels against the hospital tiles faded away.

I must have slept because when I opened my eyes, the pink curtains had been pulled back and sunlight flooded the room. I moaned and slammed my eyes shut again.

"Hello."

I bolted wide awake. Ryan sat at the side of my bed in a wheelchair, watching me. I was suddenly overcome by a very strong urge to pull the blankets up to cover my hideously ugly hospital gown. Not that he looked much better, head and hands wrapped like a mummy's, the gauze splotched and yellow in spots. What skin I could see on his face was an angry red and greasy with ointment. His eyelashes were completely gone. At least he was dressed, though, wearing a loose, white shirt and pull-on slacks. "Going somewhere?" I asked.

He tried to grin, but winced when the skin around his mouth wouldn't let him. "I gotta get back to work. I'm still on the clock."

"No, seriously. Are you okay to be discharged? You're looking kinda green."

"Ah. That." With effort, he shrugged. "They aren't . . . authorized to give me certain pain medications in here. Don't know what secrets I might divulge."

"But you're . . ." I gestured to his bandaged state.

"I'll be fine. I'm being transferred to a military hospital where they will give me plenty of lovely drugs. In fact"—he gestured gingerly with his head— "Mario and Luigi out there are waiting to deliver me right now."

I glanced to the hallway where a couple of burly men in sharply pressed white uniforms stood like twin Roman statues glowering at us, caps tucked under their respective hairy arms. "You sure they're not hauling you into some prison somewhere?"

"Have you ever *seen* a military hospital?" He tried again to smile.

"So you're really okay? The last I saw you—" I closed my eyes. I didn't even want to think about it.

"I'm good," he said quickly, and then leaned forward in his wheelchair, the fake leather seat squeaking beneath his weight. "Listen, I just wanted to tell you that you did a great job."

"But I got it wrong."

He shrugged—as much as he could, anyway. "So did I. But the important thing is that we got it right in the end."

"I *didn't*, though. I would have—"

"There's no going back, Aphra, only forward. Don't worry about what might have been. What's important is what *is*. You helped to bring down a dangerous organization. You should be proud of that."

I pleated the sheet between my fingers, trying to think of the appropriate response since I thought he was completely wrong.

"I was serious in Seattle when I said you should consider following in your mom's footsteps. You'd make a good operative."

"Oh, no. I—"

"Just think about it. Let me know if you ever change your mind."

"I won't," I said.

Someone tapped on the door. I glanced up and went all warm inside. Seth stood there, hands dug deep into the pockets of his jeans.

Ryan nodded to him. "Mulo."

Seth nodded back. "Anderson." He took a couple of tentative steps into the room and looked past Ryan to where I lay. "I just . . . came to say good-bye," he said.

Ryan backed his wheelchair away from the side of my bed, gesturing for Seth to take his place. "Sure. I gotta take off, anyway." He reached out a bandaged hand, and Seth shook it carefully. "Good luck to you, Mulo."

Seth gave him one of those tough-guy raise-the-chin-to-acknowledge-the-statement things. "See you around."

With one last glance at me, Ryan rolled out of the room. Seth stood watching me for a moment and then approached the bed warily, almost shyly. "How's the leg?" he asked. "Your foot?"

But I didn't care about those things. "Where are you going?" I blurted.

He perched on the edge of the mattress and picked up my hand. His fingers were warm and rough against mine. "We're going home," he said. He pasted on a smile, but it couldn't mask the sadness in his eyes.

I almost didn't dare ask. Given their past experience, I could imagine—now that the Mulos were free to come and go as they pleased—that the last people they would want to know their whereabouts would be the Agency. Or the offspring of the Agency. But I had to know. "Where's home?"

He looked into my eyes for a long time and then touched his free hand to my chest. "For me, it will always be right here." Then he looked away, as if he was embarrassed by what he'd said. The light from the window lit him from behind, giving him an almost ethereal appearance—unearthly and beautiful . . . and impossible to hold on to. When he raised his blue eyes to mine, I wanted to cry.

"My parents miss their families," he said softly. "They haven't seen them for over twenty years. . . ."

"How long will you be there?" My voice sounded small, pathetic.

"I don't know how long they'll stay." He cleared his throat. "I plan to start college as soon as I can."

"Where?" I whispered.

He lifted one shoulder, watching me from under his dark lashes. "Depends on where I get in. I don't exactly have regular transcripts to offer."

I laughed to hold back the tears. "Yeah, I can see the admissions board now, reviewing your extracurricular activities . . ."

"They wouldn't be able to see them." He grinned. "The file would be sealed."

"Even better." I laughed at the thought. "You'd be a man of mystery."

"James Bond!"

"Ha! Maxwell Smart." My smile quickly faded and I closed my fingers around his. "I'll miss you."

He raised my hand to his lips. His breath was hot on my skin. "I'll miss you, too."

I couldn't hold it back anymore. A single hot tear escaped and rolled down my cheek.

"Hey. What's this?" Seth cupped my face in his hand and wiped it away with his thumb. "Your meds must be getting to you."

If I could have sat up, I might have held him close and

hidden the rest of my tears on his shoulder, but with my leg strung up in the air, the most I could accomplish was to reach out for him, sobbing like a baby.

He gathered me in his arms and curled around me like a leaf. "You know," he said in a husky voice, "guys hate it when girls cry."

"I'm sorry," I sniffled.

"No. That's not what I meant to—" He held me away from him. "I was just trying . . ." He growled in frustration. "Look, you're not getting rid of me this easily, all right? I'll be back. I just don't know when."

I could only nod and grab handfuls of his shirt to pull him close to me once more. I closed my eyes, wanting to capture that moment in my memory forever, to tuck it close like a photograph so that I could take it out and relive it again and again and again.

Mr. Mulo came to the door and cleared his throat. I held Seth tighter.

"I'm so glad to see you're doing well, Aphra," Elena Mulo's voice said.

I released my stranglehold on Seth and looked up at her. *Well?* I was dying inside. "Thank you," I murmured.

"It's time to go now, Seth," she said softly.

I reached up to touch his face one last time. He held my hand against his cheek and turned his head to kiss my palm.

"Don't worry; I'll see you sooner than you think." He

laid the kiss in my hand flat on my chest, over my heart. He didn't have to say the words.

"I'll be waiting," I whispered. And then he was gone.

Mom and I flew back to the island together. I wasn't sure how Dad would be, seeing her again. I think he felt just as hurt and abandoned as I did when Mom stayed with her job instead of coming with us when we moved to the resort. But when he understands what she went through to protect us, maybe he can forgive her. And maybe if he knows how much I just wanted our family to be together again, he can forgive me for lying to him, for disappearing. I've learned that if you love someone enough, you can figure a way to deal with almost any situation.

I talked to Caraday before we left Italy. If she figured out that I had thought she was a traitor, she never let on. She got a medal of commendation from the Agency for what she did in Varese. I hope that makes her feel better about the scars she will carry for the rest of her life.

Me, I'm working hard on my homeschool packets. If I complete enough of them, I might be able to start sending in college apps this summer. I don't know yet where Seth will be going, but I figure if my grades are good enough, I can be accepted anywhere.

I guess that's one good thing my mom taught me through this thing: *Be prepared for whatever may come.*

EPILOGUE

I sit on the beach, watching the whitecaps curl toward the shore. It feels good to be back home, but I would kill to be able to dive into the water, to swim down and down and leave everything else behind.

The doctors say I can get the cast off in three more weeks. That's three more weeks of torture.

I close my eyes and turn my face to the warmth of the sun. I taste the salt in the air and listen to the steady *shush, shush, shush* of the ocean. *My* ocean. My island. My home. And yet . . .

There are times I feel like the island can't contain me anymore. Mom and Dad have a long road ahead of them. Five years apart is a long span to bridge, and sometimes I feel that I'm just in the way.

My fingers curl around the envelope in my hand. It's a note from Ryan. There is an assignment he thinks I could help with. He wishes I'd reconsider.

I don't know.

I just might. . . .